PRAISE FOR ELISSE HAY

Rory is officially one of my new favorite urban fantasy and supernatural suspense characters. She's smart, powerful, insightful, and tough—and full of care for those who need defending. I'd want her on my team for sure. Elisse had me at the Shakespearean title and locked down ownership of my heart and soul on page one with this fantastic story and lively prose. Her books are insta-buys for me from now on!

— LISA EDMONDS, BESTSELLING AUTHOR OF THE
ALICE WORTH SERIES

THUNDER, LIGHTNING, RAIN

SOMETHING WICKED
BOOK FOUR

ELISSE HAY

Holding the space is perhaps the kindest, most empowering thing you can do for someone. This is dedicated to those unsung heroes at our side.

AUTHOR NOTE

This story was written on the Wadawurrung lands of the Kulin Nation and is set in the lands of the Bunurong Boon Wurrung and Wurundjeri Woi Wurrung peoples of the Eastern Kulin Nation.

I pay respect to First Nation Elders past and present. Sovereignty was never ceded.

CONTENT NOTES

This book contains content that may be distressing for some. Extensive trigger warnings are available via the author's website, and most distressing content will be linked to the main character's healing arc, including mentions of interpersonal and intimate violence. If you have held the space for someone while they healed and still feel the bruises, consider checking the trigger warnings.

If at any point you become distressed or numb, please take a break and reach out to your supports. Your wellbeing is important.

ALSO BY ELISSE HAY

The Something Wicked Series

Foul is Fair

Villains by Necessity

Met by Moonlight

Thunder, Lightning, Rain

Fate Untethered

Untempered

MET BY MOONLIGHT SUMMARY

To ensure continuity, if you didn't read *Met by Moonlight*, what you need to know is:

Rory is now employed as a custodian, rather than a caretaker. This means her office is more central, she works specifically with high risk clients, and she has more responsibility. She's part of a trio with Lilith and Aspen, who was brought on for her case management and social work background.

Other custodians include Shepherd, as well as Fritz and Maadai, who were both new in *Met by Moonlight*. Maadai is a senior witch from Uganda who has stepped into the role of District High Witch (or District High Magi).

We learned that Gerrard, Rory's dad, has been overworld and features in confidential files held by the United International Bureau of Magi.

Faeries attacked, and Rory saw herself reflected oddly in various pools of water. Rory's primary focus was Ryan, who briefly was District High Wizard. His manipulations and the impact of their conflict was the source of a majority of the content notes. Ryan was abusive, and assaulted Rory.

Rory's primary support network, including Dad, Oma, Lilith,

Aspen, and Taig know this. Shepherd and Maadai also are aware of what happened. Her people all understood she was the victim of a series of violent crimes and responded supportively.

A woman rift-jumped into SuperSec and released all the prisoners. Rory informed Beo that Duke was likely free. She then fought in a duel with a fae lord, who she killed. She took the fae's sword. During the same duel, the others fought Ryan, who was killed by Taig.

Taig and Rory are together.

Finally, Rory got a cat. Her name is Eclipse. She's black, orange, and adorable.

CHAPTER 1

$\mathcal{I}$ didn't even make it to my appointment before my phone lit up. In today's episode of shit I didn't expect to deal with: steaming fresh ursathrope client, picked up by the cops before his file even landed in my inbox.

Aspen and Lilith were irritated by the way this client's transfer was unfolding. I was too, for the client. But I was also secretly glad to have something urgent to handle. Emergencies I could manage. Emergencies were easy.

You didn't need to think during a crisis.

Ignoring the rapid-fire messages pinging between my coven members in our group chat, I listened to the receptionists' friendly greeting on the other end of the line.

"Hi, my name is Rory Gold," I said, into the phone, swaying with the tram on the way to the police station. "I have an appointment with Jenna." I blanked on my psychologist's surname. "At nine?" I offered, hoping that information would help them identify the right person.

"I've got you right here, Rory," said the receptionist, the words light and cheery. "How can I help you?"

"I've had something come up," I said, not even bothering to try to sound apologetic. "I won't be able to make that one, I'm sorry."

"That's fine," she said. "I'll let Jenna know. Our cancellation policy will be implemented, but you can fix that up next time you're here. I see you've got another appointment next week. Did you want me to put you on a list in case something comes up sooner?"

Their cancellation policy and I were well acquainted. I shoved down the guilt. I *could* have made the time for it.

But I didn't have the *energy* for that work. Not today. Not after I'd walked endlessly through my dream toward the bridge where the boy I'd grown up with had been killed by a lycanthrope. Not when I'd eventually reached that bridge, unable to breathe through the terror, unable to look away, and found the High District Wizard pressing play on the speaker. Not when he'd looked at me across the bridge, the nineties rock anthem filling the air, and I knew what was coming next. He'd open his mouth to speak to me. And I was going to listen.

I'd woken with that knowledge vibrating through my cells, my heart hammering and the air like molasses. Taig had killed him. In real life, Taig had killed him.

But my body remembered what that man had done.

"No, next week is fantastic," I told the receptionist, and my tone was so chipper I cringed. *Too far, Rory.* They'd told me to fake it until I made it but I don't think they knew just how much faking that entailed.

"See you next Tuesday, at nine," she said, and *her* enthusiasm was the perfect level for a receptionist to a MIA client.

I swallowed down the shame. *Darkness held back by a thin layer of glass. Hands on my shoulders. His voice, demanding I sit.* The words slithered through my head and my hand tightened on the strap I held to stay upright on the tram. I scrubbed away the lingering feeling of plastic table against my cheek before shoving my phone in my pocket. I had a job to do.

I was the last one to the station, and went with my coven into the observation room. I saw the long, lingering look Lilith sent me. Aspen hid her concern behind a professional smile that was as much for me as it was for the uniformed officer who escorted me. I gave them both a brisk nod.

They wouldn't ask questions I didn't want to answer. Not here. But I could hear them, anyway. Those words crept into the quiet of the room, made louder by the background murmur of the city around us. I crushed down the slither of shame and coiled one hand around my keys. The metal bit into my palm. *You're fine. You can do this.*

Our new client's profile picture hadn't done justice to his size. He sprawled behind the desk on the other side of the two-way glass, flannel shirt open to reveal a clean, worn singlet beneath. A huge thatch of hair climbed up his neck and covered his jaw, broken by old scars.

The list of crimes he was suspected to have engaged in was even bigger than he was, and familiarity tugged at the back of my brain. I'd worked with plenty of shifters since I'd moved to Melbourne, but something about this guy in particular reminded me of a lycanthrope I'd always have a special place for in my heart.

As I watched, he cracked his neck. First one way, then the other. I could hear it popping from behind the glass.

He wasn't Beo. I drew in a deep breath, struggling with the wave of nostalgia and the compassion that went with it. *Head in the game, Roars.* The bigger they are, the harder they fall. And they all fall to Aspen's unconditional positive regard.

Or my knife.

I caught the impressed look Aspen shot me. *He's huge,* she mouthed, then gave me a firm nod and tapped her own chest, indicating she'd take him.

As if he could hear my thoughts he leant forward, the movement pulling the shirt tight across his shoulders as he folded big, scarred hands nonchalantly. His eyes turned directly toward where we stood, hidden.

He couldn't see us, but he didn't need to. Super hearing, super strength and super thick body hair, the perks of being an ursathrope.

That tug of compassion came again, and I let it sit in my chest, though it felt a little awkward tucked up under my ribs that still ached from hitting the mats badly last night.

Lilith reached around me to position her phone screen where both Aspen and I could see the report she'd highlighted.

Benson Hurtfield, during the police interview regarding the aforementioned incident, assaulted the wizard there in capacity as caretaker. This was found to be a provoked attack. Hurtfield's caretaker survived.

'Survived'? The compassion vanished. I put my hand on Aspen's shoulder and when she rolled her eyes, I rolled mine back and jabbed my finger at that line.

Aspen had the trauma-informed shit. And I kept her alive so she could make change.

Before she could complain I slipped past her. Grim determination took the place compassion should have, but it did the same job for today.

The detective who'd brought Benson in opened the door to the hall for me. I didn't recognize her dark eyes and long, straight black hair. She'd come from up north and had a rep for getting to the bottom of the nastiest shit—and living to write the reports. Seemed like a solid upgrade from the late Detective the-most-sensitive-part-of-the-penis-is-the-man-attached Clint. That wasn't a high bar, but, hells, I didn't have time for them.

She let me into the interview room without comment. As the detective put her hand on the doorknob she arched a brow at me, checking to see if I was ready without speaking. As if Benson couldn't hear us anyway.

"Thanks, Detective Delyan," I said, tucking my hands into the pockets of the long, loose jacket that turned my Custodian lupetec armor into a fashion statement rather than a war declaration.

If my fingers coiled around my wand, I didn't think anyone would blame me for it.

She opened the door and stepped back, letting me have a clear view of Benson in person.

"You lost," Benson said, dismissively, as he looked at me.

I strolled in and relaxed in the chair opposite him, using body language to say I was safe. That's what Aspen said. Safety cues? Was that the name she used for it? "Did I?" I asked, making sure my shoulders were soft and my movements were unhurried as I got myself comfortable, flipping the loose jacket over one knee, shifting my butt on the metal chair.

"You argued over who had to come in. And you lost."

Yeah, he'd made us. That damned compassion threatened me again. He assumed I didn't want to be there. "I mean, I feel like I won," I said with a shrug, inviting him to share in my amusement. "They have to sit there and listen. I get to chat with you. Seems like I got the good deal. Doing is always better than watching, right?"

He didn't smile. "I didn't do it."

My belly twisted painfully. *Remove foot, then speak. Top work, Rory.* I ignored the slither of shame that coiled around my throat. *Own it. You have to own it.* "Oh. That. No. I wasn't talking about the"—I nodded at the sheaf of notes Delyan had left on the table, seeing the strategically positioned names of Benson's two children in his view—"assault that they wanted to chat to you about. Just generally. Anyway, I'm not a cop."

"You're a witch."

It wasn't a question so I didn't bother confirming. "Name's Rory." I withdrew my hand from my pocket, leaving the wand behind, and offered him my palm. "I'm one of the custodians you'll be working with as you get settled in Melbourne. And I'll help smooth over these sorts of misunderstandings."

Because it *was* a misunderstanding. If this guy had committed the crimes they were investigating, skulls wouldn't have been cracked, they would've been unrecognizable pulp. And it damned well better not be the first of many.

He didn't shake my hand. "Smooth it, then. I have to get home."

I nodded and tucked my hand back into my pocket. "They're checking with people, confirming what you told them about locations and whatever. It takes time."

I knew he had kids at home. He didn't want me offering to check on them, I suspected. Again, I thought of Beo and his pack.

"So you're useless."

"Today," I agreed, not trying to hide my own irritation at the reality of that. "Sorry, mate. Figured I may as well pop in and say hello anyway, see if I could get you a hot drink. They have passable coffee here."

He sat back and the chair creaked beneath his weight.

That's a no. "We can catch up later," I said, easily, so he knew what'd be coming next. Predictable was safe, apparently. "Make sure you've got what you need so you and yours get a solid start."

He raised his brows and sent a droll look toward the door.

I followed his meaning easily enough. "Yeah, this isn't ideal," I acknowledged. "Your file landed in my inbox at nine. They had you at eight-thirty. I'm a sore loser, I have to say, but VicPol beat me to the punch this time." And fuck the cops for jumping to conclusions... including *my* cop.

A derisive snort was his response.

Achingly tired, I wondered if maybe I should've let Aspen do this. "Can't blame you for being annoyed about it. Just like I can't blame the cops for being suspicious." *Out loud, anyway.* "We all know there are folks around who deserve their suspicion, and there are people in my chair who do, too." *Including me!* I shrugged, bitterness settling into my bones. "It is what it is, but from here on, you're mine, so I'll be—"

The table caved with a scream of metal as he surged to his feet and drove his fists into its surface. My heart turned over in my chest as the twisted metal gave one last half-hearted squeak. His face was so close to mine I could smell the shaving cream he'd used.

Adrenaline burned through my system. Spells simmered in my mind. I didn't blink.

"I. Am. Not. Yours."

Fucking shitfuck. I felt my pulse drumming in my throat as if it was happening on the screen to a character I liked. "You're no one's property," I agreed, hoping like shit the cops wouldn't storm in and escalate this. My voice didn't shake.

His eyes flickered toward the two-way mirror, narrowed, then came back to me. He pushed off the table and it shuddered, somehow standing despite the force he'd used. With a last, threatening look at the glass he straightened and paced away.

My gaze got caught on those deep dents from his fists. It didn't help me to gather my thoughts and channel some Aspen. "I'm sorry I upset you." Silence. He stood on the intense side of seven feet and was built like a brick shithouse. I stayed seated, but reached down and picked up Delyan's notes that had fluttered to the floor to escape his attack. "You are a citizen of Australia and as such you have the right to safety and autonomy. I want to be very clear that is not in question, as long as you're following our laws." I lined up the corners of the notes as I spoke, businesslike. *How's that for safety cues, Aspen?*

"But here I am." The words were full of disgust and I couldn't blame him for that.

I folded the paper crisply. We'd need to get him some help with that temper. "You're right," I agreed, knowing damned well he'd hear the regret in my voice. "Like I said, I'll work on it."

"Then go work," he said, fury vibrating in the words.

We were definitely not kicking any goals as a team today. I stood, feeling about as useful as a pile of dog shit, and hating it. Hating the whole fucking system. "Chat soon, mate," I said heavily, letting myself out.

In the hallway were two beat cops, guns out and no doubt loaded with silver bullets. I got a grim look from one and a grin from another.

If I'd known their names, not just their faces, I'd've thanked them for being ready to step in... and also, for *not* jumping in. I gave them a nod I hoped they interpreted as one of gratitude as I went back to where I knew Aspen and Lilith would be.

My witches emerged and fell in beside me. We went deeper into the precinct together. "Next time," Aspen murmured, "*You* will never question it, not *it is never going to be questioned*. You can't vouch for other people. But nice work. Gold star for not murderising him on the spot and bonus points for not even blinking."

He would've heard my heart go off even if I didn't outwardly respond, so the praise was meaningless but the feedback wasn't. "I can't let him go around intimidating folks like that anytime someone says something he disagrees with. We'll be looking for carers for his kids in a week."

"We'll work on him," Aspen agreed firmly. "When he doesn't feel like his back is against a wall."

Considering his hair trigger, I wasn't sure we'd have all that long before our options would run out.

CHAPTER 2

"All children deserve an education of course," the principal was telling Aspen. The enrollment form in front of him filled out in precise handwriting declared it was for Jessica Hurtfield. "And I'm very keen to support in that regard. Jessica's information is yet to arrive from her language school in Brisbane, however we've already had some concerning correspondence from her old teacher."

"Regarding Jessica's behavior?" Aspen asked, scratching out notes as they spoke.

"Among other things."

I resisted glancing at my phone to check the time. Or my socials. Fuck doing this dance again with another arsehole who didn't want to learn. "So we need support from the get-go," she agreed, while I sat there like a bump on a log. "We'll support an emergency application for funding."

The word funding had him paying attention and I barely resisted rolling my eyes. "She'll need extensive assessments. I can put in a referral to our SSOs and see when we can get that happening."

Aspen nodded briefly. "We'll get those done privately. I've got a few good people I can call on, but thank you. I know the SSOs are spread thin."

"Of course we'd make any reasonable adaptions she needed, with or without funding," the principal said calmly, wisely not denying how chronically underfunded the public system was. My respect for him went up a tiny amount. It was still a negative value. He *had* to say he'd make reasonable adjustments. It was literally the law.

I knew what the practice looked like.

"Of course," Aspen agreed without inflection. I resisted shooting her a wry glance, knowing she'd be thinking the same as me. And her respect meter was still negative for him, too. You knew this shit when you grew up with someone. "When is Jessica's start date?"

My phone buzzed in my pocket, a reminder that the world beyond my job existed. My ribs felt one size too small for all my internal organs. I wished I'd had a chance to go to the office so I could've left my phone behind.

He paused for a moment and I tried to figure out what I'd missed. "We will need to process her application, wait for information to be sent across, and schedule another intake meeting before we can set a date."

Of course he did. "Term three ends this week," I said, in case Aspen didn't know. The perks of being a teacher's kid—constant exposure to holiday countdowns. "We want her in by day one, term four."

The principal's gaze cut to me. He sat there in his expensive suit with an expression of concern sitting on his face as if it'd been stuck there by an amateur artist wielding a cheap, dried-up glue stick. "We want her to start when she's most likely able to achieve success. The term start would be ideal from a curriculum perspective, however—"

"Term four it is," Aspen said, smiling. "I'll have those reports to you in the next two weeks. You'll have time to look over them and decide which class would work best for her."

"I can certainly review any information you send me," he agreed, not standing to finish the meeting. "And process her enrollment. However, setting Jessica up for success is my primary concern."

Sure it was. They danced for a bit longer and Aspen was already calling the best clinical kid psych we had on our books as we walked out, arranging for assessments.

I dialed Benson's number. I knew he'd been released this morning, but we hadn't had anything to offer him then.

I still wasn't sure we did now. But it was irrelevant, because I was prompted to leave a message by an automated service. I recorded a crisp voicemail and we grabbed Lilith on the way to his place.

His flat was uncomfortably close to mine, which I saw Lilith noting warily. "You moving in with Taig?" she asked as we approached the building opposite and down one from my own little home.

Seriously, we had a pissed off ursathrope and she was worrying about my love life? "We aren't even official," I told her, annoyed. "And that's beside the point."

She rolled her eyes. "How many nights have you spent apart since Samhain?"

I didn't answer that. It was only three weeks. Three weeks didn't make us de facto. Even if he did bring me coffee in bed.

Elders, I had no idea what my life was.

We fell into formation as we reached Benson's door. Aspen was the bright, personable face, Lilith and I protecting her flanks. She lifted her hand but it opened before she could knock.

The man filled the entire space. He loomed over us, unlike another man I remembered who had filled space similarly, but opted not to be imposing. Benson had a long way to go.

"What?"

"I'm Aspen," she said, lifting her custodian license. "This is Lilith and you've met Rory. I'm hoping to chat about how we can help you get settled."

His eyes narrowed. "I am settled."

Maybe in another situation that ridiculous statement would've been funny, but I just felt for the guy. He had the deck stacked against him. We all knew it. There wasn't a thrice cursed thing I could do about it right now, either.

"In terms of processes to help Jessica and Robert's transitions to school and kinder, in assisting you to find work, that sort of stuff." She sent him a sunny smile. "Can we come in, or would you prefer to make time to chat at the office?"

"No."

The door closed.

I had to admit, as annoying as that was, I'd probably do the same.

"It doesn't have to be today," Aspen agreed calmly. "But we do need to speak to you. Lilith, when can we stop by next?"

Lilith brought up her calendar, pointed at the complicated scheduling we had over the next few days. Aspen pulled a face at the name of the wizard causing a lot of the issues. *George.* "Benson, I'm going to come by at eleven tomorrow. If you'd rather meet somewhere else, or a different time, you're going to need to tell me."

The door wasn't opened again. No noise came from inside.

"See you tomorrow at eleven," she told the wood, then turned and jerked her head toward the stairs. "What's the range on ursathropes' hearing?" she asked me, holding out her hand for a stick of gum.

"No idea," I admitted. "Good enough he heard you talking through that door easily."

She nodded and said nothing else until we were on a tram back to the office, the city passing us by slowly. "I rescheduled tomorrow's appointment with George," Lilith said, putting away her phone. "Put the new appointment in our shared calendar."

"He'd be hung over as shit at eleven anyway," I reminded her, because she looked annoyed. "It's probably for the best."

"Yeah, but we need to talk to him before we can lock in the date for him to tour The Cottage," Aspen told me, as if I didn't know that. Which was fair, really. We had to try. Trying was our job.

"He's already said he doesn't want to go to rehab," Lilith reminded her. "No matter how nice it is. I agree it needs to be done, but I don't think trying to cut corners to force it earlier is worthwhile."

Aspen shrugged, because she would never agree with Lilith's pragmatic view. She somehow juggled unconditional positive regard with high standards and made it look easy. "Anyway." She blew out a breath and looked at me. "We need info on ursathrope culture."

"And what went down in Brisbane," I added.

"It's in your inboxes," Lilith told us, hitting the button to bring the tram to a halt at our office. "If this one goes south, it's going to get *really* messy. And not just in terms of admin."

Messy is my middle name. "That's nothing new," I reminded Lilith.

The lack of response made me second-guess my statement. Were they sitting there, trying to figure out what to say? I'd meant for it to be a joke, but they both sat, straight-faced. Before I could clarify to lighten the mood, Aspen said, slowly, "Not many of our families have little kids. Lilith's right. It feels different. That probably isn't fair, but..."

"That's nothing new, either," I said, hating the bitterness that had seeped into my soul at some point when I wasn't looking, but glad they didn't appear to notice. "I need a coffee." And sleep that wasn't broken by nightmares.

CHAPTER 3

$\mathcal{A}$spen checked her phone. "I'd better run," she told Zane, with a friendly smile. "Thank you so much for the information."

The 'information' had been rapid-fire speculation and folklore based on ursathropes. She did the polite farewells and headed off, once more avoiding going into the Playground.

I wondered if Zane had finally figured out that all the silver she wore and all the meetings she kept brief...it was specific to lycanthropes. He stood beside me, hands on his hips, frown on his face, watching as she strode off toward the tram with her head up and one hand braced against the bag at her hip.

"What's up?" I asked him, when he didn't move inside immediately.

He tilted his head, just a little, toward me. "You probably can't see him."

Adrenaline washed over me and I breathed it in deep, felt it sink into my bones. Zane was being watched? Or was *I?* "Probably not. Can he hear us?"

"Definitely." Zane smiled, slow, dangerous and utterly mirthless. "You know his alpha as Duke."

The adrenaline turned to ice. *Afternoon sun and the murmur of the bush. The press of my sleeves, rolled up to my forearms.*

"He must be short on things to do, or getting wiser and realizing that mangy bastard isn't worth dying for." Zane looked down at me, and the smile softened. "I figured not everyone needed to know."

By *not everyone* he meant Aspen, and I felt sick to my stomach. I was too tired for this shit. I needed information. How often, how long, where. But I didn't press him. Because if I pressed, I'd need to report, and if I reported, cops would get involved, and if cops got involved, Zane would have to justify his existence.

"Shit."

"Yep." He sighed and slung an arm over my shoulder. "Come throw me around, hey, make me feel better?"

I snorted, ignoring the way my skin crawled and let myself be guided with only some token trash talk. *Look into it later,* I told myself. And I'd have to, because those lycans had all but torn up this pack in its previous iteration only six months ago. But right now, throwing Zane around sounded far more productive than worrying. He'd've told me if there was anything urgent going on, after all.

All the way home my mind moved between how to help Zane, and how to win over Benson. Zane probably would need the police, and then evidence. Or to survive another attack. I had no doubt they *could*, but I'd rather they didn't need to.

As for Benson, the obvious answer was his kids, but from the reports we'd seen, we wouldn't get within shouting distance of them without court orders or a full Retrievals team.

Benson was the kinda guy who figured out what he had to do to tick the boxes so he didn't get tossed into SuperSec—much like Zane—but he kept everyone at a distance, unlike Zane.

Whether Benson had been working for vampires or fae, I didn't know, but I knew how both teams used lycanthropes as shock troops in their wars. It made sense they'd use an ursathrope to do heavy lifting in the battles that raged between their factions, and the guy felt, to me, like a veteran who hadn't had the support of someone like Beo to hold him together when things went bad.

I'd just let myself in when Taig appeared in the hallway outside my door, carrying groceries. The sight of him, with his day's worth of stubble and the cop-mask that hadn't yet slipped, made my heart sit lighter in my chest. *Speaking of veterans who hold folks together.* "Hey," I said, leaning a hip against the door and giving him an exaggerated once over. "Come here often?"

Some of the hard lines bracketing his eyes softened as a smile touched the corners of his lips. "Been known to," he said, and that up-all-night voice sent a shiver down my spine. I tipped my neck back and his eyes flickered to my exposed throat, his smile widening a little as he saw the invitation in my movement.

I stepped back to let him in. "I should have a shower before I take this any further," I said, shutting the door behind him, but it was a question, not a statement.

He set down the groceries and said, words mild, "Want help to wash your back?"

Everything else fell away and I stepped back, peeling off the layer of clean clothes over my sweat-soaked underlayer. His eyes tracked my progress, I watched the way his fingers moved over his buttons. Heat coiled low in my body. He'd used the damn hair-grab swoop kiss on me this morning before work and had left my knees weak for ages.

I wanted what I'd been promised.

We left clothes like breadcrumbs trailing away from our responsibilities. I saw them a moment before I stepped into the bathroom and the evidence of our discarded tasks reeled me ruthlessly back to the present. What about those forgotten grocery bags? And my gi needed a wash. The application I'd forgotten to send off for my centaur. I'd been tagged in a post I hadn't yet reacted to, too, and—

"How's your day been?" Taig asked, then turned on the water to heat.

I felt sick, suddenly. And I felt betrayed by my own body.

Again.

I swallowed it down and pulled my hair out of the tie that sort of held it back. *Fuck you, body.* My skin wanted to crawl off my flesh and down the drain. I didn't know *why*, of course, that would be too convenient. Had Ryan done something to me in the shower? Under a similar light? When he'd been asking me about my fucking day? Was I just irrevocably broken?

I didn't know, my brain wouldn't fucking *let* me.

Taig stood in the shower, making room for me under the water, waiting patiently for my response. How had my day been?

How was every single day, ever?

The future stretched out before me, and it made me feel hopeless.

"Busy." I forced myself to take the step into the not-yet-warm water and it sank its teeth into me, chasing away the doubt. "Let's talk about it later."

His expression had changed, though he had a hard-on. "Sure." But he didn't reach for me. There was no grin. That softness was still there, but now it was tempered with worry.

Bitterness lanced through me. He thought he knew what was going on. He didn't.

I pushed those thoughts away hard. My body was mine, and fuck any tiny part of my traumatized brain that had forgotten that. I adjusted the heat and reached for him, tugging him toward me and leaning into the faintest hint of desire.

The touch of his lips was cool and his skin warm. He let me press myself against him as I traced his lips with my tongue, wanting to throw myself into this head first. But his response wasn't as whole-hearted as I wanted.

The need was there, a pounding urgency in my temples, a tightness in my chest. It said *run, run, run!*

And my head said *toward him.*

But he just reached for the body wash and rubbed our noses together.

The steam was fogging my head, or my own desire was, maybe. I hooked a leg over his hip and angled my pelvis. One of his arms went around my back, holding me safely. He made a noise of pleasure, but it was the sort of sound he made right before he fell asleep wrapped in me. Not the sort that said *hold on to something, witch.*

Frustration gnawed at me. I checked the urge to run my hands up his back. I didn't think I'd be able to resist using my nails, and that wasn't something he liked. His eyes turned to me and he held the soap in his hand out of reach of the water.

The tightness in my chest increased at the question in that silent offer. "You don't have to," I said, working hard to keep the sting of rejection out of my voice. He didn't know the clawing, ripping impatience, the fluttering *escape, now* that beat at my ribs.

I wasn't going to tell him.

"I like touching you," he said, slicking those suds over me.

It was slow and sweet and the opposite of what I wanted. My body wasn't a temple, it was the local fucking pub. I tried to breathe, but there was a lump in my throat.

Yesterday after work he'd railed me against the tiles before we'd even got the water on. He'd held me up when I wanted to ooze down the plug afterwards. And he'd been all like 'are you okay?'

As if a few orgasms ever hurt anyone.

But maybe I was actually pretty stinky. I reached for some more soap and got to work with determination, refusing to hear the alarms in my head. Into the space left behind the guilt rushed in, choking me.

"I'm sorry," I said, but that was all I could manage.

"You don't have anything to be sorry for," he said, gruffly, wrapping me in his arms. Locking my limbs in place I relaxed my muscles and did my best to accept that hug. His hands firmed on my waist, and relief crashed through me as I arched into him. When he kissed me, I dove deep, drowning myself in sensation.

Taig was in the habit of giving me everything I wanted. Especially himself.

He made taking pretty easy.

CHAPTER 4

There was no lingering warmth after our shower sex, just annoyance that my hair had got wet and now I had to do all of the things to keep it tamed.

I considered hacking it off as I zipped up a hoodie to avoid unsettling the wrapped towel on my head, keeping it out of the way. I kind of liked the idea. I'd look great bald. Or with super short hair.

There was an itch under my skin feeling and today the fucking hadn't been enough to ease it.

It usually wasn't.

I pulled on socks, wondering if I was making a mistake staying with Taig. I liked his company, but we weren't exactly compatible. And the connection was…weird. The first time we'd been together I'd felt so *with* him. Now I so wasn't.

Maybe I'd just grown out of him.

A flutter of panic danced around my chest at the thought even while clinically I went through the things Taig knew that I didn't want him to spill. The man could see me put away for life, if he wanted to.

Eclipse brushed up against my legs and I absently ran a hand over her spine. She meowed at me, disapproving that she wasn't getting more attention. I tried to re-focus.

Shoving down all my misgivings I stood and went out to the kitchen, Eclipse picking her way around my feet as I went. Dinner simmered on the stove and spices fragranced the air. Taig had unpacked the groceries and started on dinner, and I'd been sitting there thinking about myself. I was such a fucking bitch.

"Hear you have an interesting client." Taig lifted the chopping board into the sink, rinsing it off. "There was no fae activity over the weekend."

I hadn't heard of any, either, but as a supernatural detective, the things that popped up on Taig's radar didn't always pop up on mine, and vice versa. And talking work was…easier. "Good to know. Quiet on all fronts."

"Never use the 'q' word," he said, shooting me a quick smile that I tried to return. Tears threatened to rush forth from nowhere and I looked down, swallowing them away. *You're fine, witch. Head in the game.* I had no reason to be sad. At least, no reason more pressing than it had been half an hour ago, and I'd been fine then. "Either you're out of onions now, or Eclipse has chased them under your couch again." He put a coffee beside me and paused for a moment to admire how Eclipse jumped up and sat on the stool beside me, warmth in his expression as he looked between us.

My belly was a hot, hard knot. I didn't want the food. "Are you planning on transferring to Sydney?" I asked, before engaging my brain, then hid behind my mug and wondered if my phone might go off. I could use a contract. Cash was always good. *I can't do this.* I crushed the thought without trying to identify what *this* could even be. There was no good answer.

"No." His fingertips skimmed over the back of my knuckles and I felt the touch like a rope, tethering me to the present. "No, I'm not." I glanced up at him and he was propped against my bench like we were chatting about our weekend plans. My internal alarms were screaming at me. I forced myself to breathe. *It's Taig. This is fine.* "The offer vanished when Davies did."

"Oh," I managed, somehow. "What a coincidence." Ryan Davies had known Taig was my rock. *Of fucking course it did.* There was nothing in my life that man hadn't tried to interfere with. I turned my hand over, trapping Taig's fingers in mine for a moment, caught between the urge to cling and crush.

Time ticked past. I stayed there, frozen, holding his hand. His fingers were just kind of cold, and I felt like I'd turned on my speed charms. Too slow, and simultaneously too fast, to exist. My skin felt strange.

"God I love you two," Taig said, with a happy sigh, squeezing my hand then reaching for the package of chicken breast and a knife, smiling at us as if sitting and watching him work was the greatest gift we could give him.

There was a circle of the hells reserved for people like me.

Don't run. Don't run. You're fucked up. Just sit and heal and choose later. But don't run.

I swallowed down the coffee and shifted on the stool. The pounding I'd asked for, and received, left my body achy. But not achy good. Just achy.

He moved around the kitchen in an old, thin t-shirt with a tea-towel thrown over his shoulder. Wet, his auburn-and-salt hair was a dark brown. He reached up into my pantry for a spice and pulled the shirt tight across the muscles in his shoulders. The strange, dark scar across his back was just a shadow on his skin from here, but the sight of it was engraved in my brain. The uneven, jagged edges. The puckered, thready black in the scar tissue that didn't make sense.

I hadn't asked what it was. He'd very clearly avoided talking about it. But I knew it wasn't a human mark.

My lover had a vampire brand.

Another swallow of my coffee didn't wash away my guilt. I had scars, too. Some of them were weird. He'd never made me feel less for them. And I should've been noticing the way the fabric stretched over his shoulders, the bands of muscle on either side of his spine, the flex of his biceps, and the curve of his arse. Now it was too late and he had the bowl held against his wonderful soft belly as he stirred briskly. Some of the contents puffed up and left a fine spray of flour on his shirt.

He didn't know he was about to have his heart broken.

You should run.

But I didn't know who the thought was directed at. My body ached and I felt sick.

I went to take a sip of coffee only to find the mug was empty.

"Heard you made an impression on Sofia."

Sofia. Sofia Delyan, the new detective who I'd met. Sort of. I latched onto the conversational gambit. "Oh yeah?"

"She said—direct quote—'that witch has balls'."

I rolled my eyes and he grinned, comfortable playing along with the topic. I stood, needing to do something aside from deconstructing why Delyan was paying lip service to the outdated concept of testicles linking to courage.

"What'd you say? And what are you making?"

He smiled down at his chicken. "Biryani and naan. You don't have chickpea flour." There was no accusation in the words but I felt a flare of impatience anyway. I had limited space and my cupboard was full of critical ingredients for potions. Chickpea flour wasn't on that list for me and it was literally my house.

"What makes you think I said anything to Delyan?" he asked. I snorted in disbelief, letting out some of the frustration that constantly gnawed at me, and started to tidy up after him. "I just told her it was news to me."

I groaned, even though it wasn't the worst response he could've managed, and could be taken a lot of ways. "Please tell me that was where it ended."

"She doesn't know we're a thing, so she explained what'd happened." He passed me a spoon and came in for a kiss. Frustration hummed through me while I forced myself to stay still and let him brush his lips over mine. I was trying to do things. Obviously that didn't matter.

"There was a bit of attention given to what happened with your ursa, so you were the topic of a few conversations. I reckon she'll have heard about you and I by tomorrow."

Uncertainty trickled through me. I scrubbed at the stubborn high tide mark in the cup he favored and ignored the unease. My warning system wasn't trustworthy.

"Are we a thing?"

"What, you don't want to be a thing? Then me and my biryani are going home. Might kidnap your cat, too, she's learning manners." He prodded the chicken and my heart sizzled, too, twisting and heating painfully. "You should cook the rice. I always screw it up."

I drew in a deep breath. "Shit." He was settling in and I was halfway out the door. But the look he sent me was so full of acceptance that I couldn't quite say that. I did manage to say, "You know I go hard, right?"

The corners of his mouth twitched as he turned his gaze to the water running over the chopping board. "No. Really?"

I chewed on the inside of my cheek as I got the rice going. I didn't really know how I went anymore. The reality of it made me feel… tired. "We never talked about what we want." Maybe there would be some obvious unsolvable conflict I could blame, rather than tell him I was getting bored?

"Do you know?" he asked, taking out the chilies.

Everything was still pretty raw, after what had gone down barely a month ago with the last High District Wizard, Ryan Davies. And the tiny detail of Taig murdering him in cold blood.

There wasn't much point in worrying about that, though. Not when I would've done the same myself, probably. But maybe that'd help when we split ways.

So, refocusing, I said, "I know we're both in high-risk jobs that have shit hours." He made a noncommittal noise and I poured approximately the right amount of rice into the dish to cook it. "You've got a kid already. So I know you lean that way."

"Do you, just?" he asked, seemingly casual.

Is this a trick question? I paused for a moment to try to assess whether those words really held as much bite as I thought they did, but he had his cop face on and I felt as insightful as a brick. So I just asked, "Don't you? Want kids?"

"Not so much I'd walk away from an amazing person if they didn't want kids," he told me. "We've got time to figure out what we want. I'm not feeling like that's the issue."

That casual acknowledgement was a well-placed blow and I paused while unnecessarily stirring the chicken to feel the huge, gaping hole in my chest.

Future possible children weren't an issue. But there *was* an issue.

I had no idea where I'd come from. I knew my dad was a wizard who hid his strength to keep anonymity, and nothing about my mother.

Well, that sort of gap in the family tree had roll-on effects. I hadn't yet had time to figure out what they were. And, honestly, I had bigger issues. I wasn't looking at any of that.

But he wasn't, either.

Did I want to be with Taig?

The future swirled in front of me, nebulous and terrifying. I didn't want to look at it. I wanted a path I could charge down.

A tray scraped as he slid it into the oven and I let out a long breath. I knew myself well enough to acknowledge if I set off to do a thing, I'd do it. And the path Taig was suggesting was probably the safest, most sensible path I could possibly charge down, right now.

I wondered what my therapist would say about that, but we were busy talking about Brandon, my all-but brother who had died horribly in my arms. Because that was fucking traumatic.

I scrubbed the feeling of tacky plastic table off my cheek. "If we're official," I told Taig, letting out a long breath. "And we're exclusive, I can swap out my STI charm. I wouldn't mind having another Blowback or a Deflect."

He glanced up at me, studying my earrings. "They'd be hard to match with something else. I'll get tested before you remove that one. Seems fair."

The man just made everything so easy. He always had. It was the reason he was so dangerous. "So—yes, we're exclusive, we're a thing, we're getting comfy," I confirmed, hands on my hips.

"Yes, Rory," he said, tossing the discarded bits of chili as he passed by me. "We're a thing, we're already comfy because you wear all of my shirts, and I look forward to waking up with you curled around me. Can you make the raita while I get this finished up?"

My head spun. "Your shirts are comfy. And they have cute sayings on them." We should probably look at moving in together. Talk about how we'd navigate finances. That was the responsible thing to do, right? The thought of having a tangible goal like that was strangely comforting.

"True. And I love you in them. Even if it means I need to buy more. So we're sorted. I figured I'd suggest you leave a few sets of clothes at my place in a week or two, ease you into the idea."

Who eased into ideas? *Just keep going. That's how you get this done.* "Yeah, that would work. Except now I'm onto you." I was saying a hard no to kids for the next twelve months. I stole a piece of cucumber, thinking about the timeline there. I had a few years before the body clock thing became relevant. It was probably a good time to be looking for financial stability, such as it was in this end-stage capitalist hell.

"This works too," he said, and I had no idea what he was talking about. "I'd see if you want a kiss, but you don't need chili on you. Got word that your new client's got some cash jobs."

He'd basically proposed to me a few weeks ago, but he'd been drugged up on incredibly dangerous witch-hunter potions. I'm pretty sure he'd marry me if I suggested it, though. Did I want that?

I thought of the organization that went into weddings and cringed back from the idea. There was just no way I could keep all that straight. I didn't even buy green bananas at the moment.

So instead I went back over the conversation I'd been mostly ignoring. "Client. Benson?" My ursa.

"Yeah." He stepped aside so I could grab a spoon for the yogurt. "Bouncing is what I'm hearing. Rumors he's been offered some jobs doing knee-breaking work, but not sure if he's taken them."

He'd be a fantastic kneebreaker, but I paused over the mint and tried to imagine him willingly leaping into that world. Being a bouncer for cash was one thing. Getting involved in collecting drug money was a whole different situation. "He's got kids. Six and four."

Thank fuck I didn't. I paused for a moment to imagine the TV going, shoes on the floor, backpacks vomiting educational paraphernalia, constantly interrupted thoughts and unmet needs.

Nope.

"I don't want kids," I told him, turning back to the mint. "Not for awhile. Maybe not ever."

He paused for a moment. "A very small part of me is sad," he said, slowly. "But I think that's the stupid part of me that doesn't have to live in reality."

"Don't insult my favorite detective," I said, absently. "So, Benson, kids."

Taig made another noncommittal noise. "And no partner on record. Came Overworld solo with the kids. Went through the camps with them. Took about four years to be processed, so the youngest must've been pretty new."

I scowled at him. "How come you get this shit? This is information I need."

He eyed the knife in my hand warily. "Stand down, witch, I'm a sharing caring kinda guy."

I rolled my eyes. "I don't dice people accidentally, Taig." I hacked up the mint furiously. *Fuck it.* I was going to have to pull VicPol's records now, which meant I'd have to sift through what they had and compare it to what the Brisbane police had sent to us. If I had any energy left at the end of that I'd be siccing Maadai onto them. As our new Head District Magi, a grumpy email from her meant a lot more than one from me.

"He's branded," Taig told me, quietly. "Vampire property, Spring clan."

A chill went through me. I didn't look up, though. I didn't let that strange mark on his back take up my whole brain. "Ex vampire property."

"Yeah. Ex."

"That would've been nice for Delyan to tell me," I muttered, irritated. Or anyone, really. It was sort of important.

"She doesn't know," he said, the words neutral. "The photo of the brand was part of his processing in the camps. I recognized it." The chill became ice. *Are we doing this?* I looked up at him, but he was cleaning the board, bustling around.

My heart ached. "Want to talk about it?" I offered, forcing myself to focus.

He shot me a quick, slightly amused look. "No, love. No, I don't. But thank you."

Relief rushed through me, soured by guilt. I shouldn't have been grateful for that. Maybe I should've looked into his past already. I could call in some favors. Lift some files.

My feet felt naked, suddenly, without my boots. I could go for a jog and call Nic. He'd hook me up. Why hadn't I ever done that? Taig had done it to me. Should I? I didn't *know.*

He was hyper focused on the cooking naan and I crushed the urge to rush off, scrubbing a hand over my face. He needed me. I knew what that was like.

"Okay. I don't know, either, then." It was easier not to know anything than to explain *how* I knew it. And really, it wasn't a whole new world of information that would change the way we supported Benson.

But it was a tiny piece of the puzzle about the man I was now in a steady relationship with, who had been Overworld, had a mark I knew wasn't human, and was very twitchy about vampires.

"Too easy," he agreed, voice neutral. "Keep your eyes out, though, because vamps don't like losing what's theirs." He cleared his throat as I scrambled to figure out how to respond. "How's the rice? My chicken's done."

I leant into the normal for him, the rhythms of everyday, and stuffed down my own impatience. We ate on the couch and flicked through some shows. The evening melted away and I ignored the sense of *this is wrong.*

It wasn't wrong. I was just too broken to recognize good, for now.

CHAPTER 5

The kiss Taig had pressed to my lips was washed away by the coffee's bitterness. I looked down at where Eclipse was curled half atop my feet beneath the rumpled covers and imagined my lover putting on his detective O'Malley face, glancing both ways before opening his car door, and heading off to his early shift as the city woke around me.

Notifications lit my phone up and I swiped them away. I knew what today was and I didn't want to do it. Instead I read my emails, caught up on the latest outrage on social media, and got into an online argument with a dude who probably didn't wipe his arse.

Somehow I managed to run late for my psychologist appointment. I had a particular set of skills.

"How're you going?" she asked me, with a smile.

"Great," I lied, because that was what you did.

"How have the nightmares been?" she asked, opening up her notes.

Had I had nightmares last night? Was it the night before? It was all a blur. "They're okay." Because I knew she was going to ask, I said, "Distress level about five."

She made a note. "Where are you feeling it?"

In my bones. Grief tugged at me. I didn't say those words, just waved a hand at my core, where the heaviness sat, holding me down. That was enough truth for her, wasn't it?

She nodded, passing me the tappers to start the EMDR. "Is there anything you want to work on today?"

Shame was slippery in my belly. *Cheap body spray and plastic on my cheek.* I shook my head.

She nodded. "We'll stick with what we've been doing, then." I felt myself sink a little deeper into the cushions, relaxing with relief.

Did she know?

If she did, she gave no sign of it.

"Thinking of Brandon, now. Remember that moment you realized one of you would die. The way the sun felt on your skin, and the quiet of the bush after the flock of birds faded out."

My own words in her mouth felt like foam bullets hitting me from a kids' gun. I sat in the room that smelled of vanilla, on that soft couch, feeling the weight in my guts and the ache in my bones. But it wasn't Brandon looking across the bridge at me I saw. It was Ryan, his expression one of concern.

"What's your distress level?" she asked, quietly.

I drew in a deep breath, feeling sick, and forced my brain back to Brandon. I had to put a fucking number on this shit. "I don't know. Six."

"Notice that."

The tappers in my hands went off and I tried to just sit with the feeling, but birds screamed and a table stuck to my face as I tried to push away on arms that barely worked. I kept my eyes fixed on my hands. My hands, half-hidden by the teal knit top I was wearing. My forearms, encased behind the soft fabric. Not exposed by a rolled-up shirt.

"What are you noticing?" she asked me.

"My shirt," I said, honestly, and there was a catch in my voice.

"Notice that." And off we went again, on the cycle.

I was supposed to picture putting my shit into charms and closing the box on them when I was done. But the stones in my head cracked.

"What have you got on for the rest of the day?" she asked me, as I mopped away some of the tears that always seemed to linger during these sessions.

The thought of even looking at my calendar made me want to sob like a child. But I didn't need to. A million small tasks awaited me. Notes I hadn't yet made, calls I needed to return, emails I needed to respond to, forms I had to complete and send off. Steps I needed to take down that hallway. A break room I'd have to sit in. An office I'd work in. The sun would creep across the sky and ease itself down beneath the horizon.

Sometimes I saw it happen from my skin. Sometimes from the other side of the window.

"Work," I said, standing.

She didn't look happy. "You can always call if you need anything, Rory."

Sure I could. And she'd do her best, I had no doubt.

I tapped my card. Closed the door after myself.

I wasn't healed.

It was a slow process, sure, but I was good at expediting unnecessary bullshit. And this was unnecessary bullshit.

I was done with it. Done with looking at my job and feeling like I couldn't put one foot in front of the other. Done with looking at the man holding me and wondering if I could ever love him. Done with the fury and impatience.

But I didn't know what to do now.

The morning sun hit my face and the weight of my phone in my hand was a ball and chain. The quiet lane looked the same as it had when I'd walked in. It'd look the same when I was dead, I expected. Anyway, it felt wrong.

I didn't know what to do, but I knew what I couldn't do. And that was going in to work, slapping on a professional face, and taking care of business.

My options spread out before me, and they all fucking sucked.

A low-slung red car cruised to a halt in front of me, and my mouth went dry as I reached for my wand. Ah, the age-old solution to everyone's problems. Adrenaline.

That was probably at the top of the list of shit I really didn't need.

But when the window buzzed down, I saw Nic lounging behind the wheel, one arm draped over the passenger seat. "Get in," he said. "The coffee's going cold."

I didn't hesitate, sliding in beside him and taking the coffee in the cup holder associated with my seat. "Hey," I said, because I had to say something.

"I know I lied. Deal with it." He eased us out of the lane and into traffic.

That wasn't the normal response to 'hey'. But this was Nic. "Lied?" I asked, my head aching and the adrenaline still humming in my veins.

He glanced over at me, eyes narrowed. "Yeah. Told you I wasn't Watching you anymore."

Ice ran through my veins. "You're still...?"

He held up the battered old handmade necklace I remembered flicking out of the way when I applied pressure to a neck wound, the same one that'd hit me in the nose not a few times when my legs had been over Nic's shoulders.

Pulling myself back into the present left me feeling exhausted. Or the ebbing adrenaline did. His hands were back on the wheel, now, but that necklace stayed atop his fashionably weathered shirt. The beads there glowed softly, tied together like drops of dew in a spiderweb. It looked like it'd been modified since I'd seen it. Not to increase the number of charms, but to remove some. Two, I suspected. I didn't wonder who he'd cut off, because my eye was drawn to the dead, flat stone that hung like it actually understood the laws of gravity.

He still wore the charm for Brandon.

Tears filled my throat and I looked away because I didn't know if I could keep them off my cheeks. The city blurred around us. New-car smell and Nic filled my head and part of me wanted to step back in time, to when we'd squeezed every single moment for joy until we were wrung dry.

Instead, I drew in a deep breath, and felt the softness of the leather beneath my butt and thighs.

He'd told me he'd stop Watching for me. I hadn't blamed him. It had gotten messy, fast. When you did everything top speed, and so did your partner, and you both went into a tailspin? And losing Brandon had been the sharp turn that'd sent us onto a near-fatal path.

"I'm sorry," he said, eventually.

I'd figured he'd keep Aspen and the few of his family who'd stayed on our side of morality on the charm web, so he could read their futures. I'd been shocked to find out years ago that I'd even warranted a spot on his family web.

Then we'd gone and fucked it up. Literally.

"How often have you been checking in on me?" I asked, wondering how much of what'd gone down he'd read.

"Just every now and then, between jobs." He shrugged. "Taking you off would've meant taking B off."

Looked to me like he'd cut off one of his uncles and cousins, but I could have been wrong. He'd told me who they all were at some point, but I hadn't thought much beyond the fact the man had me in his family web.

And he still did.

"Thanks," I managed to say, sounding more or less normal. I knew he'd be looking out for Aspen, of course. "I'm still not going to ride your dick ever again."

I expected him to laugh, but when I glanced over he was frowning a bit. "That was a joke, right?" he asked. "You don't actually think I'm here to fuck you?"

Since when did Nic get serious? "No." I hesitated as he sped around another car on the freeway, assuming he had the demerit points to burn or he knew there were no cops in the vicinity. "Why *are* you here, though?"

He shrugged, taking his icy drink from the holder. "Felt like a good day to go bush."

I drew in a breath and resisted the urge to ask about the futures he'd Read. We'd done this often enough that I trusted him, and speaking about the maybe's that we were trying to dodge didn't help anyone.

"Don't suppose you know what went down during Samhain?" I asked him, trying to keep the question casual.

He cocked a brow. "I don't do pasts, Sunshine. Only futures. All I got is you're fucked up. I did hear another King Ratfucker went missing in your vicinity."

The sound of the gunshot and Taig's voice saying *troll cartridges* smashed simultaneously through my senses and I squeezed my eyes shut as if I could block my ears somehow with that reflexive motion.

"Your coffee's going to go cold," he said, again.

I swallowed and reached for it, ignoring the swell of unease. It just tasted like coffee. Nic wasn't going to try to spike anything.

"Samhain was touch and go with us," he said, settling back. "Bang might be out permanently. Waiting for the docs to assess her performance with her new prosthetic."

My heart ached for her. "I'll see if she wants a training partner."

"You just look after you," he said, in his irritating leader-who-reads-the-future way. "I thought we were making small talk. Anyway, her next assessment is tomorrow morning."

I wondered if it'd be a good thing to reach out and wish her luck, or if it'd just make her feel vulnerable. I knew the way Aspen had asked about my therapy sessions didn't feel great. How are you supposed to respond to that? *'I think I only used four tissues this time, but I also dissociated twenty minutes in, so I think that's a net loss'?* Yeah, no.

The coffee sat heavily in my hand, so I put it back in the cup holder and let my head dip back. The last of my strength ebbed, and I dozed.

Maybe I woke every time I felt Nic brake, but those little rushes of whatever stress hormones bled away swiftly. I measured their impact in the too-quick heartbeats that punctuated my rest but couldn't have said what the final count was when I came awake with a proper jolt as his tires hit gravel.

My neck hurt and my mouth was dry, but I was entirely aware as I took in our location and situation in an instant.

"Morning," he drawled, as another car passed us on the narrow bush road. "Sorry to bore you to sleep."

I didn't bite. We were driving still, he'd just moved over to allow the other car to pass by. Soon he moved back into the center where it was sealed and continued on, no longer flying as he had been on the freeway.

Nic respected 'roos more than cops. That was what happened when things were legal for a price, and you could pay it.

"Your phone's been going off. I turned it off so you could sleep, and I let Aspen know you're with me, but if there's anyone not connected to her…"

My heart sank. They'd all be worrying about me. I took my phone from where he'd put it on the charger and fired off a few quick texts so they'd all know I was okay.

"Where are we going?" I asked, expecting Taig would ask as soon as he realized I wasn't at work.

Rather than respond, Nic lifted his hand and pointed to a half-melted sign beside the road. I saw the name of the national park on faded tourist-attraction brown. *Beehive Falls.*

My head spun.

I hadn't set foot in that patch of bush since Brandon had died on the bridge a few meters from those falls.

"This is what you read?" I asked, the words coming from far away.

"Best future for you, bitch," he drawled, capping off his bottle. "Kinda flattering that it involved me, I have to say." He shot me a quick shit-eating grin that didn't distract from the worried creases in his brow. "I'll come up with you, but there's a lot of possibilities after the first two minutes."

Since he wasn't in his nigh-impenetrable lupetec, I assumed they weren't likely to be violent options. "Okay." I considered asking him for more info, even knowing he'd say no, because information could skew outcomes. Instead, I downed the now cold coffee as he eased us into a carpark.

He didn't sit and think about the track ahead or the what ifs. He didn't need to. That was one of the many perks of hanging out with an Oracle.

It also helped me to get moving when I just wanted to sit and drink it in and talk myself up. He tossed me a bottle of water and led the way along the walking track leading up into Mount Difficult.

There wasn't enough air, but it wasn't because of the pace he set.

The wind was cool, and the cloud cover was heavy. There'd be rain overnight. I kept expecting to feel the afternoon sunlight, but I didn't.

I couldn't remember this part of the track. I'd been levitated out, in shock from blood loss and shitfuckery. Because even with Brandon's sacrifice, I hadn't really been a match for Duke. I'd held him off, temporarily. That was all I could do.

My team had kept my heart beating. I hadn't thanked them for that. Not ever.

And I still couldn't, either, because Nic was a half-step ahead of me and the words were caught somewhere between my lungs and my lips. Maybe that was why I couldn't breathe.

The rocks slipped under my sensible flats but I kept my balance. Nic didn't even glance back.

Because you can do this, Rory. I stopped, bracing my hands on my hips. My heart was pinging against my ribs like a fucking faerie and I could feel the clammy sweat beneath my boobs and arms. I hadn't worn a polyester shirt, but I may as well have.

I rubbed my palms against the fabric of my pants, feeling the softness. I picked out the scents of dust and healthy decomposition, the clean smell of the air away from the city. I listened to the bush and heard nothing except wind in the leaves.

Slowly, I breathed in, then out, then in again. I counted those breaths out, trying to extend myself the way Aspen had taught me. I could never remember how many seconds an out breath was supposed to be.

I was pretty sure I was winning just because I had a go, though.

The crinkle of plastic made me glance up to see Nic waiting up ahead, taking a drink of water. He didn't have his phone in his hand, but he had a detached air about him all the same. Not like when we were on a hunt and I fell behind. Like we were bored and waiting for our meal at a café.

When you were with the equivalent of a barometer for trouble, normal behavior was good.

"I bet you're feeling so smug right now," I said, realizing he was going to gloat about this for years.

He grinned and shrugged. "Not often I get to rescue you anymore."

I straightened, blowing out my breath without counting this time. "Don't get used to it." And I made sure I paid attention to the fine sandy soil with the red clay beneath, feeling them through the soles of my shoes.

He didn't hit back, just ambled along beside me, skimming through his bird identification app every now and then.

I didn't remember if he and I had ever been on a normal, low-stakes bushwalk. Maybe we'd had a picnic, once. Or at least we'd made out beside a lake. That was pretty much the same thing.

"You're getting boring," I told him, amused at the thought.

He rubbed a hand through his hair. "Got me some grays. Pretty cool."

How he linked boring and gray hair I wasn't sure but I knew better than to argue. "What'd you do on your last day off?"

"Looked at houses."

I resisted the urge to laugh, and when the bitterness rose in the wake of the mirth I was glad I'd kept it to myself. "Find anything good?"

"Couple of options. Nothing that I consider to be 'the one', you know?"

I didn't, because I'd burned through my savings when I'd been unable to work after Brandon's death. I'd never been in a position to own property. "What're you looking for?"

He shrugged. "Something with some space so I can walk around naked in peace."

I knew the bravado was skin deep. Slamming doors, barking dogs, the crunch of gravel under boots, the hum of vehicles could all set us off when we got back and the hypervigilance hadn't eased yet. He wanted space to patch up his psyche when he returned to normality.

But he hadn't said that. He'd said he wanted to be a nudist. So I humored him and said, "That's a lot of sunscreen you'll be using. Factor that into your budget."

He snorted. "Come on, Sunshine. You're talking to the ultimate forward planner."

Who'd had his heart broken by yours truly. I focused on my breath for a few steps, and my pulse didn't race the way it had earlier.

I could see the break in the trees up ahead, the rocks that jutted out of the bush. Fear hummed under my skin. And wasn't it ironic that the thing I was most scared of was myself?

CHAPTER 6

$\mathcal{N}$ic stood beside me, shoulder to shoulder. Together we faced the new bridge that had been built to replace the one smashed during the murder of our best friend. The wood didn't look new…and the steel bones of the structure looked serious.

It wasn't the same bridge that Ryan had appeared on, in my dreams. And there was something powerful about that.

I don't know what I'd expected, but I didn't feel it when I looked at the bridge with the rocky outcrop on the other end and the creek below.

I could've pointed to exactly where Duke had stood, doing his Lycy the Bogan impersonation. I could've pointed at where I'd knelt beside Brandon and tried to hold his broken pieces together. And, for all Nic's claims around only Reading the future, I hoped he wasn't looking back to that moment.

The air in my lungs left in another slow breath and I stepped forward alone onto that bridge and stood there in the lack of afternoon sun. The calm of the bush was bittersweet.

Brandon wasn't there, of course. He was in our hearts and memories, in the occasional turns of phrase and the little mannerisms, in the stories shared and good times remembered.

"I feel like I should miss him more than I do," I said, slowly.

Into the quiet after that statement the bush breathed around us, just a normal weekday without any tourists or excitement. Beautiful, peaceful, and nothing like what I saw in my nightmares.

"I'm assuming now you said that out-loud you know how ridiculous it is."

Was it survivor guilt? I didn't feel it every minute of every day, which would've made more sense, considering how it'd gone down. And as weathered as this timber was, it had only been two years. Here I was, not even crying. I'd cried yesterday when I'd had no toast to go with my eggs, but I couldn't cry where Brandon's life had ended?

The railing was smooth. I wondered if I could boost myself over this one the way Duke had done. The angle was a bit different, now, and I'd been putting in a lot of gym time.

When I glanced over at Nic he was leaning against a tree on the carpark side of the bridge, his eyes on the clouds and an expression of intense concentration on his face. He was Reading something, but I didn't know what.

I did know, from how relaxed he was, that he must've been here before. Driven by that thought, I asked, "When'd you come?"

He blinked a few times. "About six weeks after he'd passed."

Our relationship had probably been a fiery ball of wreckage about then, but I wasn't sure. Time was weird. "Been back often?"

He shook his head. "Just that once. Brandon wasn't here. I couldn't feel him, you know?"

I did. And I was glad of it, now.

"I thought I'd lost you both, here," Nic said, straightening. "For a while. Took some time for me to get used to you not being around."

For some foolish reason that was what made the tears come back. He'd never said anything about it. We couldn't talk sensibly when we were both hemorrhaging. "Same."

He shrugged. "I'm glad you're still here." He paused, and I felt the weight of his attention like a warm blanket. "Keep being still here, okay?"

I opened my mouth to assure him that was my plan, but the words were caught in my throat and I didn't know why. *I'm working on it.*

"I don't need you." He flashed me his trademark shit-eating grin, his blue eyes sparkling for just a moment before the mirth melted away, to be replaced by uncharacteristic seriousness as he said, gently, "But my world's better with you still kicking around."

My heart turned over. I reached for him and he folded me into his long, lean arms. His hug was just a little awkward and a bit too familiar. But he was safe. "I miss you. I don't miss the work."

"You miss the team," he corrected. "But anyway, I'm still here. You can always drop me a line. We can go microdose and people watch while eating fast food."

The idea was so far from the emotion-wrought bushwalk that it shocked a laugh out of me, as had probably been his intention, and I stepped back only to find him passing me his keys. Unease swept through me, but his expression was relaxed.

"I'm going to get a call out," he said, bumping his forehead momentarily against mine in a rare show of affection. "Look after her. I'll be back in the next week or so to pick her up from Melbourne, probably."

How had I dealt with this guy? I watched him walk off with his self-assured swagger, confident he'd played every single move right... because he fucking had.

He always did, right up until he didn't. And then we paid in blood and tears.

I tucked his keys into my pocket and turned back to the bridge as I listened to his steps fade into the distance. When he got the call his voice drifted back through the bush and reverberated off the rocks. The ghost of his brief conversation made me feel isolated.

The wood beneath my fingertips was cool and smooth. My steps sounded strange on the planks without my boots on. Almost tentative.

My heart sat heavily in my chest. I'd been tired and sad before this. Now I was tired, sad, alone, and hours away from snacks. What the fuck sort of self-care bullshit was this? I was doing it wrong.

But I crossed the bridge and hesitated where Brandon had stood, gun cocked, because I'd been nervous. And the day kept slipping away, painfully normal. There should've been some whisper of him. It would've been fair. Maybe I could've put him to rest after a good display of grief.

I didn't trust the little voice that told me to keep looking for peace, but I was here, now. So I followed where my feet led me and wished life was as simple as the films made it seem.

There were long shadows in the gully where Brandon had been thrown, where I'd somehow managed to scramble down. Where I'd tried to put pressure on his wounds and been unable to reach my healing magick without collapsing wards. Where I'd taken on a lycanthrope with nothing but a silver ceremonial knife and a whole lot of terror.

But standing in that place I didn't feel the afternoon sunlight on my skin. Not the way I had that day. There was no smell of blood. My hands weren't tacky with it. The birds were silent.

Sure, my stomach turned, but it felt like a normal level of response, really. So I stood there while my feet started to ache and sat with the feeling, watching the shadows move as the wind rustled the leaves above, sending sunlight dancing into the dark. Maybe that was as cinematic as my grief could be, some pretty, twirling shadows.

I drew in a breath and was surprised that it didn't shake. Brandon was gone. I hadn't clawed my way out of that gully myself, but I'd bought myself time for my team to get there. I'd been over it often enough I could identify every single time I'd zigged when I should've zagged. I'd played it over and over in my head so often it was basically timestamped.

Brandon was still gone. Brandon would always be gone. That was how it worked.

I scrubbed my hand over my face and turned away from the scene, toward the waterfall the area was named for. Across the sharp cut-in I thought I could see chunks of rock where bullets might've damaged the face of the area. In the gully I thought I could see downed trees that had started to decay, covered with moss and mushrooms. The waterfall was flowing, but it was only a peaceful trickle.

I'd stood there, on that rock. He'd told me I was jumpy.

I plonked my butt on it and looked up at the clouds crouching over me, but there was no wisdom to be had there.

"I'm not jumpy," I said, just because I could.

And I remembered the night I'd signed on with the Custodians. The way the alarms had rang in my head, but I hadn't heeded them. I remembered the way Ryan had looked at me over the entire congregation of magi and smiled, holding our jobs in his hands, and I hadn't listened to myself.

The tears burned and I let them, because this felt like the lesson I had to learn. Not that Brandon was gone. I knew that.

I wasn't jumpy. I was anxious, sad, and fucked up. I'd learned hard lessons and I might've learned them too well, or a bit wonky, but I'd done it to get through. I was pretty sure that's what Aspen had told me. It felt true.

With the rock cold and hard beneath my arse I sat and stared at the fine stones in the pool of water at my feet. I wished it was as simple as turning back the clock. Just go back to that exact moment where I'd known something was wrong, and then been gaslit. Was it gaslighting?

It didn't matter, because there was no such thing as time magic. There was no way to get back there and take what I knew. And fuck living through all that shit again.

I wasn't stronger, now. I was tired, angry, and jaded. But I sure as shit had some finely honed skills from all the surviving I'd done.

Sure, I'd give it up if I could in exchange for peace and quiet. That wasn't an option, so I needed to apply that shit I'd learned.

I needed to trust myself. Because I wasn't just jumpy.

CHAPTER 7

Driving Nic's car was a whole experience. I still winced when I saw how much it cost to fuel the trip back to Melbourne. I paid for parking, and trusted him to have insurance.

I was going to rebuild myself. Whether I'd be better than ever, well, I doubted that was how it'd work. But I'd be good. And the first step was practicing listening to myself.

I listened to my body when I got home and folded myself down on the ground to hold the purring, welcoming Eclipse. I listened to my body and shoveled in real food even though I just wanted to eat some chips and fall into bed. I listened to my body and hauled arse out of bed in the morning rather than sitting on my phone scrolling endlessly, and didn't have to rush.

Maybe I did know how to do this self-care shit. Pat cats, eat snacks, shower for half an hour. I didn't even need to worry about therapy for another week, which was a straight up win.

No one gave me shit for having been off work with little to no warning yesterday. Lilith went so far as to buy me some cake and summarize what'd gone down so I didn't have to read over the notes.

"Not like Benson minded that we couldn't make it," she said, with a shrug, ignoring the disapproving look Aspen shot her.

It was midday when we approached Benson's place again. My gut said the ursathrope wasn't going to play ball. I wasn't surprised when Aspen knocked to no avail.

"We need to lay eyes on those kids," Lilith muttered, grimly, on our way out.

I turned it over in my head, trying to figure out how I felt about that. Were they in danger? It wasn't like Lilith to identify when a glass was half-empty. Had I missed something?

Before I could decide, Aspen said, "We need to work with him." She shot us an annoyed look, as if we were part of this problem. "Otherwise he's going to feel threatened and lash out and they'll lose him."

Lilith lifted her brows at me, but I held my hands up in peace. "He got them through the camps," I told them both. "He's not used to having anyone on his team." That didn't mean I liked giving him time, but I didn't think he was a lost cause just yet.

"Ah, you got that info too?" Lilith nodded, shrugged. "Sorry. Meant to forward it on. Got sent across late last night—VicPol, because apparently that got lost in the transfer."

"His move from Brisbane was abrupt," Aspen said, looking between us. "Why? You two seem to be in the know."

Lilith shrugged. "Nothing in the reports."

"My source didn't mention it."

Aspen grinned. "Mm, he's your *sauce*, is he?" I arched a brow and jumped onto the tram, then held a spot clear for the two of them. "Oh, don't be coy, we both know who you're talking to. Any other info?"

I thought of the brand I'd found an image of in the files and what I was, and wasn't, supposed to say. *My boyfriend's been vampire fodder* didn't seem like a great opener. "Only that he's rumored to have picked up cash work. Bouncing, maybe."

"Where?" Lilith asked me.

I shrugged. "It wasn't that specific. But I'd put ten bucks on it being in shouting distance of his kids."

"Are ursathropes paternal?" Lilith asked us, unimpressed by my challenge. "He's giving coercive controller."

"Zane didn't know much," Aspen admitted. "They'd been all-but wiped out where his pack came from, so he's working from folklore."

I thought again of that brand and the way he'd crumpled the metal table like it was tissue paper. I thought of Zane, so gently protecting Aspen's feelings, never letting on that he knew how terrified she was. Was the difference just Beo? Was it just having someone to hold the space? And, if it was, would Benson's children be okay, even if he continued to struggle to connect?

"He brought those kids over here with him. He would've had to jump through hoops to keep them."

"First choice is always education and support," Aspen added firmly.

Lilith shot me another look over Aspen's head. It was our first choice, sure, but it wasn't our only one. And if shit went down, I didn't want them being collateral. But I wasn't decided yet, and I objected to her assuming that I was assuming. We were all asses.

Lilith's mouth was a hard line, though. "He can be educated and supported away from them."

"You're jumping the gun," Aspen told her flatly, but I stayed silent, studying Lilith's expression. "He's defensive and scared. I would be, too, and so would you. We need to be present, nonthreatening, and build a relationship."

"Sure, I'll build a relationship with his door." I resisted the urge to kick Aspen. Something was very wrong with Lilith, or this client, for her to be speaking like that. "Meanwhile, we want those kids to start school. The older they get, the harder the transition is," Lilith said, flatly. "If he's stopping them from accessing education—"

"So we work fast," Aspen cut in, annoyed. "I need to make some calls. Let's go clubbing tonight."

I breathed deeply. Oh, he was going to love having us rock up wherever he was working. "I'll see if I can narrow down where he might be."

Lilith sighed, running shining black nails through her hair. Today it shone a brilliant blood red. Her bathroom probably looked like a murder scene when she had a shower. I approved. "I'll see if I can get some options for his work that are more legal. And will suit school hours."

"He's not getting government payments either," Aspen reminded her. "I have those forms printed. We can pre-fill a bunch of it with what we've got and make an appointment to get him in to finalize it at the local branch."

"Local branch is trash," Lilith said, with a dismissive flick of her fingers. "I'll get him in with someone I know when the time comes."

Aspen snapped her fingers, grinning at us. "See? We can do this."

"*We* can," Lilith agreed, and the inference wasn't lost on me. We could lead our ursathrope to water, but we couldn't make him enjoy the view.

I needed to ask some questions of my favorite witch. She wasn't going to love that, and I didn't know I would, either, but something was up. Meanwhile, I thought of that barely leashed fury, the vampire brand, and the speed in which our ursathrope clients had relocated from Brisbane. "I'm going to go see Wesley." Lilith wouldn't say boo in front of anyone. Possibly even me. So why not progress what I could?

Their eyes swung toward me in horror. "How will that help?" Aspen demanded. "We need to know where Benson's going to be tonight."

"Yeah we do," I agreed, feeling mildly sick. "We also need to know what could be coming for him."

"You're thinking vampires?" Lilith asked, her eyes narrowed.

I shrugged. "I don't have a fae on my list to ask, and it'll be one or the other." There was enough truth in that statement that the rest of their questions dried up.

"Can we go this afternoon?" Aspen asked, looking at her calendar. "I have a twelve-thirty with Zane's teens' Inclusions Officer and I'm really hopeful those young folks will be able to attend this time."

"I've got this," I told her. "Off the clock." Both of them took this silently. The noise of the city washed in around us, ebbing into the cracks left behind. But I was too raw to just leave them there like that, so, keeping one eye on the tram stops, I said, quietly, "If he knows something, it's going to be unofficial. We know his motivations align with ours."

"We know he could obliterate the entire city in a night," Lilith said, flatly. "We know we're an ongoing amusement to him."

"She's right," Aspen said. "I'm all for unconditional positive regard —but that guy is on a different level."

They weren't getting arguments from me. "Fuck," I muttered, shouldering my bag. "It doesn't hurt to ask, right?"

"Is that a rhetorical question?" Lilith demanded. "Because it shouldn't be."

Less than an hour later Wesley opened the door to me in his leather pants, sunglasses, and nothing else. Not even *socks.*

I ignored all that dark, muscular flesh. I'd be dead before I staked him if he didn't like what I wanted to ask.

But it still felt good to be doing something.

"I've got you a coffee brewing, Rory," he said, angling his face over my shoulder toward where Aspen and Lilith usually stood during our check-ins. He'd only officially been on my client list for about a week, and he was the least work of them all.

And the most dangerous.

"You speak my language," I admitted, shoving the nerves down. "I was hoping to chat to you, Wes. Off the books."

He sent me a bit of a smile. "I love those chats. The last one was quite spectacular."

It wasn't a comfortable memory. "Yeah, you're even better than your word." He'd been pivotal in bringing a dangerous—and possessed—wizard into the open so we could take him out. And it'd cost me my one free favor.

But maybe this wouldn't be a favor. "I'm curious about the vampire courts. Is that something you're comfortable talking about?"

He flicked his fingers in a graceful move of dismissal. "Comfortable, yes. Interested in? No. Tell me instead about Samhain." His smile grew. He was in front of me, empty handed, as I slid onto a stool, then he was in front of me again with a coffee in his hand with only the tiniest flicker of movement.

My hair swayed from the rush of air in his wake even as he slid the coffee carefully into position in front of me. As if he didn't move faster than sound, he leant on his elbows, those sunglasses showing nothing except my own pale face, mismatched eyes and windswept curls.

The most dangerous ones always made the best coffee.

"Samhain." The fae lord in the Fitzroy gardens...with a side of murdered wizard. Surely this ancient vampire who had a strange obsession for pop culture didn't know about the murder.

We knew how to hide our tracks.

No, he just wanted gossip. "Feels like a fair trade. You tell me what you know about the Spring court, and—"

"No." He was smiling, and the word was gentle, but there was no wriggle room in that one syllable. "I'm done with them, Aurora. Unless," he nudged my coffee a little closer. "This is a favor you're asking of me. You know I'm fond of them. And, as luck would have it, I am peckish."

A chill ran down my spine. Well, there was that line very clearly drawn. "I'm not feeling that strongly about it. But I can tell you Samhain was chaos. More so than usual."

"Mm. I heard. You resemble her."

Everything in me froze.

"The Spring Court, you say," Wesley went on, as if I wasn't struggling to breathe. "Most humans don't know about our Courts for long." He cocked his head a little. "Don't die. I like you."

The ring on my finger that protected me from his Charisma grew warm and a wave of pure, physical desire washed over me. I tried to ignore it, but a part of me reveled, wanting the world to fall away.

He'd either be utterly abysmal or totally mind-blowing in bed. And I hated that I wondered which it was.

I lifted my coffee and shook myself. "Dying isn't on my to-do list."

And fuck my hormones. I didn't have time for this shit. "What do you mean, I resemble her?"

He reached over and ran the back of his knuckles over my cheek slowly enough that I could've evaded. His skin was cool, like metal early in the morning before it'd soaked up all the sun's warmth. I'd never taken the time to notice how touching a vamp felt before. I'd always been pretty busy trying to kill or not be killed.

"You're so sweet." His grin flashed. "I'm sure you hear that all the time."

The burn of desire was there. But it wasn't what either of us were focusing on. He was feeding from me, somehow, despite my magickal protections.

Who am I like?

My head spun but I held steady. "Is this another favor?"

Did he know my mother?

"Is what a favor, darling?" He nudged my coffee closer, his expression one of concern. "Are you okay? You've barely tasted it." I looked down at the cup and saw myself reflected back, expression impassive. *His fingertip stroking down my cheek. The pressure of his hands on my shoulders and the tacky plastic surface of a table sticking to my cheek.*

He knew her.

Or he thought he did.

There was nothing in the coffee except coffee. Why would *Wesley* bother to *drug* me? It wasn't like he needed to. Not that Ryan had needed to.

My stomach rolled.

"I didn't want to mention anything earlier," he said, his words relaxed as if he ripped people's lives apart every single day.

He could. He *had*.

I ripped myself back into the present. I had reason to be suspicious of people in general. That was an issue for later. Who the fuck was he talking about? I took a giant gulp of coffee and it burned the whole way down.

"...but I must say, I'm not sad to see the back of Wizard Davies. Never liked that man."

He couldn't read minds. He couldn't know about Ryan.

"We hope he'll be found soon."

He wouldn't be. When Taig killed a man, they stayed dead and gone. But I didn't need Taig being dragged in on murder charges, now, did I? Then who'd cook for me?

He flicked his fingers. "Wizards come and go. Covens are forever."

I arched my brows. "Facts." I cared more about how he'd linked the concept of a 'she' and Davies.

"I feel like Hallmark should put that on a card for Solstice," he said thoughtfully. "I'll make that happen. Maybe some mugs, too."

"If you're getting things printed, I'd like some badges for us custodians. Name and pronouns. I wouldn't cry if they were silver. Call me paranoid." Was the opportunity gone? "Wizard Davies wouldn't approve, but that's okay."

He laughed again and ignored my gambit. "If that's what you'd like. I go by he/him, but I'm happy for they/them too. My pin can say Wes."

He was running rings around me and I was done with it. "Well," I finished the coffee. "Thanks, Wes, for your time. It's nice to chat."

"It is," he agreed, wandering beside me with the fluid grace of a cat as I headed for the exit. "I hear you've got a new client. I'm sure he's got nothing to do with today's visit."

For fucks' sake. Was there anything this man didn't know? "I've always got new clients," I told him easily, not even lying.

"Now, Aurora, you aren't usually coy." He opened the door and angled himself out of the sunlight. "He won't respect you unless you can hold your own against him. Have fun, darling." The door was shut firmly in my face before I could even begin to consider how to respond.

I was getting sick of doors closing in my face. But this specific door I wasn't going to kick open.

CHAPTER 8

Fuck this new leaf bullshit, I'd stomped all over so many of my internal warnings it was a wonder they even worked. And that was just while hanging out with Wesley, much less the rest of the day. How the fuck was I going to unlearn everything?

Frustrated by so much time spinning my wheels, I got home and went for a jog, cranking the tunes and letting the cold spring air sear my lungs clean.

Benson wasn't answering his phone. He'd paid rent for a month, plus the bond. No one had seen those kids since they'd left Brisbane.

For all I knew, they were dead. Or sitting in the bottom of a cupboard, terrified.

And I kept forgetting to feel my feet hitting the cement and the air rushing into my lungs as I ran. For just a moment I imagined how the street might look if I kept on running into oncoming traffic. The trauma the first responders would carry with them from scraping me off the bumper of the cute red hybrid that was speeding toward me. I tripped over a raised piece of cement but caught myself, well and truly away from oncoming traffic. One of my earbuds was unsettled. I jammed it back in as I jogged in place beside the lights, waiting.

I'd never been grounded in my thrice-cursed life. What the fuck made me think I could start now?

I'd narrowed it down to three clubs that he could be bouncing. Assuming he was even on tonight, who was looking after his presumably still alive kids?

I got a message from Taig that interrupted the song and I glanced down with annoyance as I jogged in place, waiting for lights to change. *Busy tonight? Slow one at work, so I might even be half human.* Traffic whizzed by. A woman pushing a pram had stopped beside me. She pointed to the grassy park over the road, trying to distract her grumpy child. I followed her gaze, but the familiar bedraggled garden and equipment that had survived since the eighties didn't make me any more cheerful than it made the kid.

Usually I was free and Taig knew it. That was just a polite 'can I come over?' Well, not tonight. *Going clubbing,* I sent quickly.

The lights changed so I set off on the home stretch. His response came through but I didn't pause to look at it.

What the fuck had I thought I'd get, going to Wesley? You didn't get mercy from vampires who were older than our fucking country. And now I'd tipped my hand. Who knew what he'd tell anyone else about me.

…would he tell…*her?*

In the dying light of the day I saw a familiar huge form in the playground and my focus honed in.

I couldn't see details from the distance, but he was clearly pushing a kid on a swing. My heart just about stopped. Benson. *And his kids.*

Before I could even change direction his head swung toward me. He had a kid under each arm and was charging out of the park faster than I could've shouted 'stop, Custodians!'—even if I'd had my damned badge.

Well, fuck.

I stood, breathing hard, watching him vanish around some bushes in the direction of his apartment.

Lilith was going to be pissed I couldn't vouch for the kids not having black eyes or cigarette burns on them, but they were alive.

And he'd been pushing them on a fucking swing.

I walked back, my mind spinning over that level of resistance. He hadn't just glowered at me, hadn't postured or puffed up, he'd fled.

The kids were the lever.

I was going to get my arm ripped off if I tried to pull it, though.

What was it about *this* client that was getting under Lilith's skin, anyway? We always kept an eye out for black eyes and cigarette burns. Did Benson resemble someone she'd known? Was his cologne the same, or the way he tied his shoes?

The reek of Clint's supermarket body spray filled my head and I squeezed my shoulders up to my ears and shook my head. *Nope.* Bro had been a murder charge in waiting. At least that was one skeleton no one could exhume from my closet.

Cheered, I put aside the memory of the cop and checked Taig's message. *Girl's night, or?*

Right. Clubbing. *Work.*

Quickly, *Want someone on your 6?*

I almost shot back something suggestive, but the idea of flirting annoyed me right then. *Got the team. Probably won't be back til late.*

Almost immediately, I got, *Would it be weird if I came over for a little while? Hung out with Eclipse and waited?*

Was it weird? We were a thing, but we could be separate, and I had zero patience right now. That wasn't anything to do with him, but it would still impact how I interacted with him, and that wouldn't be fair. I took the stairs to my apartment two at a time. On this evening's episode of shit I don't want to deal with; dress codes when you're pretending to go clubbing while sussing out a traumatized ursathrope.

I dialed Taig as I dug through my clothes. "Hey," he said. "You're on hands free."

"On your way home?"

"Yeah, going to adult a bit. Want company later?" he offered.

I held up a leather jacket. Over top of my lupetec armor, with boots, it'd do. "Not sure if it'll be a late one. Probably simpler to wait until tomorrow."

"Sounds good. I'm in Samhain mode still, I think. Also, I realized I haven't told you today that you're magnificent. So there's that," he said, like we were discussing the weather.

I felt some of the worry melting. "You're sweet."

"Also bitter. Excellent balance of flavor."

The laugh bubbled in my chest. It didn't make it out, but I appreciated his humor. I realized I wanted to keep talking to him, to tell him about the curve balls and brick walls I'd encountered, to hear his responses. Given my earlier impatience, that knowledge sat oddly.

I'm not just jumpy. I let out a long breath and wriggled my toes in the confines of my runners.

I was human. It was okay to be human. And I didn't think I'd been too much of a dick. Did I need to acknowledge that I couldn't really tell, right then, how shitty I was? Or was that overkill?

"You there?" he asked. "Sorry, just turned off the car."

"Yeah. Yeah, I'm here." *Don't rush this.* I didn't know how to sit in this space and didn't have the heart to figure it out right then. "So, what're you wearing?" I asked, teasingly.

He laughed at me. "That's my line." Had he seen through me? "Are you accessorizing your lupetec?"

"Actually, yes." I looked at the jacket on my bed. "I'll send you a fit check."

"Always happy to help quality control," he agreed blandly. "I'll let you get ready. Take no prisoners."

"Rarely." I blew a kiss and tossed my phone onto the bed.

There. I hadn't told him to fuck off and stop hovering over me when I was actually fine. And I hadn't asked him to come over later, to bring a few changes of clothes. I hadn't made plans for tomorrow. I hadn't committed to a white picket fence in the suburbs.

I mean, I didn't necessarily *not* want any of that, although I could think of nothing more dull than re-painting a fence after some witty person drew a giant dick on it for the um*peen*th time. At least here, I was on the third story and any dicks on the brickwork took some effort.

"Don't go too hard," I said, out loud, breathing deep. "You're not jumpy."

Elders, sometimes I felt like a timebomb.

I got my shit together, more or less, and was ready to roll at nine when Lilith rocked up like the total fucking badarse she was. Her lupetec was worn under a corset and long velvet skirt.

She looked me up and down. "Hiding in plain sight?"

"He's going to smell us anyway," I said dismissively. "Besides, I have a lot of eyeliner on."

"Yeah you do. It's almost even, too."

I rolled my eyes and shut my door. "Let's get this over with."

She grinned and fell into step beside me, just like old times.

The cold of the evening didn't bother me in the lupetec. We just strolled along past the line to the first club, eyeballing the door staff and continuing on when there was no Benson-sized guy looming anywhere. Surely, he'd be on the door? "I don't want to actually wait to get in on the off-chance someone is having a blue by the bar," Lilith said, just as I'd begun wondering how efficient we were actually being.

"We could log the cost as work receipts," I reminded her, but I didn't love the idea either. "Is it bad I want to get home to my cat?"

She shot me an amused glance. "No Taig tonight?"

"No, no Taig tonight."

"Huh." We didn't bother waiting for a tram, just walked toward the next club. "You and he, you okay?"

I tossed some hair out of my face and shrugged. "Sure. We're good. Why wouldn't we be?" This time the look she shot me would've stripped paint. I stuffed my hands in my pockets and ignored the way my belly rolled over. I wasn't just jumpy. I was just carrying shame that wasn't really mine. So I let go of a breath and tried to leave it behind me. "We weren't really—you know. On. Before. So."

"So he doesn't have to unlearn anything."

"I guess." I cleared my throat. "My nose is cold."

"Of course it is. The air is cold. How's therapy?"

"Fine." It was fine. "I'm going again next week." She knew that, though. It was a very obvious two hour block out of my day on a weekly basis, and I'd usually come back with puffy eyes, or just dip out for the afternoon entirely.

I couldn't imagine having more responsibilities, or a less flexible job and less cash, and trying to heal from this shit. Talk about herculean efforts.

"Still having nightmares?"

"Yeah." Shit. Why did I have friends? It was one thing to decide to own my shit and another thing to get interrogated on the side of the road. "Look, can we talk about something else?"

She shrugged with dignified elegance and strolled on. "You know I love you, right?"

Something about the way she said that, or the hard lines of her face as we strolled out of the streetlight's reach and into the shadows, sent a chill through me. "What?" I asked, warily.

"You need to slow down on the rule breaking," she said, in a quick exhale. "This afternoon, with Wesley—the rules are there for reasons, Roars."

I bristled. "They're cut-and-paste from social worker bureaucracy and they don't fit our work." And anyway, they were bullshit.

She stopped, her breath misting, her hands deep in her jacket. "Look, I get it, okay? But remember how Zane's kid got fae-attacked?" I nodded sharply. I'd healed him. I'd covered up for him.

They'd been using an undeclared rift to move things to or from this world. I had no idea why. I had a vague idea where.

And I definitely knew how illegal it was.

"And how you were blackmailed?" she went on, her head tilted ever so slightly, her eyes narrowed.

I folded my arms, feeling sick. "By the same guy who registered my cat under his name."

"The point is, Roars, breaking rules hurts us." She started walking again. "Would he have found something else? Yes. But he found your weakness, fast. I know you looked the other way when Sammy wasn't getting to school."

Of course I did. "The kid was fucking traumatized, Lilith."

"Yeah, and if we'd documented that and pushed for support, it might've helped in the long run," she said, frustrated. "I love you, witch. I do. But the rules aren't going to change if we don't point out that they have to."

Frustration, and also shame, gnawed at me. "It isn't fair our people have to pay the price right now for someone else to benefit later."

She let out a long breath. "No, it isn't," she agreed, grimly. "But they already are, Roars." She glanced over and stepped into another pool of light as her expression softened and the frustration ebbed.

The shame did not.

"Sammy's now dealing with other complications," she explained, gently and entirely unnecessarily.

I knew they were. The meetings, the catch-up work, the disapproval. I was buffering what I could, but I couldn't be in the classroom with them.

As for Zane…

"He wouldn't have been sent to SuperSec," I acknowledged, feeling like six kinds of shit. He could've just said the faeries attacked them randomly. He didn't have to mention the rift at all.

I'd been too busy keeping Paulo alive to think straight.

"He might've," Lilith said, quietly. "But we'd have worked our guts out to minimize the impact on all of them." We would, sure. But not all caretakers had the resources, the energy, the know-how and the heart. Did that mean that we should be the ones driving the change?

I knew the longer the rules were in place, the harder they'd be to shift, too. Right now the dust was settling on legalization. Things would become 'the way we've always done it' at some point. We needed to get changes through. The sooner, the better.

Lilith was right, and the humiliation made me want to hurl.

I'd made everyone's life harder.

"I'm not expecting you to follow every single policy to a T," she said, tiredly. "But can we keep it to just bending the rules every now and then?"

I swallowed, glancing up. "Okay." The knot in my throat didn't want to let the words out. I ignored it. "You…might need to remind me. Because…" I wasn't used to worrying about procedure anymore.

She slowed as we looked toward the brightly lit sign of our next destination. "Thanks," she said, softly. "And I'm sorry."

I shrugged, burying my hands in my pockets the way she had. "I never said I was good at my job."

"You are," she disagreed, then paused. "No, you're good at being a good person. But we want systems in place that don't rely on us being good people."

That might've been even harder to hear than I was just doing a shit job, and I had no idea why. I cleared my throat, but that lump sat there anyway, making my eyes water. "Found him, anyway."

Lilith nodded. You couldn't miss the over-seven-foot mountain that was Benson. He towered over a guy doing I.D. checks.

I tried to shift my attention. We had an illegally employed shifter, here. Policy dictated we drag him in, give him a slap on the wrist, report him to the tax office, and then start fresh.

Which probably wasn't the worst idea, on the page, but the reality was that we had no leverage with this guy. No trust and no relationship to lean on.

But maybe we could at least rebuild his trust in our procedures?

I tugged on Lilith's elbow, just lightly, and we backed up. The wind was in our favor; we might get away with it.

I should've told her about how he'd reacted in the park. I should've, but I hadn't wanted to rouse Lilith's suspicions. And maybe that was unfair of me. Of the two of us, I knew who was more sensible. But still, the guy was being protective. Wasn't he?

Policy, though. "I ran into him this afternoon," I admitted. "Almost literally." I explained the situation briefly, then said, into the silence that followed as we walked back to the tram stop, "I need to note that, don't I?"

"It won't hurt," Lilith said, and there was a grim note to her voice. "And if something does happen to those kids..."

We were covering our arses.

Elders.

"Anyway, he's working at a half-decent place, I guess," she said, once the tram was carrying us away. "We check in regularly, see if he can hold that down. It's something. Illegal, but something."

"We should report it."

She shot me a quick look. "I will report seeing him at the location. If he's still doing the cash in hand work in two weeks, then we report him for cash under the table work." The words were emotionless. I bet if Aspen was there, they'd have been directed at her.

"We can twist some arms, get them to offer him an actual job," I said, leaping up onto the tram and making space for her. We usually waited a bit longer before we went in with boots on, but if she was deciding on deadlines, then we didn't have time to kill. "Even if he's just on as a casual, it'll be fine. And he can claim the tax-free threshold."

"He won't just be working one job," she told me with a sigh, sitting back. "Not at bouncer rates, not with two kids and rent to pay in this area. But yeah, we can try."

She didn't think he'd like it. Maybe he wouldn't. But laws were laws, as she'd just reminded me.

"Kids are alone," Lilith said grimly. "Bet."

"We can't go check."

She shot me an annoyed look. "Wow, really?"

I shifted, uncomfortable. Aspen was going to be pissed we hadn't made contact, but he was working the door. What, was I going to stand in line to chat to him?

Lilith looked away, her mouth drawn in a tight line, and I rocked opposite her rhythm with the tram. She wasn't usually this short. "You okay?" I asked, unable to avoid addressing how weird she'd been acting.

"Yeah. I'm fine. You're the—" she stopped mid-sentence, but I felt the rest of her words like a blow. *The fucked up one.* That's what she'd been about to say.

It hurt, but I had armor on. "No, that's bullshit. What's eating you?"

Her brows arched. "Nothing. I just think this guy is dirty and don't want the kids to pay for it. I don't know why we're covering for him so hard."

We literally covered for all our clients like this. Hence the talking-to I'd just gotten. I settled back, studying her. "Are *you* having nightmares?"

She flicked her fingers at me and her nails flashed under the harsh lights of the trams. "I'm fine."

"Whew, that good, huh?" I reached into my pocket and dug out an old packet of gum to offer her. "I've got a bag of chips back at mine."

Her expression softened, just a little. "Fuck you, witch." But she took a piece of gum and tipped her head back. "Maybe an Eclipse snuggle. If she doesn't leave hair on my skirt."

"Cat hair is like highlights for witches."

The tiniest smile touched her mouth. "Yeah, no. Actually, I'm pretty tired. I might just cut and run. We did the thing, right?"

"Right." She wasn't a cut-and-runner.

"Cool. Well."

"Vince waiting, back home?" I asked, trying to keep it casual.

"Yeah. Well, at his. That's where I'm going." She shot me a look. "Why?"

I shrugged. "Nothing. Sounds nice. He's a good dude." And she wasn't going to be alone.

She looked down. "He is." But I didn't buy the way her shoulders softened. It didn't seem like *relaxing*, to me. It felt like *collapsing*. And that worried the shit out of me.

Then she seemed to shrug it off and stood, letting out a huff and tossing her hair. Whatever was eating her, she wasn't telling me about it tonight. I got that. But damned if I was letting it go.

"So." I stood at my stop and she climbed down after me. "Fuck off then, I'll eat my own chips. You know I've always got more if you want to visit. Where'd you park?"

She waved a hand down the block so I wandered with her over to her car, waved her off, and as soon as she was gone sent Aspen a message. *Something about Benson's case might be triggering for Lilith. Keep an eye.*

I got back a check mark almost instantly, and the reply came through just seconds later. *Don't know her tells well enough yet. Bring me up to speed tomorrow. You two ok?*

I snorted, stomping up my steps. *No, I'm texting you from the grave.*

Straight away, *if anyone's capable of sending an SOS about a friend from the grave it's you so don't screw with me Sunshine.*

As if I'd send an SOS if I could just text. Who even knew Morse Code anymore? I mean, I did, but I'd had to learn basic military shit for Retrievals. I was pretty sure I forgot more than I could remember.

Tired, I typed, *Love you.* I opened my door and let myself in as her response flashed up on my screen, a bunch of heart emojis. I just felt hollow as Eclipse meowed happily in greeting, unaccustomed to me being gone at this hour.

"We're good, right, girl?" I asked her, hitting the lights and going to get her some kitty snacks. She meowed happily at me and wound around my legs as I squeezed the packet into her bowl, filling the apartment with the funk of the food. "We can act like normal people, right?"

She didn't bother to respond, face down in her pile of vile looking mush. I tossed the wrapper and got myself ready for bed. Alone. Right then, it was exactly what I needed.

My bed was cool and smelled like him. We'd curled up here like two pathetic bugs hiding from the light. I listened to Eclipse moving around in the dark, and wondered if this weird lack of feeling was a me thing...or a me and Taig thing.

My phone buzzed but I ignored it, listening to the city settle around me. I wasn't jumpy, but I was pretty fucked up. A gunshot, a vamp bite, those things were obvious and fixable, or at least over quickly. I didn't even know what of my current situation was me... and what was the fucking trauma.

Wesley knew who my mother was.

And that had come up in conversation whilst talking about Samhain.

I closed my eyes and felt the tension thrumming in my body. Surely, that didn't mean what I was thinking it could mean.

Eclipse leapt up onto the bed and curled up beside me, purring. What the fuck did I do now?

I felt dirty.

Loud knocking on my door was a welcome relief. The adrenaline that washed through me made me feel alive. In control.

Chemicals, I told myself, furious at my body. *Trauma*. I felt the cheap carpet under my feet and the harsh light that irritated my eyes. My heart was hammering. Normal response, really, to a knock on the door in the small hours.

I pulled open the door, half expecting to see a member of my coven.

Benson Hurtfield loomed over me, his shirt taut over bulging muscles, his face carved in lines of fury.

Maybe it was the fact that I could still feel the cheap carpet under my toes, or the fact that it was nice to have proof that I wasn't just jumpy, but I saw the humor in the situation.

Propping my shoulder against the door, I refused to feel self-conscious that I was only in a shirt and underwear. It was a good shirt; maybe I'd adopt it from Taig. *Abortions are healthcare* was this one's message. Anyway, when you knocked on a witch's door at night, you got what you got.

"You just going to glower at me?" I asked, a little amused at the way he huffed in my direction. "If you need a cup of sugar, I'm all out."

One of his massive fists tightened and Wesley's one titbit ran through my head. I didn't really want to go toe to toe with this guy without my wand and the idea had warning bells tolling in my head. Maybe poking the bear wasn't a good idea?

And how the hells was I going to document this without getting the hot-headed lump tossed behind bars?

"Stay away from me and mine," he growled.

I wished I could've feigned a yawn. "Checking on you and yours is literally my job." I held up a hand, scowling. Aspen would moan at that. "Wait. No. Helping you and yours. The first step is checking, though. I need to know how to help, you know?"

He put one hand above where I was draped on the door and leant in so close I could feel the heat of his breath. "Stay away. Or I won't. Are we clear, witch?"

I raised my brows further. "Look, I get we aren't buddies. I actually didn't mean to intrude on your park time this afternoon; I was just jogging. Tonight… yeah, mate, I'm going to check on you, because I care." Maybe that was a slight exaggeration, but not a lot. I cared on a professional level.

He bared his teeth. His very large, very shiny teeth.

My heart ached, suddenly. "Want to come in?" I asked, stepping back with a sigh. This was going to need paperwork, probably. "We can figure out some ground rules, since we're practically neighbors." And who cared that it was almost two in the morning? Not like I'd been asleep.

"I eat witches for breakfast," he said, flatly. Somehow, I kept my laughter in. Dudes threatening me with a good time were my favorite. "We aren't negotiating. Stay. Away." And he cast his eyes over me in an oddly disconcerting way, as if weighing me up and finding me totally wanting. "Next time I won't knock." And he turned and left, every step making the floor creak with the power of his stride.

Well, fuck. I shut the door the adrenaline started to ebb. I had a few charms on me, of course, but he probably *could've* eaten me alive.

Eclipse emerged from the shadows, watching silently as I went and made myself a cuppa I didn't want while my mind turned.

If I reported him for that threat, he'd be done. We were well protected as custodians and I had enough friends that it'd be taken very seriously.

He was terrified. But that didn't make that exchange okay.

I wasn't trained to handle this shit. But something about the way he'd grabbed his kids this afternoon played on my mind as the kettle boiled. He was the kind of guy used to bringing nukes to knife fights. So he'd brought his nuke. Except this wasn't a knife fight and he didn't know it.

My mind turned over my conversation with Lilith and I stared into my mug as my feet got cold. Tiredly, I reflected how I didn't make milkshakes specifically so people didn't show up in my yard. I'd stepped over professional boundaries in the past and it hadn't worked out well for *anyone.*

How could I respond in a way that aligned with policy and the long-term best interests of Benson, his family, and the wider community?

I couldn't. Because that was a threat, and threats weren't okay.

So, I'd just build a fucking bunker.

I went into my room and grabbed my phone, quickly assessing my options. Lilith's charms were shit, and anyway, she had a bee in her bonnet over this guy. Maadai wouldn't stop lecturing me until the sun came up and my Oma was hours away.

The phone rang only briefly before I heard Shepherd say, on the other end, "What's wrong?"

I smiled a little at that. "Can you come over?"

Without hesitation he said, "Be there in fifteen. Need emergency services too?"

"Non urgent, Shep." I wanted to hug him for it, though. Shepherd wasn't one to lecture. He just got shit done.

"Non urgent at two in the morning?" He snorted. "Text me if I need anything special." And the line went dead.

I gathered up suitable crystals for charms. Shepherd wouldn't run his mouth at the wrong time.

When he arrived I'd just finished making his tea. He was carrying his staff and I heard Taig's voice in my head wryly noting that breach in protocol.

And then I saw Arthur behind him.

My eyes narrowed. "Fire power," Shepherd said with a jerk of his thumb to indicate Arthur by way of explanation. "What's going on?"

"Hi, Rory," Arthur said, awkwardly.

Shit, I didn't miss him being my boss. "Hi, King." I let Arthur in, since I didn't have a choice, but shot Shepherd a venomous look behind Arthur's back. "Thanks for coming."

Arthur glanced at me, color flooding his cheeks.

I paused for a moment as he looked away, clearing his throat. He wasn't carrying a torch for me; we'd scratched that itch. So, maybe

Shep hadn't been asleep when I called. "Thank you and sorry," I said, with a wave of my hand. "I need to ursa proof my place, Shepherd."

His brows snapped together. "Hurtfield? Lilith said he's a piece of work."

"I'm reserving judgment." I shrugged, waving at the crystals. "It probably would've kept til morning, but I didn't want to risk it." And anyway, action felt good.

"How did he get your address?" Arthur demanded as Shepherd scooped up crystals in one hand and the tea in his other. "Why haven't you called the authorities?"

I rolled my eyes at him. This was why I'd called Shepherd. "We kind of are the authorities," Shep said mildly. "I'd be keen to know how he found you so fast, too."

"He lives basically over the road. He probably followed my scent trail." I shrugged it off. "Or spotted me and followed, but I doubt he'd have needed to. Am I going to need to put those against studs, Shep?"

"Yeah." He shot Eclipse a smile as she leapt up onto the bench. "Hello there. You can't play with them, beautiful."

"When'd you get a cat?" Arthur asked, surprised.

"Before Samhain," I said, vaguely, not wanting to get into Eclipse's origin story. It wasn't her fault Ryan had been a pile of human fertilizer and given her to me just to weaponize my affection. "Make yourself useful and help me find the studs, King. I'm going to have to tape these things to the plaster."

Arthur looked at me, horrified. "It'll ruin the paintwork."

I patted him on one beautifully sculpted shoulder and realized he was wearing Shepherd's shirt. "So will an ursa," I reminded him with patience I didn't feel.

That mollified him a bit. Shepherd tossed him the first charmed crystal and I pulled out the tape, ignoring the way he winced.

By the time they were done I was wide awake, my body kicking into Retrievals mode. I ate mechanically as I went over my appointments for the day and fired off emails, knowing I wouldn't sleep like this. Chores melted before me and I was incredibly productive and deeply disconnected.

You couldn't win them all.

Benson opened the door to us at eleven. "I'm here, and I don't need your help," he said, flatly, then shut it in our faces.

I pulled up my phone and kept working on the email I'd been halfway through while Aspen did her thing. And I kept what he'd done to myself. It seemed easier, for now. And anyway, I was protected, thanks to Shep.

"How many more strikes before we talk to his boss?" Lilith asked us, back on the tram.

Aspen, looking tired, shook her head. "We need a new strategy. Until we come up with one, we can do daily house calls. We know he's home, and we know he's working."

"We know of one of his jobs," Lilith pointed out ruthlessly.

"So we ask around, see where else he might be." Aspen frowned at Lilith. "What's the name of the club he's at? I might know someone who knows someone."

I sat back as they strategized and watched the city whirring by the window.

How in the ever-loving fuck were we supposed to hold our own against him in an ethical, trauma informed way? And was I going to be able to get back into my own skin today?

CHAPTER 9

"Where's Taig?" Aspen asked, halfway through the lunchbreak we were taking in front of our computers.

"Work," I sighed, avoiding her glance. We were both buried deep after George experienced a public breakdown. "So I've got a line on another person who was there that night—they party pretty regularly together, apparently."

"Name?" Aspen asked, around a mouthful of corn chips and guac.

"I'll email it through." I glanced at the clock. "George must've dumped his car, or the cops would've picked him up already." Speaking of cars, I needed to pay yet more money for parking Nic's overpriced baby in the local lot.

"Or he's got a broom," Aspen said, grimly.

I arched a brow at her. "You really think he'd use such a feminine mode of transport?"

She grunted in agreement. "So he's not alone."

"They've checked at the ex's place, right?"

"They said they did," Aspen said. "I've got it on our list for tomorrow."

Tomorrow was there before I had a chance to get myself out of whatever heightened snowball I was in, but at least I knew I was in it. That was an improvement, right? And with the trauma-and-drug-fueled maelstrom that George left in his wake, the tomorrows just kept melting into each other as we tried to wrap supports around someone who'd spent their whole life avoiding being vulnerable. After a whole however-many-hours of doing my job, I stared into a sink full of cereal bowls and coffee cups. I'd had food earlier. I knew I had, even if I couldn't recall what it was. I wasn't hungry, but my pants were sitting lower than usual.

But I didn't have the energy to cook. My bowls were all accounted for. I could pour cereal into a mug, but then I'd be in trouble tomorrow when I wanted coffee.

Before I could talk myself out of it, I started running the water. Even if I just washed *two* bowls, that was okay. Food for today and tomorrow. And then...

I needed to talk to Taig. I *wanted* to talk to Taig. Little chores were so much easier when he was around.

My mind ran over the barriers we were encountering in George's case, the interactions I'd had with other services, the reports we'd done. I paused, wondering if I'd noted that conversation at about three thirty with Housing.

I hadn't.

But I didn't let myself pull my hands out of the sudsy water, because if I noted that, I'd get sucked back in. And I just needed *two bowls*. That was all.

Blowing out a long breath, I scrubbed at the ceramics. The two bowls sat, sudsy, on the drainer beside me. I'd rinse them, but first I reached for another, and some spoons. I was probably low on spoons. *Just do a few.* It was okay to just do a little bit. Then I'd eat, and I'd text Taig while I ate, and tell him that I missed him.

Just the thought of him was calming. I could imagine the feel of his arms, the way he'd smell. There'd be a coffee at my elbow and he'd say something sweet to Eclipse. My world was a better place just for giving him room to exist in my mind.

Sudsy, but clean dishes piled up. With the other side of the sink clean I ran the water there, too, preparing to rinse. I wondered what he'd been up to that day, and what he'd made himself for dinner, or whether he had a late shift. When had we last messaged?

He'd be worried.

Shame tugged at me, but I didn't let it get its claws in. It had kept me away from him for days. He didn't deserve that. I'd call him as soon as my hands were dry.

I looked back at myself from the surface of the water. I looked calm and collected, and something about that felt like a knife twisting in my guts. With a steady hand, I dipped the last bubbly bowl into the water. My eyes moved to my phone, over near the charger. From my peripheral vision, the reflection continued to stare at me. Calm and collected.

Pausing, bowl dripping on the bench, my eyes locked on the device but my attention on that image, I tried to make sense of what I was seeing and was ripped back to that conversation with Wesley, days ago.

You don't say *you look like her* except about a family member. If she was a family member, and she had something to do with Samhain...

If my father had returned from Overworld...

The air became thick and my brain was slow. I wasn't jumpy. I was hurting, and scared. I couldn't deal with the next step in that reasoning. Not in the midst of George's acute situation and trying to figure out what to do with Zane to keep Aspen from knowing about Duke. The stress hormones had me caught in a dark vortex of *just survive just survive*. I didn't know what to trust. Things were wonky, right now. I'd get it back on track.

Resolutely, I finished the dishes. I filled a bowl with clean water and called it rinsing, and didn't bother to dry it before reaching for the cereal. *Just do what you have to. One step at a time. That's how you make progress.*

I ate. And then I dropped that bowl into the freshly-empty sink before I collapsed into bed, exhausted.

Three days after Benson knocked on my door we were walking

away from his apartment, yet again, having slid the government payment forms under his door. Lilith turned to me and said, "How's Taig?"

There was nothing idle in that question. Aspen's attention honed in on us. I looked between the two of them, pausing mid-email, sensing a trap. "Why?"

"He mentioned he was worried about you," Lilith told me, with a shrug that wasn't as nonchalant as she made it out to be. "Says you've been silent."

"I literally texted him this morning," I objected. "And last night. And a bunch of other times."

Aspen's brows jerked sharply, and, not for the first time, I hated that I worked with my best friends.

Pretending not to see the look they shared, I shrugged it off. I hadn't ghosted him or anything. "Got a gargoyle coming on-board," I said, to change the subject. "I'll update the files so it's all there. Meeting tomorrow at ten."

"Nuh-uh." Aspen snatched my phone out of my hand. "You're not sleeping."

With a roll of my eyes, I snatched it back. "Obviously, I am not, like most people at two-thirty in the afternoon on public transport. Did we make any progress on Benson's other employment?"

"Not yet." She leant around me to peer at Lilith. "You coming to Rory's place tonight?"

Alarm bells rang in my head. "Hold up. I'm not entertaining. I have sleep to catch up on."

"Yeah, wouldn't miss it for the world," Lilith agreed, blandly, as if I hadn't spoken. "What're you bringing, Aspen?"

I held up my hands. "No one's bringing anything. I'm being boring tonight."

"Chips," Aspen said to Lilith. "And wine."

"White?" Lilith asked. "I'll bring red if you bring white. And I'll get the ice-cream."

I wasn't going to get out of this, short of a fucking Retrievals contract. "Okay, look." I cast a glance around the quiet carriage, annoyed I was being put on the spot. "I have big feelings. And also no feelings. I need time to figure them out."

"Told him that?" Lilith asked, as if the sanctimonious witch didn't already know the answer.

Aspen squeezed my knee and sent me a sunny smile. "We'll have lots of time to talk it through with you tonight."

The thought made me feel vaguely ill and I shrugged it off, diving back into my emails.

We were almost back at the office when Aspen's phone rang. I didn't pay much attention, just making sure she got off at the right stop and keeping pace with Lilith.

"I've got a meeting with Jen's AOD worker in fifteen," Lilith said, glancing at the time on her phone. "Can you follow up on the Wrights' email?"

My tired brain whirred on that one for a minute. "Sure. I might give Val a call first, because she mentioned she was going to follow up with the real estate agent this morning for clarification. I want to make sure we aren't scrambling to find them a hotel room at witching hour."

"Of course," Lilith agreed. Then, "Maybe Taig can help get the intervention order expedited."

I didn't roll my eyes, but it was a near thing. It wasn't in his jurisdiction and wasn't a supernatural crime; Taig couldn't do a damned thing about the Wrights' situation, and I wasn't going to ask him, either. And anyway, wasn't she the Rule Queen?

"Hey," Aspen called, hustling to get to the elevator even though Lilith was already moving her foot to hold it open. "Plot twist. Our big boy might be doing prize fights." She slid into the lift and tapped away at her phone. "Not sure, and it's not close, but might be worth having a look."

My heart sank. I'd been called in to investigate the aftermath of one such gambling ring when I'd been with Retrievals, and I'd helped secure a few key players in another.

"Well, that fits," Lilith said, disgusted. "Tell the damn cops. Let them mop it up."

Aspen nodded firmly. "We sure as hell will. If it's him, and if we can't get through to him after one go."

Lilith opened her mouth to argue. I looked between them—one irresistible force, one immovable object.

"Hold on," Lilith began.

Stepping back a little, I cut in with, "When?"

"—we can't actually help a guy who's getting cash by—"

"Tonight," Aspen said, and my phone vibrated. "That's the location."

"—beating the everloving shit out of people," Lilith finished, the words hissing out between her teeth.

The elevator dinged open and I spotted one of the Alcohol and Other Drug workers waiting. "Your appointment's early," I told Lilith. "I'm going to go check it out." And escape from the heart to heart I didn't want. "See if he's redeemable." And I met her hard look calmly. "Been there, done that, know what I'm doing. Hi, Lorraine." I lifted my hand in greeting and swept my smile from the AOD worker to Lilith. "Let me know if you need me."

Aspen split off from Lilith, sticking to me like a burr. A big-hearted, bright-eyed burr. "I've got a change of clothes in my car. I'll dress down at your place. We can go together."

Oh hells no. "I'll keep it low-key—"

She snorted. "Keep the bullshit for someone who knew you after you were toilet trained, bitch. You go alone and you'll probably end up in those pits or on the front page again. No. I'm coming. And you're feeding me after work, too."

"You're the cutest immovable object I know," I told her, not trying to hide my annoyance. She air-kissed at me and breezed past.

Aspen seemed pretty confident it was Benson who was participating, and it wasn't like the state was full of ursathropes—they could've had him on display just for being alive and people would've come.

The address was more than an hour out of Melbourne in an

eastern area that looked like bush and hills. I sat there looking at the map page on my laptop, studying the area.

Usually these sorts of things were held in industrial or run-down commercial areas. Easy to access, easy to blend in. This was an isolated farm shed on the back of someone's property. And I didn't like that vibe.

When Aspen swept in and set a coffee before me I barely even noticed. "This is weird."

She cocked a brow and propped a hip against my desk, leaning over me. The smell of her herbal tea made my eyes water. She made a thoughtful noise in the back of her throat and sipped at the foul brew.

"How much do you trust the person who told you about this?" I asked her. But there was no reason for a setup, and that's why I was confused. We'd pissed off plenty of folks, sure, but short of the ursathrope who'd paid me an early morning visit, there were no specific threats.

She held up a hand, wavering it back and forth in a *could go either way* sort of motion. "Him, sure. But he was told by someone else."

Who'd probably been told by someone, who'd been told by someone. It's how these things worked. I stood and paced the room, unsettled. It'd have to be a pretty good showing to get the punters out in profitable numbers. Or an established, trusted organizer. And considering Benson had only been in Melbourne a hot minute, I doubted he had those connections yet.

"What're the risks?" Aspen asked, crossing her legs as she leant against my desk. "Worst-case I can see, it's a trap."

I nodded confirmation, wishing Lilith could get done and get in here.

"Seems unlikely, but not impossible," Aspen mused. "So, I'm the best driver. You're on rear guard, Lilith's on point. We'll burn rubber if it goes to shit." She paused halfway through straightening. "When. When it goes to shit."

I couldn't help but laugh at her pragmatism and the deadpan way she delivered that. "Some things never change, huh?"

"Yeah," she agreed, looking at me from where she was half hidden behind a wedge of blonde hair. "And some do."

. . ' ' 0 0 ∾ ' '. . 0 ∾ ⟵ ' ∾ ∾

IT WAS A SHIT PLAN, but with Aspen spear-heading it, it was marginally safer than what I would've come up with.

"So what I'm hearing is that you're dissociated," Aspen said, her tone gentle while her fingers tapped impatiently on the wheel.

I glared at the back of her head. She and Lilith had somehow beat me to the front seats and I hated it. "I'm getting things done."

"At what cost?" Lilith asked, as if the answer was obvious.

"It's fine." I didn't have the energy to argue. "Let's just get through tonight without being made. I'll work on the rest tomorrow." But there was no way Benson wouldn't make us. The question was whether he'd call us out.

Maybe I'd make him a nice pot of tea for when he visited later. And be prepared to kick his arse.

Aspen's lights swept across the tiny, unmarked dirt road that led up between the eucalyptus and I was transported back in time to another place and another vehicle, with another sibling.

Brandon was gone. And the woman wincing as her car hit every pothole in the road was all he'd left behind. That wasn't me being jumpy. That was the truth.

A wave of nausea swept through me and I set my teeth against it. She wouldn't have let me come alone, and much as I hated to admit it, she was right.

Still, Lilith and I could hold our own. We had in the past. Some places, talking didn't help.

I watched in silence as the bush unraveled around us endlessly. If another car came the other direction, on this narrow track, with that bracken...

When we saw lights ahead the tension only cranked up another notch.

Lilith turned and pinned me with her eyes. "Three's a good number," she said, threateningly.

I leant forward, propping my elbows on my knees, and tried to breathe. I couldn't hear any warning bells in my head but I didn't know if I would, or if I'd damaged my alarm system.

No. I hadn't damaged it. I took a moment, forcing myself to reframe that thought. I didn't know whether *I'd survived harm done to me* that had damaged my alarm system. I hadn't done it. It wasn't my fault.

Aspen guided the car over grass to a makeshift park. There were a lot of other cars here, and that surprised me about as much as Lilith's reminder.

Was it my fault that I hadn't listened to those alarms, before I'd been hurt?

The shed looked like it could've held a lot of machinery. Tonight it wasn't, though. Two guys in their forties stood out the front, smoking, bottles of beer in their hands. One of them cracked a grin at Aspen as we got close and stepped forward to offer a hand in greeting. "Hey. I'm not your daddy."

I was already intercepting, shoulder first, forcing him back. I loved a good game of patriarchy chicken and didn't give a shit that a bit of beer slopped over me as he scrambled away, keeping his cigarette out of my hair.

"Have I been out of the scene for too long?" I asked them, as Lilith opened the door and shot the guys behind us a warning look. "Or are their lines getting worse?"

"Oh, didn't you see my shirt?" Aspen asked me, doing a quick spin and tugging her artistically slashed shirt a little lower. It read *I'll only call you Daddy if you disappoint me like my father.*

Trust Aspen. "Low profile?" I muttered, irritated.

She just grinned. "Have you seen her?" she asked, jerking her thumb toward Lilith, majestic and eye-catching as ever.

"It's not a competition," I reminded them, when Lilith opened her mouth to deflect, leading us toward the bottleneck of people beyond the fuckboys, waiting to get inside. "You're both gorgeous and they're skeezy. I shouldn't have blamed you, Aspen." I paused next to Aspen in line, shocked at myself.

Shocked, but kind of happy, too. I'd just victim-blamed Aspen, which, fuck, I didn't even know how much shit was in my brain I needed to unlearn. Was it subtle? She'd have called me out if it wasn't subtle. Anyway, I'd caught it and corrected it. Because I needed to make the part that re-attributed blame correctly more obvious. I needed to make the quiet part louder.

Getting in was easy. That was the least of it, really. I guess we didn't look like cops, anyway, and these places were run by bookies who had better escape plans than we did.

The lights were huge and harsh, and the shed was full of layers of crates arranged to provide a view of a circular fighting pit. Tears pricked my eyes at the rush of pride I felt at having identified and dealt with just a tiny bit of my own shit. Two big cats were in there taking swipes at each other and I just stood there wondering how many more little rocks I'd find in my pockets weighing me down.

"Drinks," Aspen said firmly, steering us through the crush of bodies to the back where a makeshift bar was exchanging cash for bottles.

Lilith and I fell into formation behind her. I knew damned well Lilith's hand was on her wand, same as mine. My boots were on my feet, a comforting weight that held me attached to the ground while the crowd flowed around us.

I wasn't a lost cause.

There was a competitor's area, but it looked like some sort of back room, or possibly just a side door to an outside set up. Curious gazes slid over us and then away.

"Two lagers," Aspen said to the woman behind the trestle table. "And a sparkling water."

"I call the water," Lilith muttered.

I shrugged. I'd drunk a few liters of coffee already, and adrenaline said I didn't need to put anything else in my system. I could nurse a beer, though.

"We've got spring?" The waitress asked.

Aspen made a show of being disappointed but went along with it eventually. And, as soon as we had a little breathing room, she said to us, "Found him?"

"Outside," Lilith said. "If he's here." And, what she didn't say, *he'd better not be.*

A wave of noise came from the crowd and I glanced over to see one of the felinethropes had shifted back to her human form and was holding her hand to a wound high on her shoulder while the winner roared in victory.

The crowd went off for the blood and barbarism as I glanced around again, looking for familiar faces.

A tiny, pointed heel came down on the toe of my boot and my attention snapped forward.

Wesley was standing in the ring, applauding the fucking victor.

Wesley. Our motherloving ancient vampire.

"Well, shit," Aspen said, disgusted, and twisted the pry-off cap on her beer.

The victorious shifter turned back to his human form to flex and pose while the defeated one was half-dragged off by her friends. And Wesley smiled like a proud father the whole time.

"Excellent showing, Cadaver," he said, and I felt the vampire's charisma pulling at me even in the crowd.

"I am not drunk enough to not see this," Aspen said to us, mildly. "But I think I want to be."

The ramifications of seeing Wesley not just attending but *running* an illegal fighting pit started ticking through my head.

Wesley could kill everyone in this shed, humans and supernatural, before a drop of blood hit the floor. And I was cold to my bones.

"...next fight," Wesley was saying, and the crowd was listening closely. "Cadaver here just isn't up for it."

The shifter beside Wesley shook his head and whatever he said to Wesley didn't reach us.

"What's going on?" Lilith asked. "Aside from a truckload of charisma?"

"He's using it to MC," Aspen said, frowning. "And he's trying to get this guy to fight someone else."

"There's a werebear," a guy offered beside us, sending us all a friendly smile. "Haven't seen you three before. Want me to show you around?"

"Thanks, no." Aspen half-turned to me. "Let's go outside, get some air."

"Yeah, I'm going to vape," said the charming individual beside us. "I can keep you company. Dark out there."

"Not as dark as the inside of my trunk," Aspen told him, with a big smile. "Or so I hear. Lead the way, Lilith?"

Lilith sipped her water, shot friendly guy a decidedly unfriendly look, and turned toward the exit.

Benson was here… and so was Wesley.

Had Wesley known Benson was in the pit fighting scene when he spoke to me? How long had Wesley been overseeing this? What did he get out of it? What else was he involved in?

Much as I wanted to help Benson, keeping Wesley on track was critical for everyone's survival.

As soon as we hit the biting spring air, Lilith turned to us and asked, "We bailing?"

"I want to talk to him," Aspen said, the words firm. "Or at least be seen. You can wait in the car if you want." And she lifted her beer in a half-joking toast. "It's okay. I got this."

Lilith's plastic bottle crinkled in her hand as Aspen turned and swaggered off around the outside of the building in the direction of the competitor's area.

"I'll keep her alive," I told Lilith, my head still whirling.

Lilith said nothing, just stormed after Aspen, her leather skirt accentuating the long strides she took to keep up.

Fuck, everyone thought *I* was the loose cannon.

I had to jog to catch them. "Plan?" I asked Aspen.

"Leverage," she said.

"We'd have that if we went and took his kids," Lilith pointed out, the words cold. "And they'd be safe."

"Temporarily." Aspen led us through the parked cars and across the hard packed dirt around the shed where no one lingered. "You know what foster looks like for supernaturals."

"Zane would take them."

"Zane's got a house full of teenagers. These are little kids." Aspen took my beer and before I realized what she was doing and tipped most of it out, then emptied hers completely, thrusting both bottles into my hands. "Follow my lead." I was still juggling the bottles as we rounded the corner where we came face to face with a huge, barely clad, heavily tattooed man sitting on a camp chair and messing around on his phone.

"Can't come here," he said without looking.

"We just need the bathroom," Aspen said impatiently. "Benson will vouch for us. You ask him."

The guy didn't look up. "Nope."

"She's going to puke and if I have puke on me how am I going to get laid?" Aspen demanded, hands on hips.

That got his attention. He gave Aspen a once-over, amusement tugging at his mouth. "Have trouble getting off, come find me. I finish at three. I'll do you in the shower."

"Chivalry lives," Lilith muttered, disgusted.

I was about to have a go at acting like a drunken embarrassment, which probably suited me, when Wesley appeared beside us. "My favorite witches." He kissed my cheek. I felt the cool pressure of it as I saw him simultaneously beside both Aspen and Lilith.

The sight almost *did* make me puke.

"You're here for the friend you asked me about?" Wesley asked me, smiling. "Because that would be perfect. No one will fight him, you see. I understand he spent his last fifty getting a ride out here. Such a shame if he returns home empty handed."

My mind instantly went to emergency help we could organize and what food they'd need with their not-human bodies.

"Witches?" The bouncer stood, surprised. "Sorry. Didn't recognize you. Come in."

"We aren't fighting," Aspen said. Her hand rested on my forearm and gave an unnecessary warning squeeze. "We don't have those sorts of powers. But we'll gladly use the bathroom."

Wesley cocked his head at me. "Well, your loss. Maybe I'll find another competitor for him. Toilet is round back, little one." He pointed in the other direction.

Aspen made a frustrated noise. Before she could continue the show, I heard myself asking, "How much is he fighting for, Wes?"

Wesley shrugged. The movement made his leather vest shift over his bare chest in a move that was pure sex. Tumbleweeds blew through my hibernating ovaries.

"It's fine, we were just—"

"He gets three grand for a showing," Wesley told me, with an apologetic air. "Plus winnings. Non-lethal combat, of course. I'll leave you to use the facilities. Enjoy the show…safely. A pleasure, as ever."

And the jerk vanished.

Numb, I followed Lilith as she steered us away from another gawker. "We aren't fighting," she said flatly.

I'd been set up.

Shit, he knew how to play me.

"Wesley told me Benson wouldn't listen until we showed him we were worthy of respect," I told them, my lips cold. *Afternoon sun warm on my skin.*

"I'm sorry but that's way too convenient," Aspen told me, her hand a vice on my forearm. "Fuck, I'll give him three grand."

But maybe it made sense. And it wouldn't surprise me in the least if Wesley had fed information to Aspen's source somehow. The man… the *vampire*…had pulled through for me in the past.

I wished I'd asked why he was here. It wasn't for the money.

On a whim I stopped in front of a generic man, smoking under the stars and floodlights as he scrolled on his phone. His buddies were probably all vaping inside. This guy apparently preferred Classic Ashtray taste. "Hey, I'm new." I offered him my hand and, shocked, he stuffed the cigarette between his lips in his haste to take it. "You been coming here long?"

"Awhile," he said, holding my hand for an awkward length of time. "What can I help you with?"

I shifted back a little but still couldn't breathe well through the funk. "The guy in charge. He's a vampire, right?"

He grinned at me and cocked his hip. Impatience simmered and I was glad of it. That was a normal reaction, wasn't it?

"Why, yes he is. I can probably arrange you to meet him if," he sent me a bit of a smile, "You're into that."

I was so far from being into vampires that parcels from there would take six months to arrive. "What was this place like before he started?"

He scratched at his beard, raining ash on his denim jacket. "More fights, for one. Not the display ones. You three wouldn't have been safe. You know what men are like."

"Not all men," I offered, with a smile.

He lifted his beer in a toast and smiled back. "What's your name, sugar?"

Sugar. Who called anyone sugar? "Thanks." I turned back to my coven and saw they were already following my thoughts.

Wesley wasn't just here for the cash or the ego boost. He always had another motive.

Aspen and Lilith had followed the conversation and looked as happy as I felt about it. "Fuck," Aspen said, blowing out a hard breath before adding, somewhat calmer, "We're going to be very visible."

I looked at Lilith, bracing for her objection. Instead, she said, "I told Maadai we were doing this as a check in...sort of. We're covered to be here."

How the fuck she'd swung that, I had no idea. "Do we have to report this?" I asked, quietly.

Her eyes flickered around, as if looking for threats. "Maybe. It depends."

I didn't ask her what it depended on. We were cleared to be present. If we were recognized, we had cause to be here.

Whatever Wesley was doing here, it wasn't just entertaining himself.

"I was coerced," I told them, numb.

"We," Lilith corrected.

But Wesley had only spoken to me.

A gorgeous young person appeared in the doorway. The child star smiled at us and the bottom fell out of my belly. *Fae.*

"Wes says you'll want him?" The young faerie said.

"This is absolutely a trap." Lilith's words were soft enough only for our ears, and any shifter in the place who cared to listen, as we were swallowed by the chaos and violence within.

"Yes," I agreed. "But I don't know if we're the prey, the bait, or the knife." Elders, I'd walked right into this. "While you two figure it out, I'm going to need silver."

CHAPTER 10

$\mathcal{A}$spen had done her share of competition fights. But competitive fighting against humans was a world away from brawling with supernaturals.

Neither of them argued that I was the best at not dying.

The fights rolled before me and I barely paid attention. A gold-haired, double-jointed fae competitor ripped half a siren's scalp off. A bird shifter shat on a cockatrice and then got carried out on a stretcher.

I listened with half an ear as the fae talked us through the rules, stripping off my charms methodically. Nothing I hadn't done myself was allowed. No charms, no potions, no nothing. And I had no silver weapons. Not until Aspen slipped me a heavy silver necklace. I wrapped the metal around the knuckles of one hand. I'd probably break my damn fist if I hit him with it, because I hadn't worn my lupetec gloves. But I could heal a broken fist.

Non-lethal was the brief. I could do a lot of spells that were non-lethal, but not many that'd force an ursathrope to submit. Chop off an arm? Suffocate him until he passed out? Burn him to not-quite-death? I didn't give a shit about being disqualified, but I didn't want to do lasting damage.

I grabbed my phone and tapped in a quick message to Lilith. *Can you transmute this chain into something useful?* I asked, then hit send and stared at her until she took out her phone out and read my message.

She gave a nod, and held up a few fingers, asking for time.

We weren't cheating so I could win. We were cheating so we could all win. And I wasn't going to lose a moment of sleep over it.

We stayed in the crowd rather than going around back with the competitors. If we'd tried, Benson would probably rip my head off there, and there wouldn't be a pot for him to collect.

A few guys around us got mouthy. Aspen dealt with them while I tried not to overthink, holding my wand firmly. I needed to get a good silver spike to hang beside it on my keyring in case Wesley played me again.

Fuck, I hated knowing that was a real possibility. But when he'd been around longer than I could trace my family tree, he had access to a lot of tricks I didn't.

The crowd shifted and I caught a glimpse of a familiar face that made ice run through my veins. But it couldn't have been Taig. The hair was wrong, the profile wrong, and he'd never…

I straightened and looked harder, because I *wasn't* just jumpy. In the man's place, when the crowd shifted again, I caught a glimpse of a classically beautiful woman.

There was a gnawing unease in my gut that I didn't ignore, but I did turn my attention back to the ring. Taig had a brother, but he was in Queensland, I was pretty sure. It hadn't looked like Taig, exactly. And he was working late tonight anyway.

But something niggled, low in my brain, and I listened.

A drunken, "Hey," from behind me made me turn and bare my teeth at the human cumsock who had been annoying Aspen. The guy sneered in response, flicking his gaze over me, as if he wouldn't do me dry if I gave him half an opportunity. Happily, I took the hair-tie Lilith thrust at me and scooped up my curls. Wesley's fae helper hovered nearby.

"…give you, Teddy," Wesley declared.

Teddy. What a stage name.

I didn't need the impatient tugging hands on my leggings to know that was my cue. I shrugged out of my jacket and Aspen grabbed it. "Fight your fight," she said, the words hard, as the fae kid ushered me forward.

Tightening the tie in my hair and hoping it'd hold, I followed the fae along the narrow dirt path alongside the makeshift ring, my heart drumming in my ears.

Benson was there, wearing lupetec trunks and staring at me with ice cold fury. Old scars puckered his body, leaving silver streaks in the hair that covered his chest and belly. I recognized the long-healed puncture marks that covered his flanks as lycanthrope bites and the jagged scar in one shin as the mark of a compound fracture.

I didn't like any of that.

"And the Wicked Witch of the South East!" Wesley said, taking my hand holding my fist aloft.

Was I going to like this vampire's objectives?

I gave no shits about the roars of the crowd or the gross comments. But I gave a lot of shits about the way Benson stalked toward me, his muscles banded with fury.

"I'll manage this," Wesley told me smoothly. "You're in that corner, darling."

The adrenaline made my skin prickle and my heart race. I followed his instructions, focused on what I needed to do. Non-lethal damage.

Did this even make sense? Was I turned around and inside out?

"Oh, she's not wicked," I heard someone say from behind me. "She just needs someone to teach her what a good girl does!"

My stomach turned and I rolled my shoulders aggressively, feeling the lupetec hugging my flesh, the pinch of my hastily restrained hair at the back of my head. *Supermarket body spray and red wine.*

Fury whipped through me and I shook my head at myself, tightening my fist around the silver chain that was my only fucking weapon. As soon as Lilith transmuted it, it'd be marginally less pathetic.

Assessing whether Benson was engaging in illegal activities made sense. Figuring out what Wesley was doing in a way that didn't immediately set us up as enemies made sense. Getting Benson some cash and then pleading coercion and never doing it again made sense. Shutting this whole fucking operation down without getting any of our clients offside made sense.

But standing on the other side of the ring to my client did not make sense.

Get it done, Rory. I limbered up my hips and wondered if Nic had known I'd end up here. His Oracle skills were excellent, but only for the short term. Unless he'd done a lot of study while I'd been gone, he was clueless.

It was nice to think that maybe there was a purpose I just didn't know yet, though.

The ursathrope hadn't stopped looking at me. Teeth half-bared, chest rising and falling rapidly, his fists clenched beside him.

My heart ached for him. We were both flies in Wesley's web…for now. I gave him a nod of acknowledgement, but he turned and spat. Unfortunately, he turned away from Wesley, but I didn't blame him for that.

The vampire, apparently satisfied, left Benson's side. "Witch. Teddy." He positioned himself neatly in the center of the ring. The vamp had the skills to be an amazing announcer. I didn't want to know if his charisma could extend to halting fights, though. The thought made my skin crawl.

On the other side Benson cracked his neck.

Nostalgia swept through me. Brandon used to do that, too, just to piss me off. He thought it made him look tough.

I suspected Benson did it to loosen up.

Putting aside the memories, I shook my head and sighed. "I don't like this either," I told Benson, hoping he'd hear me.

"Fight!" Wesley crowed.

I glared at him out of pure reflex.

Benson stalked forwards, still in his human form. The silver necklace warned against my skin, biting into my knuckles as I pressed it dramatically to my lips.

It slithered in my hand in a way that made my guts turn, but I didn't look to see what Lilith had turned it into, just acted like that spell was mine. Elders, I loved my coven.

Benson's nostrils flared, but either he didn't know the smell of my magick or he didn't care, because he didn't call me out. I raised my fists and came forward a few paces, mostly so I could see what it was I was now holding.

One pretty silver knuckle duster, complete with spikes longer than Lilith's nails.

She really didn't like him.

With the weight of my wand in my other hand, I watched him move. There was no way I wasn't bending the rules here. The baying crowd faded. My mind turned them into quiet eucalypts and slow shivering leaves against bark, and that made it okay, somehow.

"Come on," I invited, quietly. "We both know you've got me."

He straightened. "How can I not kill her?" he roared at Wesley. "She's a wet tissue!"

The crowd went off at this and I couldn't help but smile a little. *Gravity sucks, unless you're me,* I thought, breathing just a little magick into the spell. *Then it fucking blows.*

He went down on his knees, crushed by the weight of my spell.

I straightened and around us the wind blew louder. "I don't have a lot that's not going to hurt you," I admitted, watching him brace his hands against the ground, the veins on his neck popping out with the force he was using to stop from eating dirt. "But I'll do my best."

The look he shot me was pure venom.

I stood, hand on my hip, feeling bad for him. "Did you want to…" I waved a hand and saw my keys were still on my wand. If I lost them I was going to be pissed. "Give up?"

His answer was to reach out with one hand and drag himself toward me, centimeter by agonizing centimeter.

Alarm skittered along my skin. That spell crushed pretty much everything alive. I'd pulverized my foot when I caught myself in one I'd dropped during my early days with Retrievals. *That* had been a very badly positioned ward. If I'd been in that circle, my skull probably would've been pulverized.

Of course Benson was magickally enhanced, so I knew he'd be fine. But still, the guy was a fucking tank.

"He's gonna make you crawl, bitch!" someone shouted nearby, cutting through the mental calm of leaves that weren't real, jolting me back into the present. "Get back to the fuckin' kitchen, whore!"

I cared a lot more about the man making slow, undeniable progress toward me, murder in his eyes, than I did about that cum stain.

"Oh, shut the fuck up!" I heard Lilith roar. "Or I'll fuck your dad and give him a son he'll actually love!"

I let out a shocked laugh and half-turned to the guy who'd taken the full force of her anger. She and Aspen stood in a pocket of calm, surrounded by frenzied shitstains. Her face was twisted in fury like I'd never seen it. I didn't need to heckle him. His buddies had all turned on him already, laughing and shoving, driving home those words.

Wesley appeared at the heckler's elbow, his smile polite, his glasses reflecting the big, soulless lights. And the guy went from red to white at his sudden arrival.

Around Wesley, the group of them fell silent. Curiosity had snagged my attention on the scene longer than I could afford, though I wasn't the only one. The entire crowd was focused on the vampire rather than 'Teddy' and I.

They were here for blood, after all.

Uneasy, I shifted my attention back to Benson. I knew he'd hit the edge of my ward when his mouth twisted in a smile.

Cool and normal. I stepped back and considered re-casting it. Would he shift if I canceled it? He would be on me in a moment and, at this point, I didn't know how much he cared about lethality.

Shit, if I'd been forced to crawl along the dirt under bone-crushing weight, I doubt if I would, either.

I didn't have much choice. If I got pushed into that ward, I'd be done, which left me limited space to move. So if he was going to get out, then we'd have to dance.

As it will, I thought, bracing myself. *So shall it be*. And I leapt at him.

I was met with a solid wall of muscle but before I could use my dusters I was flying, pain exploding through my chest as he counter-attacked. *Gravity sucks and I sure don't*. I caught hold of the net at the top of the ring and clung, struggling to draw breath.

This is why I wore lupetec at every opportunity.

He stood beneath me, staring up at me with disdain. And then the edges of his form blurred.

I shut my eyes and sucked in more air. I had no idea how long an ursathrope shift took. If I looked into that otherworldly void I'd be sick as a dog. If I didn't look and he was a thrice-cursed giant bear, I'd be dead as doornail.

How high could bears jump though, really?

A gust of air was my only warning that ursas shifted a lot faster than their lycan kin. I let go from my hold on the wire but held the spell.

Fur, steel and agony met me. My body knew the moves, even if it didn't know this game. I slipped away from him and hit the ground lightly, letting the spell fizzle as I looked up to see him hanging off the same wire that'd supported me. Somehow it wasn't sagging under his weight.

And they say drop bears aren't real. I straightened, rubbing at my ribs. "You pack a punch," I admitted, hoping that was trauma-informed. The bruise I'd have tomorrow sure would be.

He moved, climbing over the wire with speed that made me wish fervently for my time-slowing charms. If I could've passed them off as mine, I would've, but Wesley knew they weren't.

But my Oma hadn't raised a jellyfish.

Through this shield you can't touch me.

He dropped, crashing against my barrier and thrown away by his own force.

It barely slowed him. Again, I cast my anti-gravity spell and narrowly avoided his charge. It wasn't until I was upside down with a face full of hair and a burning scalp that I realized how close I'd come.

There was no way those claws were non-lethal.

I flipped away and felt the weight of him hit the net, releasing my hold and landing hard. He was less than a second behind me. Reacting out of pure instinct, I dropped my Impenetrable Ward around us.

The flick of one scarred ear showed he knew I was casting, though I didn't speak. I didn't have time to think about it because he charged at me.

I danced back and the sound of his claws against the edge of my ward clanged like a car hitting a church bell. He staggered back, shaking his head.

An idea bloomed.

There weren't a lot of ways I could take him out without killing him. I wouldn't win if we kept dancing, because I only needed one misstep to be done.

Teddy had very sensitive ears.

If I could disorient him long enough to sink a silver spike into him, I'd be on equal footing. And I didn't hate those odds.

"Hey," I said, strolling around the edge of my ward. "I didn't come here for a hair-cut, friend." That was going to hurt when the adrenaline died down.

He lifted his paw, decorated with a mess of black curls he'd ripped out of my head, and blew the hair off his claws.

This time he was more cautious, feeling the edge of the ward, brushing up against it. I should've dropped this one in the first place, but how was I supposed to subdue him like this? Through boredom?

With every moment he was in the ward he was trying to puzzle his way free. I had to admit, he would've been a terrifying foe, if he was actually my foe.

Surely he'd figure out he wasn't.

Amused at my own thoughts, I stepped over the edge of my ward. The magick crackled and ran against my skin, welcoming me.

He lunged. I side-stepped out of the way and ignored the agonizing noise as he hit the edge of the ward. The impact still reverberating in my skull, I went hard.

The first blow with the silver-studded knuckle dusters made him roar in pain and stagger into the ward, causing another massive church bell toll. My heart was in my throat as I threw myself over his back, scrambling for purchase, using those knuckle dusters like climbing spikes. He hurled himself against the ward attempting to crush me, but it slipped over me harmlessly and gave me a split second to drive those spikes into his neck.

This isn't trauma informed. The thought was slippery and purpose poured through my veins.

When it came, I felt his shift in my bones. The magick in my cells vibrated, a very specific sort of torture. I closed my eyes and locked that gut-wrenching nothingness he'd become in my guard, breathing through pain that set off explosions behind my eyes and made me clench my teeth against a scream.

His neck was thick and strong beneath my forearm when he coalesced. The nausea threatened to undo me, somehow, though I hadn't opened my eyes. I didn't need to. I knew these moves and I hung onto that with everything I had, trusting to my body even while the fibers of my being threatened to unbind.

Once more he tried to crush me against my own ward. The toll rocked through us both. He clawed at my arms but now he was just a man, pierced by silver, and I had him in a rear naked choke. Spots swam before my eyes. Puking on your training partner was bad manners.

"Tap," I told him through my teeth as he writhed.

The noise he made was one of rage, not submission.

I tightened my grips. The pulse pounding through his huge chest I could feel drumming against my thighs. Every beat of his heart said *no.*

He was going to fight me to the bitter end. I hated that for him.

"Tap," I told him, furiously.

Whatever he said in response was lost to the language barrier. He tried to drive his head into mine, but he was slow, now, and weak.

My heart ached. Old scars were smooth beneath my arms. I could smell the man, soap and sunlight.

He wasn't going to give in. I knew it. Sick to my stomach, I let out a long breath. He fell like the mountain he was and if I hadn't been in lupetec I'd've been badly hurt, but it was just another bruise now. I struggled out from beneath him and grabbed his feet, lifting them to return the blood to his brain.

I didn't know if I could fix this.

There must've been another way. His ankles were too thick for me to get my hands around. I propped his feet on my shoulders, shaking from the after-effects of his shift fucking with me. It didn't matter. We were committed.

In that moment, with his hairy legs on my shoulders and the contents of my stomach wanting to escape one way or the other, I looked down at his deathly pale face and wished I'd stopped for just a few more minutes and thought this through.

Wesley appeared, laughter in the corners of his mouth, reaching for my hand to declare me the winner.

I shrugged him off, furious. "Help me," I demanded.

His brow twitched in amusement. He didn't help, but he did step back with a grand, sweeping gesture. "And the Wicked Witch has it!"

Benson's eyes snapped open to the roar of applause. Exasperated, I dropped a silence ward around us.

His eyelid twitched in the slightest flinch. He yanked his feet off my shoulders, but he didn't kick me as he pulled free.

I stayed upright, a fresh spurt of adrenaline racing through me as he got to his feet. Blood ran from those wounds unchecked. He let them bleed freely and just towered over me, his gaze unreadable. Then he swayed a little and I reached out in of sheer reflex to steady him.

Again, he flinched back, his jaw tight. But he didn't take a swing at me.

"It's noisy out there," I said, regretting having grabbed him. Regretting the entire shitshow. He'd be riding the adrenaline, just like me, and I hadn't checked in. "I've got some water in the car. Want?"

He looked at Wesley working the crowd on the other side of the silence ward, the people standing and cheering. "Do I have a choice?" he asked me.

I raised my brows. "I'm sure you do. And this is one of them." I shrugged and pulled out the hair-tie that was still tangled in my hair. "We'll hang around for a while. Think about it." I collapsed the ward and winced at the wave of bullshit blood frenzy.

Letting myself out the same way I came in wasn't an option. The net had been sealed. So I followed Benson out the back into a poorly lit, marquee. Ignoring the suspicious looks sent my way, I went straight out into the cold air and breathed it in deeply.

The nausea was still there, but at least if I chundered now it'd be in relative privacy.

"Fuck," I breathed, putting a hand to my aching ribs. Lupetec had saved my life at least twice tonight.

"Fancy armor, for a witch."

I didn't jump, but it was a near thing. Benson was at my goddamn elbow, watching me.

"Basic black. Good capsule pieces. Dress it up, dress it down." I shook my head, hoping Lilith and Aspen would find us, and eased the silver off my now-aching hand. He was buttoning up his flannel shirt, wounds completely open.

Something about that made my heart hurt.

"Can I catch a lift?" he asked, briskly. "Since you basically live next door."

Paying for a ride share from all the way out here wouldn't be cheap, and Aspen was going to kill me if I said no. Lilith would kill me if I said yes. "Can't see why not." *Hah. I found a loophole.* "I assume I don't have to fight anyone else."

He shot the building an irritated look. "Vampires," he said.

"Vampires," I agreed, starting back toward Aspen's car. Surely, she wouldn't be long. "How're winnings paid?"

He snorted. "Wesley will find us."

Wesley didn't, though. Aspen and Lilith did. And when they got close, Aspen tossed me my jacket and a heavy reuseable supermarket bag.

"You're going to need at least some of that to fix your hair. It's a mess."

I shrugged, but my scalp, reminded of the injury, started to burn. "We're giving Benson a lift," I told them both.

"Cool," Aspen said, easily. "Well, it's past my bedtime, so let's get on the road."

Lilith said nothing at all. Yet. Just climbed into the back without a word.

When Benson went to go around the other side I shook my head and pointed at the passenger side. She wanted to sit behind him, she could. I wasn't fighting her for it. Anyway, I still had the blood-slick silver weapons. Before I could figure out how to reduce the mess, something made me look up.

Taig.

Except it wasn't Taig. His hair was a ruddy brown, not the salt-and-pepper I knew, and he had a full beard. But I couldn't mistake the way my heart rolled in my chest.

And then I saw Delyan coming out of the shadows, and it all clicked. The beautiful woman who'd got in my line of sight. The strange not-quite-right profile of his. They were both undercover.

Well, shit.

A group of men came out, laughing, their steps so light they barely touched the ground. They were all doing pixie dust for sure. And if I'd just gatecrashed Taig's sting…

"Hey, Wicked Witch!" one of them said, laughter in their voice. "I'll nap in your thighs if you want!"

If Taig and Delyan, and who knew how many other cops, hadn't been there, I probably would've put a choking ward on that specific space cadet. But they were, so I just flipped him the bird and climbed in on the other side of Lilith.

Aspen cleared her throat. "Well, I think it's your shout for pizza, Sunshine."

"Sure." I gave no fucks, just tried not to look at Taig. I definitely hadn't told him I was going to be here. I didn't recall if I'd even responded to him when he'd told me that he was working late tonight. When had he said that? Yesterday? The day before? It was pre-planned. Of course it was pre-planned. Had any of the arseholes I'd run into been undercover cops I hadn't even looked twice at?

Fuck. Fuck.

Fae coercion wasn't a defense in court. It'd get my head off the chopping block with Maadai, sure, but not VicPol. I could claim Wesley had threatened me, but not only would it be a lie but no one would want to believe it, because that meant they'd have to arrest Wesley. Which was like attempting to arrest the fucking sun.

I rested my head back against the uncomfortable cushions and breathed through the nausea and the pain.

I'd just beaten an ursathrope, solo. More or less solo.

I was a fucking *baddie.*

Potentially a baddie about to be tossed into SuperSec.

But I pulled out my phone, feeling the adrenaline ebbing, and opened up my messages to Lilith.

Nice weapon. I owe you.

Beside me she shifted. I watched as the glow of her phone lit her perfectly made up face. She read the message and tapped out a quick response. *You scared the shit out of me.* Her words glowed white against the dark background of my screen.

Part of me wanted to reach over and hug her. Part of me wanted to grin. I did neither. Better than being full of shit, I typed, threw a few emojis in for good luck, and hit send.

I didn't get another response. She settled in beside me as we bumped and scraped our way over potholes in silence. The car rode lower with Benson onboard, but no one commented on that, or on what had happened, or on what might be about to happen.

The silence wasn't uncomfortable, at least not for me. I checked out my hand in the flickering freeway lights on the way home. I was going to have some bruises to show for tonight, no doubt about that. But I'd got off pretty lightly.

"Hey, Aspen," I said, an idea floating into my brain. "If I get Dierdre to make Benson up a potion to help with the aftereffects of the silver, can we swing by and grab it on the way back?"

"Sure."

So I pulled out my phone again and called Dierdre, who sounded sleepy but happy to help.

By the time we got back to Melbourne it was very late, but Dierdre responded to my message and met us in the underground parking lot of her apartment, folded up in her robe, her pajamas peeking out the bottom and a reused plastic bottle glowing in her hand.

I tried not to worry about whether this might be the last time I'd see her.

"I got it," Aspen told us all, climbing out and leaving the car running as she jogged around to Dierdre.

"If she saw you, she'd be taking you in and giving you healing potions," Lilith said to me.

I had no doubt. I also had no doubt that Aspen had gone because Lilith and I were best positioned to skewer Benson if we needed to. But I didn't think we'd need to. And anyway, I'd done my skewering for the week.

Aspen passed the bottle over to Benson as she climbed back in. "Sip away at that. Apparently it should be enough for two or three desilverings and will be good for six months, after which time the effect will start to reduce."

"I don't need this."

"Maybe not, but your kids need you to be ready to meet their needs, and we want to set you up to do that," Aspen told him serenely. "Feeling less like trash will probably help."

I kept my amusement to myself as he uncapped the bottle and, without another word, took a pull.

We had access to his one lever, now.

"On that topic," I said, trying to keep my tone as nonchalant as Aspen's, "I'm sure you want to get home immediately, but I'm happy to patch you up first. I'm sure the kids will smell the blood on you, and I know how off-putting it is to have a loved one come home banged up. Smelling like blood and being visibly wounded is different."

Also, I wanted to maximize the wins we'd had tonight. Because I hurt like hellfire, and I wanted that to be worth something.

"I don't need healing."

"Yeah, but," Aspen shrugged. "It'll take ten minutes. And like Rory said, it'll protect your kids a bit." He didn't argue with her, just looked out the window and took another pull of the potion. "Is that okay? We can take you to the office quickly. We've got some field kits."

The field kits at the office were generic and also would be a lot more than ten minutes. I opened my mouth to tell her that my place was closer, then closed it with a snap.

Regardless of whether he knew where I lived or not, I didn't need him feeling any comfier than he was with the whole *let's visit my custodian* thing. But I did need to tell them both that he knew where I lived, probably.

"So," Aspen said, lazily. "You okay with this, Benson?"

His response was a grunt.

Aspen's grin wasn't directed at anyone in particular. "You sure you're up to do a healing, Sunshine?"

"We could call Bernie," Lilith added, quietly.

"I'm fine. Lupetec ate most of the force." Or enough of it, at least. That wasn't what Aspen had meant and I knew it, but it was the answer she was going to get.

I could deal with my own trauma responses if it meant chipping away at this guy's resistances...and reducing the fear his kids carried when he left their sight.

CHAPTER 11

$\mathcal{B}$enson stood in the kitchenette, his eyes on the wall of windows that overlooked the city and his expression fixed in the middle distance as Aspen and Lilith washed his wounds clean. The kits were fine, but I added a few pinches of garlic to offset some of the physical damage the silver had done. I didn't have a rusty spoon to stir it with, but I pricked my finger and dropped a bit of blood in the mix.

Modern, standardized magickal recipes wouldn't allow that switch, and I understood why. But this was kitchen magick.

Anyway, I was probably about to get hauled into SuperSec.

The elevator chimed, signaling the pizza I'd ordered had arrived, and Aspen set aside the cloth to go and get it. I'd ordered more than we needed.

Slapping on the poultices didn't take long. His wounds were relatively clean. I hadn't done a lot of damage, despite the silver. "I can magickally heal you," I offered him, as I worked. "But it'll make you sleepy. Potentially very sleepy."

"No."

It was what I'd expected. "I can magickally boost what I'm doing now. Very minimal negative side-effects. Basically like having a glass of warm milk."

He snorted. "I hate milk."

I resisted the urge to slap the mixture on a bit harder. He didn't have to be grateful, but there was an excessive amount of grumpiness considering we were all now unlikely friends. "Look, these wounds are the least of it. Those muscle aches you've got aren't going to—"

"I know." He half-turned his head and met my eyes. "I'm fine, witch."

"Fair enough," Aspen cut in, smoothly. "If you change your mind, let us know. You've got our phone number. And I'll be stopping around tomorrow afternoon to help you with the forms to get some government payments happening—"

"I don't want to be owned by your government," he said, the words stubborn.

Aspen nodded, taking a slice of pizza and crossing her leg as she leant back in the chair, the picture of chill. "Same. We can talk about the things you're required to do to be eligible, and you can make an informed decision about what you apply for. Because there are some payments that require nothing from you that you haven't already given them, since you're a citizen."

He made a noise of disbelief. "Are we done?"

"Side note," I said, quietly. "Being beholden to our government? Way less problematic than being beholden to Wesley."

That made him pause. Lilith's nails tapped irregularly on the edge of her cup in the silence as I worked.

"Stop by before four," he told Aspen, when I passed him his shirt. "But after ten."

"I'll make it work," Aspen said, while I resisted doing an air punch. *Fuck yes, learning how to speak ursathrope.*

"We'll give you a lift home," she went on, going to wash her hands.

He stilled, though, his eyes going toward the elevator and every muscle tensing.

I hadn't dated a lycan and learned nothing. My wand's weight settled into my hand and the adrenaline rushed through my tired system, pushing aside the pain and weariness.

Aspen went to reach for her keys and I stopped her, holding my fingers to my lips.

"They were there tonight," Benson said, directing the comment to me, his voice quiet.

"Did they follow us?" I asked him, struggling to make sense of this.

He shook his head. "Not that I could tell."

I wouldn't put it past Wesley to rock up at our workplace in the middle of the night, but I doubted Benson would know about him before he hit us. So I nodded to show him I understood, much as I could, and walked him down the hall. The rooms on either side of us were lit with the glow of the city. With the harsh office lights shining from behind us and the late-night quiet of the building, it wasn't surprising that my skin crawled.

I wasn't jumpy. I knew what could happen in these walls on a night like this.

Flexing my aching hand to remind myself I'd just taken down an ursathrope didn't help, especially with my nose full of the healing kit I'd sabotaged to heal said usathrope.

The elevator door slid open as we got close. Out of the corner of my eye I saw Lilith in a doorway on my diagonal, positioned so she could cast. The sight made my heart sit lighter in my chest.

I wasn't jumpy, *or* alone.

I opened it and stepped back, spells swimming in my head.

Taig stepped out of the elevator and the bottom dropped out of my stomach at his expression.

He was alone, and that worried the shit out of me. *The sound of a gunshot. Ryan's body falling through the rift.* I stepped back to let him through. There were some red patches on his jaw but his hair was back to its usual auburn with gray streaks.

He offered me one of two takeaway coffee cups, his gaze skimming over Benson, Aspen and Lilith. "Sorry, folks," he said, as if it was just a normal social call under totally normal circumstances. "If I'd known there would be a crowd, I'd've taken orders."

"No crowd here," Aspen said brightly as I hesitantly took the cup. "We were just going, weren't we, Benson? Lilith, you want a lift too?"

Lilith's eyes back on Benson, she said, "Yeah, thanks."

"Take the...wait." I hustled back to the break room, taking the bag I assume held the fight money and the extra pizza I'd ordered and thrusting both at Benson.

If everything went tits up after that cursed pit-fight bullshit... Would Taig want to go on the run with me?

Did I want that?

Benson didn't move, staring at me like I was a puzzle piece from a random set.

"Go," I said, waving my hand at it. "I couldn't take it. It'd be a whole official thing. So."

Ignoring that completely, he stepped just a little closer. "Are you safe with him?" he asked, the words a low, threatening rumble.

There was no way the ursathrope was trying to look after me. Against *Taig*, of all people. "Of course."

"Your heart hasn't settled," he said, even quieter. "We can't smell fear, witch. Not exactly."

But he sort of could, too.

I met his eyes, struggling to sort through the rush of emotions. Guy had run from me a few days ago. Now he was checking in on me.

"It's a complicated personal situation," I said, so quietly I was confident no human would've heard it. "But I promise, I'm not unsafe."

"Your body promises otherwise." But he moved away from me, still eyeballing Taig. "I'll be up the road," he said, to the room at large, the words not a threat but a promise.

That was a complication I really didn't need.

"Cool, well." Aspen shot me a sunny smile. "Let's go, Lilith, before my car turns into a pumpkin. Hello and goodbye, Taig!" And she breezed out with a cheery wave.

Lilith paused for a moment next to Taig, though, and said something I couldn't hear that made his eyes burn holes in me.

Maybe I should get him some drops for that?

The sound of their steps faded out and I reached for something, anything, to do. The elevator dinged as I carried mugs to the sink. Taig's steps echoed down the hallway as water splashed over my hands and the colorful ceramics. The table in the break room had been changed. The whole feel of the building was different. Plenty of days I made myself coffee and it was all good.

But Taig rested one hand against the surface of that new stained pine table. I could see it in my peripheral vision. And there were shadows. I hadn't been scared of the shadows for a very long time.

"How fucked am I?" I asked him, and while it was the surface level, legal bullshit that was in the fore of my mind, that wasn't my only thought.

I wasn't jumpy. Some of the shit I'd survived had left restless ghosts in the fibers of my being. And tonight I was too drained to exorcise them.

"Fucked?" he asked, frowning. "Why would you be fucked?"

"I just fought in a pit-fighting competition," I pointed out, feeling sick. Maybe he hadn't been looking. Maybe no one had recognized me.

Maybe he was seeing the ghosts.

His eyes narrowed. "Stokes told us it was strategic to minimize risk, that you weren't really participating."

The knot in my belly just tightened. "Did he?"

He blew out a breath. "Can we compare notes on the way back? I've done a double and I'm wrecked."

He looked it. I took my coffee and fell in beside him, glad to have him between me and the shadows. "Must admit, when I heard you were getting friendly with a vampire who predates the Western world, I was a little concerned."

I didn't answer until we were in the elevator and the office was safely on the other side of the steel doors. "He played me."

Taig turned to me, *crowding me.* The fury in him chilled me. Behind me, the steel handrail bumped against the small of my back. "Tell me."

I held up a hand. The other curled around my wand as my heart kicked. "Whoa no. You don't get all," I waved a hand at his chest,

"Mister Misogyny on me." Spells swam through my head but there was a limit to what I could cast in this steel box.

The elevator dinged open.

His hand reached out, white knuckled, and grabbed the door to hold it open. But Taig didn't move, staring at me with those piercing blue eyes in a way that made my skin crawl.

Any spell I could cast on him right now probably wouldn't be non-lethal. And the fact that I even started to sift through my options made me want to puke yet again.

Instead, I side-stepped around where he stood, clinging to the steel frame, his eyes fixed on the buttons behind my right shoulder.

I didn't breathe until I was a few meters away in the foyer. He still hadn't moved.

You ought to run. But the thought was tentative. Running, from Taig? My heart raced. Would Aspen have left already? I reached for my phone, my hand shaky as I tried to tap my unlock sequence.

He straightened and turned toward me. His steps were crisp.

Run, the voice in the back of my head breathed. Grief and confusion had me frozen. It wasn't a big deal. I'd done plenty of poorly thought-out, risky shit in the past.

His hand caught my arm just above the elbow and I came to a halt, bracing myself. "You haven't spoken to me in days," he said, flatly, as the blood roared in my ears. "You show up in the middle of a bust in some sort of alliance with a vampire I don't know about and you damn near got your head ripped off by a client you've barely even mentioned to me. I'm Mister Impatient, sure, but this has got *nothing to do* with gender roles."

I looked, very deliberately, at where his fingers were biting into my arm. And I didn't loosen my grip on my wand, even though my nerves prickled at the pressure he'd used.

He let go of me and stepped back, deflating. "Right. So that's where we're at."

Fury rolled in my belly. "I don't know what conclusions you're jumping to, but I'm happy to have a conversation with you. One without grunts and growls and more bruises than I already had."

Something flickered over his face. "Okay."

He wasn't back from whatever spinout he'd been caught in, like he'd been—

Triggered. Like maybe he had trauma. Maybe around vampires. *Nice fucking work, Rory.*

I scrubbed a hand over my face. "Can I catch a lift home?" I asked him. "It's actually a pretty short story, but I'm beat, too."

His nod was stiff. "Sorry."

"Yeah. Me, too." I hated that I was hyper aware of where he stood beside me, and not in the sexy way. But he didn't say anything else until the car doors had sealed out the city and the engine hummed as gentle background noise.

I explained the situation in the detail I had, and he listened in silence, pushing the speed limit and running every orange light we came to.

"Well, as far as we knew, you were doing exactly what had been organized to protect your clients," he said, at the end. "Someone said they'd checked in and you'd been signed off by Maadai."

Elders. "Why would Wesley set that up?"

He parked and cranked the handbrake harder than he needed, but I pretended not to notice. "I don't know, yet. Come on. You need to clean those wounds. I'll make you pancakes." But there was a bite to the words that stopped me from relaxing, even once we were inside and Eclipse was threading her way around us, greeting us with her meows and touches of her paws.

I showered briskly and went to find my own first aid for the agony in my skull. Taig was making pancakes with a ferocity that irritated me. I'd given him cool-down time. He was on private property that was warded for protection. Really, if Wesley decided to kill us, we were done regardless of *anything* we could do, but the point wasn't the real danger, it was whatever his lizard brain was telling him.

"What've you been up to?" he asked, tone mild, shoulders stiff beneath the windbreaker I'd never seen before.

My mind skipped back to the accusation of being out of touch. "Work. Like I said." And I tossed some salt into a bowl. Objectively, I could admire the way he stood with his feet set and his shoulders back, ready to start swinging. But the only part of me that was wet were my hands as I dipped them into the water.

"Work? All day, every day?"

He knew damned well what my routine was by now. But I didn't want to get into a pissing match with him. "I'm a busy witch," I said, keeping my tone mild.

"You're something," he agreed, but it was said with grief and he paused to look at me. "Are you okay, Rory?"

Not only had the last of my frustration melted away as he softened, but so did all the layers of armor I hadn't even known I'd been wearing. "I think so." The air I drew into my lungs sat heavily, but I could do it. "A bit battered. You?"

He glanced up at me, and the smile that touched his mouth was a little bitter as he said, "I prefer crumbed."

Maybe it was supposed to be funny. I was going to need to figure out how I felt about him losing his shit at me, earlier. And I was going to need to make sure I didn't do the same to him.

I blew out a breath. "You had me worried."

He shrugged a bit in a somewhat self-deprecating fashion at odds with the lack of expression in his eyes. "Next time you want to go a round, maybe remember I'm harder to knock out than that."

Unease climbed under my skin and I listened to it, pausing and meeting his eyes. "Are we on the same side still, Taig?"

He slid some pancakes onto the plate. "I thought we were." The ceramic base of it grated against my benchtop as he pushed it gently over to me and he leant on the bench as if I'd landed a few hits. I didn't remember taking any real swings. "But you're not letting me in, Roars."

I opened my mouth to object and, without even looking up, he angled the spatula in his hand precisely at one of the crystals taped to the top of my wall.

I closed my mouth with a snap. I hadn't told him about Benson's late night visit. Or about going out there tonight. I wasn't in the habit of checking in with him about everything, but that had been some big oversights. If I was in his position, I'd have my nose out of joint, too.

So I blew out a breath and copped that one, turning to the pancakes in front of me. "That's fair, and I'm sorry." And I really was. I didn't know the name for whatever the sticky black emotion was that slithered through me and made me feel small, but it was the cousin of grief and the step-sibling to shame. "I'm trying," I admitted, and the words burned my throat and my eyes. "I'm not good at it, but I'm trying. And honestly, I need you to, as well. I don't know if it's fair or not, Taig, but if you take swings I'm going to swing back." He was wearing his cop face, but his shoulders were hunched and his breathing quick. My heart twisted. This probably wasn't the best time to do this, but I was committed, now. "I'll get better at that." That's what experience had made me believe, anyway. "But right now, I've got no buffer." And the reality of that made the tears burn painfully again.

What I was asking him for maybe wasn't entirely fair, but it was still what I needed for now. And I was working to not need it for long, wasn't I?

The stove was turned off with a flick of his wrist and he walked over and stood beside me. I could feel the warmth rolling off his body, but he didn't touch me. "Thank you for telling me," he said, softly. "For what it's worth, I'm re-assembling my own support network. I've lost a couple of them in the last five years."

Elders. I laughed, but the sound wasn't joyful. "Look at us, being responsible and shit."

He picked up a pancake and inspected the crispy edge where he'd shallow fried it. The smell of vanilla drifted gently into my head and it made me want to curl up and cry while stuffing my face. I was pretty sure he'd be okay with it, but I didn't like the snot to comfort food ratio I predicted I'd ingest.

"Do you know the statistics on how many couples split in the first year after sexual assault?"

I just shook my aching head. I couldn't keep doing this tonight.

"I saw sixty percent, somewhere." He offered me the food and I took it from his fingers because it was easier than trying to redirect this conversation.

How often had I contacted him over the last few days? How busy had I *really* been? I couldn't even remember what I'd done. It had been a blur.

I'd gone into survival mode. I'd barely slept, but I'd got a lot done. And I needed to come down from that.

"I haven't been able to find the information again," he said, almost apologetic. "I've looked. I remember it was in a pamphlet I was given at a training session years ago." I looked up and the shadows under his eyes made me feel like six kinds of shit. "They didn't list the reasons. I wanted to find out if it's because statistically the most likely perpetrator is a male partner but I don't know. I don't think it's that simple."

The pancake tasted like dust and sat in my mouth like mud, but I swallowed it. "I'm working on my shit." And if there was a bit of defensiveness in my response, I felt like I'd earned it.

"I know you are." The statement was almost puzzled. "I don't know what the risk factors are. I can't manage them if I don't know what they are."

My heart about broke. I was just so done with this, so I held up my hand jokingly. "Me! Pick me!"

A frown creased his brow and, impatiently, he thrust the pancake at me. "Don't, Rory. I'm trying to have an actual conversation with you."

He was obviously not done. I ate another pancake and watched the pulse drumming rapidly in his throat. There had been another time he'd been a bit short with me...only one. I couldn't remember when it'd happened, but I wondered, now, if it had something to do with vampires.

He opened his mouth and I put my fingers over his lips, shaking my head. "I can't, Taig. Not tonight."

That should've been it. I knew it should've been. Even having been in his shoes, if someone had said that to me, I'd have withdrawn if I couldn't stop.

But his eyes closed and the pancake in his fingers crumpled as his chin tipped upward, jaw clenched. That I could see the artery in his neck throbbing worried the shit out of me. I couldn't remember the spells to help heart attack victims. I needed to do my magick CPR refresher.

"Can I give you a hug?" I asked, because it was about all I had.

A beat later I was crushed in his arms. He clung to me, his face buried in my neck. I was rocked aggressively back and forth and just held on, feeling the hard gusts of his gasping breaths and helpless to do anything except just wait it out.

"I've got you," I promised, but even as I did, I wondered if he'd be better if I let him go. Grief rushed into the wounds in my soul. My bones creaked as he squeezed me harder, as if he could hear my thoughts, and pain from my earlier injuries flared. "We're okay." *More or less.* "We're okay for tonight." That was true. I cradled his skull and rocked with him, pressing kisses to the softness of his cheek above the high-tide mark of his beard as he shook in my arms. I swallowed down whatever feelings were trying to choke me. I couldn't separate them out. I couldn't feel them properly. "We need sleep." It was the best thing I knew to reset our brains, and the closest I could come to solving this problem. He smelled like blueberry vapes and sweat.

It was hard not to mentally separate the shaking, snarky mess of a man from the one I'd fallen for. But I refused to let that thought coalesce in my mind, as if it were a spell I could avoid putting power into. Because I probably smelled like blueberry vapes and sweat twenty minutes ago. And hurting people hurt people.

I wasn't the only one who was imperfect, here.

"You're wounded," he said, the words small and reedy in his sexy, up-all-night voice my undoing.

I could deal with his anger. I couldn't deal with his sadness.

"Yeah." I'd never found comfort in lies, and doubted he would, either. We could find comfort in each other. I circled my hands on his back, feeling his heart trying to claw its way out of his chest where we pressed together, breast to breast. I hoped mine called to him. Tired, maybe, and fucked up, but okay. "Not too badly, though." His breathing settled, and he let me rock us slower, now. I made sure I did big, slow out-breaths.

His heartbeat gradually ebbed to follow the rhythm that mine set. His arms were still locked around me like the jaws of life, as if he wanted to climb inside my skin. He made a noise that was heartbreak and worry and fear all in one, the noise of a wounded animal.

The wounded animal in me responded with a rush of compassion. "Maybe you can kiss me better," I suggested.

Taig drew in a violent breath and his face turned, lips lingering over the sensitive point on my neck.

I expected a roaring leap of lust, but instead relief coiled through me, and compassion. The shadows carved into the hollows of his cheeks and the way his hair hung over his forehead, the bite of his hands and the way he looked at me like the whole world. Blood pooled low in my belly, but the hunger didn't scream, it murmured, and I pressed myself against him. I could feel the cold floor beneath my aching feet, the scrapes and bruises across my body, and the force of his desperation as he clung to me. My heart swelled so much that it was a wonder it could still fit in my body.

"I've got you," I promised him, as if the words were a spell I was finessing, and the breath he'd sucked in released in a woosh as tension melted from his limbs. My head spun. I held him up as his weight shifted, suddenly. "I love you."

He raised his head and tears were on his cheeks as he rested his forehead against mine. His eyes were still closed. I ached, hoping it was because he was trying to find himself, rather than hide. "I know you do," he said, without infliction. "I know it, but I need to hear it sometimes, Rory."

I didn't flinch. I'd earned that, and more. To think, days ago I'd been wondering if we were done. To think, if he said it to me I'd be out the door. To think, I didn't know if I could even contain all these big feelings, or what in the world I could possibly do with them.

I buried my nose in his hair and found the remnants of the smell I associated with him, beneath the stress and chemicals of tonight's shitshow. "I love you, Taig." The fear was there, but I refused, tonight, to sit around waiting for the other shoe to drop. "Can I take you to bed?"

He nodded, wiping his face with his shoulder, letting me slowly rock him toward the military neat bed I'd left behind this morning.

I didn't recall making it, but I wanted to recall messing it up.

We were plastered together so hard that getting my hands to the buttons of his shirt was going to be some work. "Can I help undress you?"

The sound of him swallowing was loud in the peaceful darkness of my bedroom. "Yes."

Keeping my belly pressed to his soft one, I yanked the bottom of his shirt free from his belt. The fabric bit into my aching hands. I stopped him with his thighs against the bed and stripped off his shirt, encountering no resistance.

His breathing was ragged still, but the tears had stopped. His skin was soft beneath my hands, a little tacky where he'd sweated into his shirt, cool where the chill of the November evening had settled over us. Impatiently I pulled my own shirt and pressed us together, belly to belly.

"I know I can't ask for more," he said, and I stilled in my mission to plaster myself as closely as I could. "I know I can't. I'm trying not to."

It hurt to think I'd put him in this position. I hadn't even stopped to notice.

"I don't have a lot more," I admitted, safe in the dark and sealed against him. "I'm trying to find it again."

"I know." He let out a long breath that shook. "I know. You're here, now." He framed my face with his hands, his touch gentle, his fingers wet from tears. "Thank you."

There was the shame, of course, that I'd hurt him. Maybe that was normal. But I wasn't carrying that right now. I'd never pretended to be perfect and I was finding my way, same as him. So I took it at face value and just nodded, leaning into his desperate kiss.

Like a drowning man drawing air he breathed me in, and I gave him what I could spare.

His belt gave way to my fingers. Happily, he shifted so I could get rid of the rest of his clothes, toeing off his shoes. He left the laces done up. He *never* took them off without untying the laces.

"Is this okay?" he asked me, still backed up against my bed, his balance precarious. In the darkness, I couldn't make out his expression clearly, but it wasn't his neutral face. He was here. He was vulnerable.

And yet, *he* was asking *me* if I was okay. I didn't know if I should laugh or grieve, or whether it should just be par for the course. Perhaps all three. Naked, I wrapped him in a hug, enjoying the toe to crown contact. Our hearts didn't quite beat in time, but they would again. I tried not to wonder why we were out of sync. Whether it was fear of me, or for me.

Whether it was justified.

To silence my own thoughts I pressed my lips to his, but he hesitated, and I circled back around to his question. "This is okay," I said, hoping he still trusted my words. "For me."

He nodded, his belly pressing into me as he filled his lungs. Then caught when his cock rubbed against my thigh. "I want you."

The thrill of pleasure I felt at those words made the air in my lungs ignite and my heart melt. He was defenseless and open in a way I wasn't accustomed to. A large part of me wanted to seize on that vulnerability. I struggled against the desire to shove him back onto the bed and take until his heart beat only for me, until every doubt and fear was gone and it was just us, in the moment.

"Do you want a few minutes?" I offered, like the fucking adult I was. My lips were still wet from our kisses. I wanted to feel that wetness everywhere. "Some space?"

"No." He held me closer again. "No, I don't want space. I want to be yours."

He wanted it to be simple. He hadn't used the words, but, Elders, I knew that feeling. The *'just make it okay'* feeling. And I couldn't make everything okay, but I could sure as hellfire make right now a whole lot better.

"I'm taking that as consent until you say otherwise," I said, because I wanted to be crystal clear.

He let out a surprised laugh and I stayed there, still, waiting for him to say, "Good."

Steel fused into my bones, but I held myself back. When I pressed him down, my hands were gentle. He went down in a controlled, almost relaxed tumble and lay spread across my bed like a sacrifice, gazing up at me like I was his god.

Uneasiness twisted inside of me and while I didn't know why, I knew it was there for a reason. But it didn't apply to us tonight. I ran my hands up his thighs and over the curve of his hip bones, kneeling over him as I felt the resilience of his flesh, the density of his muscle, the heat of his body. The fine hairs on his legs, the smooth scars, the curve of his belly. I pressed a kiss to the side of his navel and he drew in a quick breath, shuddering under me.

Deliberately, I moved across to one of his scars and pressed my lips to the side of it.

He hadn't received magickal healing for it. Not quickly enough to save him from those big, ugly marks.

Fury pulsed in me, a slow, dark drumbeat that I wasn't familiar with. I ran my lips up his belly, up that scar. Whatever had hurt him had better never cross my path.

My mind went to the scar on his back. To the shadows in his eyes.

He'd been a witch-hunter. I'd been a vampire slayer. We were a match made in the seventh level of hell for anyone who tried to get between us.

I ran my fingers over his skin, fighting to keep the rush of fury leashed as I made my way up his body and seized his mouth, laying claim. His lips opened hungrily beneath me and I sucked his tongue into my mouth. His moan was caught somewhere between us, captive. It sent a chill up my spine.

He was already mine. I didn't know how long he had been, or when it'd end, but I knew the truth in that moment, as he shuddered under me again. Warm and pliant in my hands, needing gentleness and care, I tempered my fury and ran my fingers over his jaw and buried them into his hair.

I cradled his skull, though he was on the bed and didn't need me. I felt the strength in the bones.

He and I, we both knew how much a body could take. We knew how little.

Tears pricked my eyes and I pulled back, resting my forehead against his. *The smell of blood and afternoon sunlight.* "I'm glad you're here," I told him, and if it was a bit hoarse, who could blame me?

"I'm glad we're here, together," he said, his hands smoothing up my back. "Even if the journey hasn't been ideal so far."

I couldn't even imagine an ideal journey. Picnics and rainy days, polite conversations and laughter. Not holding him down on my bed in the dark as my body screamed to avenge, to satisfy, and to heal.

Turning my mouth back to his I traced the familiar line of his lips that never made promises they couldn't keep. And my heart broke. And my heart healed. He grabbed my hips and arched into me as if he couldn't bear a millimeter of our skin to be apart. As if I was his air, and he'd been suffocating.

Settling my weight more firmly on him, I put aside the rage and hurt. Compassion coiled in my belly. The hunger was a simmer, not a boil. He caught my lip between his teeth and my body responded. But it was his ragged breathing and vice-like grip that made my heart sing.

Taig wanted me. All of me. The bumps and scars, the grief and joy, the lightning and the rain. The thought was terrifying, but also thrilling.

"Roars," he said, against my lips, but my name was a plea.

I smiled, holding him a little firmer between my knees, directing his movements. "I want more than minutes," I told him, as he'd told me once, long ago. It felt like another life.

"It's yours," he promised. And I believed him.

My ribs still ached, and I hadn't properly dealt with my hair. But we were resourceful people. I straightened and climbed higher, guided by his biting hands on my hips higher, higher. I didn't need his encouragement to settle over his mouth, but he held me there, anyway. His lips locked on my clit and his hands bit into my flesh as he clung to me like a starving man, consuming me with single-minded desperation. I breathed it in, drew it deep, and felt my response ignite in my veins.

Breathing quickly, I wondered if our hearts were in sync, now. I wondered if his brain was quiet. I wondered how long he could possibly maintain that level of suction and that mind-melting rhythm of his tongue.

I wanted to stroke the hair away from his face, but my hands shook and my movements were hurried. A dark slither of something crept into the back of my brain and I acknowledged it, pulling back and dragging air deeply into my lungs. He wasn't a victim, and I wasn't an abuser.

But I could be. I could be, and the reality of that made nausea grab me by the throat and my knees feel weak.

I could be, but I wouldn't.

His hands bit deeper into my hips. "More," he panted. "Again. Please."

The dark slither was there, still. I could feel the clutch in my belly and the pulse beating too fast in my throat. But I put it back in its place, focusing on my breath, on my body, on the man beneath me. If he kept grabbing me like that, he'd end up doing more damage than Benson had.

He was where he wanted to be. And so was I.

I didn't know if I wanted to laugh or swear at him so I did neither, just panting. "Hands over your head."

He'd never let me go so quickly, falling back and arching his spine as I crawled off his face and sank back down over his belly. In the darkness I could make out the sharp lines of his face, but I didn't need to see his expression. He was safe with me, and he knew it. The rush of that made my head spin as my body throbbed.

I leant over and clasped his wrists despite the dull ache in my hands. So he'd know what was happening, I said, out loud, *"Heavy as guilt but harming none, anchor this space."*

The rapid in-drawn breath and flex of his arms let me know he was testing the small immobilizing ward. But I didn't move until he said, again, "Yours."

I wondered if that was to make me feel better, or him.

The thought of working him to a fever pitch pleased me. I reset-tled so I could reach more of him, only to be distracted by the gleam of moisture on the tip of his cock.

A dangerous mixture of surprise, pleasure, lust and love swept through me and I froze, trying to decipher what all meant. The infor-mation wouldn't compute, though, and he was lying there, panting, helplessly waiting.

He could've moved, of course. The ward was on a small part of his hands. Whether the man knew how to do a proper backwards roll or not he could've got himself into a number of positions despite my spell. But it wasn't about truly locking him down. It was removing the choices he needed to make, and encouraging him to be taken.

My heart sat, hot and swollen, in my chest as I leant over and with no fanfare whatsoever took the tip of his cock in my mouth, tasting that moisture.

The noise of pleasure he made came out between gritted teeth.

I ran my tongue along the delicate slit, searching for more, then swept my tongue down the underside of his shaft just to hear the way his breath grew labored.

He didn't have the patience for me to work him over properly and my goal wasn't to push him. Not this time. So I straddled him, one hand guiding his cock and the other planted in the center of his chest. His pulse hammered at me as I slid home.

This was where we belonged, tonight. I wasn't just jumpy. I knew that was true, in my soul.

With his hips locked between my thighs, I set a slow pace, grinding myself against him. My own moisture and the wetness from his lips slicked our bodies. I closed my eyes, feeling the heat connecting us, moving between us with each rolling motion. The various aches and pains dimmed. I could feel the tiny flurries of cold air against my hot skin where it was damp and where it wasn't yet. I could feel every cell in my untouched breasts and the ache in my nipples. I could feel every part of our skin that touched and every part that didn't, too. I could feel the ghost of his mouth urgently sucking my clit, the way his tongue swept around me. I could do it again. He'd take me gladly.

Would he enjoy it enough that he'd come, too? While I rode his face?

Our gasping breaths mingled. Beneath my palm, his heart beat the same ragged tune. He stared up at me like I was his entire universe and I was. I could've taken everything. I could've done anything. The trust, the power, the way he panted for me, the taste of his pre-cum on my lips and the smell of sex and sweat made every cell in my body burn.

"Roars," he said, helplessly. It was an offer. It was a plea. And I wanted nothing more than to take, and give. My hips rolled, grinding us together.

All I could see when I looked were the depthless pools of darkness where his eyes were lost in shadow. I'd never be able to explore that. I didn't need to, though. Because he could, and return to me.

I took him over the edge, and only tumbled after him when I knew he'd made it safely.

CHAPTER 12

"Morning."

I sat up, blearily taking the mug and phone Taig passed me. But I couldn't sit up properly, because Eclipse was a warm, comforting weight on my feet.

He returned after a moment and settled on the edge of the bed, creases still on his face from sleep. We sipped in silence until he scrubbed a hand over his face. "I've got an afternoon shift," he told me, around a yawn. "Might go home, do some washing, get some groceries."

"Responsible," I acknowledged, fighting my own yawn. "I need to get into the office. Maadai will want to know what happened." And maybe she'd even throw some healing at me. My scalp throbbed.

"We need a Wesley management plan," he agreed. "Want more coffee?" I finished what was in my mug and he took it, pressing a kiss to my lips that lingered, deepened, then grew. "You make it hard to get out of bed," he said, not unhappily.

My body remembered the joy of last night, but that wasn't all we'd had. "Not recently."

Taig didn't disagree or point out how few days it'd been since we'd last had sex. There had been a difference, and I was glad I wasn't the only one to notice it. But he just pressed another, lighter kiss to my lips and said, "You've been making progress. It isn't linear, and it's incremental, so I doubt you see it. But this is all shit you know. You'll get there." He stood, taking my cup with him. "We both know that. It's really just about the road you take." He turned, and, without even looking at me, added, "And who you take it with."

The barb burned as it slid home. Had I earned that? I didn't know, but I thought it was shit regardless. I reached down and stroked my hand over Eclipse's fur. I'd made it clear who I'd wanted to walk down this metaphorical road with, hadn't I?

At least I had last night.

I wasn't really in the right space to be making fifteen-year plans. But maybe it hadn't been such an unfair shot after all. It was true.

Halfway through easing myself out from beneath the most majestic being ever to exist, my phone lit up. Eclipse raised her head, blinked at me in deep disapproval, and launched herself off the bed.

Cautiously, I answered. "Hello?"

"Don't come in this morning," Maadai said from the other end. "You're working from home or out of the office until I've taken care of this."

I knew it wasn't going to be simple. "I'm sorry, Maadai."

She snorted. "You're sorry you got caught."

She wasn't wrong. "Also sorry to make your life harder," I admitted. "And maybe Benson's."

"He does enough of that himself," she agreed. "This will be the one and only time. Won't it?"

"Yes." And I meant it. "I'm okay to still be on the clock? We've got some people we were hoping to visit who might know about George's whereabouts." And if he was there, I didn't want Aspen and Lilith doing it without me.

Maadai hummed in agreement. "That is fine. I just do not want you walking in here when I'm trying to put Jerome in his place."

My method of dealing with wizards wasn't really ideal, so if I was being exiled due to lack of diplomacy, well, that was fine. "Cool. I'll set it up with my witches. Thanks, Maadai." I hung up and sat there with my legs going numb due to the weird angle, trying to figure out how I could've done anything better.

Really, the fight was the problem. Everything else we could've justified. Maadai was going out on a limb to back me up, and Wesley had laid the groundworks. If I hadn't gone along with his plan, I wouldn't have known quite how deep Wesley was and how much he'd set up.

Taig came back in and I took the coffee he passed me. I couldn't speculate with him, and the reason for that was scarred into his skin.

"What's news?" he asked me, making the bed as I gulped down some more coffee and tried not to worry about that.

An unfortunately powerful vampire who's meddling in my affairs. In a good way. Maybe. "I need to stay clear of the office this morning," I told him. "I'll have to tee something up with Lilith. I expect Aspen'll run a bit late."

"She's living way out, isn't she?" he asked me, idly. "Why don't you two rent together?"

I shrugged. "Working together and living together? I love her, but one of us would die in a week. Worse, our families would visit unannounced."

His grin was quick and still sleepy. "Maybe she could take over this lease for you, and you could stay with me. My family never arrives unannounced."

My brain went utterly blank.

He gave the cover a final tug, pressed a kiss to my lips, and said, "Think about it. I'm heading home." Eclipse chose that moment to rub herself against my leg and he crouched to give her a quick scritch. "Let me know what happens with the vamp and we'll chat tonight, yeah?"

"Yeah," I agreed, because what the fuck else was I supposed to say except *hold on buddy I'm still in second gear here.* "See you soon. May your groceries be affordable."

He scoffed, stole another quick kiss, and left.

Eclipse's paws on my bare shin were warm and soft with tiny pricks from her claws as she looked up at me.

I couldn't breathe. I just looked down at my beautiful little cat and felt the whole world spinning around me.

Yesterday he was snapping and snarling, then letting me fuck his brains out, and today we're talking about moving in?

"I'm not just jumpy," I told Eclipse. She mewled at me. "Right?" Her claws sinking deeper into my leg was her answer. With a wince, I put down my coffee, scooped up my familiar and went to check on her food.

Two hours later my workday began when Lilith arrived with a giant, sugar-loaded iced coffee and heavy steps. I took in her unusually plain outfit of black jeans and light shawl over her lupetec shirt. One of her nails was held on with medical tape.

"I made muffins," I told her. "Mostly because I'm bored. I didn't have as many raspberries as I thought, so they're kind of basic."

She nodded. "Sounds good." Looking around my apartment, she let out a breath, her posture softening. "Aspen's late, yeah?"

"Yeah." I passed her the muffin I'd already put on a plate, and watched her from the corner of my eye. "You okay?"

"Just tired."

"Tired because you can't sleep, tired because you're using all your energy to keep going, or tired because we're existing in end-stage capitalism?"

She considered it for a minute. "All of the above?"

I nodded and hoped she couldn't tell I was assessing whether her cheekbones looked particularly sharp because of how she'd used highlighter today, or because she'd lost weight. "Is it something about Benson?" I asked, trying to keep the question casual.

She shook her head and turned away to set up her laptop on my table. "Not his fault."

That was both a no and a yes. "Intention and impact aren't the same though."

She shrugged and took the muffin I nudged at her. "My dad reached out recently."

I tried not to react, because this was perhaps the second time since I'd known her that she'd let the shield down at all. "Oh yeah?"

"I don't want to go into it," she told me, dismissively. "He's not a great guy, you know?"

I did know, and I wriggled my bare toes against the floor. "It's a lot, growing up with that." The flavor of 'not great' didn't really matter, here.

She flicked her hands dismissively, making dark blue glitter on her nails shine. "It was whatever. But he reached out. And it's been weird. It'll stop being weird soon, I'm sure."

I nodded, nursing my coffee and hoping Aspen stayed away long enough for us to finish this conversation. "Want to tell me about the weird?"

"No." She pulled her muffin apart. "I don't want it to be a big deal."

Elders, could I respect that. "No worries. But thanks for telling me."

She shrugged. "Sure." And popped some muffin in her perfectly painted lips. Immediately, Lilith pressed a hand to her mouth to contain a cough. "Shit, Roars." Her eyes watered. "What did those muffins ever do to you?"

Shocked, I grabbed my own muffin. "What?" But before she could answer, I tried it and nearly gagged at the heavy, salty mess with vague raspberry overtones. I spat it out and took the muffin from her. "I bought a few kilos of salt to make pickles," I said, knowing immediately what I'd done wrong. "I'm so sorry."

She made a noise that might've indicated forgiveness around her straw, washing her mouth out with heavily sugared coffee. I reached for my mug to do the same.

Such a silly little thing. I tossed the batch in the bin, and tried not to think about favorite headphones that were still missing, somewhere, or the jacket I'd left in a café weeks ago, or the way I'd almost walked out without paying for the items I'd been holding in my hands.

I wasn't jumpy, but I wasn't healed yet, either.

I blew out a breath, grabbed the big tub of salt that I'd decanted into an airtight container, and wrote SALT on it before I forgot. Even if I was fucking up, I was working on it.

"Nic's stopping by in about twenty minutes," I told her, before I forgot that too. "I need to give him his keys."

She nodded. "Want me to go get some raspberries and we can have another go?"

I could feel the lino beneath my feet, then, and the mug in my hands. That was Lilith for you. "Fuck that. I actually want a good sausage roll. I'll hold out until we're on the move."

The ghost of her usual smile touched her lips. She slumped back in the chair and started clicking through tabs on her laptop, her coffee balanced precariously between her hand and the edge of my table. "Okay. We'd better figure out the incident reports, then."

By the time I'd explained the updated situation with Wesley, we only had time to do the most basic parts of the report before Nic rocked up, looking like an action hero during the at-home lull with a scabbed cut on his brow. True to form, he wore a lazy grin, well-worn jeans, and his hand hovered close to his wand.

I let him in and wondered how often I'd been that person in others' lives. I kinda liked being on this side of the door.

"Heard some witch took out an ursathrope in an illegal pit fight last night," he said, instead of 'hello'. "I also hear she was hot, though, so it couldn't be you."

I held up my hand, bruised from the knuckle dusters, and just so he didn't miss my intent, flipped him the bird, too. "Where's my coffee, you jerk?"

"Aspen's bringing breakfast," he said, gleefully. "I caught the train." He shuddered, then held his palm out.

I dropped his car keys across his lifeline and realized I hadn't forgotten to pay for the parking.

Salt looked just like sugar, really. It wasn't a big deal.

Happier, I closed the door after him. "Nic, Lilith."

Nic gave her a friendly nod, then clicked his fingers at her. "Wait. You helped fight those possessed witches a few months back. With the angel."

"Yeah," Lilith said, sipping her drink. "Rory gets me into trouble."

With a laugh, Nic gave me a quick, one-armed hug. "And out of it, at least sometimes, right?"

Lilith made a non-committal noise and turned her eyes back to her document, but there was the hint of a smile on her lips, and it made me feel lighter.

"Want coffee while we wait for Aspen?" I asked Nic.

He waved me off, having spotted Eclipse curled up in the center of my couch. "Who is this?" It was a rhetorical question. His hand was already outstretched. "Oh my elders, Sunshine, she's adorable. Look at you. Aren't you just the most adorable pussy I've seen all day? Yes you are."

Eclipse, understanding the situation, rolled over and stretched out, not even opening her eyes as she accepted the worshiping touch of his fingers.

I could still remember when I'd sat on Brandon's back step while Nic sobbed about the death of his family dog. My teenage heart would probably always have a soft spot for a man who could cry like that. Even if he *had* grown up to be a jerk.

"Why is your witch beating up big magickal bears, hey?" he asked Eclipse, pouting as he spoke. "Why would she do that?"

Lilith's lips twitched further as Nic flopped down on the ground, better to adore my cat.

"I bet she couldn't even keep the cash, hmm. I bet she didn't. She should've been home snuggling you, you beautiful little baby."

Before the sweetness made me vomit, I said, "It didn't exactly go to plan, but it involved a couple clients of ours."

Nic rolled his eyes, not looking up. "The ursa? And the vamp is yours, right?"

"I'd be in breach of confidentiality if I discussed that."

He snorted. "Okay, sure, excuse me, Ms. Professional Witch." I wasn't sure if I preferred the cutesy pet-talk, or sarcastic Nic. Eclipse opened her eyes and put a firm paw on him. From his wince I assumed there were some claws involved. "I'm sorry baby. Did I stop talking to you?" Her ears went back and he winced again, beginning the careful extraction process. "Okay. Message received. Sorry. Won't happen again." Clear, he rubbed his arm as he shot me an annoyed look. "You could've warned me she's your guard cat."

Ignoring him, Lilith said, "What time was the fight?" Her fingers never slowed as they danced over the keys. "Nine-fifteen?"

I had no fucking idea. "Sounds about right."

"I'll say between nine and ten," she said, after considering it. "We arrived at eight forty-two, so."

Nic came over and leant on the back of a chair, one leg crossed over the other at the ankle, looking like some sort of model going for the rugged wizard aesthetic. He peered at my screen, but didn't interrupt while we filled out our form from our viewpoints.

I heard Lilith's phone vibrate a few times, but she didn't reach for it. A few days ago, I wouldn't have noticed that. I tried to remember how often I saw her scrolling during work hours. She did it, of course. Riding the tram, waiting for a meeting or whatever. I'd also seen her ignore notifications plenty of times.

A knock came at the door, and she flinched, bumping her laptop into her coffee.

Nic's hand whipped out before her cup hit the ground and I felt my own rush of adrenaline answer that almost-violent movement. Not because I gave a shit about cleaning up some spilt coffee, but because, even after all these years, my subconscious still took its cues from Nic.

"Sorry," Lilith mumbled, taking it with an unusually clumsy hand.

"Don't worry about—" he began.

He staggered back, the blood draining from his face as he hunched over, clutching his belly. The stones in his eyebrow rings blazed.

I jumped up, the bowl that had held my muffin mix a few hours ago now used as a catch-all as I thrust it under his face in time for his first gag. Lilith was on her feet, too, her coffee splattering across the floor as she surged into action.

"Coming!" I shouted to whoever was knocking at the door, hoping it was Aspen. Eclipse raced away, her tail fluffed up. In her haste to turn a corner she smacked into the wall and Lilith started at the noise.

Lilith, her eyes everywhere, said, "What—"

"Oracle shit," I told her, as if this was totally normal, putting a bracing hand against Nic. He was shaking like a leaf and I felt time slow in response to his distress. But there were no obvious attacks to defend from, nothing I could do. The fabric of his jacket was heavy beneath my hand. He was lean beneath it. "Can you let Aspen in?" I angled Nic away from the spilled coffee so it didn't get tracked everywhere, taking in every threat, assessing every outcome. "Watch my laptop charger."

"Sure. Yeah. Of course. I'll clean that up," she promised over her shoulder, running for the door. "I don't know what happened."

I did, though. I just hadn't seen it happen since he was a teenager. Seeing a pimply-faced wizard toss his cookies on the skate ramp seemed, right then, lightyears away from us, now. I was wearing a *suit*. We weren't young kids learning to control ourselves anymore.

Nic took the bowl from me, heaving without vomiting. The stones in his eyebrow rings glowed as the charms worked to protect him from whatever backlash he was experiencing. There was sweet fuck all I could do, and the fury of that turned to fear as first one, then another stone cracked, going dark as the charms gave way.

"Oh my God," Aspen said, charging in. "Nic, are you okay?"

He nodded, leaning into me. "Fine," he said, and then gagged again. "No. Actually no. Not fine." He shook his head and I squeezed his shoulder. "I gotta sit down."

Before I could start to figure out how to make that happen he'd collapsed on his arse, hunched over the bowl. He hadn't actually vomited, and didn't have a blood nose, so I just kept a hand on him and ran through options in my head.

Involuntary Readings were always ugly, and potentially lethal, but I suspected the worst was over. Even if it wasn't, there was nothing anyone could do now.

The sound of water running made me glance over to find Aspen filling a glass.

I let her put it beside Nic, knowing it was more for her well-being than his. He probably did, too, because he managed a smile for her. "I'm coming good," he promised her, weakly, and put the mixing bowl down with hands that shook. It clattered against the floor.

There was no color in his face still, but as I watched him stretch out and put an arm over his face, a knot loosened in my belly.

And, crisis averted, my mind went to what possible Reading could've knocked out a professional Oracle who lived and died by his ability to control his magick.

The sound of Lilith wringing out the mop drew me out of my thoughts before any possibilities could form.

"We were just doing the incident report from last night," I told Aspen, who took the hint and stopped hovering, pulling out her laptop. "What time is our first appointment? Twelve?"

"I've got to take a phone call at twelve, yeah," she said, resolutely looking away from Nic. "I was thinking we could visit Benson before that, but after will probably give us more leeway."

There was no way Benson would let us hang out for the hour we'd have spare between rocking up to his, and Aspen's meeting. If by some miracle he did, it wouldn't be a big deal for Aspen to phone in. But the decision was driven by neither of those factors, so I said nothing.

"You need to update her on what you told me," Lilith said. "And the cops, too."

I pulled a face. If I told the cops I wasn't actually taking protective measures when I climbed into the ring, I was fucked. If I didn't tell the cops, Wesley owned me. Since he basically owned everyone anyway, that bothered me a lot less. But maybe that was my dysfunctional traumatized brain?

Nic's hand closed over my wrist and I froze.

"Vampire," he told me, his eyes squeezed closed. "Fuck."

My heart turned over in my chest. "Bad?'

He shook his head firmly. *Not bad.* Relief rushed through me as he grabbed the bowl, knocking the water over and hurling what looked like a coffee and some sort of pastry with maximum noise and stink.

Grimly Lilith opened the windows. "Does he have a Guide?"

"He *is* the Guide," I told her, moving away as he kept on heaving.

"Great." She snatched up the coffee Aspen set in front of her. "If he dies, I'm cancelling on my entire fucking day."

"Fair," I agreed, the word lighter than I felt.

Aspen fidgeted with a different, not-transmuted silver necklace, twisting it around her fingers as we all stood around, waiting for Nic to finish puking.

If I'd been good with charms, and had the right ingredients, I might've been able to throw something together, maybe. But any charm I made was way more likely to cook his brain. Considering how hard it was to find Nic's brain, that was a whole skill.

It felt like hours waiting for the vomiting to stop, but he settled back eventually. With shaking hands, he pulled off his bracelets and the necklace charmed with our essence.

Only then did I understand what'd happened.

"He was open," I told them, in case they hadn't figured it out, too. "His charms triggered a new Reading and he's too wiped out to deal with it. We can't touch him for a while."

"Done," Aspen agreed, swiftly. "Five years? Ten?"

When Nic didn't even hit back, I figured he was too weak to move, so I went and disposed of the puke. It wasn't the first time.

Upon returning I was met with the sight of him still on the floor, but now cozily tucked under a blanket, his head on a pillow. I filled up a drink bottle and put it in eyesight, but there wasn't much more I could do without touching him. "We'll be back later," I promised. "Don't drown in puke, okay?"

"'Kay."

Since my morning was about as good as it was going to get, I tucked my phone into my pocket, grabbed the bakery bag Aspen had brought with her, and suggested, "How about a visit to a very old, very irritating client?"

CHAPTER 13

It wasn't Wesley who opened the door, but a sweaty guy with blown pupils whose shirt wasn't on straight.

"He'll be with you in a moment," he said, breathlessly, letting us in. "Go through to the sitting room."

From the color still in the guy's cheeks, Wesley wasn't done feeding on him. I caught Lilith's quick look and knew she was regretting just rocking up, same as I was. Even if Nic had indicated we were okay.

Considering Wesley could move faster than the speed of sound, the fact that he kept us waiting for almost a full ten minutes seemed like a statement. Beside me, Aspen was aggressively responding to emails. Lilith stood near the blackout blinds, a position that would've been a power move against a younger vampire but, considering it was Lilith, was probably her subconscious flair for a good silhouette.

Eventually Wesley walked in, stressed denim riding low on his hips and mirrored aviators hiding his eyes.

"By the pricking of my thumbs," he said, his smile slow and seductive.

"Hey, Wes." Aspen quickly tucked her phone in her pocket and stood. "How was the rest of your night?"

His smile widened. "Perfectly legal. Yours?"

"Same," I said, and even Lilith's lips twitched. "Don't even know how that happened, do you?"

Aspen shook Wesley's hand before folding herself back into her chair, shooting me a quick look that was a politely veiled 'shut the fuck up'. "We understand you're working with VicPol," she said, settling comfortably. "We were surprised. Generally, we support our clients with interactions with law enforcement."

Faster than I could follow, Wesley was reclining across another overstuffed armchair, stretching his long body like a cat. "Didn't they tell you?" he asked, lazily. "I was so sure they would. My apologies. Tragic oversight. Would you like the badge number of the constable I spoke to?"

"Oh no, that's—"

I had my phone in my hand already. "Go for it," I told Wesley, feeling grim. Aspen, catching on, didn't say anything.

He rattled it off without pause, then, "His surname is Allen. Two L's."

"Seems that due diligence hasn't been done," Aspen said, slowly. "That's a shame. I'll definitely look into it in the next few days. Thank you for having that information ready."

"Of course." Suddenly he was on his feet, running a hand through his hair in a way that made the muscles in his abdomen and shoulders ripple. "Anything else, Custodians? No? My Feeding List will be modified slightly in a few days. I'll send it through as soon as I've completed my own research into the candidates so you can check from your end."

"Fantastic, thank you." Aspen stood and we paced quietly behind her. "Are you planning on working on any other cases with VicPol in the next week, Wesley?"

He reached out one finger and gently air-booped her nose. "You'll be the first to know, little one."

She stepped back, her expression smooth. "I'm glad you're in a good mood, Wesley, and that you're comfortable with us. But I have a right to my personal space."

"Of course." He stepped back, sweeping his arm toward the door. "Have an excellent day. Excuse me if I do not step outside with you."

I wondered, as we left his home, how long it would take him to die if he *was* in the sun.

"Why does he want Allen to go down?" Lilith asked, while Aspen checked the time of the next tram.

That was what I wanted to know, too. "We should definitely find that out before we place a complaint. Especially given the conversation between Wesley and this constable isn't one we were privy to."

"I don't like being a pawn," Lilith said, her eyes narrowed. "I really, really don't."

Neither did I, but we were like children in charge of a nuclear weapon. "We're in no rush, and we don't have to act on anything." I shrugged. "We'll case note exactly what happened, right?"

"If we don't follow up on that, we're breaching policy," Lilith reminded me. "And maybe he did have a conversation with this guy. Who's to know if the cop has been Charisma'd to forget and take the fall? Or to lie if asked?"

We could speculate about Wesley using his Charisma to do pretty much *anything*, and that was why we were so utterly fucked.

"I need a sausage roll," I sighed, scrubbing my face. "And to check in on Nic. We headed to Benson, since that was at least a *brief* waste of time?"

Aspen made a noise of annoyance. "I'm logging into this meeting. Lilith, you right to go suss out our situation with Maadai?"

Lilith nodded, re-settling her laptop bag higher on her shoulder. "Want me to look into Allen, too?"

"We're all on *that*," I said, but my mind had returned to Nic. "I'll see what Taig can tell me. You two good to check with folks you know?" I looked specifically at Lilith, who had some good connections.

She nodded, as if it was already a foregone conclusion. And there was something about her razor focus that was achingly familiar to me.

She didn't want a big deal, though, so I wouldn't make one. We parted ways. There wasn't a snowball's hope in hell of getting a decent sausage roll, so I stopped for potato cakes instead.

Nic was still where I'd left him when I returned. Sleeping on my floor was probably no worse than he was used to, and Eclipse had curled up by his ankle. He opened one eye when I removed the still-empty puke bowl from beside him.

"Sorry to worry you."

Me and my bag of potato cakes sat beside him. I stretched out my legs and bit into another batter-covered slice of fried potato. "Haven't seen you that fucked up in awhile."

It was the understatement of the year. He struggled upright, his back propped against the wall. Eclipse remained resting, a ball of fuzz and love now nestled between his feet. "Shit," he breathed, then winced and grabbed the water bottle. "I need to organize new protectives."

Chewing thoughtfully, I looked at the cracked, darkened gems adoring his brows and the pallor beneath his tan.

I'd done a good job of not freaking out, really, considering he'd been smacked with a bunch of information about important futures when he'd touched one of my best friends.

I chomped on crispy batter and soggy spud, starting to regret my choice of fuel. "So, Lilith, hey?" I asked, stretching my legs out and getting as comfy as the floor would let me. I needed to vacuum. I wondered if Nic could see that, considering how thoroughly his circuits had been blown.

He let out a long breath. "You're her friend, right?"

"Yeah." I eyeballed him, waiting for the other shoe to drop. When it didn't, I said, "I'll rip the throat out of anyone who hurts her, so if I wasn't in the futures you Read, go back and have another look."

He shook his head though. "She's fine. I don't usually get sucked so far into the future anymore." He swallowed loudly and I felt better knowing whatever was tying him in knots wasn't Lilith's future. "I'm going to screw this up, Rory, what I'm going to say."

"You Reading that?" I asked, but regretted the jab the moment it passed my lips. "Sorry, Nic." I resisted the urge to rub his shoulder. "It's okay. Just say it. It's me you're talking to, right?"

He nodded, scrubbing a hand over his face. "I got smashed with the next probably fifty years, Sunshine." And when he looked up at me the cost of that magick was evident in the lines carved in his skin and the shadows in his eyes. "And also some snippets of the past."

That made me stop chewing. "What?"

He swallowed. "It was hazy." He took a mouthful of water, apparently choosing drama over answers. I stomped on my frustration as he gazed, brooding, out the window. At some point I'd thought that was kind of hot. Now it was just irritating. Maybe I was getting old? I shifted so my legs got better circulation and tried to remember the last time Nic had gone *backwards* with his Readings. I was pretty sure it'd landed him in the hospital as a teen trying to Read what had happened, or was happening, with his upfucked parents. No one had told me anything and I hadn't exactly been super chill back then, so I couldn't really blame them.

"Do you believe in past lives?"

I tried to check his pupils, garnering a dramatic side profile view of his very nice jawline. Unable to make them out, I asked, "Are you high?"

He shot me a dirty look. He certainly appeared to have come out of a bender arse-first, but he'd looked normal when he'd rocked up. "Your friend is my soulmate. Cut me some fucking slack, would you?"

"She is?" Excitement, then terror raced through me. "She's got a boyfriend."

He nodded, taking another mouthful of water. "He's a good guy."

"Wait. Are you telling me that you and she are like, soulmates across various lives?"

He shrugged. "Dunno. I might just've misread it. I damn near hit overload." He scowled at the glass of water. "I don't know if soulmate is right. Undo that. Love of my life." He brightened a bit. "Yeah. She's that. Or she could be."

Considering he'd met her twice in passing, the adjustment was probably a good start. I took another bite of my lukewarm food, mostly chasing the salt, and turned that over in my head. Reading people's relationships was a messy business. No one actually wanted the truth. Nic was by no means an expert on long-term readings.

When it came to the next twelve hours, he was good. The next six, great. The next half hour he could read like a champion chess player sitting across from a six-year-old. But that was a *very* specific window.

"Could you be mistaken?" I asked, thinking of the quiet happiness Lilith had found with Vince. Then my mind went to the *weirdness* she'd flagged. I opened my mouth to tell him, then stopped, swallowing the words with the half-chewed potato.

Nic apparently understood what'd been going through my head. "Look, we can't break rules here. And she can't know. If it happens between us, great. If it doesn't happen, maybe I get a new friend, and to hang out more with two old buddies I don't see enough."

My heart ached for him, but I nodded, feeling sick. If I tried to fuck with anything, not only would it potentially mess up their future but it wouldn't be fair on Lilith.

He let out a long breath. "And, on that note, I hear they're trying to set up a task-force for the city. Alongside local cops. You're getting too much attention. They want to separate your bad-arse from law enforcement."

"My bad-arse is climbing into bed with a Supernatural Detective every night," I told him, and he arched a brow. "Good luck separating us."

"Figured. Haven't seen you kiss an angel out of too many blokes." He set down the empty drink bottle and groaned, rubbing his head. "You know how hard it is not to ask everything about her?"

In sympathy, I offered him the last potato cake.

"I don't know what I can tell you without tipping over the wrong domino and making them all fall wrong," Nic said, taking it from me without thanks. "I *hate* this. This is why I kill trolls and vampires for a living."

That certainly wasn't what Retrievals' job description was, but I didn't correct him. After all, I didn't know what he could tell me, either. "I'm not very good at being neutral," I admitted. But I really didn't know if I was even on a team. They could be happy separately. Apparently, they could be happy together. Whatever worked?

He took a bite and sniffed. "You can't intervene."

I thought of the brief moments of vulnerability Lilith had shared with me. I doubted she'd let me even if I wanted to, and I was proud of her for that. "She knows what she wants," I told him, suddenly unconcerned about it all. "She'll look after herself."

He held up his hands in surrender. "Look, I'm over here trying not to be a puddle because I just saw myself at fucking seventy or some shit with a big-arse table all set for the grandkids at solstice, okay?"

I felt warmth swell at the image. But I asked, "How was it decorated?"

He frowned. "Pretty. She was in a tracksuit and was mixing something in a huge bowl. Reminded me I had to put the dog away so she didn't get hair on her dress after she got ready."

That sounded exactly like Lilith and it surprised me to feel my eyes burn to imagine it. He sounded…content. Peaceful. "Did you? Put the dog away?"

"Oh, fuck," he breathed, rubbing his head. "Most choices led to *no*. Few led to her actually being upset. If this doesn't end up happening because we sat on your dirty floor eating bad potato cakes and talking about the love of my life's decorating tastes, I'm going to be incredibly pissed. Just so you know."

I resisted the urge to hug him to me. "So, looking for a place in Melbourne, then, to go with the new job you need?"

"I'd been thinking of wrapping up Retrievals," he said, scrubbing his face. "Stepping back from the team is hard."

My own lingering feelings of guilt and shame around that weren't helpful to him. "No one is irreplaceable."

"I can literally Read the future and see who they'll put in my spot," he said, bitterly. "Each time we roll out, there are less safe paths for me to travel. But if I'm not there?"

I looked at the sprinkle of grays in his hair, the depth of the lines beside his eyes. "Imagine how you could help Aspen and I, though," I offered, quietly. "If you were close."

He shrugged, running a hand over Eclipse's back. "You're not exactly in mortal peril."

Well, if he needed a reason to look after himself… "I'm still standing because Taig shot himself full of M-Barrier to take down the High District Wizard who'd raped me and was going after Aspen next, Nic. We could use your help."

His eyes snapped up to my face and for a moment I was terrified he'd try to Read what had happened. "He's a witch-hunter?" he asked, all business.

"He was."

"Well, fuck." He let out a long breath. We sat in the shared quiet for a while.

Was that the first time I'd said that, out loud?

The world didn't stop turning. The house didn't burn down. It seemed painfully normal, really. And it was, statistically speaking. I hated that for us.

Nic flopped his head back against the wall. "They won't let me work just anywhere. I'll have to stay government. Being an Oracle is the most litigious path in existence."

There were good reasons for that. I was grateful that he was a problem solver, not a comforter, in that moment. "Considered going into teaching?"

He frowned a little. "What, like, training up other Oracles? You know they keep us on tight ropes."

"I was thinking magick studies in general." The idea had some serious appeal. "Imagine, instead of Reading various death and dismemberment, you could instead Read various ways to support and help your students be the best magi they could."

He passed back the half-eaten potato cake and I took it, mostly because I didn't want it to end up being puked all over my floor. "Maybe. I'm guessing there's a bunch of soft skills I don't have in those fields."

Considering he'd been the coven's secret weapon, then military, then special ops... "Cool thing about soft skills is that they're learnable." I stood and offered him a hand up. "Hells, maybe you could be a custodian. Come chill with me."

He snorted. "I'll look into teaching, thanks." On his feet, he gave Eclipse a last pat and then scooped up his charms, surprising me by glancing toward the door. "Elders. You punched a hole in my whole fucking week, Roars. That's the last time I ever lend you my car." He scrubbed a hand over his face again, like he was trying to rub off the after-effects of the magickal tidal wave he'd been dunked by. "Actually, I don't think I can drive." He steered himself toward my couch and fell into it, his long legs dangling comically off the edge. "I'm sorry."

Happier he wasn't taking unnecessary risks, I filled up the drink bottle, disposed of the soggy potato cake, and set to work on his shoes.

By the time he looked relatively comfortable Eclipse was already asleep on him again, curled on his back behind his head. Nic had the seal of approval.

In years gone by I'd've been able to contact his charm-maker, get them cooking up some new protections. I'd've got him into my bed and cleared my day to care for him. But times had changed.

I pressed a kiss to his temple and then to my beautiful little kitten. "Be safe," I murmured to them, brushing the last of the dust and cat hair off my pants and turning back to my life.

· · ' ' 0 0 ◐ ● · · · . 0 ● ◐ ● · ● ●

GETTING JESSICA READY FOR SCHOOL, given our short window of time, wasn't easy. In theory we could throw her in and hope she could swim. That seemed like a crap thing to do to a kid whose life seemed, from the outside, to have been nothing but chaos.

Benson's apartment was small and what furnishings he had were entirely kid-focused. A tiny table with two tiny chairs and some modeling clay figures atop was the extent of it. The kids were on the floor on their bellies, working on a puzzle.

There was a fridge, but no pictures. There was a television propped against the wall. An old alarm clock glowed in one corner of the bare bench. A stack of plastic cereal bowls were drying on the metal part of the sink. It looked naked without some sort of rack on it to hold the bowls up.

Jessica and Liam stared at us. Aspen breezed over and folded

136

herself down, picking up a puzzle piece. "Hi," she said, the word directed at the puzzle. "I'm Aspen. I think I've got a piece of one of the birds."

Lilith and I turned to Benson, whose eyes were glued to Aspen. "Can I get you a drink?" he asked us, without moving.

"No, thanks." Lilith put a folder she was carrying down. "We need to talk employment."

I managed not to show my surprise at Lilith's bluntness. "We know it takes time, but we do need to start the processes to get you moving toward employment and financial stability," I explained, as his eyes dipped to the pieces of paper. "We also need to do a few more things to sort Jessica's school."

His jaw tightened. "Humans wouldn't need to."

Plenty would, however the core of the complaint was fair, so I didn't split hairs. "For now, you do," was the best I could offer. "How'd you pull up?"

His eyes flickered over to me. "Fine. You?"

I didn't want to say anything in front of the kids, and I didn't miss the dark look Aspen was sent me, but at the same time… the guy had been publicly beaten. Building his ego up a little didn't seem like the worst thing to do. So I pulled a face and put a hand to my aching ribs. "Yeah. Fine."

His expression didn't change. Maybe his ego was more secure than I'd expected, or maybe he actually gave no shits. "Can we do this outside?"

Both the kids froze, looking up, their expressions hopeful. Aspen was already on the move, making suggestions, scooping up papers and ushering everyone into the sun. The kids flanked Benson, who had one hand on each of their shoulders, and Aspen walked alongside Jessica.

"I think that's a wren," she pointed out a small, cute little bird. "I love the way they hop." She mimicked a few hopping steps, smiling.

The kids didn't comment at all, much less join in, but she scooped up a leaf and was twirling it, apparently engrossed.

I took my lead from the other two and kept my mouth shut until we made it to the playground. "Lilith, you want to do an obstacle course?" Aspen asked her, brightly.

Lilith, to her credit, didn't point out the generous platform heels on her boots. "I love obstacle courses," she said, hands on hips. "But I've never been to this playground. I wonder what the fun parts are?"

Jessica's eyes flickered to her dad, then back to Lilith. "I can show you?" she offered.

"I know the *best* parts," Liam said, scowling. "I want to take the human!"

Jessica froze and Benson's eyes flickered around. Without a word from anyone, Liam went pale shrank, putting his hands to his mouth.

"All right, then," Lilith said, nodding. "Better show me. I'm Lilith, by the way. What's your name?"

Benson gave a tiny nod, and Jessica locked her hand over Liam's wrist like a shackle. As the three of them walked off toward the playground I could feel every step of Lilith's majestic boots on my heart as it stayed there, trampled amongst the tan bark.

We couldn't talk without the kids hearing, but fuck I wanted to unpack that.

"Lilith's found four job opportunities that roughly fit the soft skills and interests you filled out on the intake form," Aspen said, tucking her hands into her pants and cocking her hip, as if she was talking about the weather and not a requirement to keeping this guy out of SuperSec. "But you filled that out a few years back, now." She shrugged, angling her face so the wind blew her short choppy hair away from her cute but impractical wet lip gloss. "We'll get you signed up for government support, too. It won't be much, but it'll be a bit of a buffer."

Benson's eyes flickered briefly from his children to me, narrowed with suspicion, as if he wanted me to ratify Aspen's words.

"It's really not much," I agreed. "They'll make you jump through hoops, and good luck surviving on it with any quality of life. But I'd rather be doing that than getting into bed with powerful underground organizations. Our government is a lot less scary." Certainly less scary than Wesley. "We can also help more with government stuff."

His answer was to fold his arms and turn his eyes back toward where Liam was currently hanging off the playground. Lilith was poised beneath where he dangled, an expression of deep concentration on his face and his cheeks red.

"I'll show you what we mean about the hoops," Aspen said, tucking the folder under her arm with finality. "So you understand what'll be asked of you, and when."

A quick nod of acceptance was the first sign of Aspen getting her hooks into him. I wondered if he knew it.

She didn't gloat, of course. We'd do it later, probably over chips with dramatic reenactments and iced coffee that might or might not have a few fingers of something more, like the classy witches we were. I breathed a little easier, thinking about it.

"What are the jobs?" I asked her, because I genuinely didn't know.

Aspen shrugged. "Mostly laborer type stuff. One had the potential for an apprenticeship. It was for a landscaper, I believe. She tried to focus on finding opportunities that worked with school hours."

Everyone's eyes were glued to the kids as Liam scaled a climbing frame with all the confidence of the happy go lucky four year old he was. I wondered what a bystander might think. I wondered how closely Aspen and Lilith were watching not Liam, but *Jessica* watching Liam.

My time in Retrievals hadn't geared me up for this. Why the fuck had they even given me this job?

"Kinder hours are different to school hours," Benson said, like that was a full stop on the conversation.

"Of course," Aspen agreed, frowning. "A lot of kinders have child care facilities. Maybe we could investigate whether Liam's does."

It did. Lilith had checked already and we'd discussed their rates and government rebates. She was going to put it together so Benson could see what it would cost him and make an informed decision. It sounded like we'd need to make the strings attached to that support explicitly clear.

Benson snorted as Liam leapt clear of where Lilith waited and hit the ground running, laughing gleefully as he kicked tan bark in his wake.

Playing tag in today's playground wouldn't be like when I was a kid. I wondered idly how the social dynamics would shift to account for that. "Problem with child care," he said, nodding to where Liam was now launching himself off the slide at high speeds. "They can't deal with him when he's like this. Imagine if he shifts when he's tired or grumpy."

I didn't put my hands to my aching ribs. I couldn't imagine a temper tantrum from a little ursathrope being a zero casualty situation, and the thought of the pressure that put on these kids made me ache for them. They deserved to be able to grow up without fearing they might accidentally murder someone.

"He's too young," Benson said, with finality. "He's home with me, or Jessica."

"I wonder if there are shifter-qualified daycare centers," Aspen mused, folding her arms beside him. It was a genuine wondering, this time. "Seems like a lot for Jessica to carry, worrying if you're coming home, and what state you'll be in." He opened his mouth, but she flicked her fingers. "Of course you know that and you don't have a choice. But I wonder if we could find another way forward. One that'll let them both just be kids, you know?"

His mouth closed. For some reason, *I* was the one he sent a dirty look toward.

I was already at the next step in the thought process, though. "Trinity has her Working with Children Check," I reminded Aspen, quietly. "She basically runs a daycare already. Even if this isn't something we can get up and running in time for Liam…"

"Good thought, and I'm going to start figuring this out right now." She pulled out her phone and turned away, tapping out a quick message.

The next look Benson sent me was suspicious, and I realized I'd skipped over a kind of important piece of information. "Trinity is a lycanthrope we know," I told him, wishing I hadn't used her name at all. Client confidentiality. *Next time.* I'd get better at this shit eventually. "She's solid. And she's been in a similar situation to you, except with more kids."

He grunted, and I followed his gaze to see Liam staring at another kid like a deer in the headlights as they tried to convince him to play. Doubtless, something that was high risk and high energy. Lilith was there, introducing herself and modeling how to do the basics. But I still didn't blame Benson when he left us to go call Jessica back and take Liam by the hand.

Aspen, phone dangling forgotten in her hand, opened her mouth as if to call him back, then closed it firmly and turned back to the message.

"I'll call Trinity," Aspen said. "She's with East now, isn't she, Roars?"

"Uh." *Shit, I should remember this.* "West, I think. Maybe check her files." My phone buzzed and when I glanced at it I saw a brief proposal Aspen had sent through, CCing the office.

"We don't want these young shifters isolated in shifter-only groups," Aspen murmured to me, folding her arms. Benson returned, holding both his kids' hands and looking like something out of a horror film as he walked along with them in his shadow. "But I don't think shoving them in with only humans is going to work well, either. I suspect diversifying staff and taking a top-down approach is the way to do it, but…"

I thought of the amount of supernaturals we had with *any* formal qualifications, much less university level ones. But I could also imagine a siren would be amazing in childcare. *Okay everyone, nap time.* Elders, I could go some of that. "It'll take time," I said, instead, keeping that thought to myself.

"Too much time," Aspen agreed, her tone dark but her smile bright as the damned sun as she turned it on the kids. "Time to go home?"

"Yes," Benson said, flatly.

Aspen shot him a cocky grin. "Challenge accepted. Hey, you folks brave enough for me to drag you into a grocery store? I need some oranges for a thing I'm baking tonight."

She was so full of shit, but they followed along behind her to the local fruit and veggie grocer.

Lilith lingered out the front, typing rapidly into her phone as I stayed on lookout by the inner door. My phone buzzed in my pocket with the messages going off in our coven group-chat. I watched as Aspen taught Jessica how to sniff the flat bit at the top of a rockmelon to see if it was good and wished I could participate in the conversation. Being the muscle of the group was fun sometimes, but mostly involved me standing around and being watchful.

"Maybe I should upskill," I mused, as Benson accepted the whole watermelon Aspen and Liam lifted off the table, his face straight as they giggled. It looked like more fun than keeping an eye on the gangly kid behind the checkout to see if he was snapping his friends or filming Benson.

"Thinking of going into childcare?" Lilith asked me, not looking up. "I think there's rules about caffeine consumption."

I snorted, trying to imagine anything worse. And that was *without* any limits on hot drinks.

Liam was carrying a bag of pears and Jessica had a selection of greens, including sprouts. They moved on to compare tomatoes, with Aspen describing how the truss ones differed from whatever the cheaper ones were.

Bored, I grabbed a hand basket and strolled over, holding it out and accepting the greens.

"...why those ones smell faint," Jessica was saying, of the cheaper tomatoes. "Why are those ones *yellow?*"

I could see a session in the community garden in our future. I glanced at Benson, thinking I'd share my wry amusement, but his attention was razor-sharp and I wondered with a jolt what they understood of our world's food.

There were so many witches I knew who'd *love* to show them a spot of basic gardening, if they were actually keen.

With that thought in my head, I leant a bit closer to Benson and murmured, "Landscaping will involve construction...and gardening."

He just shifted the watermelon to sit under one bulging arm.

By the time we left, they had a decent supply of produce and happily walked beside Aspen. They waited little birds as she broke into a pomegranate and passed them each a chunk to pick the arils from while we hauled the shopping.

Lilith's phone rang and I thought heard her greet Trinity's caretaker before she fell back.

Benson kept pace beside me. He'd probably understand why I was considering skilling up. There just wasn't much call for muscle in everyday life.

Though the kids were happy for us to come in, he stopped us at the door and took the groceries with a stiff "Thank you."

"Can I pop over tomorrow?" Aspen asked, brightly. "Same time? Hopefully I'll have the information mentioned by then."

"Sure," he agreed, but it sounded like *fuck, no.* "Goodbye."

Aspen's smile didn't slip as the door was closed in her face, as I'd expected. Aside from popping some pomegranate seeds into her mouth with more vigor than needed, and taking a few grinning chews, she didn't say anything.

She was going to be unbearable later.

Lilith met us at the door back to the street, phone away and expression pensive. "Got the all-clear to chat to Trinity. Sounds like she and her pack are doing well."

I nodded, because I'd expected no different. "Cool. Want me to book it in, or?"

"I'll touch base with Trin, see when she's free." She shook her head, mouth twisted in disgust. "Did you hear how he blithely parentified Jessica?"

I had. I could also see his options were Buckley's and none. "Living on government payments won't get them far. The biggest barrier to people leaving poverty is poverty itself."

"I know the statistics," Lilith said, irritated. "But that little boy is home for, what, two more years? Surely he can find a sitter."

I shrugged again. I didn't know how rebates worked, or whether there were many supernatural babysitters. "That's why we're here to help, I guess."

She shot me a wary look. "Just because you beat his hairy arse doesn't mean I trust him."

He had a long way to go, but I figured I wasn't anyone to be throwing stones right now. "Fair."

She shot me another look. "You okay?"

"Yeah."

"Not really," she corrected, the words a little gentler.

"No, not really," I agreed, impatient. "But you know. It'll be a process. I'll follow it."

She accepted this with a long sigh. "I got you, Roars."

Gratitude warmed me. Beneath my shoes I could feel the concrete, and the breeze tugged at me, full of the promise of spring. I wasn't jumpy, and I'd get there in the end. "I got me, too."

"Good." She shot me another look, this time of approval, before glancing to where Aspen had fallen behind. "What the fuck is she up to now?"

It was the age-old question, really, with us witches.

CHAPTER 14

I was trying to figure out if exposing Nic to Lilith again, or just paying for a cup of coffee, was a better choice when my phone rang.

Glad to postpone such a weighty decision, I ignored the uncharacteristically impatient look I got from Lilith and said, "Why hello, Detective. Are you clocking off?"

"I wish," he said, on a sigh. "I was hoping to grab the three of you. Official business."

There was a sinking feeling in my gut. Of our current caseload, Benson was the most likely to get heat with the cops this minute, and while he'd been tucked in safe and sound with a few kilos of fruit and vegetables less than ten minutes ago, he'd also had plenty of time last night and this morning to get up to shenanigans.

"We're about twenty minutes down the road." I paused, my mind ticking over possibilities. He should've been clocking off soon, so it was potentially urgent. "Near my place now."

Aspen was standing in the shade of the tram stop while Lilith checked the timetable. On the other end of the line, Taig offered, "We can swing by your place if you don't want to make the trip. Or steal Arthur's meeting room. Save you some travel."

If he was willing to come to us, right now, it was urgent. But there was no way I wanted to be writing minutes at my own table, even if Nic *wasn't* there. That didn't seem like a good separation of work and life. "It's fine. Make us hot drinks, and we'll see you soon."

"Thank you. I appreciate it. Delyan or I will meet you out front."

They were *both* working it? The sinking feeling became a knot. "Cool. Catch you soon." I hung up on his polite apology and turned back to the other two. "Taig. Something's happened. He offered to come to us."

Aspen winced. "If this is about Benson, I'm going to be pissed. It's too early to be modeling how to repair a rupture."

"Yeah, like that'll be our biggest problem," Lilith said, sounding tired.

"I don't know anything." Which was a pretty accurate statement for me a majority of the time. "Except that Taig and Delyan are waiting for us, and they'll have mediocre coffee." Again, could've gone for a lot of my life right now, bar the Delyan part. The thought made joy sit lightly in my chest.

"Shit," Lilith muttered, watching as the tram pulled up.

Aspen shook her head. "Here I was feeling hopeful for a minute. If we could get Trinity doing even informal childcare it'd be a game-changer. But actually having a proper center? That'd be a dream. I bet we could get a grant for her to study Early Childcare, or get qualified as a Kinder teacher. I wouldn't want her having less status than a human in that sort of facility, so we'd need to make sure her voice would be heard."

Considering we hadn't spoken to Trinity yet, it seemed like Aspen was getting a bit excited about it all. Bearing the bad news didn't seem like a me problem though, so I just focused on getting into the tram without sustaining grievous bodily harm.

"What do you think of assessments for Jessica?" Aspen asked us, offering a pack of gum around. "I've got a child psych who's offered to make a bit of space this week." I was pretty sure that was basically magick, but before I could comment, Lilith steered the conversation somewhere useful.

"What're we looking for?" Lilith asked her, taking a stick of gum.

"I'm no expert," Aspen demurred. "But I think dismissing her presentation as purely trauma without exploring options isn't fair."

I tried to think of this presentation Aspen had identified, but couldn't. When I looked at Lilith, though, she was nodding. "I'll take your word for it," I said, because if she wasn't an expert then I was a three-week-old potato that'd started to sprout. "Will it help her in the short term?"

"Probably," Lilith said, on a sigh.

Taking pity on me, Aspen explained, "The modifications we'll ask for will be focused around increasing her sense of safety. I'm going to assume she doesn't have a PDA profile, so clear routine and explicitly teaching social norms and all the strategies should be successful."

Didn't that make sense for a kid who hadn't grown up fully enmeshed in our society? Before I could ask if thropes could *have* Autism, I saw Lilith's phone droop in her hand.

"What's a PDA profile?" Lilith asked. "And aren't you disrespecting Autistic people's experiences by lumping Autism and trauma in together?"

Typical Aspen, not only did she not get upset at the question, but she looked genuinely pleased as we paused the conversation to navigate off the tram again. "I don't honestly know if what I just said is disrespectful. It's what I hear from Autistic people, but no community is a monolith, you know?"

Lilith kept pace beside me, her hands tucked deep in her pockets.

Aspen hit the pedestrian walk button on the next road and turned to Lilith. "PDA is Pathological Demand Avoidance. I don't know much about it, either, just that it seems like another trauma response. Often goes hand-in-hand with Autism, but needs a very different approach. Routine is king for a lot of folks with Autism, I hear, unless they have a PDA profile, and then flexibility is where it's at. That's the extent of my knowledge, but it could be entirely wrong, and I need to skill up a *lot* if we ever come across someone with it."

I listened with half a brain, trusting the two of them to let me know if I needed to focus in. Ahead the police station squatted amongst crowded shop fronts, half-hidden behind the newly land-scaped gardens that emphasized Australian native plants. There were some scathing observations I could've made about that, but the conversation didn't pause. I walked in the shadows of two awesome witches, and I was content there.

"Would you be interested in PD?" Aspen asked, turning to me. She had her phone out. "I'm asking Maadai what our budget is. There are some good orgs around, and I'd like to hear some 'own voices' presenters."

"Yeah." I wasn't a monster. Of course I wanted to learn. "Unless either of you two can relay the critical info so we can make the budget go further." Really, I was the least likely to have it soak into my brain. "But yeah, I'd like to know more. And if there's potential crossover with what we're doing, it'd be really great." And that was true. I didn't want to be Retrievals full time, and it wasn't just because I couldn't hack it.

The *push* sign on the door to the station seemed deeply symbolic until Lilith's hand landed square in the middle. She shoved it open, making her skirts swirl dramatically around her calves.

I let out a deep breath. I wasn't losing my mind. Well, maybe I'd already lost it. If so, it wasn't necessary for happiness. And anyway, I was finding my way back to myself.

The door to the side opened and Taig appeared, his face lined with tiredness. His gaze rested on me for just a moment longer than usual. His expression didn't soften, but I felt, for that single heartbeat, the connection between us like a tangible thing. I breathed it in deeply, filling my lungs with warmth and gladness.

Shit was fucked, but at least I had good company.

"It's like coming home," Lilith declared in counterpoint to my own thoughts, her hands on her hips as she surveyed the police station, complete with a grinning receptionist.

"We've missed you, too," the receptionist said, with what sounded like genuine warmth.

Aspen shot me a quick look behind Lilith's back, but whatever she was hoping to convey to me I didn't get.

He was in another horrible navy suit. If I ever got a say in the matter, they were all being cycled out. They made his brilliant blue eyes look flat and boring, and the auburn in his hair seemed a dull brown.

And I couldn't believe I found space in my brain to think about the man's clothing selection when I had far bigger problems.

"Long day?" he asked us, leading us toward a corridor.

"Busy one," Aspen agreed. "You?"

"The only kind we have." He opened the door and stepped back for us to file in. "I got you all a drink as thanks for coming on such short notice."

Delyan lifted her hand to us in greeting as we all picked chairs around the table. "I got notes," Lilith told Aspen, pulling out her phone.

Shit, I wasn't even trusted to do that.

I shook that thought off and reached for the coffee Taig had made me with gratitude. Predictably, it was just right. I sat back as he chose the chair opposite me, beside Delyan.

"Okay," Aspen said, sitting back. "Who're we talking about?"

"Wesley Stokes," Taig said, the words entirely neutral.

Ice crystallized in my veins. The one dude who could flatten the whole city. Again.

"Again?" Aspen breathed, mimicking my thoughts and pinching the bridge of her nose.

"Should I note that?" Lilith asked, wryly.

I let out a long breath and met Taig's eyes over the table. "Please tell me it's just about his connection to that pit fighting fiasco?"

He shook his head once, cop face intact. "He was questioned and very helpful on that topic. Did you get the report?"

"Not yet," I said, exhausted. It would've been the easiest solution. "What's happened?"

"Kate Bonnell, a registered volunteer on Wesley's Approved Feeding list, has been reported missing by her partner. He was in here last night and this morning. She never came home."

Aspen sat back and looked at Lilith and I, quietly deferring to us.

We did, after all, have an unbroken record of not dying at the hands of our own clients.

Lilith drummed her nails thoughtfully as she met my eyes, her bottom lip between her teeth. We both knew we couldn't actually take Wesley down. The vampire could probably annihilate the whole damn country and still make it home in time to arrange his charcuterie board.

But he also had no reason to kill anyone. And if he was going to kill them, he wouldn't have done it so obviously.

"He can break my charisma proof charm," I began, slowly, ticking through our options. "I'm going to need to crank that up if we're doing this."

"We could do a Circle." The words made Lilith's mouth twist like she'd just suggested having pickles on her hamburger.

A Circle would be as useful as a single bucket of ice-cream after a breakup. "Before we make plans," I said, pulling us back, "Is he being arrested, or questioned?"

Taig and Delyan exchanged a quick glance. "Questioned," Delyan said, finally.

I didn't like that one bit. "You know once we show our hand, it'll be impossible to bring him down?" I asked them both, bluntly. "Maybe, if we have the drop on him, we could do something."

"We would've called in Retrievals if it was more formal," Taig reminded me. "I know you three can more than hold your own. But."

The way the man could turn 'but' into a full sentence made me smile. "If you call in Retrievals, they'll probably send at least three teams." They'd need them. "I'm assuming you've exhausted every other avenue."

"Pretty much," Taig said, heavily. "We don't like to send civilians in to check on potential suspects."

Delyan opened her mouth as if to object, then closed it again. I saw the quick glance she shot him and wondered how he was holding together.

"We've got it." I caught the look Aspen sent me, underscored by the slight quirk of her brow, and shrugged it off. We had a solid relationship with Wesley. We'd talked to him just a few hours ago, and he thought he had the upper hand.

He did, but that wasn't the point. Nic had said he was okay, so I was going to trust Nic's Read and hope it was okay in the mid-term, not just okay in the moment.

"How illegal would it be for us to go fishing? 'Oh, just checking up on your Feeders, noticed this one hasn't been home, was she going on holiday' sort of thing?" I asked the table at large. "He mentioned his list earlier. It isn't a stretch."

The way Delyan and Taig shared a quick look made me glad we were all working with people who cut down on the need to throw words into the air. That was convenient.

"We could probably overlook that," Delyan said, grudgingly. "There's room to…adjust protocol in cases like Mr. Stokes', due to the nature of his potential."

Aspen ran her hand through her blonde mop and fell back, looking at me. "He's least likely to rip your heart out. You'd better take point on this one."

I saw Taig's throat work as he swallowed, but his expression didn't change. I ached all the same. "No worries," I lied, nodding to Lilith. "You've kept those minutes brief, right?"

She held up her screen. "'Asked how recently we've spoken to Stokes' Approved Feeding volunteers. Some limited concerns around one client's whereabouts. Offered to check in.'"

That wasn't a totally inaccurate summary. I saw Taig draw in a deep breath and nod in agreement, but he was a little paler than he'd been before.

"Cool." Under the table I reached out and pressed my foot over top of his. When his gaze rested on me I chose to believe he looked more relaxed for that small offering of comfort. "Guess we've got us a late afternoon trip to Saint Kilda beach."

"In terms of safety measures," Taig began.

Lilith waved her hand at him as she stood. Her charms glittered. "We've got this," she said, but not unkindly. "Let us work, O'Malley. We'll get back to you."

"I'm off soon," Taig said, standing. "I can do a drive-by if you tell me—"

"Please don't," Aspen said, with a wince that she mostly hid with a hand-wave and a smile. "Don't worry, we'll call in the rest of the coven if we need. Won't we, Rory?"

"I'll call you when I'm done," I promised him, ignoring the professional setting and acknowledging, silently, the man had a lot of reasons for that stress. "And I'll let you know before we go in, too, okay? But it's going to take us time, so don't expect anything for at least a few hours."

"Also." Lilith shook her phone. "I want to go visit a few of his other Approved Feeders. It'll save lying, because you're shit at that, Rory, and it might give us information. Anyway, it's literally our job."

"Unscheduled visits?" Aspen asked her, pulling the door open. "I'm going to need snacks. Shit, why did I wear heels today? Let's start with Leticia. She's the closest, I think."

As their chatter rose and fell, all I could see was Taig standing there, cop mask on. Probably freaking out underneath.

I offered him my hand as they ebbed out of the room. His expression softened. "No heroics," he said, quietly.

Right then I had less than zero interest in being a hero. "No," I agreed. "It really will take time. It might even need to wait until tomorrow. If he took her, she's dead."

"And if he didn't," Delyan said. "Which, statistically, is highly likely…"

I didn't roll my eyes at the woman because Taig was lifting my fingers to his lips. "Stay in contact."

We both knew what silence, in this situation, could mean. With the hand he gently released, I drew a line over my heart like a kid.

CHAPTER 15

The day was fading but the chill was minimal outside of the cop shop. Lilith was on the phone to Maadai, Aspen was logging our destinations into the journey tracker, and I just wanted to breathe.

If it came to fighting, we'd have one shot at Wesley. I'd rather give that job to a couple of Retrievals teams. Fuck those odds.

It didn't make sense, though. Wesley didn't need to kill anyone, and if he did, he had the connections and resources to make them disappear.

"Taig's got a thing about vampires, hey?" Aspen asked as we waited for a tram.

"Yeah," I agreed, though she already knew the answer. She was fishing as to why and I wasn't going to tell her. That wasn't my secret to share.

"Guess he'd have reason," she mused.

I glanced pointedly at the four-tiered silver necklace she wore. The silver rings. The silver bangles. The silver piercings. Aspen had reason to be wary of lycanthropes, after what happened to Brandon. And I didn't discuss that with anyone, either, even though it unsettled our thropes.

She scowled and flicked her hair over her shoulder.

"Wonder what his link with Benson is," I mused out loud. "And did we figure out why he's got a hard-on for that cop he tried to sic us on earlier?"

Lilith shot me an annoyed look. I hoped my lack of professionalism hadn't been overheard by anyone without a sense of humor. And also that I'd eventually get a filter. Feeling guilty, I shoved my hands in my pockets and followed behind them.

Leticia's place was chaotic as ever. Her teenagers had either multiplied, or they were having some sort of social thing. She stepped out the front and shot us a sunny smile as she closed the door after herself. "Hey," she said. "Everything okay?"

"Just a routine check-in." She hid the lie behind a quick shrug and a cheerful smile. "Semi-routine, because we try to shake it up occasionally."

"Oh. I thought this might be about Kate."

I managed not to react, and Aspen asked, with the perfect amount of casual interest, "Kate?"

"Yeah. We've got a group chat," Letitia said, and I saw the not-quite-idle look Lilith slid me. "She was really active in it from the get-go. She seems like one of these super social people, you know?"

Aspen made a noise of agreement. "I envy their energy," she said, wryly.

"Girl, same," Letitia laughed. "But yeah, I just thought, with what happened…"

"What happened?" Aspen asked, the picture of innocence. "If you've got time."

She had time. Either she was worried, or avoiding the teenagers inside. Either way, totally fair. "Oh, well, it wasn't much. Just Kate got a new boyfriend. Actually, she'd been seeing him for ages, but they went exclusive? Anyway, she swapped a few of her shifts with us, you know? He wasn't keen on it and we were like, 'it's about you not him', but." She shrugged, pausing for a moment as if searching for something polite to say. "Easy to see from the outside."

My belly twisted. Run-of-the-mill creep boyfriend was a lot easier to nail than an ancient vampire.

Maybe it said how much I trusted Wesley that I'd rather bump into him in the woods than a run-of-the-mill creep.

Aspen worked her for a bit while Lilith drifted away, digging out her phone. By the time Aspen was done, Lilith had the boyfriend's name, date of birth, and place of work. "Boyfriend did it," Aspen said, her tone still as chipper as it had been with Leticia. "Let's go visit, hey? Pretend we don't know anything?"

"Active investigation seems bad to mess with?" I reminded her, then felt weird to be the voice of reason for possibly the first time ever. "I mean, we can if you want. I'll hold him, you punch?"

Aspen looped her arm through mine and rested her head on my shoulder for an awkward, but sweet, moment. "You're tired."

I was tired to my fucking bones. "It's fine." But it was nice to know that we wouldn't be going toe to toe with Wesley all the same. "I vote we go straight to Wes, get it done."

Lilith raised her brows at us. "Really? We've got enough to postpone until tomorrow, if the boyfriend isn't dirty."

The way Taig had pressed his lips to my knuckles made my ribs feel like they were a size too small. "I think we just go and ask," I said, resigned. "We're like ten minutes away now." And Taig wanted to know. "But I can do it solo."

The eye-roll I got in response was intense. "Whatever." The tram was busy and we traveled in silence until we got off at the top of the vamp's street. "Is this a Wesley thing, or a generic vamp thing?" Lilith asked me, and I knew the insightful damned witch must've been following my thoughts. "Taig's hidden it well."

I shrugged, because he hadn't explicitly said, and anyway, secrecy. And, while I was thinking of it, I flicked Taig a message telling him to look at the boyfriend and that I'd give him a call after we'd finished with Wes.

There was another hour or so of sunlight, but Wes opened the door all the same. "My favorite witches, back so soon," he murmured, stepping back. "I was just thinking of making a fruit platter. You don't have any allergies, do you?"

"We aren't here to impose," Aspen said, her expression open as she stepped in. "But thank you for the offer."

I tuned out the back and forth as we followed Aspen and Wes in, feeling fury pounding at my temples.

Wesley made no sense and yet it all made perfect sense. I hated it all.

He knew my mother.

He knew about Ryan.

He'd set me up.

"...is doing well now?"

The conversation around me paused. I tuned back in to find them watching me expectantly. "Yeah," I agreed, vaguely.

Wes was beside me before I'd finished that single word. "Are you okay, Aurora?" he murmured, mouth unsmiling, my own pallid reflection staring back at me from those heavily mirrored glasses.

I opened my mouth to tell him I was tired and realized my makeup was smudged and my hair looked like I'd stuck a fork in a toaster. I didn't like staring at myself in his glasses. "It's been a long couple of weeks," I said, instead, giving myself a shake. "Sorry."

"Yes, with Benson last night." A smile tugged at his mouth, as if he knew that wasn't it. I didn't bite. "I've no doubt he's been a perfect gentleman now, though." And he sent Aspen a speculative look. "You're single, aren't you, dear? Ursathropes do like to partner off."

Aspen held up her hands in a sign of peace. "Well, I don't."

"Shame that these two are taken." Wes' hand settled on my shoulder for the briefest moment. "So, if you're not back about Benson, and we've already had small talk today, then this is an official visit."

"Kate Bonnell," Aspen said, hands in her pockets. "Switched up her schedule a bit recently?"

He let out a long sigh and paced away. "Oh, yes. Shame, really. But I can't say 'don't listen to the rat-bastard' when she told me about him, can I? I'm hardly an unbiased party."

Lilith tapped away. "Any info we can pass on to the cops?" she asked him.

He glanced at me again, brows arched. "Is she okay?"

"Missing," I said, trying to keep it as simple as I could.

His head tilted ever so slightly. "Then why am I speaking to you, and not the police?"

"They haven't done the basic checks," Aspen lied glibly. "Next of kin, that sort of thing. She was scheduled on Wednesday?"

His hand tightened fractionally on my shoulder. "She came in distressed. I've a feeling I should go have a conversation with your lover, Rory."

The way his tongue rolled over the word *lover* did delicious things to my insides that made me want to gag. "You and me both," I agreed, shaking my head. "But the sun's up. I'll call him. Maybe he'll try your fruit platter."

"Maybe you could both try it," Wesley offered, a smile tugging at his mouth.

Over his shoulder I saw Lilith arch her perfect brows and had to grin. "I think there's a line between personal and professional that might be blurred by this conversation, Wes." There was no way I was nibbling on *any* fruit this guy offered, but refusal could offend, and upsetting an ancient vampire didn't sound any easier than just playing nice. "So let's leave it there, hey?"

Look at me, having professional boundaries and shit. If I'd had any energy left for it, I'd have given myself a pat on the back as I hastened us back out the door.

A few texts to Taig to let him know we were all alive and that Kate's boyfriend was likely the guilty party didn't take long. I hand-balled what info I could via official email and clocked off, making a bee-line to a fish and chip shop.

Lilith and Aspen would have the paperwork side of things covered. I settled in to wait on a rickety little iron chair as I scrolled mindlessly on my phone, letting myself float. I wondered how Taig was doing. I wondered if Kate would be found.

Eventually my name was called and I picked up my butchers' paper bundle without pausing in my scrolling, trudging outside. The weather would be good soon. And Taig had booked us in for a holiday somewhere at some point, hadn't he? Perhaps it was testament to how tired I was that the image of *SomePoint, Far East Victoria. Population: you* flashed through my mind. I don't know what it said about me that there was an emoji with heart eyes on the sign.

This is fine. I hauled my food closer, wondering if shopping at a fish and chip shop twice in one day was a symptom of some deeper problem. But really, there had been neither fish *nor* chips in my earlier meal, so it didn't really count.

I steered toward the tram, pulling up an empty seat opposite a group of eshays, heat from the chips warming me through my jacket. Hot, salty carbs made my mouth water, and listening to the losers in front of me waste their youth made me smile. Maybe I wasn't totally dead inside. There was hope yet. For me, anyway.

My steps were light as I climbed off the tram and headed home, finding Nic lying on my couch stroking Eclipse, their expressions blissful.

"She's my cat," I reminded him.

"Hi, Sunshine," he said, not even opening his eyes. "How am I feeling? Oh, better, thanks to this majestic, healing familiar of yours."

I snorted and dropped the chips on the table, but damned if my heart didn't melt a little as my kitten's head swiveled to track me, her big, liquid eyes full of contentment.

I wouldn't hate to see that look on Lilith's face. *Bad friend.* I wasn't matchmaking. *Nope. No siree.*

"Is that chips, *again?*"

"I didn't have chips earlier."

Nic was still pondering on whether he could let me off for being technically right when my work phone buzzed.

If it wasn't for the Kate situation, I wouldn't have answered. Taig had my personal, but Deylan would call my work and I didn't want to risk missing an update.

Benson's name cleared distractions from my mind. "Hello?"

"I have people over the road," he said, the words a low rumble.

I paused, sifting through the various things that could mean. "They're a threat?"

"They have my name in their mouths."

A chill swept through me. "I assume you don't know them."

"If they come up the stairs, I'll gut the first one and wrap the others in his intestines as a warning. If they make it to my landing, they're all dead."

"Okay, but that's kind of messy." I wondered what Aspen's response would've been. "How about I, I don't know, see if I can get them picked up by the cops?" I was halfway out the door and waving to Nic, but he was on his feet with Eclipse curling up in the warm spot he'd left on the couch, his eyes on me. "They've committed some crimes, right?"

His answer was a growl that made me roll my eyes. I motioned for Nic to bring my chips, because they'd be inedible by the time I got home, and set out at a brisk pace toward his place. "How many?" I asked him, as Nic caught up, scanning our surroundings with the focus of a hunter.

I'd fallen for him. It was possible Lilith would too. But she was way more sensible than me, so maybe she wouldn't. Not like it'd gone well for me.

"Four." The word was practically a growl. "In a car over the road."

I didn't like that, and for the first time I realized the gravity of what this might mean. "I assume you didn't give them your address."

He snarled into the phone and I gritted my teeth. "Okay, I need to call the team. I'm a few minutes off. Keep the evisceration on hold for now." I hung up and blew out a breath. "Elders," I muttered, bringing up the messaging app I used with Lilith and Aspen and calling them both. "Hey," I said, as they answered.

"I'm in a crowded train," Aspen told me. "Keep it G rated."

"Benson's identified a threat over the road from his apartment," I told them, briskly, hoping my words didn't carry far. "Lilith, I'm going to need to extract."

"On my way. Grabbing some extra crystals in case I need to hold multiple illusions." My heart sat lighter at that.

"I'll book the emergency accommodation," Aspen said. "And shoot through the address. Hopefully I'll be back in time to help everyone get settled."

"I'm going to see if I can nail these losers." I felt like we should've put our hands into a circle and shouted 'Go, team!' but I settled for, "My chips are getting cold for this, just so you know."

Aspen's noise of compassion told me she was firmly in professional mode. I hung up, my eyes on the car ahead.

"Got their plates," Nic told me, flashing me a quick glance of his phone screen with numbers shown clearly. "Sent it through as a text."

"I missed having a helper," I told him, and he rewarded me with a flash of that dangerous grin. His pupils were a normal dilation and his color was a lot better. "You okay?"

"Depends on what we're up against."

I rolled my eyes and dialed the local station. "The lumbering support of the law," I told him, keeping the car in my sight. "This is Custodian Gold," I told the receptionist. "I've got a current situation, police presence required." I rattled off the address. "Magi on sight, ready to act protectively, target is Benson Hurtfield. Appears to be a hate crime, four unidentified male aggressors, possibly armed."

"We'll have someone there soon, Custodian," she said. "Call triple-oh if you're in immediate danger."

If I was in immediate danger I had better things to do. "Sure. Thanks." I hung up and took a handful of the chips Nic offered to me. The bastard had ripped straight into the paper, rather than unwrapping the precious bundle, layer by layer. It'd keep them warmer longer, but they'd be soggy.

Lilith could do better.

"This isn't the worst," he mused, chewing on a chip and looking off into the distance, like he was bored and waiting for someone. "What's your pay like?"

It wasn't a joking question. "Not as good as yours. But the adrenaline crashes happen a lot less." I wondered how long it'd take to get a cop out here. I hadn't specified they come without a badged car. "Reckon I can get their names?" I asked him, considering the situation.

He shot me a grin. "Come on. At least *one* of them would give you their number, surely?"

If they knew the local scene, they'd know my face. "Safer if you try."

He waved it off modestly. "You're too kind."

Would they be locals, though? Benson had barely been in Victoria for a fortnight.

They'd followed him down. I knew they had. It felt right.

Chilled, I guided Nic to wander past the car, making a show of checking my phone and looking around in annoyance. "Where are they?" I asked him, loudly.

"I don't know." He overdid it a bit with the confusion, but that was okay. I didn't love him for his acting skills.

I got myself into position so I could see all four passengers of the nondescript sedan. At a rough guess, they ranged from thirties to fifties, and all wore casual clothes.

I picked the guy in the back with thinning hair and made eye contact through the car window, channeling every drop of fangirl energy I had. "Holy shit!" I said, to Nic. "Oh my God, is it – it *is!*"

On the way over to the car door, I did a quick body scan. My heart was steady. No sense of dread sat in my belly, just some chips. I was energized, but of course I was.

Everything was okay in my world.

Time to pass that privilege along.

"Hello?" I tapped on the glass. "I watch you every week! Oh my God!" I waved at the guy as his expression went from alarmed to confused. "Hello? Oh my God, please, could I get your autograph?" And I did the obligatory happy dance, holding my hands to my face. I wasn't the best at puppy eyes, but I gave it a red-hot go.

After glancing at his buddies I knew I was good when amusement touched his lips, not derision. *The safety of the patronizing guidance from a middle aged dude.* "I never expected to meet you," I gushed. "I'm so sorry. I can tell you didn't want to be identified, but *oh my god.*"

Lilith would've given me props for faking it so hard.

"Now, what's your name, sweetie?" he asked me, unfolding himself from the car and then hitching his jeans.

Oh, fuck. "Rory." I turned and waved a hand. "He's Nic. He isn't my boyfriend. We're just hanging out together."

Nic looked apologetically at the guy. "Hi. Sorry. I don't know what got into her."

"I just…I'd love it if you have a moment to autograph something for me?" I didn't have a notepad, but the butcher's paper worked, and he had a pen. "I don't mind if it's your stage name or personal name," I prompted, as he hesitated. "I don't know what your personal name *is*." Elders, I was pretty good at this. Proud of myself, I couldn't hide my grin. "I'm free tonight. And tomorrow. If you've got a phone number. Or a way to contact you?"

"I think you might have the wrong person," the guy said.

From the car, one of them called, "Give your fans what they want, C."

I leant around him and shot the guy a thumbs up.

The driver was in his forties. Snake tattoo on his left hand. Light scar on the opposite curve of his chin. Dark eyes, brown or hazel. I stored the information away later, hoping it didn't fall out of my brain before the cops rolled up.

"I don't usually do this," the guy in front of me said, signing his name with practice that looked, to me, to be authentic. "But if you give me your number, maybe I'll see if I've got time to hang out."

"Oh." Well, fuck, that wasn't what I wanted. "Of course." I took the pen and his hand, gently writing my work number onto the skin there.

Rough palms. This guy did physical work for a living, or had an intense hobby. *Supermarket body spray.* I wriggled my toes in my shoes and breathed, reminding myself of how little danger I was in. "Could you text me?" I asked him, trying to look at him the way Eclipse looked at me for wet food. "To check I got it right. I just." I fanned myself. "Like I said. I watch you every week."

He pulled out his phone slowly. No rings on his hands, no jewelry, basic watch. "What's your favorite part of the show?" he asked.

Good question. "Oh, I love the community." He was typing my number into his phone and I wanted to crow with delight. Next step, getting them all to bite a chip so we had DNA. "How everyone interacts. I'm probably not your usual target audience," I admitted. "But all my friends are men, you know?"

He relaxed a little, shooting Nic a quick look. "How about you? You a fan?"

Nic shrugged. "No offense man. I have no idea who you are."

I shot him a dirty look. "Nic's just leaving. He's more of a ball sports kind of guy."

"Don't you want to finish?" Nic asked me, offering up the chips.

"Oh, I couldn't keep you," the guy said. "There you go, darling. You've got my number. Mind if I talk to you later tonight?"

Oh, he'd be talking to someone much sooner than that. "Absolutely." I hugged the autograph close. "Come on, Nic, we'll go in and get them."

"Oh, you're coming too, now?" Nic asked, with the perfect amount of amusement.

I punched his arm and waved back over my shoulder, steering him into Benson's building so we could step out of sight and guard the door.

"Reckon that signature is real?" Nic asked, once we were out of the wind.

I stole a chip and checked my phone. "Possibly." I flashed him the text I'd got, laughter in my chest.

"I can't believe he went in for that," Nic breathed, shaking his head. "Maybe my cup size isn't enough for this line of work."

I snorted, catching sight of Lilith striding along the street, wind whipping dramatically at her skirt and hair.

Nic drew in a deep breath and I shot him a cautious look, remembering the whole magickal backfiring shit that had happened. "You've had a rough one, hey," I mused, glad I wasn't the one who'd seen a million versions of the rest of their future.

"I like 'em rough," Nic said. But the words were a little unsteady as

Lilith lifted her hand to the door, meeting my eyes through the glass. Nic lifted a hand. "Hello again. Want a chip?"

Lilith brushed her hair out of her eyes and looked at the offered food, confused. "I see why you get along with Rory." She tossed me a crystal and started up the stairs. "What'll it be today, Roars? We need an illusion suitable for six."

"Drinking buddies," I decided, because I was feeling pretty confident. I could pull off that swagger. "Turn us all into mediocre guys, Lilith."

"I guess that's one way to avoid questions," she agreed, dryly.

The kids had backpacks on when we arrived, and Benson carried two large duffel bags. I'd left Nic down the bottom near the door as lookout, expecting I'd need to convince Benson to go.

"Can't fight here," Liam told me with the sleepy air of someone discussing their bedtime routine. "Dadda says there's a baby next door."

The ground fell away beneath me. While Lilith gave them her brisk run-down of the illusions she was about to cast and what they'd experience, I checked where the fuck we were going.

Aspen had grabbed a hotel room for the night and sent through three choices for month-long accommodation. Her note above it said, *Offer Benson these choices once safe.* Beneath that, another message said, *Got the room key, waiting in lobby. Shepherd on his way. Maadai alerted.*

Like a well-oiled machine, we were.

When I looked up from my phone, I was in a room with two nondescript women wearing cozy jumpers with their hoods up, a short, thin dude, and another painfully mediocre guy with a beige shirt beneath his jacket. *Supermarket body spray.*

"Ready?" asked Mister Beige.

I held out my hand. Lilith plonked the crystal in my palm and began murmuring. Prickles crawled over my skin as one of the women took the hand of the short, thin guy. Lilith was clever. No one would ever expect Benson to be that stature.

With the address plugged into my phone and silent navigation active, I took the lead as she wrapped up the spell. We plunged back down the floors without speaking.

"Hold up," Lilith said, as we approached where Nic waited. "Let me just finesse this guy a bit."

Nic did a double-take, hearing her voice coming from Mister Beige, then grinned. "Shit. You didn't mention you were friends with an Illusionist, Sunshine."

Lilith muttered something humble, shoving a stone at Nic's chest. "She likes to keep a low profile," I said, in an attempt at humor that earned a dark look from Lilith.

Maybe I wasn't doing my finest work today, but, fuck, there had been a *lot* of today.

"Hey Nic," I said, after Lilith finished up. "Reckon you could Read the next two minutes? We need to get out without drawing attention."

His face, now aged, crinkled with worry. "What's at risk?"

"Two small kids," Lilith muttered.

His expression cleared and his eyes, even behind the illusion, locked onto the middle distance as he worked his magick silently. It was a low blow, and not one I would've taken, but *I* wasn't his soulmate.

He said, "Wait for a horn blast to our right before we head out. We're taking the first left."

I nodded. He didn't have a blood nose that I could see. That was good enough.

A few moments later a horn blared and we stepped out into the crisp November air. I fell to the back without checking in, Nic taking the lead, and Lilith herding Benson and the kids.

The car was still there, and the driver had glanced at us, then away. A cop cruiser was trundling slowly by, but seemed to have been distracted by the blaring horns further along.

This is why I liked to hang out with an Oracle.

We got onto the correct tram and I knew Nic had continued to do micro-Reads along the way. I hoped his Eclipse snuggles had restored him enough to make that safe, but there wasn't much I could do from a few meters behind him except trust.

It didn't come as easily as it used to. It hadn't since I'd tried to hold in Brandon's lifeblood. When I stopped to think about it, with the city around me and the concrete below me, in my own little pocket of quiet, that wasn't so strange. In fact, it felt almost right.

After Brandon had died I'd hated that the sun came up like nothing had happened. I'd stood in a grocery store wondering how normal people could do normal things. The rage at the unchanging world had almost eaten me alive.

That had been part of my grief. Still, it was kind of comforting to think that my entire world view had shifted to *trust your judgment* in such a dramatic way in those moments. Even with Ryan, where he'd run circles around me, I'd known things were wrong. I just hadn't acted on those instincts. He'd made me doubt them.

I'm not jumpy. It was, perhaps, my new mantra. And it felt right.

Nic stopped opposite a tram stop three blocks away from Benson's place and I suddenly realized the arsehole wasn't holding my chips anymore.

"You're good from here," he told us. "Drop the illusions around that corner. Tram should be here in just under four minutes. Go straight there, no stops. I can't vouch for any side-trips." He kissed me on the cheek and grinned, making me wonder what my costume was. "I'm heading home. Your couch sucks. Nice to meet you all. Bye."

It was on the tip of my tongue to ask him to message me when he got home, but I bit it off. "Thanks, Nic."

He waved, the illusion concealing him melting away to the quiet sound of Lilith's spellcasting. I wondered if that might be a bit symbolic, or if I just had a case of confirmation bias happening.

Either way, I had bigger issues right now. Like figuring out what kind of men were arrogant enough to come for an ursathrope.

CHAPTER 16

There wasn't a lot of settling I needed to do at the hotel room when we got the Hurtfields there. Benson had packed some activities for the kids, so they sat on the floor doing a puzzle inside the Silence Ward I'd cast on them, with everyone's knowledge. They didn't look comfortable.

Neither did Benson, perched atop a tiny chair beside an equally tiny table. The cops on this case weren't ones I knew well. Aspen was with Benson, wearing her serene bomb-defusal face.

Lilith was over with the kids, intently puzzling alongside them. She'd already written up the reports, much as she could. I needed to do mine, but fucked if I was wrestling with the forms on my phone.

Which meant I had nothing to do except stand around and speculate wildly.

At least, since we weren't dealing with vampires, I wouldn't need to deal with Wesley or a triggered Taig over this matter. The guys hadn't been faeried, or they wouldn't have been able to deviate from their programming.

The most likely culprit was humans. Except Benson didn't know anything. Allegedly.

I remembered the way he'd rocked up at my doorstep, the way he'd looked at Taig when I'd been patching the big ursa up. He wasn't the kind of guy to outsource his problems to law enforcement, but that didn't mean he shouldn't.

I watched him staring at the steely-haired, soft-bellied cop who led the questioning. Benson's face was expressionless, but there was coiled power in the man. This time, if he smashed a table in front of me, I doubt my heart would've kicked.

What did that mean?

Tiredly, I picked a stray strand of hair off my arm and opened up my phone. If he'd had run-ins with some humans, there would be some sort of trail. He'd quickly slipped into Melbourne's pit fighting scene, so starting with bookies from up north was probably a safe bet.

I'd only sent one email asking for information from his old caretaker when things started to wrap up. It was a kindness, really, because it was late, and those kids had already put together all their puzzles twice. For a third go, they'd flipped all the pieces facedown, going off shape alone. They seemed like they were making progress, which was low key terrifying.

Everything about this was low key terrifying.

On the tram on the way home, having split with the cops and my witches, I noticed the crawling sensation under my skin. Once I became aware of that dissonance there was no way I *couldn't* notice it.

I watched street signs flick past, my belly in a knot. There was no reason for this anxiety spike. I wasn't jumpy, but I'd learned some lessons too hard. They didn't apply here. I was fine.

Puddles of light spilled out from beneath street lights. This late in the year, the dusk was long and the shadows indistinct. I wasn't scared of the dark. I wasn't even scared of what hid in it.

I was scared I'd fall apart.

And maybe a small part of my brain remembered the night I'd met Ryan for the first time, before I'd been struck down by the migraine that hadn't been a migraine at all.

My keys were a solid weight in my fist. I drew in a deep breath and forced myself to stop and look up at my ugly-arse apartment building of aged bricks and gray cement. *You're here. You're safe. You're okay.*

Up the way, a driver neatly parallel parked as a trio of cyclists whizzed past. The ground was solid beneath my feet, my hair a warm weight against my back.

I still felt that buzzing sensation under my skin.

Fuck it. I started moving again. I'd dig out the grounding exercises my psych had given me and start working through them. That was what you did, right? But not on the fucking footpath like a lunatic.

Gritting my teeth, I shook my head, wishing I could dislodge that word. *Trauma brain is braining. It's okay. I'm okay.* I couldn't even find an alternative word to correct myself in my head, though.

A car door opening close by made my heart rate spike and my system scream. I spun, falling into a defensive stance. The world moved slowly around me, like I lived in stop motion. But the frames flicked too fast and surely I was missing *something* –

Taig stood there, expression neutral. "Just me," he said, his hand hovering just beyond my elbow as he guided me toward the entry without touching. "It got late, hey?"

My feet carried me, somehow. I couldn't breathe. "Yeah. Days are getting longer."

"Good long evenings, soon," he agreed, opening the door and ushering me in. "And it'll get warm, too. There's a place with finger lime gelato a few blocks over. It's best as a mid-afternoon refresher on a hot day."

I couldn't make sense of the words. The keys were ungainly in my grasp. Finding my front door key was way more challenging than it should've been. How long had I lived here? And I really had a choice of four keys. It wasn't that hard. I tried to force the correct key into the lock and felt the metal give, a little. *It shouldn't be this hard.*

You're struggling. You're going to be okay. I let out a slow breath. "Can you?" I asked Taig, passing the keys over.

"Sure." He boosted the bag I hadn't realized he was carrying a bit higher on his shoulder and took them. The noise of the metal clashing against the nub of my wand and the rings holding it all together set my teeth on edge. "I feel like something cold. Want to crunch some ice with me?"

I couldn't think of anything less appealing, but I also couldn't think of anything *more* appealing. "Sure." It opened for him on the first try. I needed to get him a key.

That thought made me realize… "Were you waiting for long?"

"Only about twenty minutes," he told me, locking it after me and putting the keys back in my palm, wand first. "Joyce always works slowly. I figured I had time to get some adulting done." He went to my freezer. I followed along behind. Maybe the ice was a good thing, I didn't know. But I knew I wasn't in the right state to identify what good was. I could trust Taig.

Maybe I shouldn't have, because he didn't dry his hands after washing them, and popped the cubes straight into his palm. They, of course, stuck.

Mine came off relatively easily, but he pulled a face that made amusement thrum in me as he tried to pry his off. When he failed to unstick it, he held his hand up and put the whole cube into his mouth, holding it while it melted. "You didn't see anything," he said, around palm and ice.

I crunched on mine, taking in the scene. The total lack of dignity, the drops of melting water down his front and his expression of concentration all made me feel a little lighter. I grinned at him, wincing when I got some tooth pain from the ice. "Ugh. I think I need to visit a dentist."

He shuddered. "Save me from dentist bills." He held out the tray of ice with his free hand. "You better get yourself the next one."

Amused, I took one of the loose cubes and popped it onto the safer side of my mouth, then gave him an awkward kiss. "Shower," I told him, around the cube.

He nodded. "You eaten?"

"Yeah." There had been some food. Not meal amounts, but as much as I could stomach. "Help yourself if you haven't."

I didn't hang out to chat further. Instead, I let myself into the bathroom and shut the door behind me. The crawly feeling was gone. The world moved in stop-motion, though, sort of?

Looking at myself in the mirror, I blew out a long breath. Whatever fresh hell this was, I did *not* agree to be here, and damned if I was hanging out for long.

"You got this," I told myself. "Just...after some sleep." Even bad witches needed to recharge.

I was hyper aware of the feel of fabric as I peeled off my shirt. The sound of the zipper of my pants was loud in the quiet of the bathroom and I suddenly couldn't breathe.

Pants hanging off my hips, zip still in my hand, I felt the cold against my bare skin and suddenly wished I couldn't. It wasn't right. *Something* wasn't right.

The tears were right there and I didn't fight them. *You're okay.* I locked the bathroom door and turned the shower on to heat. *You're tired. You're stressed. You're okay.* But I wanted to dive under a towel and hide in the corner. Turn out the light and claw off my skin.

My pants slid off too easily and my movements were hurried, trying to keep them from landing in the puddle that had somehow appeared on the ground. My reflection in it looked strange. Fabric tangled in my shoes but somehow I didn't fall. *Slow down.* I adjusted the shower so it didn't flood the bathroom and left my clothes to soak up the overflow. *You're okay. You're okay. You aren't right now but you will be, which basically makes it a net average of okay.* Witch math.

The water washed away the tears and the feeling of cold prickling air against my skin. I breathed in the steam and tried to convince myself it was some sort of health thing when I stayed in there past the five minute mark. And the twenty. I let the tears come, washing away the waves of grief.

A knock on the door and a quick, "Want a cuppa?" made me realize Taig was probably worrying.

"I'm okay," I told him. *I'm not jumpy.* "I'll need a bit longer. Just getting my head back on." *You're a fucking boss.* Aspen would be so proud of me for communicating.

The thought made me cry more.

I wasn't jumpy, but maybe my body remembered things my conscious brain didn't. And maybe my subconscious brain had made connections to try to keep me safe. And maybe the whole thing was just a tangled mess I'd eventually sort out. I didn't fucking know.

Taig was in bed when I got out of the shower, tired and hollow. "When are we going away?" I asked him.

He lifted the covers and smiled at Eclipse as she leapt into my spot, then looked at me pointedly and strolled over to make room for me.

I went with their unsubtle suggestion, climbing in beside them. "Less than a month. You put in leave, right?" he asked me.

"Right."

Taig settled beside me, waiting as I plumped my pillows. "I'm glad you're here," he said, in the dark.

My eyes burned. I curled up around his warmth and breathed in the smell of him, enjoying the texture of his skin under my hands and the softness of his belly under my leg. There was something so wonderful about pressing pause on life and just existing, here, with him.

CHAPTER 17

Warm and safe, I clung to sleep a little longer, snuggling into Taig. He made a pleased noise and tightened his arm around me. When he kissed me his face sandpapered mine and I woke properly.

"Morning." I pressed a kiss to the soft skin above the irritating stubble and wriggled away. "Coffee?"

He pulled a face. "I'll get it. You can snuggle in."

I couldn't, actually, but he was already getting up. He slept lightly. Some of us never learned to shake that habit.

"Did you get decent sleep?"

He nodded, halfway out the door and dressed before I'd even stood up.

Eclipse yawned beside me, then jumped down and wandered toward her food bowl, clearly ready for her breakfast.

As I prepared it she rubbed herself against my ankles and purred. Maybe I was a well trained human, but I was happy in servitude to my feline overlord.

Taig delivered the coffee to me as I continued to stroke her while she crunched on her breakfast. "You cuddled me all night," he said. "And she slept tucked into the back of your knees again."

I smiled at the image he described, but in the back of my mind I wondered again how he was sleeping.

I wasn't the only fucked up one under this roof.

"Picked up an extra shift," he said, as I straightened. "I expect I'll be seeing Hurtfield today, from what I heard yesterday."

I needed to see if that loser from yesterday had texted me. Instead I wandered into the kitchen and began to make my second coffee.

"I'm keen to get to the bottom of that," I admitted, as Taig pulled out the eggs.

"Noted." He rummaged for a minute in my fridge and I wondered idly what Wesley might know about this new issue. "Where's your spinach?"

"It was slimy. I have fresh herbs?"

He accepted the switch and moved around me, making some sort of egg concoction I didn't attempt to identify. "Why is it you don't use the Sharing spells?"

I hadn't had enough caffeine for subject switchups like that. "Because."

He shot me an amused look. "That never worked for anyone."

I downed the last of my drink and progressed the next, topping his coffee off so I could get out of his way. "You mean the physical or the emotional Share spell?"

"Both."

Whether that was annoying or it was just morning I couldn't tell. "Emotional Share is a whole 'nother level of personal. Also, it's distracting. You don't realize how much you have going on in your head until you Share, you know?" He might not, so I added, "Like, I might be low key annoyed from something that happened hours ago, or whatever, but mostly just happy. But if you suddenly got access to all of that you'd ask not why I'm happy but why I'm annoyed."

He frowned, as if he might object. I waited for him to assure me he was different. He just waved one hand for me to keep going before opening the jar of sundried capsicums. Fancy eggs today. Maybe it was an occasion.

"Anyway, it's just a lot. And the physical Share is the laziest way to fuck, honestly."

He paused, knife in hand, and looked at me with confusion. "Laziest?"

"Yeah." There was something funny about the way he was so completely taken aback by that. "It's basically a safe-guard against shithouse sex. I'd rather not be used as a masturbation sleeve, even if I get the magickally-induced mutual enjoyment."

He set the knife down, studying me. "I never even stopped to think about that angle."

Of course not. *Everyone* thought about multiple orgasms and simultaneous climaxes. "Yeah. And, like, think about it logically." I paused to sip and he started chopping herbs and capsicum again. "The way you and I often have sex, you'll get me off at least once before you come."

He was nodding, a wry smile on his lips. "If you come, I come, and then I've got recovery time."

I propped my elbows against the bench. "Some people can brute force it, but yeah. It's not half as sexy as everyone thinks." Who would've thought magickal shortcuts had drawbacks?

"So it isn't that you're unwilling," he said, the words neutral, "But that you don't want to problem-solve the complications at this time."

I didn't love the implications there. Sitting back, I folded my legs and cocked my head. "Is there a problem?"

He glanced up from the chopping again, raising his brows. "I don't know. Is there?"

My heart turned to a chunk of ice in my chest, because when he spoke, I didn't hear his voice. I heard Ryan's.

I kept the responses I wanted to hurl at him in my throat and filled my mouth with coffee, forcing myself to take time, to feel the press of my thighs where they were folded and the way I could wiggle my bare feet. My kitchen stool stuck to my arse where my underwear had ridden up. Because I was at home, and it was now November. I'd left Ryan in the chaos of Samhain, and he was never coming back.

I wasn't jumpy.

"It seems like there is, Taig," I said, and I was proud of my voice for sounding so damn calm. "Because you're talking to me like I'm shit, and I'm not okay with that."

He froze. I watched his professional mask settle over his features. His knuckles very briefly went white on the handle of the knife. It was so quick I barely felt the responding spells swirl in my head before he set it down and braced his hands against my bench. His fingers left pieces of basil and parsley across my countertop.

I didn't worry about that. He was pretty good at cleaning up his mess.

"I didn't mean to make you feel pressured," he said, meeting my eyes. "I'm sorry I did. I know I need to communicate about sexual topics with more consideration, and I screwed up."

Yeah, that was a learned apology. I vaguely wondered if I should apologize for calling out his crap with zero tact, but dismissed the idea. "Okay." Words were one thing, but I wanted to see him learning from his shit. I was. He could, too.

"Would it be better if I did these chats via text?" he asked, with his cop face in place. "I'd have more chances to read over what I said and you could respond when it worked?"

Elders. "Taig, I can talk about sex. I just don't want you giving me attitude because I say no. *Especially* when I actually go to the effort of explaining *why*."

He blew out a breath. "That's fair." He finished up the mess of what I now suspected was omelet fillings. "I'm genuinely worried I'm going to trigger you and not realize it one day. I'm consistently concerned that you'll go into freeze, I won't know to stop, and I'll re-traumatize you."

Anger turned to guilt in an instant but I struggled against it. His feelings weren't my responsibility. I was doing the work.

"I'd really value the extra safety net of a peek into your experiences. But it's a two yes, one no situation and I get that. I'm sorry I didn't take it gracefully," he said, the words holding the perfect dash of regret.

That makes two of us. I kept that to myself and dug deep for an adult response to this responsible conversation. "I haven't Shared since I quit having questionable hookups in my early twenties." Except with Nic. But I didn't think Taig would like to know that it had been *different*. Nic was a wizard. It was what it was. "Maybe it'll be something I can come at later, but right now I'm struggling to be okay in my skin, much less having yours to figure out, too."

His mask had softened, and he looked tired, beneath. "That makes a lot of sense." Again, I refused to hold onto the guilt. It wasn't mine. "I wanted to float another idea with you. Is now an okay time?"

I glanced at the clock. My alarm still hadn't gone off, and wouldn't for another twenty minutes. I *could* go into work early, but why the fuck would I do that? "Sure."

"I meant," he tapped his own chest with a hand holding an uncracked egg. "Emotionally."

"Oh." With the guilt set aside, I was left with the seeds of wariness that hadn't sprouted, and a lot of grief. Maybe I was just jumpy, maybe he was just healing, maybe we'd be totally okay. Maybe not. For now, I smiled at his earnest expression, though it probably wasn't the most convincing. "Yeah, O'Malley, let's talk about sex."

He nodded and began cracking eggs. I resisted the urge to go get my herb knife and mince the last of the fragrant greens. Instead, I dug out some bacon. *It's a day for overkill.* Lilith would tell me this was an omen, I was sure. We'd see if she was right. "The night before last, when I got all fucked up? Having you take over was hot as hell."

I hummed in agreement, but I didn't want to dance around this. "You want to go there more often when you aren't triggered?"

He nudged me with his elbow. "Shut up, you're ruining my spiel. I've rehearsed this."

"Should've rehearsed the lead-up." As soon as the words were out of my mouth I winced. "Sorry, that was unfair."

"It was perfectly fair," he disagreed, tossing eggs in the bin. "I've lost my stride now, so here's my thinking, in verbal dot points." I'd never heard of such a thing, but I liked the concept. With bacon sizzling, I stepped away as he whisked eggs. "It's hot as fuck and can feel really cathartic to let go. Or take over."

"Tick."

He nodded, pouring the egg into the pan. "It needs to be done safely, right? We need rules around shit."

"You know how I go with rules," I said, to make light of it. I paused, remembering the gnawing stress of the other night, and also how hot it had been. "That's a joke. I'm not fucking around with consent."

The look he shot me made heat rush through me. "I really liked that. More than I thought I would. That you made it really safe, the other night, I mean. Your joke was whatever." He paused for a moment. "That was harder to say than I expected. I'm sorry, Roars, I'm not doing this well."

I blew out a breath. "Cool." Had I never checked in with him like that before? I was sure I had, which meant he'd been so raw he'd *really* needed it. I was both glad I'd done right and terrified I could've done wrong.

"Tick."

The laugh lines at the corners of his eyes grew as a smile tugged at his lips. "My proposal, then. A phrase to start and end the session. One of us would propose, the other would agree, and it ends when either of us indicate it should."

"Basic." I tried not to watch the way he was ruining my favorite fry pan. "Is that heat good there?"

"Hm?" Taig adjusted it slightly. I stepped back, because he'd clean up after. If my pans didn't live as long, well, he could always buy new ones. His birthday had to be coming up at some point. Maybe I'd give him his own set to torch. "I was trying to figure out what opting in might mean for the bottom person, and I'm having a hard time identifying general guidelines aside from 'go with the flow'."

I thought of what I'd wanted from him. I hadn't really known, at the time. It had all been by feel. But it had really been about acceptance, and enjoyment. "I think that's it, though, isn't it? You're saying 'yes until no' rather than 'no until yes'."

He pointed my spatula at me, eyes bright. "Exactly."

I wasn't sure I was entirely comfy with that idea, though, remembering the other night. I'd known he'd been happy to participate because of his body language. But if I'd restrained him earlier, and his hands hadn't been clinging to my hips, would I have been comfortable to sit on his face?

I turned it around in my head a bit as the food sizzled, then said, "I'll probably tell you what I'm going to do. Maybe not asking for permission, exactly, but giving a bit more warning."

"Yeah. And that's hot too, so that's a win." He was pulling out the fancy cheese he'd brought over a week or so ago and it was a good thing he used it now because I kept forgetting it existed. "I'm happy for you to take the lead and be the sub, sometimes." He punctuated his words by shutting the fridge with the nudge of one knee. "I don't think I'll always be in the mood for it."

If he'd tried to tell me otherwise, I'd have called him a damned liar. No one was in the mood for anything all the time. Except possibly coffee. "I'm cool with that." I watched him fumble the cheese, and wondered if this was a bigger deal than it felt to me. "Thanks, Taig."

He looked up at me, wrap in one hand, cheese wheel in the other, brows raised. "Why?"

I swallowed down my worry. He'd been smoother than this when he'd asked me to marry him. "This feels like a big deal." I needed to acknowledge that. I was pretty sure that was kind.

"It's a trust thing, right?" he asked, simply. "Just so we don't misunderstand anything, I'm not saying you *don't* trust me if you don't want to do something. I'm saying by chatting and deciding stuff like this, we're trusting each other to do what we agree to."

I waved that away. I hadn't felt a moment's pressure from the man, otherwise I wouldn't still be here. *I'm not jumpy.* I settled deeper in my seat, comfortable with that knowledge. And he didn't want me to make a fuss, so I wouldn't. "Okay, so you're fine for me to take control. I'm fine to take control." I thought of those days I'd desperately wanted for him to just fuck away reality with me and struggled with that, a bit. "I haven't really thought this stuff through, Taig. I don't know what I'm doing. I don't think I've got the world's greatest relationship with sex."

"Would you like a raincheck on this chat?" he asked, turning back to the cheese. "I saw a sale on cat towers I wanted to show you."

The memory of Ryan offering to take me cat toy shopping floated through my mind. That was *exactly* the reason this was so cursed dangerous. He'd offered me a low-pressure way out, and instead it just brought home my options. I considered explaining all of that to him as he tore up the cheese, but instead opted to sit with it a moment.

"I'm worried," I said, slowly, "that I'm going to be fucked up one day, and be like 'hey Taig come fuck away the sad', and I'm going to agree to something in the moment that'll hurt me in the long run."

His hands stilled. "You aren't broken."

I rolled my eyes. "I'm aware of that." *Most of the time.* "The point still stands."

We stood there, the noise of the city seeping into the quiet space around us as we both considered that problem. Despair got a claw into my guts and I took a deep breath to dislodge its hold. This *wasn't* a forever problem. And it wasn't an unmanageable one, either.

But I'd been doing it before Ryan. The one that leapt to the fore of my mind was the time I'd pushed poor Arthur to fuck me against his desk. That situation could've gone so badly wrong.

The cheese had started to ooze. I liked cheese, but that wasn't appealing.

"I'm asking this without judgement," he said, slowly, and my gaze jerked away from the cheese, up to where he watched me with his brows drawn in concern. "But do you think that's a risk that would be unique to some power play?"

The despair turned to shame and I took another deep breath. "No. No, it wouldn't be. But the risks are greater." I thought of the way Arthur's fingers had bit into my hips and felt mildly ill. "Aren't they?"

"Whatever is decided," he said, with confidence, "it's better to discuss it than not. I know there are plenty of times that you reach for me instead of going for a run. I'm fine with that, as long as it doesn't do harm."

Of course he'd known. Probably before I'd figured it out, myself. "I'm sorry."

"It's easier on my knees than going jogging with you," he said, with a shrug and a bit of a smile. "It's hard when you bounce straight out of bed, though."

I nodded, knowing there were times I'd left him gasping. Plenty of them. "I can't always stay still."

The cheese kept on oozing on the board between his palms. "Can we bounce together? I could sit on your feet while you do crunches, or read you a recipe while you cook?"

There was no question that I'd taken hits from both vampires *and* lycanthropes that hurt less than that offer did. "I should've asked for that," I acknowledged. "I am feeling so mature right now Taig, who the fuck am I?"

He snorted and turned back to the cheese, pulling a face. "So we agree, where possible, that we do an activity together afterwards, but it doesn't have to be cuddling. What if we choose high, medium, or low energy?"

Witty remarks floated through my head, but I put them aside. Maybe I'd never needed to be quite this real with a partner, but I'd certainly never tried to be. I felt naked. It wasn't entirely comfortable, but it was okay. Because he was here, naked with me. "Okay. But I also want to say if I'm going solo because I need to. And no questions."

He nodded. "No problems."

I scrubbed my hand over my face. "This seems complicated. I'm not qualified for this."

"Same. But so far, we've agreed to aftercare, I'm pretty sure. Cuddles, a glass of water, a shower, or activity together."

He'd acknowledged I basically used him to fuck my soul back into my body. So there was that. "You know, I'm fine with being the submissive party. As long as you check in with me." I hadn't had an issue speaking with him. He'd always stopped in the past when I'd been triggered. Even before I'd acknowledged what was happening, he'd been there. "That's usually your preference, isn't it? To take the lead? Or is that gender norm bullshit?"

The poor cheese was promptly forgotten as he looked out the window, frowning. "I don't know," he mused, quietly. "I don't like giving over control. There's probably some trauma there. It isn't sexual, but it's there."

"Thank you for telling me."

"Now I know Aspen," he said, his gaze cutting back to me and a smile tugging at his mouth, "I can hear her voice when you say those phrases, you know. It's fine. I think it's kind of sweet. I can hear your voice when she lets loose about men."

"Boundaries," I corrected, firmly. "That's what I taught her."

He didn't laugh, just took it like it was a page from my Oma's grimoire. "I'm glad you've got each other. I do prefer to lead the dance. I do like the idea of having you put yourself into my care in a, I don't know, a more *official* way? That's the wrong word."

We weren't talking about his trauma, again. I put aside impatience. "So we're both happy to dominate, and we're both happy to submit. Aren't we just ticking boxes?"

"Too time-poor to be inefficient, love." As he spoke I considered reaching over and squishing the cheese, just to show him how long it'd been out for. He'd reached for a knife, though, and was scooping it up. "I've got an idea how we can implement this."

"Can you tell me while you put that in the bin?" I asked, cringing. "I'm sorry. It just looks *weird.*"

He paused, incredulous. "It's brie, Rory, that's near it's perfect date. It's been out for ten minutes."

"It's oozing," I said, sensibly.

"Only the best cheese oozes."

"Okay. More for you. *I'm* too time-poor to spend extra time on the toilet, regretting my life choices."

He glanced at his eggs, then the cheese, then double checked the date on the wrapper. I didn't look, but it must've been well past its expiration date, because he scooped the mess up and threw it away.

"I think the simplest way to do it is for the bottom person to, by default, be super passive. Maybe I'll get lucky and get time to research safe restraints, but my training is about detaining. I know enough to know I could do real damage if I do it wrong, and that's really it," Taig said.

From the fridge, he retrieved safe cheese. I asked, "We're talking about bondage right now, yeah?"

"Yeah." He paused. "That's okay?"

"I kind of used a spell to pin you down, so."

He shrugged, scrubbing down the board quickly. "Doesn't have to go both ways, though. I liked it when you did it to me. I'd be happy to return the favor."

Did I want that? The thought of handcuffs left me cold. *Supermarket body spray.* Ropes looked hot but I didn't know if I had the patience. I couldn't really imagine him tied up. That thought took me to the next; him, tied up, and gagged. My skin crawled. "It's fine. But yeah, I can see the practical barriers. I'm sure there are products. No gags, though. That's off the table. I'm not using one on you and I'm not okay with having one used on me."

He nodded, pausing for a minute. "You okay?"

Was I okay? I stood, for a moment, feeling my heart beating a little too fast. I'd never really thought about this specific kink in a serious fashion. "Clint gagged me. It was fucked up. I still…" I looked down at his hands on the knife and the slices of cheese bending over themselves to reach the wooden board. "It's still here." I tapped my head. "Parts of it. It's low on my priority list to work through, but I'll get there eventually." I breathed in deep and put that dark, crawly feeling aside. "Maybe one day we can go there, but for now that'd be a no from me."

He shook his head a little. "I don't want to, either. Work."

He'd been a witch-hunter. I struggled against the unexpected rush of revulsion that went through me when I realized he'd probably gagged magi the way I'd been. He'd probably trained cops. He'd probably looked the other way while—

"Great, so I don't need to worry about it." I grabbed my coffee and refocused, hard. "This is the unsexiest sex talk I've had in a very long time, Taig."

He shrugged, but his expression was worried. "Getting the unsexy out of the way early is kind of important."

Maybe it was, but I was going to have a hard time getting that image out of my head, now. I swallowed a big mouthful. "Yeah. So." *Don't think. Don't react. He doesn't do it anymore.* "Ropes, hey."

"We didn't use anything like that the other night," he pointed out. "But if you're interested, maybe for Solstice I can pay for us to do some sort of rope work course."

The thought of spending Solstice with him made me feel lighter. I stopped his speech, putting a hand on his arm. "I don't know the last time I planned to spend a holiday with a partner."

Before he could respond, Eclipse had wound her way around my legs, demanding to be adored. Obediently, I picked her up and snuggled into her warm fur, ignoring the stink of her breakfast that clung to her. That wasn't her fault, now, was it?

I looked at Taig to share the sweetness with him and found him with his hand pressed to his mouth, watching us with affection. "I'm down for restraints, when I've had time to do the research," he said, turning back to the food. "You'd be hot as hell on display for me. Are you cool with that?"

"Sure. Sometimes." He knew I could use my magick defensively even restrained. *Even gagged.* My head ached. The scars I bore from Clint had nothing to do with the man, and everything to do with how shitty it had felt to be so easily one-upped by such an abysmally mid human. In that context, it didn't feel so wrong to have learned those lessons. "After Clint, it's going to need to be pretty far removed from SOP."

He didn't try to tell me that Clint hadn't followed standard operating procedure. "Sure. I'll check in beforehand to get the green light with the concept, at least until we've had a few experiences." I nodded, glad he'd offered. "I don't want work coming into the bedroom, either."

"Anything in particular?" I asked.

"No." He whisked the eggs for a moment. "Maybe. I hadn't really thought about it. Hard no for anything to do with heat." My mind went to the scar on his back and my stomach rolled. "Other than that, I don't have much that would distress me. A lot of things that'll make me feel like I'm at work, though."

I knew what those things were for me. "Like what?"

"Handcuffs," he said, with a shrug. "Name calling. Blood. Overt aggression. Bruises or red marks. Choking. Way too much choking. I'm sure there's safe ways to do that, but I'm not going near breath-play, love."

Aspen had told me some statistics around it. I couldn't remember what they were, but I remembered it was very common in intrafa-milial violence situations. "I'm going to have to think about this, and think of some suggestions." What the fuck could I do that wasn't on that list? "What about, like, blindfolding?"

"Work," he said, shortly.

Well, fuck. "Sorry." I blew out a breath. "How about if I hold you down and use toys on you?"

He frowned a little. "As long as you're safe with them all, that should be fine. You don't have any toys that are too intense."

"I'm sorry, did you just admit you've snooped through my draw-ers?" I asked, amused.

"I was looking for lube," he said. "The other day? And yes. Yes, I did. I also snooped through your medicine cabinet. You were out of shampoo, and you don't have any spare, by the way."

I felt the prickle of Eclipse's paws gently reminding me she existed, and turned my attention back to her. I was obviously going to put thought into my newfound role. "How do you feel about being pene-trated?" I asked him, thinking of some double-ended dildos I'd often admired and never purchased.

He arched a brow at me. "We'll start small, right? I'm happy to try it out. I don't have a lot of experience receiving." His words were underscored by the sizzle of a pan in his hand. I considered doing some online shopping, but discarded the idea. Those toys weren't cheap. We could try something less ambitious for a start. "While we don't really know what we're doing, and still establishing all this," he said, "Whoever is the submissive party, can stay wherever the other person puts us, or follows instructions?"

"Tick." Eclipse lay across my chest, her paws draped over my shoulder, purring and looking in the direction of the second, uncooked, batch of egg. I took a step away from temptation. *First time for everything.*

One omelet was slid onto a plate as he got the second cooking. "Just for the record, I'm cool for you to do whatever that spell was."

"Noted."

"So we're on the same page?" he asked, as if surprised.

"So far."

He nodded. "Okay, the hows. Best I can figure out, we just need to signal when stuff starts and stops, right? So I was thinking some specific phrase that could be modified to indicate who wanted to top and allow the bottom to agree."

I didn't know if I loved the language he was using. Was it accurate? Was it kind? What did I know? I had an armful of cat and the food smelled amazing. "Like what?"

"I had an idea," he said, looking chagrined. "But saying it out loud is weird, okay?"

"It probably isn't a good option, then." Was he blushing?

No way.

Watching the omelet, he said, "What if the person who wants control says 'you're mine', and then the person who agrees can say 'I'm yours'? And then when they want it to end, they can say 'I'm my own' or the other person can?"

The thought of any of that made me feel super weird too. Would it be hot, in the moment? It wasn't hot over breakfast while cuddling a cat. "The whole ownership thing squicks me out."

"That's kind of why I chose it," he admitted. "It's such a weird notion. We have inalienable rights to our own bodies, yeah?"

"We should," I agreed.

He shot me a look of understanding, flipping the second omelet. "So the whole concept is play pretend. But it can also feel sweet, in the moment. And I thought it might be important to end it with the reminder that it's all bullshit, you know?"

I thought of trying to get *I'm my own* or whatever he'd said out of my mouth when having a panic attack and didn't like my chances. "We can still go with no, pause, and so forth, yeah?"

"Of course."

"Okay, that's fine." It was just an illusion. "We can try. I'm not really sure how it'll work." I sat down and Eclipse, disliking the change of scenery, jumped off to sit on the stool beside me. "But short of like, pink pumpkin vegemite or something random, I guess it'll work?"

He ate standing up as he tidied the last of the dishes, and I became aware, once again, of the city around us.

After that conversation, negotiating how we should split finances seemed like it'd be a *breeze*. I forked up some omelet.

"What's that look for?" he asked me.

"What look?" I bit into the food and it was, of course, awesome. "You're a good cook, O'Malley."

"I like working with my hands," he agreed, blandly, that up-all-night voice rolling over the words. "And I like eating."

I pretended to fan myself, and regretted it when Eclipse got annoyed and scampered off. "Whew. Better get you a key so you can visit more often."

He laughed, taking my empty coffee cup and going to refill it as he ate.

There was no reason to withhold a key, though, and he'd sat around enough times out the front of my place that I figured it made sense. Filling my mouth first, I went around and dug through my random drawer of whatever while he topped up our coffee. I found the spare key that I'd got when I'd had the locks redone after my door was obliterated by faeries and set it beside his food. "Here." It didn't have a ring on it, but I'd been paying for speed, not optional extras.

He glanced up, spotted the key, and stopped so fast the full cups splashed over his hands and coffee dribbled over my floor. "Fuck!" Managing to set the cups down with minimal extra mess, Taig shoved his hands into the sink. I turned on the cold water, thinking of what he'd said earlier about heat being a trigger. "That was hot!" he said, through gritted teeth. It was the sort of exclamation you made when trying not to lose it at the pain, rather than trying not to lose it at the traumatic memories. Relief unfurled in my belly and I pressed my hip to his, and accepted his weight in return. Cold water washed over his hand and we watched it, together.

"You're actually giving me a key?" he asked.

It wasn't *that* shocking, was it? "You can cook *and* eat," I said, as bland as he'd been. "And you're a hard-arse who happens to make a good ally. Why not?"

He leant his forearms against the sink, looking at his hands in the running water, a strange expression on his face. "I..." he frowned a little. "I don't have a spare to give you back."

I rolled my eyes. "Fuck off."

"No, really." He looked irritated, suddenly. "I had this all planned out. How we could progress. I know you have reasons not to trust. I hadn't even thought of keys."

Why the fuck that turned me into a puddle I had no idea, but it did. "Elders, I love you."

The irritation deepened. "You're messing with my timeline, Roars."

I pressed a kiss to his lips. "It's my timeline, now."

CHAPTER 18

When we got to the hotel, Taig and Delyan were already there. Benson sat at the table with Delyan, looking over photographs. Nearby, Taig had the kids, a bunch of what looked like pre-made pancakes, and various tiny tubs of toppings that were in single use plastics and probably tasted like the waste they were stored in.

"Just a tiny bit of vegemite, mate," he was telling Liam, watching the kid trying to lever the normal-sized knife in the tiny container. "I can help if you want."

"I got it," Liam said, scowling.

Jessica sent me a look that clearly said *he doesn't have it, but it's not worth arguing*, as she bit into her pancake with jam.

Brandon had been a shit, too. He'd been older, so he'd gotten away with a bit more... for a while.

Tears I didn't expect rushed into my throat and I turned away, going to stand by Delyan's shoulder. I nursed the half empty cup of coffee I'd brought with me, but having my hands full didn't do a damn thing for my battered heart.

Taig's vegemite negotiations with Liam were improved when Aspen entered the fray, and I tuned out the by-play.

"...further evidence," Delyan was saying. "Unless you know of anything else that might help us narrow it down?"

"I've told you."

I didn't need to have been there to know what he'd told her. "Do we have much?" I asked her. "The phone number I got?"

"We know who owns the phone, but Mr. Hurtfield hasn't been able to identify the owner."

They had no evidence of wrongdoing, I assumed. Innocent until proven guilty was so inefficient. Benson had heard them speaking about him, no one else had witnessed it. We hadn't given them the opportunity to show their hand before we'd jumped on the situation. Now the *no harm no foul* rules kicked in.

They needed a *thanks for sorting this out in a way that didn't require us picking up body parts* clause to that.

Also, if the cops had spoken to the guy, I couldn't try my hand at honey trapping him. Probably lucky, because I had a lot more vinegar than honey.

"I want to assure you that we're taking this situation very seriously," Delyan began, and I zoned her out completely, running through options in my head.

Benson knew them, and wouldn't rat, because it'd get him in trouble.

Benson didn't know them, and but suspected, and similarly kept his mouth shut for safety.

Benson knew them, and planned to deal with it himself.

Benson didn't know them, and planned to find out himself.

That was pretty much what I had, and I'd figured it out yesterday. I studied his expression as Delyan wrapped it up, but he didn't give away a thing.

I waited for the cops to clear out and for Aspen to organize the last-minute appointment we'd got with a clinical child psych. I had no idea how common those cancellations were, but I hoped we got whatever she needed to get for Jessica. Snacks were packed, situations were explained. Lilith organized, on the fly, for Benson and Liam to meet Trinity. In a whirlwind of getting shit done, I juggled a few appointments we needed to shift, and bided my time.

While Liam played with Trinity's kids and the two adults stood, watching in what seemed like friendly silence, I waited. When we left and Liam fell asleep in Benson's arms as he stood on the tram, one big hand braced and looking like the child weighed nothing, I waited. When he said, "She isn't working for the fae or vamps. We'll get along fine." I waited.

It wasn't until we stopped at a park on the way back that my opportunity presented itself. Aspen was looking after a frazzled Jessica, while Lilith distracted the newly energized Liam. And Benson stood beside me, arms folded, like he was carved of granite.

Granite with a lot of body hair, and a bad attitude.

"Who is he?" I asked him.

"Why should I tell you?" he shot back, not even looking.

I didn't roll my eyes. "Because I'm on your team. And I can kick your arse."

He didn't smile. "That wasn't your magick you used. It was hers." And he jerked his chin toward Lilith. "You didn't beat me fair."

"Mate, do you think I'm a sucker? I *never* fight fair. And that's why I always win."

His eyes flickered over to me, a ghost of a smile on his lips. He considered me as Liam giggled happily, running away from Lilith's energetic impersonation of a crocodile. "No one always wins."

That went home. I don't know exactly why, because of course I was being dramatic. "I'm alive," I said, bluntly. "I call that winning."

His smile vanished, and his eyes were hard as diamonds. He looked at me as if he could flip through every thought in my brain and while it wasn't terrifying, it certainly wasn't comfortable. "I was on call with a client a few weeks ago. Liam had a bad dream. I muted, but didn't have time to shut down the camera before he walked in front of it."

I could imagine it, a quick apology, a flick of the mute button, and then a little kid with a dripping nose throwing themselves into his lap. I bet his expression had looked like it did then, in the spring after-noon. Cold and distant. I struggled to believe, though, that he couldn't have caught Liam before he was in video range. I'd seen those reflexes up close.

Still… "What happened next?"

"They came after us."

I nodded, because it was what I'd expected, from the situation now. But it was important not to assume. "Why didn't you tell Delyan?"

"I was working illegally."

That'd do it. "Clients would be liable, too." He snorted and looked back toward his kids. My heart ached for the big grumpy jerk. "What was the work?"

"Sex work."

It all clicked neatly into place, the big pieces, like his motivations, and the little pieces, like how he'd probably been throwing clothes on when he'd heard Liam, or possibly shifting form. Why he'd run so hard and fast.

"Didn't usually bring it home," he muttered. "But Liam was sick, and he was paying a lot. It was a once-off." He glanced over at me. "You'd know how it goes, when you fuck up once."

"I do," I acknowledged, trying to match his neutral tone.

He couldn't tell Delyan. And I didn't know if I could tell Taig.

"I'm going to put down a Silence Ward," I told him quietly. "Two steps in any direction and you'll be out of it, okay?" Once he nodded, I dropped the ward. The quiet was so thick I could barely breathe, but I forced myself to. "Do you think they're after Liam?"

His gaze fixed on the kids. "Wouldn't surprise me."

"Want to tell me how it went down?"

"Will it help?"

I wanted to hit him. I didn't. "It might."

He did glance at me then, briefly. "You going to roll over on me?"

I resisted the urge to flip him the bird. *Good witch*, I told myself, feeling proud. "If you thought I was, you wouldn't have told me. No, Benson, I'm not. But I need to know how these people operate."

He glanced forward again, jaw tight as he tracked Jessica's swift movements across the climbing frame. "Not sure how they found me.

Someone I worked with, I assume. I'd never met them in person. I did cam work. So I didn't recognize their scents when they started staking us out. I didn't realize who they were. And they were smart, too. They used some sort of scent canceling items, and a sound muffler. Similar to what you've done here."

Charms. Not live wards, but lingering spells activated as needed. They weren't magi, then, as I'd expected. "Goal?"

"Unsure. But I'd been working with two of them for more than six months, and one for about three, without any of this. It was after Liam was visible. That's what I can identify as the change."

I shook my head. "Back it up. What changed?"

He shrugged. "Demands to meet. Extravagant offers of short holidays, little 'come have coffee' things. Big tips, and changed expectations."

"All of them did this?"

"Yeah. Three. There are others in the group."

I let out a breath. "What's the group?"

"I suspect they hunt shifters. Not sure if it's all about sex, or if it's the thrill."

My stomach rolled. I didn't dare let any feeling into my tone as I said, "Know any of their names?"

"Not their real ones. But I know a few faces, and eight unique scent patterns."

"Are you sure? Even through the magick?" He sent me a long, dark look, and I held up my hands in surrender. "I need to check." Eight known members. "They'd be known to the police, probably." But how the fuck I'd find their names without tipping my hand from two states away I had no idea. Delyan had come from up north, but unless it was that specific district, I doubted she'd be useful. I could make enquiries about that, it'd be simple enough to rule out.

If I started searching up supernatural sex workers without being able to clearly show *why* I was doing so, I would probably have my license pulled. If that wasn't a rule, it bloody well should be. "There are some sex work options here," I offered, slowly. "If you want to continue it."

He shrugged. "It was a job. I don't have the set up here, and I don't want to do it at home. I can't send the kids away from me. I won't do it in front of them."

I nodded and changed back to my main concerns. "This is why you don't want Liam with a sitter."

He was quiet for a minute. Said child was upside down on the climbing ladder, his shirt dangling around his armpits, his hair a fine brown cloud beneath him. I steeled myself against to halt any thoughts about these people's motives. I didn't need that in my skull.

"Trinity seemed fine," he said eventually.

There were tears in my throat again. I cleared them away. "She is."

He nodded. "Cash would help her."

And having Liam with a sitter would be safer than with Jessica. "Want me to try to get Jessica into the same school as Trin's oldest?" That was probably something I could do, eventually. But wheels turned slowly.

"Jess could deal with a human," he said dismissively. "Her ursa form is bigger than you."

I braced myself, but said, "If they know to bring charms to make it harder for you to sense them, they know how to silver you, Benson."

He didn't have any response to that. He just stepped out of my silence ward, and went to go play with his kids.

CHAPTER 19

"What'd he say?" Aspen asked me, falling onto the gaudily patterned tram chair that probably hid puke stains.

I'd known the question was coming. There was no way I'd get away without an interrogation. I'd told him I wouldn't tell the cops, but these two were my *coven*.

I leant forward so Lilith was part of our little huddle. "He did sex work, sounds like online services with at least some live individual options." I recounted what he'd told me, almost exactly. He hadn't given me a lot of words. There wasn't much to cut.

"Y'know, that all makes a lot of sense," Aspen mused, standing to go first off the tram, then waiting for us to join us before she said, "I should've picked it. Also, he'd be amazing on a pole. Can you imagine with that core strength how long he could hold an inversion?"

I couldn't imagine too many poles that would be safe to hold *him*, but I didn't mention that. "We can't tell the cops."

Lilith seemed strangely relaxed. "He didn't work from home though. Except that one time."

I'd definitely mentioned that. Twice, because she'd reconfirmed already. "No."

Whatever Aspen was going to ask next she swallowed, tucking her hands into her pockets and walking quietly between Lilith and I.

"Pizza night?" I offered her. "I'll get the ice cream?"

She shook her head, her eyes on the ground. "I'm fine, Roars."

Aspen shot me a quick sideways look that was entirely unnecessary. I could clearly see Lilith wasn't fine. "The kids will be okay. We're on it, and we *are* making progress. Now we know what we're up against."

Lilith nodded and waved me away. "I misjudged the whole thing," she said. "I'm embarrassed. And I feel shit, because I assumed things. I'm not triggered."

I ached for her. "You didn't hurt anything."

She shrugged. "I'm clocking off early, okay?"

I stopped walking and she did too, hands tucked deep in her pockets. "This isn't about work, is it?" I asked her, bluntly.

She let out a watery laugh. "You're so bad at tact, Rory. No, it isn't about work. I need to go lick my wounds, okay?"

"Okay." I wished I could hug her, but she took a half-step back as if expecting I was going to try. I wasn't, and that small motion made the knot in my guts tighten. "I'm not down to lick your wounds with you but I can pack them with junk food and memes if you want, okay?"

"That sounds unhygienic and awesome for another night." She offered me her hand and I didn't realize how much I needed that small contact until I took it. She squeezed the tips of my fingers. "Blessed be," she said, the words thick, and then hurried off.

I watched the wind swirl around her dramatically. There weren't many people who could pull that off like Lilith could. I wished I'd seen her as an old woman in a tracksuit, baking. Because right then the world was terrifying and having something good to work towards sounded so comforting.

"Well, that happened," Aspen said, from beside me. "I'd recommend packing the wound with something soaked in alcohol, personally."

I rolled my eyes at her. "Ice cream doesn't give you a hangover."

"Can make you puke, though."

"You're doing it wrong," I told her, wishing I could tell anyone anything about this whole Nic and Lilith and the future thing. "She's got family shit."

"Families are shit, all right," Aspen said wisely. "Let's go do this work so she doesn't get back to a giant pile."

I nodded. "Solid plan. Then we need a safety plan around those kids."

"And the dad."

I disagreed with that, though. Benson didn't need a safety plan.

He needed an accomplice.

CHAPTER 20

Our emails were fun that afternoon. Wesley was off the hook for the missing woman on his feeding list; her boyfriend was in custody. Delyan emailed us thanking us for our help. It was cute. I was still smiling over it when I saw the next notification for a new email, this one not CCing Lilith and Aspen.

"Holy crap," I said, grabbing Aspen's shoulder.

She looked up from her own screen and bobbled the healthy juice Shepherd had delivered her. "What?" she asked, craning her neck. "*What?*"

"I got it!" I showed her the email, complete with the official governmental stamps and seals, and felt the laughter bubbling in my chest. Taig had said he'd pull strings, but that was *fast!*

"What did you get?" Aspen demanded, impatiently. "You're so annoying, Rory. I want to party too."

"It's a license to carry the fae sword." I'd forgotten about it in the chaos of the last few weeks. When I opened the attachments to find the photographs of said weapon beside rulers on a boring white backdrop, it was easy to remember the weight of the weapon, how solid it had felt in my hands.

"*Oh shit.* No way. You can't use a sword?"

"Yet." I laughed at her expression. "It'll make buying for me easy this Solstice, because training isn't cheap." But even the government respected the law of *finders keepers*. And impeccably done paperwork. Gleeful, I dug through my notes for the links to trainers I'd found when I'd been totally fixated on the idea, back when I was still all fucked up from Samhain.

That had been a damned good night.

"You can respond to Delyan," I told her, hitting *call* on my first preference of instructor. "I've got plans to make."

I went straight from work to jiu-jitsu where I rolled with my favorite lycan. "Want to come back to mine?" Zane asked me, at the end of the night when we were both sweaty and tired, and even his foster kids were looking a bit less energetic than usual. "Chris put ribs on to slow cook this morning. They should be pretty good."

"That sounds amazing." I glanced around and saw Chris ducking his head to avoid my gaze. "Is this food and chill, or food and chat?" I asked Zane, hoping there wasn't more of Duke's lycans about.

"Food and chill," he told me, wiping his forehead. "They're still around, but not focused on us."

Any interest I'd had in food vanished. "Same someone we talked about ages ago?" I asked. I didn't know why I bothered. He nodded, but I was already saying, "I'll have to grab the recipe from you," knowing I probably wouldn't. "But I'm keen to get home."

Zane grasped my shoulder, his hand firm and friendly. "Okay. You know where we are."

I put my hand over his and gave it a friendly squeeze. "Thanks. You, too." On the way home, I binged videos about sword technique. I continued listening as I did all the boring adult things after work. Taig brought celebratory ice-cream and blueberries to top celebratory pancakes.

"So you don't have to store it in a safe?" he asked, amazed, as he read through the paperwork. "What the fuck?"

"It's not steel," I said, smug. "They're accepting it under the tool category, like my knives."

He shook his head. "Boots said he'd try to get that over the line, but I didn't think he'd actually be able to."

My attention piqued, I offered him a forkful of loaded pancakes. He leant over the bench and took it from me. "Who's Boots?" I asked. He'd mentioned an old friend, but no names.

Taig waved at his mouth and I waited for him to finish chewing before he said, "An old friend. Brian Luscombe."

The name didn't ring any bells for me. "How old of a friend?" That was a considerate way to ask if they'd been deployed together, wasn't it?

Taig stirred a dollop of ice cream into his iced coffee, which was apparently his choice of celebration. "Known him more than two decades."

That didn't answer my question, but I accepted it anyway. "What does he do?"

Taig considered that question for a minute, before he said, "I'm actually not sure, anymore. I haven't asked. I'm relatively confident if I knew, I couldn't tell you."

Well, *that* certainly answered my questions. The ability to pull a lot of strings *and* secretive work wasn't bog standard military. "He was a witch-hunter."

"Used to be his job title, yeah." Cool blue eyes watched me. "He's a good guy."

A witch-hunter had helped me get a fae sword. I didn't *have* the sword yet, of course. I'd booked in to pick it up after my next psych appointment. But he'd made it so that was *legal.*

Was I on the right side?

"My life is so weird." I tried to fork up some more pancakes and a blueberry rolled away. I chased it with my fork, hoping it wasn't an omen. "Good, but weird."

"Same." He offered his hand, palm out. "It's my brother's fortieth in March, by the way. I'm going to fly up for it. Want in?"

The idea of making plans in November for March didn't seem so bizarre. "For how long? You okay if we crash at a hotel?" On the off chance I hated his family it'd make me much comfier.

"Kind of required. He's got four kids in a three bed, and mum's couch is balls." He watched me like he expected I'd bolt. "I was thinking of inviting Mia along, too, seeing if she wanted to do the theme parks."

I tried to figure out what that would look like. A few days with a random teenager doing activities couldn't be that bad, right? "Separate rooms, not just separate beds," I said, levelly. "Right?"

"For us?" he asked, frowning at me.

"Room for you and I. Room for Mia."

"Oh. Of course." He kept looking at me like I was a wild animal. I propped one foot up on the stool beside me, looping an arm over my knee as I sliced off a bit of pancake drenched in half-melted ice-cream. "You'd be okay with going away with her, though? If she agrees?" he asked.

I tried not to be insulted. "No, Taig," I said sarcastically. "I'll pay my way, if that's cool."

"Sure, if you want. My family though, I'd cover it."

Cop wages weren't that great, and I wondered if this was where we were super responsible and sat down to discuss how we saw finances being split going forward. "I'm not as commitment-averse as you seem to think."

"Want to get married, then?" he asked, straight-faced.

The level of nonchalance while joking about that kind of shit had to be admired. And responded to. So I flicked a blueberry at him, and was pleased when it left a smear of ice-cream on his shirt. "Go fuck yourself, O'Malley."

He grinned and flicked the berry back at me. "Want to watch, do you?"

I caught the innocent fruit before it ended up under the couch and didn't try to return fire. "It wasn't how I planned to spend my night, but," I cocked my head and considered him, imagining a few scenarios of what he'd offered. A few options were kind of hot. Or maybe my imagination was top notch. "I could probably be convinced, if you're feeling persuasive."

He made a thoughtful noise and picked up his glass. My heart rate kicked up as he walked around the bench and propped a hip beside me. I lined up another blueberry but didn't let fly just yet, enjoying my ice-cream before it melted.

I quite enjoyed the way he stood there, sipping like he could taste a damn thing, looking at me like he was fucking me in his head. He got bonus points for letting me finish my pancakes as his fingers trailed up my leg from where it was perched on the stool, starting at my ankle and skimming lightly up my calf. The leggings I wore were no protection from the featherlight touch and I was glad of it. Especially when he rested his palm against my knee.

I didn't consider my knees an erotic area. The smoldering look he gave me definitely changed the vibe, of course, but it was mostly just a sweet, comforting movement.

"You're cute," I said, waving my fork at him. "Thank you for feeding me."

He didn't take it as the invitation I'd half hoped he might. "You've been too stressed to eat."

I licked the tines of my fork and his lips quirked, but my heart wasn't really in it.

I'd noticed the constant supply of snacks, of course. I figured he liked cooking, or liked forward planning. It was comforting to know what was happening in advance, more so for some of us than others. Taig was a planner.

He was also a worrier, though. And yeah, I'd lost condition. I forgot to eat less now, but the two meals I'd had today were both things he'd made me.

I wondered if the protein powder he'd left her, and prepared for me in the morning, was really a flavor he didn't like. Did he like cooking? Or did he just get satisfaction from having everything just so?

Was I in a relationship with a micromanager, or a sweetheart?

"I can see the wheels in your head spinning," he said, setting down his glass. "What're you thinking about?"

"You," I said, honestly.

"What about me?"

I scowled at him. "Is this an interrogation?"

His hand was cold from his glass when it cupped my cheek. He lowered his face to mine and I lifted to meet him, touching the tips of our noses together. "No," he breathed. "Or I'd know what the fuck I was doing."

My heart tangled in my chest and the myriad of responses I could've made all melted away. The flecks of cold gray in his eyes made a hypnotic pattern amid the blue and I stayed, frozen, while his fingers scooped and twisted my hair. There was something so fabulously freeing about having that weight taken away, and the pressure that replaced it helped me to relax into the forerunners of hunger that stirred in my veins.

He twisted his face away from mine, and my breath tangled up in my lungs at that stolen opportunity. His lips whispered against my ear and I arched into him, wanting his kisses, not wanting to unsettle the delicate balance to get them. "You're mine," he murmured.

A chill swept over me, not unpleasant but unfamiliar and unsettling. A part of me started thinking about the cold, logical things. What we'd agreed, how it'd all go down, whether it was my preference, how late it was, how much we needed sleep.

The other part of me was noticing the way the stool dug into my backside and the way he was holding me, waiting.

Curiosity might've killed the cat, but this witch had nine lives.

"If you treat me right," I allowed, and I felt him grin against my ear before his teeth tugged at my lobe above my piercings.

It was on the tip of my tongue to tell him I'd rather relocate to bed when he asked, "That's yes?"

"Yes it's yes." Surely that was obvious?

His hand tightened on my knee, but not painfully. I let him reposition my leg so my foot dangled near the ground, and, when his fingers bit into my hip and pulled me up, I stood. It wasn't super floppy, though. Wasn't floppy the brief? I could've cast my low gravity spell, but I opted to see how it played out, first.

His hand gently pulled my head back by my hair, while I was

cradled against his other arm. Before my back arched beyond levels of comfort his mouth was on my neck. Heat swept through me as he scraped his teeth against the sensitive places he'd found beneath my ear, then closed his lips and sucked.

My knees went out like my strings had been cut and I barely noticed, because he had me held tightly against him. His sweeping tongue and the humming noise of his pleasure became the focus of all my attention and I burned to have him turn that mouth on the rest of me.

When he first moved I stumbled, but he lifted his head, walking me backwards and holding me against him. "I think I'm going to fuck myself," he said, and there was laughter in his voice. "And you're going to regret it."

My body was still humming. "Is that a promise?" I asked, but my head cleared enough to be mildly concerned. So far he had an impeccable record of getting me off, but we'd never been here before.

"You're terrible at following instructions." The laughter was still there. "Your job is to shut up and take it. You agreed."

I considered that as he steered us into my room. Obviously I could withdraw consent at any time, and he was just playing. "Sure. But I want you to fuck me."

He made a noise of compassion. "I know."

I blinked. *Cute? Or?* Before I could decide, he let me fall onto the bed.

I'd been half expecting it, but still couldn't stop the reflexive slap to the bedspread to break my fall. I had an excellent view of his face as he opened my top drawer and started sorting through my toys, a wicked glint in his eye.

Ah. Happily, I relaxed back, resisting the urge to put my hands behind my head. I hadn't shown him where they were, but I wasn't surprised he knew. It wasn't the sneakiest spot in the universe. Convenience was king.

Maybe I was queen?

I shrugged that thought off. Who needed a crown? I was a fucking *witch.*

He held up a string of anal beads, looking at me thoughtfully. "We're definitely going here one day."

There was no way Taig would use them like he was pull-starting a chainsaw, so I wasn't scared. "Need help to find something for today?" I asked, to make sure we were on the same page.

He waved it away. "No. Let me use my detective skills to identify which your most frequently used items are."

If he could, I'd been cleaning them wrong, and the thought made me want to cringe. I knew I hadn't, but I still had the ick, now.

"I don't know if this feels sexy," I said, hoping we could abolish that concept from my brain. I blew a stray curl out of my face. "Grab my hair and kiss me again, maybe?"

He held up a pretty aqua dildo and assessed the suction cup on the end. "No. But if you're not going to shut up and take it, at least get undressed."

I sat up and pulled off the sweater I'd had on, but paused when I saw him looking at the threading on a bullet, a jolt of uncertainty going through me. "Am I wrecking this?" I asked, rather than letting it fester.

He looked up immediately, frowning at me. "What, by being yourself? God, no, Roars. We're playing, aren't we?"

"Cool." I let out a breath. He leaned over and kissed me, a gentle kiss on the tip of my nose. "Sorry. That probably broke your immersion."

"I'll get it back in a minute," he said, and held up the bullet. "Almost new. Also, your batteries are oozy. This needs to go."

I looked at the unsuspecting little silver thing. "It doesn't bring joy, I guess."

He tossed it toward the doorway. "So we don't forget." And spent a moment looking me up and down, a smile tugging at his mouth. "It's a crime to fuck myself instead of you. Good thing I'm off duty."

That was perhaps the most dad-jokey line I'd ever got from him, and I arched my hips to make a bit of a show of getting out of my pants. He watched, his mischievous smile back. "Go on, see if you can change my mind," he offered, idly.

Something dark and gross swept through me. "Nope." I sat up, folding my legs. "Time out."

Taig set down another dildo. "I'll grab a glass of water for you."

I shook my head, letting out a long breath. The feeling was already receding, and that was such a relief that tears pricked at my eyes. "It's fine. Full steam ahead."

He sat beside me, though, and put an arm around me. I let myself flop against him obediently but dreaded the apology that too often came next. He had nothing to be sorry for. Quite the contrary, he'd been fucking amazing.

Every single time this happened.

But he just pressed his lips into my hair, and let out a slow breath. "You smell good," he said, quietly. "I'm glad you've got your normal shampoo back."

So was I. There had been supply issues after Samhain, and the one I'd grabbed as a stop-gap had made my curls impossible to deal with. I'd lived in braids for a few days. But it had cost *so much.* I couldn't just throw it out.

I relaxed back and he rested his palm against my weird belly button for a moment, but when I met his eyes he wasn't looking at me with distaste. "That's the second immersion break," I said, around a sigh.

"I like frequent breaks. And long ones. We could pretend it's Friday arvo and roll one long break into the end."

I rolled my eyes. "When the fuck have you ever worked a job where you could do that, O'Malley?"

"I've hung out with friends who've done it," he objected. "So far I haven't convinced any amazing witches to have a long lunch with me."

To get him back on track, I folded my legs at the ankle and put my hands behind my head, hoping it'd look cocky and not relaxed. "They'd probably tell you to go fuck yourself."

"Witches, man," he agreed, shaking his head, and leant over to dig through my drawer. "Good thing I love you."

"Or what?" I asked, amused.

"I might've just grabbed that sad silver bullet. I bet it was buzzy."

My interest was piqued by that description. "Buzzy?"

"Yeah. Aggressive rhythm. Buzzy." He had a big pink dildo with a clit stimulator attachment, and I loved the way he studied it like it was a traffic photo. "You'd hate buzzy vibes." And he turned the two-in-one on, considering it. "You like deep pressure."

I resisted the urge to tell him the toy he held was one of my favorites. I was pretty sure he'd figured that out from the way he turned it off and tossed it over beside me.

I'd literally told him about my pressure preference, so I wasn't going to be awed by his powers of perception, but I was kind of impressed at how he was sorting through my collection.

"This is for me, right?" I asked him, suddenly suspicious. "You're not stealing my shit, are you?"

He flicked his eyes over to me, then upended a velvet bag and sent a purple sparkly silicone dildo tumbling onto the bed. "I like the shape of this," he said, and held it up. "No additional veins. Why do they put veins on fake cocks? Just rib them if you want them ribbed."

I actually agreed. "I bought that because it was so pretty."

"I can see it," he mused, holding it up. "Goes with your eyes." He set it aside.

The air on my skin was cold, but I stayed where I was, watching as he quickly discarded a few options before coming out with a buzzer I hadn't seen in awhile, and the remote.

He was resourceful, I'd give him that.

Apparently he was happy with his selection, because he stripped off his shirt and started working on his shoes. I looked at the three options and wondered exactly where he thought they'd all go. The buzzer didn't have the flared base required to work in the backyard, and the dildo was too big to go in cold. Or possibly at all. The two in one was pretty specific about where it'd fit best.

I was considering breaking immersion again to question him about it, but a man who used the word *buzzy* for a toy surely knew everything I'd tell him?

I deliberately sent my mind to fantasy land as he undid his belt, watching the play of the last of the day's sunlight on his forearms and the strength in his back. I didn't bring my attention back until the fabric of his pants was being tossed neatly aside.

"This is where I'm glad you didn't want to do the sex spells," he said, grabbing the lube. "I think I might give you a pearl necklace, love. It'll look fantastic with these accessories." And he glanced at me quickly. "Don't you think?"

I thought it sounded like another shower and I'd already had one an hour ago after jiu-jitsu. "I think I like it when you touch me." I was a fucking grade A diplomat.

"Maybe next time you should say *let's go fuck* instead of *go fuck yourself.*" He climbed onto the bed and scooped my legs up, folding me like a deck chair.

I let it happen, and sat with the discomfort of being exposed. He nuzzled at my ankles and traced my opening at the same time and the contrast made me jump. "I'm looking forward to exploring all of you," he murmured. "Another day."

There was a game afoot, and I settled back as his fingers stroked me, tracing my opening, reminding myself I wanted to see where this would go. Another shower wouldn't be the worst thing, really. I focused on the tightness in my muscles and worked on getting them to relax, one by one. It was easier than I expected, considering I had my naked lover kneeling beside me and was entirely vulnerable and not super turned on.

Maybe that said something about how I really did trust him.

The thought made warmth sweep through me, and he pressed a longer kiss to my leg. "That's better," he murmured, glancing down at me as he brushed his knuckles against my clit, then closed his eyes. His fingers stroked deeper inside me and I felt the exploration with growing interest. He found the magickal spot at the front of my wall and I don't know what made me hotter, the way he switched from slow, explorative strokes to hard, deep circles or the way his mouth parted to take a deep, ragged breath.

As soon as he opened his eyes, illogical unease crept through me. I watched as he reached for the lube, then caught myself. *You're not jumpy.* It wasn't illogical. But it didn't fit here. Not with Taig.

His fingers were slick with lube as they dipped deep into my cunt again, then slid over my clit. The exposed wet skin was cold where the air swept over me and it made me feel painfully vulnerable. He stared down at me like I was the center of his universe and pressed his lips gently to the flat of my foot as his fingers liberally spread the lube. It was hot. It was awkward. I didn't love awkward hotness, so instead I focused on his hard cock against the back of my thigh. The angle was wrong to grab him, so I reached out to run a hand over the curve of his arse, enjoying the feel of his skin.

With almost no adjustment, he leant over my legs and kissed me on the lips, withdrawing his fingers only when he raised up a little. "You're doing great," he told me, in that up-all-night voice.

Was I? I had no idea what I was doing, but I was pretty sure great wasn't it.

I felt him reaching to where he'd put the toys. Beneath us, the bed rocked a little. He pressed another kiss to my lips, slow and lingering. I breathed in his breath, felt his gaze searing me from point blank range. He was studying every single reaction I gave, and the attention was electrifying.

"Are you scared of me?" he asked, holding my legs pressed against my chest, his expression remote.

I scoffed at the idea of ever being scared of Taig, and apparently it was the answer he wanted, because he grinned and slowly slid the toy into me.

"You like this one," he said, quietly, his grin fading. "The bag is worn, but the rope is in perfect condition. You've never bother to knot it." I swallowed at that observation, trying to remember if that was true or whether he was bluffing. Thinking was challenging, though. The clit attachment wasn't buzzing but the simple rub against my clit in time to the slow internal strokes was enough to break my train of thought. "Since you don't undo your shoelaces, it fits with your standard MO."

I did sometimes, but the correction was in the back of my mind as his tongue swept over my bottom lip. He nestled the dildo ever so gently high against my cervix and I turned my face for another kiss, liquid warmth pooling my body, chased by faint traces of anxiety. This time it was fleeting as he leant back, observing me for a moment with a bit of a smile against his lips.

When he lowered my legs gently I felt the dildo shifting inside of me, the drag and pull of its weight sending shivers of pleasure through me as it avoided ever hitting too hard against anywhere too sensitive.

"What setting do you use on this?" he asked me, the question delivered in that neutral cop voice with the up-all-night rasp that made me melt.

"Three," I said, as he adjusted my legs, clamping them together. "Never the patterns. And…five when I get close, then three again when I come." The empty hand rubbed up my belly and rested between my breasts. I didn't move because it'd unsettle the toy inside of me, but I wanted to. "I think." Maybe I should've made him figure it out, since he was so smart.

"Thank you, love." He shifted so his knees were on either side of my thighs, holding my legs together. He reached between them, settling the external part of the toy atop my clit. His fingers were warm and lingering. My nipples ached where they were entirely ignored.

"This isn't going to want to stay still, is it?" he asked. I closed my eyes as he spread my labia gently nestled it in as deeply as he could, the waves of wanting a slow rising tide. "You're going to need to stay still," he said, sounding pleased.

I nodded, and I was rewarded with him swooping down to deliver another gentle kiss. His tongue swept into the gap of my lips and I tilted my head to offer more, but he withdrew, leaning up again and sitting back. I opened my eyes to find him looking at me with raw hunger and my mouth watered at the sight of him there.

One of his fingers trailed over a nipple and electricity shot through me, making my breath catch and my thighs squeeze together.

A smile kicked up one side of his mouth and he added more lube to his palm, reaching over me with his other hand to get the remote for the buzzer.

I let out a long breath and again forced my muscles to relax as he got it started and sensation swept through me.

There was no way it was on the setting I liked, though. It was good, but not enough.

His hand closed over his cock, the smile on the corner of his mouth spreading a little further.

"Want more?" he asked.

If he was looking for begging, he was shit out of luck. "Feels pretty good," I said, and his eyes watched my lips form the words with such intensity that I felt my body responding. The sound of his hand sliding along his swollen flesh and the potential of that unoccupied hand of his sent sparks of sensation through my body. My nipples were hard, and cold, and entirely unloved. "Think you'll get my neck from there?" I asked, arching my back a little.

His eyes dipped to my breasts. "Might've changed my plan," he said, and his spare hand curled around one, making my heart sing and my breath catch, but he didn't touch the nipple and was left unsatisfied as he squeezed my hungry flesh.

"I'm looking forward to making your arse mine," he said, the words low and breathless. "Maybe when we go away I'll spread you out and spend all day getting your body used to me while exploring your collection of toys." The thought made my head spin. The man was a planner. He could make it happen. And I was okay with that. "Maybe we should just call in sick tomorrow." He licked his lips and I watched the movement hungrily. He was so damned good with those lips. I only wanted them on my nipples. I wasn't greedy. "And I'll definitely treat you right, love." He let go of my breast and disappointment swept through me, so bright it hurt. A moment later the speed of the buzzer kicked up and I sucked in a breath, struggling not to writhe.

He was grinning now, his breath coming quickly. "What do you want?"

"My nipples," I said, because it was true. It might even be enough to push me over the edge, if I could flex hard enough around the toy inside of me.

"I love the way they feel in my mouth," he agreed, his voice rasping over the words. It was possibly the most erotic thing I'd ever heard as he kept right on touching himself. "And in my fingers. I love the way you moan when I nibble."

I went to touch my own breasts and he took his hand off himself, pinning me back down. His cock pressed into my pubic mound and my head spun. "No cheating," he said against my ear. "Or I'll play mean."

"I'm not scared."

His teeth sank into my lobe and the sensation was a jolt that stole my breath. "I don't want you scared," he said. His tongue darted into my ear, making my head spin. "I want you obedient, woman." The words washed over the moisture he'd left on my flesh and I couldn't catch my breath.

"I'm not good at that," I admitted, arching so my nipples rubbed against his chest hair. "Better fuck me, hey."

He laughed, sitting up. "I'm fucking myself tonight, love."

I closed my eyes. Vibrations from my clit rolled through me as I listened to the sound of his hand against his cock and the way his breathing quickened. I didn't try to move my hands, because he might fuck himself, but he'd look after me, too.

The buzzer slipped from prime position as his hips thrust forward and I let a needy noise escape. His gaze met mine when my eyes popped open, lifting from my breasts. He turned up the speed once more, so we were both panting. I watched his movements, the flexing muscles of his shoulders, the rise and fall of his chest, the slide of his hand, and even as I crept toward my own peak I watched him climbing his, knowing he'd get there first.

His eyes dipped down to my breasts, and my nipples burned to feel his cum. I breathed and let myself be swept along. When his breath hitched and he moaned my name I soaked in every sensation of the warm droplets and the sticky roll of liquid down my skin and across my belly.

My hips begged as his breathing evened, but his hand, wet with warm lube, pressed me back down. And then his hands were on me, on my breasts, smearing the warm, sticky cum on my nipples, rolling them between his wet fingers. Shocked and hungry for it, I flexed my hands on the bed beneath me and felt every muscle in my body tighten as the heat roared through me. Beneath him, I lost myself, and I was glad of it.

CHAPTER 21

aig tugged me into the shower and I let myself fall against him, hearing the pleased rumble from his chest. "How you feeling?" he asked me.

My legs were still shaking, and I didn't really have my breath back yet. "Oh, yeah."

His kiss was lingering and sweet. "What sort of 'oh, yeah'?" he murmured. "Because I'm a bit worried, Roars."

I blinked some water out of my eyes. "Why?"

"Because I don't know all your triggers yet," he said, squeezing soap into his hand. "Want me to wash you?"

I looped my arms around his neck and closed my eyes. "Please." The one word took a lot of energy. "I'm good."

"You're magnificent," he corrected. "But that's splitting hairs." His kisses forced water to run over my face and I fixed that by turning more into him as his hands slicked over my breasts and belly. "That was okay?"

"I might've murdered you if it'd gone on much longer," I admitted.

"Figured that was a risk," he agreed, sounding pleased. "I can't really take tomorrow off, but I wish I could."

I wondered if he'd been thinking about that as he'd been spinning those fantasies. "We probably don't need all day."

"Long lunch?" he asked, and the curve of his lips against my cheek made my heart swell in my chest. "Did I get it all?"

I had no idea and it was a later problem. "Mm." I pressed closer, only to find he, too, was sticky from the hug. That'd seared cum far and wide. I laughed at the feeling, stepping back. "We're a mess."

"Yes we are." He offered me a high five and the water made it sound exceptionally crisp. "I'll clean up the toys if you want. You look pretty sleepy."

I was pretty sleepy. "You're my hero."

"We probably shouldn't meet, then," he said, and even though a part of me knew it was just the hormones, it was the funniest thing ever. I was giggling when his hand grabbed my arm and dragged me out of the water, his fingers biting deep into my arm.

Alarm jolted through me as we stood together, dripping all over the floor, and a face like mine but not looked back at us from the pool of water at the bottom of the shower.

Taig swiped water off his face and the ground could've opened beneath me, in that moment.

"That's not you," he whispered.

"No."

He looked at me in the billowing steam of the shower, searching my face wildly. "How long has your mother been staking you out?"

My head spun.

My mother.

He'd said it. It was real.

"Remember when the faeries almost ripped my throat out?"

"Yeah, I do." He looked back toward the water, and her head was cocked now in a way I recognized from the mirror. There was roaring in my ears.

It *was* real. It was all suddenly real. And I'd been about to climb into a bed that had avoided any wet spots, somehow, and sleep the sleep of the well-fucked.

"That's no magick I know," Taig said softly. "I think she can hear us."

"Probably," I agreed to the second statement, my world rushing and spinning around me as pieces slotted into place. "Hey mum, meet my boyfriend. Human custom dictates you shouldn't see his cock, so kindly fuck off."

Taig reached over and picked up a charmed bangle I hadn't put away yesterday and dropped it into the water.

The image wavered and warped. I couldn't tell if she looked amused, annoyed, or was just all fucked up. But it wasn't distortion just from the break in surface tension. It was magickal distortion, and my world shifted again.

"Look at that," Taig said, with his neutral cop-voice. "I bet your dad could tell you what percentage of iron is in that gold bracelet. But I reckon it's not zero."

CHAPTER 22

His hands were steady. Thank the Elders his hands were steady. It felt so much easier, seeing him going through the coffee-making ritual without haste or fear.

"Your dad's focus on the fae suddenly makes more sense," Taig said, stirring milk into his coffee.

I stared at the surface of my cup, wishing the pieces didn't all fit, looking for cracks. "I have no idea how it's anatomically possible."

"Same. I hope he was consenting."

I hadn't gotten to that point and my skin wanted to crawl off my bones. "Maybe he isn't biologically my father. Can I even ask him that? Do I have to sneak a DNA test?" I shook my head. I didn't want my DNA being on file, and the reason made me want to puke. It was almost eleven at night. I couldn't call him *now*, could I? "How the fuck did it take me so long?"

"Betrayal trauma?" Taig suggested. "Wait, sorry, is that an actual question?"

I scrubbed my hands over my face, not wanting to know what the fuck betrayal trauma was. "My dad didn't betray me."

"No, but this unsettles *everything* you believe." Eclipse leapt up onto the bench, her steps slow and confident, like a queen at her coronation. He stroked a hand over her spine absently, missing the full force of her majesty. Maybe he *was* as fucked up about this as me.

"You've got no issue with iron. Maybe fae genes are regressive. Maybe she's keeping an eye on you around the normal coming of age time, and you're not showing the right signs, so she's waiting." He paused, and I did too.

I didn't have fae magick. I couldn't hypnotize anyone. I didn't have a glamor. And I definitely didn't have the speed.

His hand on my waist eased me in close. I made myself stay and focus on that weight, on the comfort and welcome in that small gesture.

My palms settled on his biceps, sliding up the strength in his arms, so real and wholesome. So I leant forward and breathed him in, the smell of sandalwood and soap.

My lips found his and there was no demand, just a sharing of affection.

I could've stayed there forever, in the glow of the cheap fluoro globe, in his arms, his lips warm against mine. I hoped a part of me would. I hoped that, if something happened, one day, that this would be a memory of us I'd keep. Just the two of us having a normal night in, in love, enjoying the afterglow, planning a future and figuring out curve balls.

"Thank you for letting me in," he said, the words soft against my ear as he turned his face into my neck.

Had I? Maybe. And what did you say to that? *You're welcome?*

I probably should've called Dad, but it was too raw, still.

The idea that maybe he hadn't wanted me was a whole trip I wasn't excited to go on.

"How should I tell my dad I know?" I asked Taig, as he put the milk he'd bought into the fridge.

He blew out a breath. "Look, I've had to have some hard conversations with people in my time," he began, neutrally. "Your dad loves you. Where you come from…"

I nodded, feeling sick. "It's in the past." Except it wasn't my *past*, it was my present. And maybe it didn't feel like it for Dad, either.

Taig shrugged. "Knowing your dad?" he nudged my coffee closer to me. "I reckon you go with interpretive dance."

Tears burned my eyes. He was right. It was a ridiculous question. "Wow, so funny," I said, adding extra acid to the tone and swallowing away the lump in my throat. "You know how you said you couldn't miss work tomorrow?"

He pressed a tissue into my hand. "Already called in sick," he told me, gently. "Can't have you dancing solo."

THE SUN'S bite reminded me we were moving toward summer. Taig drove with the windows down and the tunes loud, his hand in mine. We didn't talk. We didn't need to. We'd been up half the night, spitballing what-ifs and maybes, taking the pieces of the puzzle out, looking at them, making sure they *actually* fit.

Dad opened the door as we pulled up and met me on the drive. His hug was hard and he didn't speak, just held me and rocked.

I kept the fire of fury in my heart unlit, choosing compassion over indignation for now. "I'm okay," I told him, feeling every fold in his shirt and the hardness of his arms. "I just need to talk it through, Dad."

He nodded and his hold loosened a little, but he rested his forehead against mine and didn't let me go. "You're my Sunshine," he whispered, blinking away tears. "Look at you. You look amazing."

Without the inconvenience of sleep, I'd had time to care for my curls as they needed, *and* do make up. I'd also needed to.

He sniffed and put his finger under my chin, turning my face a little. "Remember when I had to teach you how to blend down your neck?"

He said he'd done it. In reality, a combination of experimenting with Aspen and watching a lot of videos were to thank for those skills. "I remember."

"I liked it when the problems were easy like that," he said, quietly, and I deliberately kept the rage at bay. Now wasn't the time. "Come on, get out of the sun. Hello, Taig, how are you doing?"

"Can't complain," Taig said, following us in. "Tomorrow's set to get muggy, but there'll be a good storm at least. How are things out here?"

"Oh, yeah. Starting to get busy as everyone wraps things up before Christmas. You celebrate it?" He started making the coffee.

"Not religiously," Taig said, sitting down beside me at the table. "It's a good excuse to see family."

Dad met my eyes, arching his brows. My impatience flared and I held onto it tightly. "You want to invite him to Solstice, go ahead," I told Dad, waving my hand. "He's here to stay."

Dad glanced up from the milk frother and met Taig's eyes. "Heard of the Black Trio?"

I sat back and wrestled with my impatience again, spinning the coaster Dad would forget to use between my fingers. We were doing this the long way, apparently.

"All due respect, Wizard Gold," Taig said, "I've heard of a lot of magi over a lot of years."

"Wizard Gold," Dad repeated, snorting. "I'm not interviewing you, mate. You're an ex witch-hunter, though."

I knew why Dad was asking and some of my impatience lifted. I didn't know if I wanted the answer to whether Taig had helped kill members of our community, even if they'd needed to be dealt with and we hadn't had the tools, resources, or training.

I wondered, staring at the coaster spinning between my fingers, how many shitty situations had come about because of lack of tools.

"I know of the Black Trio," Taig said, slowly. "I recognized Nic's surname when it came up."

Dad set coffee down in front of both of us. "He looks like his mother, doesn't he?"

My mouth went dry. Taig had his cop face on. "He does," he confirmed, and I felt mildly ill. "I wasn't on the team that took her down."

"Most of them are six feet under, now," Dad said, going back to get his own coffee. "I hear the ones who took out Greg did a better job of it."

I'd made peace with Taig's past. I hadn't realized how much until that moment. But I knew why Dad was asking. And I knew why Taig didn't want to get drawn into it. Because, yes, he would've probably killed someone who was linked with us, somehow. The magickal community was so close knit that there was bound to be crossover.

It was probably how my clients felt about me being Retrievals.

"Thank you," Taig said.

Dad shot me a look to check that I'd caught that acceptance of responsibility, his expression friendly and his eyes cold.

"Sometimes you need someone with those skills, willing to do the job," I said, thinking of Samhain. *Troll cartridges.* "He's on our side, Dad."

"I'm on Rory's," Taig agreed, mildly.

I wondered, as I watched my Dad watching Taig, if he heard the *for now* after those words that I did, and whether it was actually there.

I wasn't jumpy.

I'd dived deep, fast. Maybe bringing Taig was a mistake. Even without all the baggage, there were no guarantees we wouldn't fall out of love. Then I had someone with all of my secrets running around the world. Taig was pretty good at keeping his mouth shut, and he'd be implicated by a lot of it, but…

"I'm going to be straight with you both," Dad said, leaning forward. "I'm not going to say a lot of things if you're here, Taig. That's nothing personal. I like you. I shouldn't, considering you just admitted you killed an old friend of mine, but, shit."

"I'm a likeable kinda guy," Taig drawled. "And he wasn't, by the time we found him."

Dad blew out a breath. "No, he wasn't. That's life. We change. Right now, you're here, perfect for my Sunshine. Who knows where we'll be in a few years."

Taig looked at me. "You want to dance solo, love?"

My phone buzzed in my pocket and I ignored it, flipping Dad's coaster some more. "Give us the generic bits together so I don't have to repeat it."

Dad sat back, nodding. "I went Overworld as part of an adventure gone wrong with a few friends back when rifts were opening randomly and the ugliness was in our face, all the time." He got up and went over to a drawer behind the bench, rummaging. "Sunshine and I came home."

I took a pull of the coffee and waited for the rest, but he came and slid a fidget toy over the table to me, falling back into his chair with a sigh.

The little yellow and white combination of cubes and wire sat in front of me, innocuous.

How did a human feel, anyway?

"Fae don't reproduce the way we do," he said. "In case you were wondering. Your genetic makeup is almost totally human." The coffee tried to crawl its way out of my belly. He'd done *tests* on me? "I needed to know if you'd react badly to iron," he said, softly. "Turns out you love a good steak." He turned to Taig and said, "Before she was on solids I'd give her a bit of silverside or some well-cooked steak and she'd gnaw on it happily for hours. Great when she was teething."

Taig made a noise of agreement. He probably hadn't heard the stories, the 'back in my day kids didn't choke when you fed them normal food' rant.

"What percentage?" I asked.

Dad turned the mug before him. "Ninety eight."

I should've been a carbon copy of him at ninety eight percent of his genes, shouldn't I? Wasn't that how it worked? Biology had never been my strong suit, but it seemed like a *very* high similarity.

I didn't ask if he'd've killed me if I was less human. I figured he would've. An enemy is an enemy, regardless of how similar your genetic makeup might be.

That was something I was going to need to keep in mind.

I didn't have time to sit with that concept before Dad said, "She's onto you now. Whatever you've got of hers, it's enough." He put his hand over mine and our hands just sat there, on the table. They didn't fit together. Or maybe they did, but had forgotten how.

He could've told me years ago, but I could understand why he didn't. It might never have been an issue.

"I thought we moved a lot when I was small because of how

volatile things were for us magi." It wasn't, though. Or at least, not totally.

The fae who'd attacked me when I'd been in the midst of Van Der Holsts' bullshit had recognized me, I'd known it. Dad had been there, ready for war, within hours.

"What do you mean, it's enough?" I asked him, letting go of all the pieces of the puzzle that I knew now *would* fit and looking forward. "What do I have of hers, except unique eyes and cool hair?" Bitch had better lipstick shades and didn't frizz the way I did. *Thanks, Dad.*

Dad glanced over at Taig, who just looked on with his cop-expression. I struggled against the desire to tell my dad to suck it up. Taig was in so deep, a few more details wouldn't matter, surely?

Maybe Dad came to the same conclusion, or maybe he figured *these* details weren't likely to be weaponized, because he said, "You broke the lord's hypnosis naturally, at Samhain. The rest of us were ensorcelled."

I filled my mouth with bitter coffee and struggled to remember that moment. It already had the fractured, fuzzy quality of something my mind either couldn't, or didn't want to, deal with. Beautiful fae opponent. Humanoid folks pouring from chalices without end. Faces in the water. Me and mine decked out in imaginary finery. They'd watched from the sidelines. Dad's skin had been covered with strange markings, the same as the fae had. And I'd *burned.*

I'd been over so many of these memories in the last twelve hours that the details blurred, but I didn't think it'd been the usual burn of purpose. What did I know, though? If it was a different type of magick, I had no idea how to consciously activate it. It seemed unlikely I I'd tapped into it until that moment, assuming their magick worked even slightly like ours did.

"What does it mean for the future?" Taig asked, beside me, and I was so glad he was there to ask it. Because my brain wanted to go back to when I was tiny, when Dad had come into my room in the night with a staff in his hand, ready to go to war with monsters scraping against my bedroom window.

"Don't know," Dad said, honestly. "Fae work kind of like ants. Rory should've been fuel for the colony."

I looked at the lines of tiredness in his face, the jovial smile that was pasted overtop and sat ill on his flesh. "Fuel," I repeated, slowly.

"Magick savings accounts." Dad drained his coffee. "From what I could figure, that's about the jist of it. They put a little in, let them sit, then drain when needed. She kept a few. Don't know how she chose them, though."

He'd been close enough to watch the process, and present for long enough he'd seen it all play out. "Did we come back alone?" I asked him, and my voice sounded weirdly flat. "Just you and me?"

His eyes dipped to his empty cup. "We did." Watching his smile slide off his face was like watching an avalanche. But he caught it, somehow, forced it back in place, his eyes overbright. "Your uncles would've loved you, but they didn't make it." He dashed away the tears that spilled over his cheeks. "Don't talk about it much. Can't. I didn't want her attention, you know? I don't know if now you're an even better magickal investment than you were as a tiny little thing, still covered in goo, or if your use has passed."

I'd had uncles.

"'Didn't make it' can mean a lot of things," Taig said, the words low and gentle. "Are they dead?"

"Yes."

I put that aside. I was less worried about whether some version of a few humans might still be alive, and more worried about whether I was an offshore bank account for a fae queen.

Judging by the show they'd put on for me at Samhain, the chances of me being worthless seemed pretty low. I wondered what the interest rates were on potato-fed human accounts. "She's watching me."

His grip on the empty mug went white-knuckled. "I can teach you a spell to end hers. I can't protect against it."

I felt sick. "You knew?"

"No." He shook his head. "No, but I've heard from others. She likes to keep her finger on the pulse."

There *were* others, then. "Like me?"

He met my eyes, the smile gone. "Don't. You're more human than most of the humans I deal with."

"Agreed," Taig said, quietly.

"I knew I liked you for a reason," Dad said, firmly, sniffing. "I don't know," he said to us both. "I really don't." He picked up his cup as if he forgot he'd drunk it all. "I've been offered a job next year at the university near you," he said. "Magi studies. Got a history class, and a casting class."

My head spun. Dad was moving closer to me, giving up his work, his life. "The house?"

He looked around blankly. "Yeah?"

"You selling?"

He shrugged. "Maybe. It's just four walls." Then he frowned. "Well, actually, there's a lot more than four, even if we're only counting loadbearing. I never understood why people used that phrase." He lifted his mug in a wordless offer for more coffee, and I shook my head. "Figured I can cat-sit for you, at least, while you're off adventuring."

While he made himself a second coffee I turned it over in my head. Taig's leg pressed into mine under the table and I pressed right back, drawing comfort from his presence. I had a million questions, and didn't know anywhere near enough about ants, or genetics, or any of the shit he'd mentioned to answer them myself.

It was the next steps that were critical, though.

"She breached SuperSec," I said, and Dad nodded in confirmation. "Why?"

He shrugged. "Allies, I assume, or distraction, or fun. I don't actually know her. No more than you'd know the killer in a true crime documentary, anyway."

Elders, I hoped ants reproduced without actual contact. I blew out a long breath. The rage was smoldering and now wasn't the time.

"I hear they've rounded up most of the humans who got out," he went on. "Van Der Holst didn't redeem himself, flattening half of Ballan."

I shrugged. Van Der Holst wasn't my issue anymore. "Know how I can train it?" I asked him. "The hypnosis-breaking magick I did?"

"No clue." He settled back across from us. "That's pretty much my hard limit, Roars. You want to walk down memory back alley with me, as is your right, we do it together, just you and me."

Was it my right? I don't know if I liked that idea, that he was required to prostrate himself on the altar of my curiosity. Yes, it was my heritage, but they were his scars. "I'm here if you want to talk," I offered, slowly. "But I don't feel like I need the action replay right now."

"I really don't want to talk," Dad said, with a laugh that sounded so genuinely light and full of mirth that it made my heart hurt. "But the offer is there. It isn't time-limited. And if I drop dead tomorrow, there's a few people around who'll reach out to you."

He *was* able to talk to someone, then. I felt better knowing he wasn't carrying whatever deeply traumatic experiences alone all this time. "Okay." I wondered if I should've reassured him, or tried to help, or something. Aspen would've known what to do. "Thanks, Dad. And I'm sorry."

"I'm not," he said, quietly, and under the table his foot bumped against mine. "I like where we're at, Sunshine. Change one thing, change everything."

My throat tightened and I dipped my head, blinking back tears. "That's not how it works," I objected, but I understood the sentiments. Even the most powerful oracles couldn't agree on how interacting with the future worked, and Dad was no oracle. "So, the fae stuff has no physical ramifications. Just a bit of magick."

"Far as I know. And apparently some stalking, too."

Fuck. "I'm going to need that spell." I let out a long breath. "I should get home, too. Is it okay if we stay for lunch though? I'd like some normal."

"Normal is my specialty," Dad told me. "I'm the most mid a person can be."

I didn't even roll my eyes at him, feeling lighter at finally hearing a bad joke. "Does that make me ninety-eight percent mid?"

He considered it. "Pretty sure you're more like your Oma. I guess being mid must be a recessive thing. You didn't get it." He stood and tugged one of my curls lightly. "Sorry, Sunshine. How about a barbecue? It's snag on the barbie kind of weather."

IT WASN'T until we were on our way home and I was sitting in the passenger seat, fighting sleep, that I realized there was one glaring hole in his story.

He had files.

He hadn't been on an adventure gone wrong. He'd been doing some sort of task. Either that, or he'd signed on when I was young, and I couldn't believe that. Not with what Ryan had said in their conversation a few weeks ago.

Whether Ryan had known about me was a piece of the puzzle that didn't fit neatly. What Wesley knew was another. One of those I'd never know, now. The other…

I glanced over at Taig, his profile clean, sunglasses on, hair ruffled by the wind and hand steady on the wheel.

He would've been reading between the lines and putting pieces into position in his own head, with his own understanding.

"Have you got access to Dad's files?" I asked him.

He glanced over, brows folded in consideration. "Your dad has files?"

My stomach clenched. "I don't know," I lied. "I thought he might. If he's been Overworld."

"Plenty of older folks danced in and out of rifts, back in the day." He shrugged. "Nowadays we just spend our time dancing in and out of social media rabbit holes."

He wasn't wrong, and that answered my question. I didn't even consider enlightening him, and that surprised me. But it was Dad's story to tell, not mine, much as he'd offered me a part of it. "What do you think?"

He wound up his window and flipped on the AC. "I think your dad overcooks sausages, has top notch humor, and is doing the best he can to deal with shit he wasn't equipped to manage." He glanced over at me. "He's doing well, Roars. Really well. But he's got good reason to be scared."

I tracked his words back to the thought trail they'd come from, which I assumed was about Dad working near us. "Think it'll help? To have him near?"

"He casts faster than anyone I've ever seen," Taig told me, flatly. "We'd've all been overwhelmed by Davies without him."

I hadn't been watching most of that fight, but what I'd seen looked like they'd all pulled their weight.

Thinking of the man they were fighting, I said, with disgust, "He was a helluva wizard."

"He was a lot of things," Taig agreed, without infliction. "I quite like the way he's feeding worms, now. Excellent career choice of his." Without changing tone, he said, "I like the idea of a cat-sitter. I don't like the idea of having your dad pop around while I'm trying to bend you over the kitchen bench, but hopefully he knows how to work a phone."

I snorted at Taig's association of ideas. "He does."

"Then I'm happy to have access to an easygoing cat-sitter." He reached over and squeezed my knee. "I'm actually kind of shocked he talked to me at all." He smiled a bit, then. "I probably shouldn't be. I've got the key to his heart, so."

I let out a long breath and wondered if that's how he felt about Mia. Before I could ask after her and what new shenanigans she was up to, my phone rang. It was Aspen, so I answered with, "Hey, what's up?"

"Where are you?" she asked, the words precisely enunciated. "In relation to Melton?"

I took the phone that Taig passed me and brought up his maps app. "Address? While I look, why?"

"George," she said, flatly. "He went into flight, and they cut off his path. So now they've got nothing left for him to do except fight. Last I heard, at the big shopping center in town, Woodgrove. I'll send you an exact location."

Fuck. I refined my search. "Twelve minutes." I told the app to navigate and Taig accelerated. We'd been following an L plater, doing a solid twenty under the limit. I pretended not to notice that we were going on the other side of the limit now. "Depending on traffic. Situation?"

"I'm on my way. Shep is giving me a lift, but I'll be at least thirty minutes. Cops pinned him down. They didn't call us until after they'd already set him off."

"Of course they didn't." I glanced down at my sundress. At least I had flats on. "I'm not dressed for combat."

"They need advice on how to help him de-escalate," she said, the words sharp and clear. "Not how to kill him, Aurora."

Whew, full names, now. Maybe this is why you didn't work with your bestie. "Message received. I'm all about the risk-min."

"Message received right back." She let out a frustrated noise on the other end. "Lilith is doing her best to get some locals on board, but they're already calling Retrievals, Roars."

If he was high and throwing fireballs, they'd need Retrievals. I didn't tell her that, though. She knew. "Give my number to whoever you're in contact with, tell them I'll be there in ten. Love you. Tell Shep to drive safe. You can't help him if you're held up in an accident, okay?"

"Yeah. Yeah." She blew out a breath and it crackled over the phone. "Sorry. There's fatalities, Roars. They're going to put him away."

If they don't put him down. Cops didn't like their own dying. Took it personally. Couldn't understand why. "We'll cross that bridge when we get to it," I told her, calmly. "We'll just do our best for now."

"I know. Okay. I'm fine, we're okay, and I'll see you soon, okay? Just go slow and easy, Roars."

Neither of those words was in my vocabulary. "Got it," I lied, without a qualm. "Love you. I'm hanging up now, ETA seven minutes, call the cops on scene for me."

"Will do."

The call went dead, and I dropped my phone. I didn't have my kit with me to change into. I had basic, everyday charms, my wand, two percent fae blood and my armor of unconditional positive regard.

As we turned off the freeway I saw the black, billowing smoke and felt my pulse start to kick.

"Well, he won't be hard to find," Taig said, neutrally. "That's something."

"You heard?"

"I heard."

I nodded and blew out a breath, wishing we'd pushed harder for the rehab visit. The way this guy had been skirting with drugs and the law, we should've seen this coming and done more. Maybe I still could.

"I can't believe I'm half fae."

"Two percent isn't half." I thought he was going to stare deeply in my eyes and reassure me, but he was doing a head check and accelerating into a gap. "I can't believe how much I love you. The fae stuff I can believe. Want me on your six?"

I wriggled my feet in my flats. "No. Less is more." And the cops wouldn't talk to him. He wasn't on duty, or one of this crew. "Maybe you can go get me a coffee."

"Sorry, Roars," he said, pulling up to a hastily laid out police barrier. "But I'm not going anywhere."

I leant over and pressed a kiss to his lips in response before letting myself out and jogging up to the nearest cop. "I'm Aurora Gold," I said, bringing up electronic proof of my job. "I'm George's Custodian."

The woman in front of me glanced at my sundress as she turned away with the radio to her lips. I waited as the crackling conversation happened to the side, my eyes on the smoke that looked like it was coming from a car-park a hundred meters away.

I should've asked how far away Retrievals was. I didn't want to step on toes.

The woman waved me in and a young guy in blue fell in beside me, pointing. "He's up here," he said, without infliction.

I wasn't calling the kid Sherlock, that's for sure. "No worries." I pushed my speed to a jog. Blue kept pace, steering us around cars and past another barricade. I heard a helicopter and glanced up, but it had the red cross of an ambulance, not the matte black of Retrievals.

If they were air-lifting out injured law enforcement officers, George's clock was pretty short. There wasn't a damn thing I could do about that now.

I was stopped by a steely-haired, uniformed officer with sunglasses on his head and a bottle of water in his hand.

"Aurora Gold?" he asked me, and he, too, looked at my dress. "I've told the District Witch that I advised against this."

Had he, now? "Against what?" I asked. Another shout went up as I saw people with riot shields move between cars, looking for cover. It seemed safe to assume George was on the other side of the smoke.

"Civilian involvement." He nodded and glanced over, squinting. "You're welcome to stay here. We can work on getting you a megaphone."

Elders, he was serious. "How far are Retrievals?"

He glanced at the guy beside him. "Waiting on confirmation of that, Custodian."

That meant they hadn't assigned a team yet, which meant the answer wasn't *in the next half hour.* "Okay." I shook my hair out of my face. "Can I have two waters?"

He glanced down at the one in his hand, then at one of his peons. They scurried off. "Anything I ought to know?" he asked me.

"If I get blown up," I said, focusing more on the patterns of wrecked vehicles than the conversation, "let my boyfriend know, yeah? Just call it through to Maadai."

George hadn't cleared a clean battlefield. He was being purely responsive, which aligned with Aspen's assessment of him being in fight or flight. There also seemed to be a central area where he hadn't caused extensive damage. I heard the chopper landing off to the side and absently held down my skirt as the wind whipped around us.

He wasn't a killer, otherwise that helicopter would never have landed.

"What were you doing when he went off?" I asked.

"The officer first on the scene was doing a welfare check," the cop answered.

"Because?"

"I understand there was erratic behavior reported."

He wasn't sober. *Fucking hells.* "Okay." The peon returned and passed me two bottles of water, their cheeks flushed and eyes huge. "Cheers." I took them and set out, juggling it so I had my wand in my hand alongside the water bottle.

There was a ringing in my ears and my throat burned from the fumes, but there wasn't a fire response unit nearby.

The car park wasn't as big as I'd thought, it just seemed larger because he'd brought down a multi-story building adjacent to it. I hadn't seen the rubble through the smoke and chaos.

Calm and nonthreatening, I reminded myself, coughing around a deep breath. *Everything will be totally fine.* He was going away for life, no question. However long that was. There would be a serious body count from this. *Shoulders soft, steps unhurried. Totally normal.* Damned if Aspen was walking into this, even with lupetec.

"Ignis flammis!"

Elders, save me from latin spellcasters. *Through this dome none shall leave or come unless it is with me.* The fireball hit my ward and encased the area in flame. I waited for a minute while it roared around me. Fireballs were making a come-back, like all things retro. Maybe I should dust off my roller-skates.

As I will, so shall it be. I set off into the smoke, waving it away. "Hey, George!" I shouted, coughing. "It's just Rory. We were supposed to hang out last week, remember?"

There wasn't another fireball immediately. The ground was hot beneath my shoes and the fumes were going to seriously fuck up my lungs.

"Is there somewhere to get a coffee around here?" I called into the smoke and twisted metal ahead of me. "Maybe we can teach them how to make macchiato the way you like. Iced, because apparently, it's summer today."

I saw movement up ahead and my heart skipped a beat as George straightened from behind a twisted four-wheel-drive, wiping his hand over his eyes. "Rory?"

"Just me." I held out my arms to show him I was alone. "Aspen's coming, but she got held up. Traffic sucks."

"Facts," he said, unironically, looking at me in a daze. "Why are you here?" I wasn't in arm's reach and I could already smell the alcohol on him.

"I was genuinely in the area." We were close enough I could offer him the water now, and it wasn't just alcohol I could smell on him.

He was covered in soot and there was what I suspected was a bullet wound in his upper arm. One leg of his pants was soaked in blood. "You were here?" he repeated.

"Kind of." I waved a hand in the rough direction we might've come from. "My dad lives over there. I was having a barbie."

"Oh." He looked at what I was wearing. "That'd look better on Lilith. The color's no good for you."

"My dad said it was cute," I complained, tucking my water under my arm so I could open his. My hands were shaking. "He always burns the sausages. You know?"

"Yeah," he agreed, but I don't know if he did. "Why are you here?"

The confusion and lightness in his tone made my heart ache. "Just checking in, mate. Seeing how you're going."

He took the water. His hand was shaking, too.

"Doesn't look like you're having a good day," I said, taking out my own water. "Want to tell me about it?"

He held the bottle like he didn't know what it was. I wondered when he'd last drank anything without mixing it first. "Those pigs," he said, his mouth twisting. "Those *fucking pigs!*" He hurled the bottle of water at a nearby car and screamed in fury.

I sipped mine, standing beside him. We watched as the water bottle pissed itself all over the bitumen. Flames crackled nearby. I could hear the chopper lifting off, headed away. I hoped whoever they were carrying lived to have a story for future generations.

From here, I'd be able to ward him if needed.

"Want to go somewhere cooler with me?" I asked him, eventually. "You can tell me what the cops did this time."

"No." He laughed, whirling. "No, they're not going to let me go."

I kept my expression relaxed. They weren't. But I held up my hands. "Look, man, I don't know anything except it's hot here, and my throat hurts. I saw a café back that way that looked good though." I waved toward where I figured there were less civilians. "We could go, get a drink, you can catch me up."

His hands went to his disheveled golden curls. "They fucking killed Pix, Rory! They fucking *killed* her!"

I arranged my features into what I hoped was compassion. I had no idea who Pix was, or whether she was real. "I'm so sorry, George."

He screamed again, whirling. *"Ignis flammis!"*

The pile of cars on the other side of the carpark went up and I hoped like fuck they were empty. *Where's the line, Aspen?* I knew where it was as Retrievals. He'd crossed it long ago. But I wasn't Retrievals.

Bracing myself, I took a chance. "Is she here, Georgie?" I asked, quietly. "I'm a healer. I can try."

He turned back to me, his eyes huge and his pupils pinpricks. "You can heal?"

"Yeah." I lifted my skirt and showed off the scars left by the lycan who'd killed Brandon. "Learned the hard way," I lied.

He stared for a minute, swaying a little, then, "Yeah. Fucking, yes. Yes. Come on. Come *on.*"

I fell in beside him as he half ran, staggering along toward the untouched area in the core of the chaos.

Pix was real. And she was beyond my skills. I knelt beside her spindly form in her party outfit. One of her heels was missing.

There was a hole in the side of her head.

"You have to help her," George said, furiously. "I can have your license pulled if you don't!"

I reached out toward him. "Give me your jacket." He shrugged it off, his movements uncoordinated. "We need to get proper paramedics in here," I told him, tucking it over her. He hadn't killed her.

Who'd shot first?

"You said you'd help!"

"I said I'd try," I corrected, calmly. "I won't lie to you, Georgie. Will I?"

He was shaking. "No. No no *no.*"

"Look." I stood, hoping I hadn't fucked up a crime scene. "You didn't hurt her. I can't heal her. We need to get people in here who can help." I took a risk and offered my hand. "I'll stay with you, Georgie."

His eyes flickered over my hand and darted around the crumpled cars, avoiding the body of his friend. "This place is *fucked,*" he said, tears in the words. "I was told it'd be quick, but people talk shit. They just want me because I've got money. They think I'm weak."

I didn't try to follow what he meant. "You're not weak." Unfortunately.

"I'm not fucking *weak.*" He whirled again and spells swam in my head, but he just threw his head back and screamed, *"I'm not fucking weak, you fuckheads!"*

I put my hand on his shoulder. His designer shirt was clean where it'd been safe beneath his jacket. Rings of sweat formed under his arms in layers, telling the story of his last day or so. He'd partied hard before he got here. "Come on. I want to get Pix help." That meant cops. "We're going to figure it out together, okay?" That wasn't a lie, was it?

He looked like he might start casting. Instead, he looked at me again, hypnotized by the yellow flowers on my dress. "You're the mean one."

"Usually, yeah. Not many people are as good as Aspen, right?"

He smiled a bit. "She's single, isn't she?"

Happily. "She is. And she'll be here soon, too. So will Lilith. We aren't going to leave you unless we're forced to, okay?"

He snorted, but walked alongside me as if his feet were out of sync with time and space. "They all say that," he told me. "They always do, though. You bitches, you all lie."

Freud would've had a field day with George. "I try not to. Sometimes I have to, though. Like when people ask if I like their art."

He waved that away. "Bitches all lie."

"Coffee doesn't lie," I tried.

"Bitch, the drugs lie most of all." He flopped against a random steel frame where trollies waited patiently. "I'm *tired*."

"I know, mate." I could see movement up ahead, riot shields and weapons. "We're almost there. We'll hop in a van and go somewhere you can sleep it off."

He squinted at me. "Do I get my own cell?"

I supposed at least he knew what the process looked like. "Probably, but I'm not in charge."

"Get me my own cell," he said, yawning. "And a decent fucking blanket at least. Shit's still spinning, Rory."

"People pay a lot of money for that," I said, mildly, glancing at the blood on his leg. It wasn't fresh, though. He'd knelt in it at some point. Maybe it was Pix's. "Lean on me, mate."

He put his arm around me and put his face in my neck, laughing. "You smell *good*."

"Yeah, no." I pried his arm off again. "We'll try again when you can show me some respect, hey?"

He snorted and stumbled along beside me. "You'll have a buncha cats before I respect bitches."

"Ah, you're an oracle now, too, Georgie?" I asked, approaching the edge of the police line. "I bet you can predict what these guys are going to say." I glanced at Officer Shithouse and waved. "George's tired," I told him. "He'd like his own cell, if it can be arranged, and a decent blanket. I can help with the blanket?"

"You're a good witch," George told me, yawning. "Fuck, my head."

"Oh." I held out my hand. "Want me to look after your wand? So you don't smash it?"

"Yeah." He tried to put it in my palm. It ended up at my fingertips and he swayed into me. "And my phone. Fuck. Where's my fucking phone?" A cop was approaching cautiously. "Oi, where's my fucking phone, you pig?"

"I'll call it," I told George, tucking his wand under my arm. "They're probably going to cuff you. We've done this before, right?"

"You don't usually show up until after," he said, around another yawn. "Fuck. I'm going to fall asleep right here. Go on then, you fat cunt. Get me a nice bed." He offered them his wrists and turned to me. "You bring me a cold drink, won't you, Renny?"

I didn't correct my name. They snapped the cuffs on and I ached. There had been things I could've done that I hadn't, I was sure of it. But if I'd been helping George, maybe I wouldn't have been able to reach the Hurtfields. "Macchiato with caramel syrup," I confirmed. "Iced. I got you, mate."

He blinked. "How'd you remember that?"

It was so vile it was seared into my brain. "I care about you, George," I told him, pacing alongside as they took him toward an armored van. A cop in riot gear held a gag in his hand and I wanted to puke. I wondered if there was anyone to follow up about Pix. "I'll be here, okay? If I possibly can be, I will."

He didn't believe it. I could see it in his eyes. Maybe I didn't, either. We both went along with it for now. "Yeah, well. Maybe a nice juice or something, you know?" He twisted to talk over the top of one of Officer Shithouse's peons. "You know, Riley?"

"I know, Georgie. They're going to want to gag you, mate," I said, my lunch rolling around in my belly. It was a minor miracle they hadn't secured him already. "I'll make sure you've got a cool drink when you get there."

"Fucking pigs," he muttered, spat at the cop and laughed.

I swallowed the tears as the ball was shoved, hard, into his mouth. He made a noise of pain. "Hey," I said, my fury hard and hot. "I need your badge number, now."

They closed ranks.

I lifted my phone, and started recording.

George stumbled toward the van. I couldn't see, from my angle, if he was shoved or if he fell. I closed the distance between me and the arsehole cop who might've cost the shitstain wizard a tooth, recording his badge number as he stood in silence.

They were already in motion, clearing a path through the abandoned, destroyed, or banked-up vehicles. They didn't care. We all knew how this would play out.

CHAPTER 23

By the time we got out of the police station, it was late, and I was grieved-out. I declined the offer of dinner at Aspen's, huddled down in Taig's jacket as we headed home.

"Can ursathropes be Autistic?" he asked me, frowning, having overheard the whole debrief that Lilith and Aspen had given me.

"We've got one specialist who says they can." I propped my foot on the dash and stretched out my neck, exhausted. "We need a speechie and a pediatrician to have an official diagnosis since she's a child, but the recommendations are relevant regardless."

"There you go." He eased into a carpark near my place. "I assume the recommendations are similar for a human?"

"They are. Because of course we've done no research, yet." I hoped it'd help Jessica anyway. Apparently Benson thought the whole thing was bullshit, and all the recommendations were common sense. Aspen had paraphrased that, but the point held. I was tempted to tell Taig to forget the information he'd overheard, but didn't want to insult him. Instead, I said, "I want, like, a week of chill."

"I'd like the rest of our lives to be chill," he told me, as we climbed out. "If we're stating preferences."

"I choose achievable goals."

He sent me a sideways look. "You reckon you can go a week being chill?"

"Yes, I do." I arrogantly flipped my hair, then struggled not to cough as the crap in my lungs shifted.

He watched me as we walked into my building, hand hovering somewhere in the vicinity of my back as if he was ready to catch me. "You should've let them treat you for smoke inhalation."

I should probably let them treat me for a lot of things. "I wanted to get home." It was weird to have him step up to my door with my key in his hand. Weirder still the way he kept me close and watched me cautiously whilst also getting the key in the lock.

"Wish granted." He opened the door. "I'm going to order in, and I'm thinking Thai."

I wasn't thinking at all, but as he followed me in and locked the door behind us, I felt exhaustion wash over me. "I'm having cereal and going to bed." And the cereal was purely so he didn't worry.

He nodded, already working away on his phone. "Go wash off the smoke. I'll be there in a tic."

I knew he was going to order me food, but if it made him feel better, I wasn't going to argue. We were both wrecked, and celebrating survival by supporting a local business seemed like a solid option, really. What's more, I could do it in my pajamas. Really, why bother complaining?

"Dinner's ten minutes off," he told me, when I emerged smelling marginally better. "I'm going to throw a load of washing on. Did you want to soak that dress?"

I waved a hand at it. "I'll try." It was probably toast, but I liked it. It was cheerful. I wasn't, right now, but that made it even more appealking. "Did you get an update from Delyan?"

He nodded. "Everything's under control. Who knew the world would keep turning without us."

I followed him into the laundry, squeezing in behind him deliberately so I could press myself against his back. I flopped into his strength while I slam-dunked my dress in the empty bucket I used at least monthly to soak clothes. My arm went around his waist and he made a pleased noise in the back of his throat as I leant a bit further around him to my jar of Oma's laundry soak, tossing some in. To one side of us, the water was rushing into the machine. The sound of it changed as he turned the tap on in front of us, filling the bucket. I cuddled into him. Just doing normal couple things was pretty fucking cool.

Taig took my hand with the last lingering bits of Oma's mix and held it under the cold water, rinsing it off. He slowly ran his fingers over mine, exploring the valleys and mountains, the spaces in between. Draped over his back, I enjoyed the sensation of his warm hand against mine beneath the water, the strange, feather-light touches knotting up my belly.

Better to block out the mess of my laundry, I closed my eyes. I felt every flex and stretch of his muscles as he turned off the water running into the bucket and took my hand, sandwiching it between both of his gently. The muscles in his back shifted as he lifted it to his lips and put the tip of my index finger into his mouth.

The sensation was strange and not in an erotic way. Or maybe it was the smell of Oma's laundry mix and the smoke that lingered in my dress. "Dinner won't be far," I said. "Should I cook some rice?"

He lowered my hand and tried to turn his head, but couldn't actually see me. "That's okay. I ordered it all tonight. It's been a long one."

He wasn't wrong. I peeled away and led us out of the laundry, going Eclipse-hunting. When the food arrived, Taig got the door and accepted the order while I worked through her usual nap places. I found her in the open, curled up in the middle of his bag, her feet stretched out in the cozy little bed she'd made for herself from his work clothes.

Before I could react he came up behind me, offering me a plastic tub of food. "She's pretty damned cute, isn't she?" he said, apparently not angry at her choice of bedding. He waited until I opened the container to pass me a fork. "I hope that shirt survives. It was comfy.

Hard to find shirts that are the right length in the arm and size in the neck."

It wasn't one of the horrible navy blue ones that made his eyes look bland as white bread, either. "I should rescue it and hang it up."

"Probably," he agreed. "But look at the baby."

She slept on, unconcerned.

"You've seen her up and about, right?" I asked. "Since we got home?"

"Fed her and played with her while you showered," he assured me. "She's getting good at fetch."

She wasn't, but if he slept better at night thinking it, I wasn't going to fight it. I followed him back to the kitchen where he'd made me what I suspected was a decaf.

My phone lit up and I saw it had a number of notifications. I lifted it off the cradle and flicked off the work emails, opening Aspen's texts.

A bunch of screenshots of Melbourne apartments with commentary about Nic's price range and specifications filled the screen.

"Your dad?" Taig asked, glancing at it and obviously making out real estate options.

I shook my head. "Aspen. Or Nic." While I ate, I scrolled back up to where the flurry of messages had started, reading the initial explanation. "Looks like they're thinking of buying together."

"They an item?" he asked, frowning. "That isn't what I got."

I shook my head because my mouth was full. "Nic was Brandon's bestie. He grew up in Aspen's house."

"Ah." Taig let out a breath. "Yeah." He stirred his curry absently. "He didn't end up in the system?"

"No." We wouldn't have let that happen, but Nic'd had a decent uncle who'd stepped in. "He wasn't close with our local coven, because the old guard don't just forgive and forget."

"Sins of the fathers bit?" Taig asked me.

"Yeah." I didn't need to mention Nic's sins weren't entirely the by-association type. Being in the grip of the number one most dangerous magick hadn't increased his popularity either. "We were good, though.

And yeah, he and Aspen, that's strictly platonic. Same as Brandon and I." And saying that didn't choke me up at all. "He's going to be sad when she pulls more women than he does." He wouldn't be, but he'd joke about it, even if it wasn't true.

"Quality over quantity?" Taig suggested, frowning. "Learn from the master? I don't know how to respond to that one." He nudged a glass of water I hadn't seen toward me. "Why's Nic buying an apartment with Aspen? Better equity to be had in the suburbs that're easy travel distance, I would've thought."

"I am no one's financial advisor," I said wryly, sidestepping the question. "I just get sent pictures of rat-infested hell holes and asked to identify the lesser evil."

"Play to your strengths, love," he said, amused, muffling a yawn. "How's Lilith? She was looking a bit pale."

She hadn't said much this afternoon, but she'd been there. "No she wasn't." He'd never see it through her make-up illusion. "She's hit a rough patch. She'll be okay, though. She'll make it through."

He nodded slowly. "You will, too. You're survivors, you two."

That word still made me feel like I was wearing someone else's skin. "I never doubted I'd make it through," I told him, putting my fork down. "It's how I get from here to there that makes me anxious as fuck." I put the lid back on my food and put it away.

He didn't follow as I got ready for bed, and I was glad for the space. The patronizing wellbeing bullshit got really hard to swallow sometimes. Especially when it was already in my fucking head. Could someone toxic positivity themselves?

I probably didn't have enough positivity to hit toxic levels, really. Scowling at my cupboard, I pulled out the outfits Ryan had bought me that had been shuffled to the end. I'd got by without them for this long. My skin crawled when I touched them. Now I needed the cupboard space.

Taig didn't comment on the clothes on the bed when he came in, minty fresh and looking tired. "Hang your shit there," I told him, waving at the spot I'd made. "Eclipse doesn't bother that stuff. There isn't as much room as it looks, but you should fit two or three changes." I scooped up the offending clothes and took them out to the kitchen, bagging them up to donate and tying the knot on that bag tight.

I could smell the lingering lemongrass and spice from our dinner, but in my head all I had was cheap plastic and commercial cleaning products. I didn't even know why.

CHAPTER 24

It was muggy and hot when I left for work in the morning. By midday, I was freezing. We hustled out of the weather into the entry of the short-term accommodation Lilith had found the Hurtfields yesterday. I'd been eating burned sausages with Dad at the time.

When the door opened to show Benson's towering form, and with my dad's words in my head, I wondered if I smelled like a faerie. The ursathrope looked between us, huddled deep in our jackets, our hands buried in our pockets. Without a hint of either compassion or annoyance, he stepped back, letting us in.

"I called. About the landscaping job."

As greetings went, it was pretty fucking awesome. "The apprenticeship?" I asked, before the others could react. "That's great!" I offered my hand for a high five, but he just stared at me. Refusing to let him get away with pretending not to know the social norm, I said, "You lift your hand and we clap in the air."

Liam scrambled away from the television. "Like this!" he crowed, and offered his hand to Lilith, who didn't leave the poor little guy hanging.

"Where were you?" he asked, hands by his sides, continuing to ignore my offer.

"Had to deal with something. It's sorted now." I wiggled my fingers. "Liam even showed you how."

He walked away and I let my hand drop, my mind spinning. Had I gone too hard, or was this punishment for not being here yesterday? *Interesting.*

"You folks have made good progress on that puzzle," Lilith said to Jessica and Liam. It was a three-dimensional monstrosity I couldn't yet recognize.

"Have you heard anything about government payments?" Aspen asked Benson, sitting at the table where his paperwork sat in four regimented stacks.

"I don't believe so."

"I can suss out your emails while I'm here," Aspen offered.

Benson glanced at me, his expression unreadable, and just sat there silently.

Yeah, I'd pissed him off.

"Let's walk," I said, standing. "We'll go grab something to make for dinner."

There was leeway in the policy ratios in situations like this. Lilith still looked up from the puzzle she was working on, her attention honing in on us.

But Benson was standing, too. He towered over me for a moment, and I was taken back to the night he'd stood in my doorway at three am, trying to scare me off.

I hid the rush of compassion by leading us out the door, while I looked up directions to the nearest grocery store. "I make a pretty decent lasagna," I told him. "I'm not territorial when it comes to recipes, either. Let's do that." It'd keep him busy for a while, too.

His legs were longer than mine, but he slowed his pace to match me after a moment. Was I supposed to wait him out? Reassure him? I should've got some guidance from Aspen, but she'd stayed with Lilith.

The smoke I'd eaten yesterday made my throat burn, and I glanced up at Benson's dark expression. "I had to sort out some personal stuff," I said, quietly. "I'm sorry I wasn't here."

"They say Jessica's brain works wrong."

I kept my face in neutral lines. "Pretty sure no one said that."

"I've watched the videos," he told me, flatly. "I know what it means. You all dance around it, but that's what those papers mean."

I blew out a breath. I was definitely the worst witch to have this conversation with. "There are a lot of videos that say a lot of things. I think Jessica is awesome. I think you do, too." He frowned, as if he'd never even considered it. "These processes, they aren't all fair, and they aren't all accurate. We're working on it, but what it says is 'this is how Jessica learns' and 'this is how Jessica thinks'. It isn't lesser. It comes with a set of strengths and weaknesses." I could hear Aspen's voice in my head correcting the word weaknesses to *barriers. Sorry Aspen. Too late.* "The rest is just there for people who like, or need, bullshit." I stuffed my hands in my pockets, coming to a halt while we waited for the pedestrian light. "And, look, some people find that info is actually comforting. It tells them *why*. It helps make sense of things. You don't, and that's okay too."

He let out an annoyed rumble, and his scowl deepened, but when he pressed the pedestrian crossing button one extra time, for good measure, his movement was gentle. "Your human schools are useless."

Agreed. "Our world is different. The skills you need are different. It isn't without flaws, but I bet yours weren't, either."

He flexed one hand. The muscle in his forearm bulged. From the corner of my eye, I saw Benson attracting the gaze of a random passer-by, who stopped at stared. Benson either didn't notice or didn't care. "I can't write. Aspen wants me to learn."

I knew, from his forms, his literacy was basic. That he could read some, but not write, except with us clearly modeling the shapes of the letters. It was a pretty standard issue with folks from Overworld, and we had some literacy courses, but adult learning wasn't easy. "It'll be good if Jessica and Liam never face that issue."

The lights sounded and we set off. I strode along in the lee of his big body, protected from the worst of the biting wind as we made our way through the other pedestrians, seeking the far side of the road. The grocery store we were aiming for was ahead, advertisements on the glass promising we'd save money.

Benson bumped into me, jostling me to one side. I caught myself, looking up quickly.

His response to my surprise was a scowl. One of Benson's big fingers with a sprinkling ofg ruddy hairs was jabbed aggressively toward the puddle I'd been about to step in.

Elders, the man was impossible not to like. "Thanks."

"You should've been watching," he said, irritated.

"I was. I just wasn't watching where my feet went."

He grunted. I dragged him around the store, grabbing required ingredients, and heard nothing except those low rumbles in his chest by way of communication until we were outside again.

"So, what's up?" I asked him. "You worried about Jessica?"

He snorted. "No."

"New job?"

"I called. I haven't got it."

I couldn't argue with that. "So?"

"They haven't found them."

"Yet." He didn't rumble at me. The lack of aggression made me study the way he was staring into the distance, his mouth a thin line. "I haven't forgotten, Benson. And I haven't decided working with you is too hard."

"Yet."

"I hope you're patient, mate," I said lazily. "You'll be waiting for quite some time if that's what you're hoping for." Unless he forced my hand, of course, the way Beo had.

I wondered, as I walked alongside the big bear of a man, how Beo was doing. I wondered how I could've done things differently, or whether it was kinder for both of us, the way it'd all gone. There had been no future in dating a client. Just the thought of it made my skin crawl, now. I could be friends, the way I was with Zane, but that was my limit. That would've been true even if Taig wasn't already keeping my bed warm.

How many warning signs had I missed, with Beo? How well had he hidden the complexity of his grief and the depth of his trauma? I blew out a breath, and wondered if I hadn't been able to see the forest for my own trees, whether I was better at woodcraft now, or whether both of those might be true.

If Beo was on my list, now, I would've been able to do more. For him, for his pack. For starters, I would've insisted he wasn't paid cash in hand. I hadn't even known that was going on until Zane took over running the classes. Permanent part-time with sick days and superannuation was a lot better than under the table.

Beside me, Benson slowly scanned our surroundings. I wondered if Beo would've wanted to do an apprenticeship in landscaping. I bet a few of the pack would've.

I hoped they had a caretaker who knew what they were doing, now.

Benson and I cooked while Aspen and Lilith did some drawing games that were apparently useful for schoolwork because of fine motor skills or some shit. I had the better end of that bargain. Their laughter was *intense*.

By the time we left, the temperature had dipped even further and I was exhausted. "You busy tonight?" Lilith asked me.

"Nope. Got a plan?"

She shrugged. "Kinda feel like chilling on the couch, spending some time on our farm."

"Yes, please and thank you." I hadn't been to her place in ages. With Vince there too, space was at a premium. "Want me to bring anything?"

"My setup is actually all unplugged because we got a different console," she admitted. "Maybe I should just bring it over and leave it at yours for a while. I only ever play it with you anyway nowadays."

Suspicion crept through me at that nonchalant offer. "That sounds amazing. Then you can get Eclipse cuddles *and* make a wine empire."

"Exactly." She tossed her hair over her shoulder. "It'll be nice to talk about something that isn't work for two minutes."

"I need to go shopping, too," I said. "Next time you're bored, maybe you can help encourage me to, you know, actually do the thing."

She looked me up and down. "You're looking better. Clothes still not fitting?"

"Clothes are mostly fitting," I disagreed, irritated. "I've just sacrificed a lot of my wardrobe to the greater good. Blood can come out, but burn marks?"

A smile tugged at her mouth. "Sure you want to take *me*?"

That sounded like a threat, but I liked that smile. "Witch, I am equal to anything you can throw at me."

"That was definitely a challenge," Aspen told Lilith, with a grin. "You're looking at apartments with us this weekend, Roars. We've got an inspection on Saturday at twelve thirty that we're excited about, and there's an open on Sunday Nic is stoked to see, but I think it's butt-ugly."

I didn't recall agreeing to that, but I probably had. "Fuck," I muttered, then glanced at Lilith pleadingly.

She shrugged. "I will judge them by their indoor plants. I'm no help."

"See that's what I'm saying," Aspen agreed. "Plants make it come to life. Nic's like 'no, it brings moisture in' and 'they make cats sick'."

"They can do both of those," Lilith admitted. "How many cats does he have?"

"Zero!" Aspen said, throwing her hands up. "And I have *rabbits,* so he *can't* have a cat!"

I tried to hide my smile. Lilith saw it, though, and the laughter in her eyes made me feel lighter than I had in days.

CHAPTER 25

$\mathcal{N}$estled deep in an office building, my psychologist's waiting room smelled like vanilla and other people's breath. It was always mildly unsettling. I didn't scroll as I sat there, listening to the chill waiting room music piping from the portable speaker. *I'm not jumpy.* When she appeared in the doorway, summoning me for my session with a smile, I braced myself.

It started the way it usually did, with a very brief rundown of shit happening in my life. The whole time, I could feel the press of my Retrievals top against my forearms. *Wine coating my tongue. The warm synthetic tabletop peeling away from my cheek.*

"Thinking of Brandon, now. Remember that moment you realized one of you would die. The way the sun felt on your skin, and the quiet of the bush after the flock of birds faded out."

I shook my head, braced. "Yeah, so, I've been noticing something else keeps popping into my brain. Something that happened recently." The words, miraculously, didn't get stuck. "A few somethings."

She picked up her stylus. The chunky knit jumper she wore dragged worryingly close to her open bottle of water. I didn't move as it wobbled, then settled, all without her being aware. "What are you noticing?" she asked me.

In my chest, my heart beat faster. *I'm not just jumpy.* "My shirt sleeves, rolled up. My wallet is missing. There's a knock at my door. Plastic table, stuck to my cheek. I can taste wine. My head aches. Footsteps, down the hall. They're different memories."

She nodded, busily writing them. "Which one is coming up now, do you think?"

"Shirt sleeves. Rolled up to my forearms." And for some reason, *that* was the phrase that stuck in my throat.

"Okay." She made a few more notes. "Distress level?"

"Five." I hated numbers.

She nodded. "Notice the feeling of your shirt sleeves, rolled up to your forearms."

I swallowed. In my hands, the tappers started to buzz. For once, it was okay, to just sit with that image and let it fade out. And in its place was the inhuman wailing Ryan had let out when Taig had shot him with anti-magic, echoing in my head. But it didn't feel like it was right on top of me.

The tappers stopped. I braced. "What are you noticing?" she asked.

Well, Jenna, my partner was a witch-hunter. He injected my boss with a carefully controlled substance called anti-magic that split the magic from the cells in Ryan's body, causing mind-ending agony. And to make sure he died, he blew his skull wide open.

Instead, I said, "Screaming."

"Notice that," she said, quietly, making some more notes.

I drew in a deep breath, let that noise reverberate in my head, and reclaimed my brain.

"YOU DON'T HAVE to come with us," Aspen assured me as we stood side by side, waiting for Lilith to join us after a meeting she'd managed for us. "You'll be wrecked tomorrow afternoon."

She didn't say why, but she didn't have to. I'd told her I was taking psych days off. I didn't have to explain *why.* It wasn't exactly rocket science.

I had more money than I did mental health, so I figured that time off was an investment in my healing.

"My appointment is in the morning," I told her, rather than bullshit my way out of it. "I want to be there when we see George. They'll transfer him from our load soon." I'd made promises to the guy. The SuperSec team would take over in a week or so, but it meant something to me. It might mean something to him, too.

Aspen nodded, tucking her phone into her pocket. "Well, if you change your mind, that's cool."

I didn't glance up from the email I was skimming. "Okay."

"I didn't tell you I was proud of you." I definitely didn't look up after that. "That's kind of the first time you've talked someone down without blowing them up first, isn't it?"

I swallowed away the tears in my throat, thinking of all the things I'd done wrong, all the things I needed to improve on. "Depends on your definition." I marked the email as unread so I'd remember to deal with it later and went on to the next thing. "It's no big deal."

She made a noise of agreement that was thick with insincerity. "Okay, Sunshine. Well, I'm proud of you anyway. You do good work."

"I blow things up pretty good," I agreed, because it was easier. "You seen the update about Damien?"

"Yeah, came through while you and Lilith were getting Jessica's school uniform this morning."

That wasn't going to work as a distraction, then. "She's worried about school."

"New schools are scary, especially when you aren't the same species as your classmates." Aspen stretched, yawning. "New kickboxing class is okay."

"Cute instructor?"

"Nah. He's a meathead." She jerked her chin toward the tram. "Here's our missing piece." Lilith stepped into sight, her batwing shirt fluttering in the breeze. "She at yours again last night?"

I nodded. Taig had stayed away while Lilith hung out, and I was glad. "No news." She wasn't talkative, but she was there. She must've been getting something out of coming.

"Did you see the update about Damien?" she asked, stopping beside us.

"I know!" Aspen agreed. "How amazing is it? He worked so hard for that score."

"Do you remember what uni he applied for?" she asked, falling in beside us. "I can't remember what his first preference was anymore."

Aspen shook her head. I wasn't even sure what course he'd been chasing. I'd spent more time with his mum, who was only slightly older than me and struggled to leave the house. The problem with witchcraft was the lack of work from home options.

"Pretty sure he's partying in Torquay with his mates next week," Lilith said. "He asked if we were going to come and check on him."

"What'd you say?" Aspen asked, laughter in her voice.

"Maybe."

I grinned at the idea. There would be a lot of very seedy teenagers in that group. "It's a big step," Aspen said, her smile softening. "He's doing well. What's our game plan here?"

We stopped out the front of the West Melbourne coven. "Officially?" Lilith asked her.

Aspen snorted. "I was at the briefing. I know the *official* line. What's our *actual* line?"

They both looked at me, and I scowled. "You want me to rip his balls off?" I asked.

"Pretty sure that was what Maadai inferred," Aspen agreed, with false humility. "I'm the nice one."

I rolled my eyes. "Shows what they know. All right." I put my phone away and fluffed my hair. "It's too hot to touch his balls. They're probably sweaty as fuck. Let's go for the throat."

"The less time I spend picturing this wizard's balls, the happier I'll be," Lilith agreed. "Allow me." She swept forward and shoved the door open. It hit the brickwork behind it with a crash.

Aspen swallowed a laugh, painting a severely neutral expression on her face as she fell in behind Lilith.

A witch I vaguely recognized stared at us from a plant-filled breakroom, her knitting drooping in her hands. Lilith didn't pause to reassure the locals, storming up to Samuel's office. He was halfway to his door when we walked in.

"Hey, Brown," I said, as Aspen firmly shut the door behind us. "We were contacted regarding the recommendation to remove Onyx's niece from his care and place her in the care of a magi family. Know anything about it?'

His eyes fluttered. His office smelled like dust and over brewed coffee, but something else, something darker, coiled up into my brain. "We're doing the best we can for all of our clients. If you need further information about Onyx's behavior—"

"We're taking the lycanthropes from your lists onto ours as a short-term protective measure," I said, cutting in over top of him. "Given the seriousness of your report, the District High Witch felt that was best. Given how many lycanthropes your district is no longer servicing, and the average age of your remaining clients, the High Witch has decided to review your coven's performance."

"Of course," he said, frowning at us. "We do annual performance reviews, as is standard."

The door downstairs opened and I smiled. "We need to review deeper than that, as there have been some serious allegations. I.C.T is here to transport work devices. H.R. is waiting to speak to you."

He looked at us like he'd finally woken up, color flaring in his cheeks. "What? What's going on?" His chest swelled with indignation. "You can't just seize all our devices! They're required for—"

"You'll get new ones," I said, dismissively. "Come on, Brown. No one keeps H.R. waiting."

"This is deeply unprofessional and entirely uncalled for, and I expected no less from—"

"Faeries," I said, lazily, and just like that, his expression went blank and he stood there, relaxed.

"Faeries?" he asked me. "Not an issue here."

"Mm-hmm." I would've felt bad for him, too, if he hadn't been working to make the lycanthropes as vulnerable as he could. "No faeries to be seen. Let's tell H.R. about it, hey?"

He nodded firmly. "And about how terrible the vampires are."

The vampires who'd been driven out already. I didn't respond, though, because Vince was down the bottom of the stairs, pushing his glasses up his nose. "Hello, Wizard Brown," he said brightly, offering a shiny new phone to the man. "Here's your new work phone. It's already got everything you need on it. I'll need your old one."

The wizard's color flared. He opened his mouth. "Faeries," I said.

His expression softened. "Faeries?" He looked down at the phone. "Not an issue here." He handed over the phone.

Was I immune to that?

Could I *do* that?

I side-stepped both thoughts, guiding him out of the coven and toward the car park. We couldn't physically drive him, but we could make sure he wasn't able to get in until the devices had been taken.

It was a damned shame Davies had started the process of changing up the District Wizards, but hadn't finished it. The whole staff situation had been locked down while Maadai stepped into his role. They'd managed to make it so the wizards in leadership were impossible to remove for twelve months.

But you couldn't be a District Wizard from SuperSec.

We waved Brown off and a moment later a police van pulled up. "Afternoon," I called, feeling pleased with how well that had all worked.

"Jesus, that timing," Aspen breathed. "That was *close*. Why are the cops so early?"

I didn't bother to respond. "There's a few witches we'll need to watch," Lilith agreed behind me, as I stepped forward, all smiles, to greet the cops. "I'm going to float."

I nodded to her as I waved them in. "How's your day been?" I asked.

"Oh, can't complain," said the uniformed woman at the front, setting down a bag. She looked around the coven we'd basically seized control of. "Thanks for your help with this."

"Our pleasure," I said, with feeling. "You okay to start from the top? We just need to talk to a few other coven members, smooth your way." *With a bulldozer, if needed.*

CHAPTER 26

In the end, a bulldozer wasn't needed to make things happen. Unplugging everyone took time, and explanations, and reassurances. It was four before we were done. By the time we stepped out into the street I was glad to be away from all the people breathing in one space.

Aspen lifted her hand in greeting. "You didn't tell us your sauce was working this," Aspen told me, with a nudge. "He's looking a bit cute today."

I followed her gaze and found Taig in a three piece with his tie loosened, the top button undone. In his hand was a to-go cardboard tray with a bunch of little cups that definitely didn't look like coffee.

"He had a court appearance." One that'd had him fighting nightmares the last two times he'd stayed over. He had sunglasses on, so I couldn't see if the shadows under his eyes had grown last night. He'd stayed at his. Lilith and I had an amazing farm, though.

"The Montgomery case," Lilith agreed, quietly. "It was a bad one." She shot me a quick, searching look.

I avoided it, stepping forward and to kiss. "Nice tie," I said, giving it a gentle tug. "I wore it better."

"I recall," he murmured, and a shiver went up my spine as he turned his smile on Aspen and Lilith. "I hope you're feeling like gelato, because I felt like sharing."

"This is mine," Lilith announced, plucking the golden pile with caramel sauce in it. "It told me so."

"Oh, you didn't have to," Aspen said at the same time.

"What'd you get her?" I asked him, jerking my chin at Aspen. He knew Lilith's preferences from my freezer. On cue, Lilith sighed happily, before scooping up an impressive amount of iced confection given the size limitations on the spoon that came with the cup.

"You can choose," he told Aspen. "There's lemon, coffee, and French vanilla."

"That's so hard," she said, but she was already reaching for the vanilla. "I couldn't take Rory's coffee."

"It won't disappoint," Taig promised me, laughter in his eyes.

I could tell, from the smug little smile, that he'd predicted her choice. I wasn't sure if I should be annoyed or charmed, but charmed was easier. "Trust you to choose the bitter option," I said, mostly to make small talk, as I accepted the little cup.

"With just the right amount of sweetness," he informed me, tucking the now-empty cardboard under his arm. "How's yours?"

I licked some of the melting gelato and he was right, it was damned good. He was watching me, waiting. I scooped some up and offered it. He accepted it without hesitation. "Mm. See?" he asked, which was a very polite 'I told you so'. I nodded in agreement, giving credit where it was due, and he wandered along with us for a few steps. "How'd you go? I hear you just took a whole coven's devices without a warrant or any pushback."

"Oh, there was pushback," Lilith said. "We just push harder."

"Thought that might be the way it happened," Taig said, like he was commenting on the weather. "You three headed back to HQ? Want a lift?"

"I'm actually thinking of finishing the rest off at home," Lilith said. "I've got a bit of a headache coming. Could do with a sleep before I try to put words together."

And Vince wasn't there. I didn't say that, but it seemed like an unusual coincidence. "Stop by Dierdre's apothecary," I suggested. "She'll have something for what ails you."

"She always does. Thanks, Taig." She waved to us, heading off.

"She okay?" Taig asked us, quietly.

"Yeah," I said, but it still made me feel sad. "Did you see Vince, Aspen? It was weird."

Aspen raised her eyebrows. "I'll catch a lift. And yeah, it was weird. They said hello, but like, awkwardly? Like they didn't know each other."

"Could be a policy thing?" he asked, glancing between us. "You're not allowed to date coworkers, are you?"

"Sure we are," Aspen told him, flicking her hand. "Controlling who people can and can't sleep with is ineffective and also cultish."

I leant into him as we wandered back toward the coven, bumping our shoulders together on purpose.

He nudged me back, gently. "Got much to finish up? I can hang out, or go grab groceries."

"I can finish it up," Aspen told me. "Consider it payment for good vanilla ice cream."

"Good guess, by the way," I told him. "But no, I'm not going to ditch you. Not yet. Four weeks, and I'm taking off. You can pay him back then."

"Where're you two going?" she asked us, as we reached Taig's car.

"Surprise," he said, and we stopped speaking as we climbed in. Aspen took the back seat without checking in and I didn't fight her for it.

It was going to be somewhere remote, I'd figured that much out. I anticipated a beach or mountain somewhere. I doubted we'd be flying, but wouldn't be surprised if we camped. As long as there was somewhere to shower and I could have coffee, that was fine. I could deal with sleeping in a swag if I had coffee.

"How's the house hunting going?" Taig asked, glancing at Aspen in the rear view. "Got a feel for what you want yet, how it sits in the market?"

"Getting there," she said, cheerfully. "We've got pre-approval, so that's exciting."

I didn't block my ears when she started talking about locations and price ranges. I was obviously her best friend, because no one else would've been as patient.

"He's been working Retrievals for years, right?" Taig asked us, when there was a gap in the conversation. "Why the sudden change of career?"

"Why not?" Aspen laughed.

Taig shot me a quick look. He knew it didn't work that way. "He'll probably talk about it one day," I said, with a shrug, not even needing to lie.

"Talk about what?" Aspen asked, leaning forward. "Do you know? He didn't tell you, did he?"

From the hunger in her tone I figured Nic hadn't spilled the tea. I knew Aspen, and she smelled blood.

She definitely wasn't the nice one.

"He Read something big," I told her, honestly. "At my place the other day."

"To do with you?" she asked, halfway in the front, now. "You two are long done, aren't you?"

I rolled my eyes. "Elders, Aspen, it has nothing to do with me, okay? It's probably location based."

"Huh." She was frowning. "He's a short-term Oracle though. How many jobs you reckon he could get?"

"Legally?" Taig asked. "Law enforcement, government level security, or teaching."

She crinkled her nose. "Really? You telling me we don't need Oracle surgeons, or…"

"I'm telling you the law, nothing more or less." He shifted a little. "Speaking of the law, mind sitting back a little, sweetheart?"

Aspen silently did as he'd asked. I shot him a quick look, but he didn't appear to notice the sudden silence. Pet-names for my friends probably needed to be worked up to, and I didn't know how Aspen would take that particular one. If it'd been 'baby', Taig would probably already be dead on the side of the road.

"Here we go. I'll drop you two off and go grab some groceries, I think. Steak and potatoes okay?"

I brightened at the thought. "I'll help cook that."

He nodded. "I'll grab enough for Lilith, if she wants to hang out." He pressed a kiss to my lips and reached over, opening my door.

I took the hint and scooted out back into the muggy air. Aspen grabbed my arm with both hands, her eyes wide. "That man needs to be a voice actor."

I laughed at the color in her cheeks. "I was worried you were going to murder him for that."

"I might need to," she said, cringing. "I don't need to have these thoughts, you know? Pretty sure that's some sort of witch-version of a sin."

Rather than burst her bubble and tell her that Taig referred to Mia as 'sweetheart', I just led her upstairs. "It's fine. I was shocked when I found out Lilith is immune."

"Fuck, I'm *barely* even into men." She fanned herself. "That should be illegal."

"Want me to talk to the cops?" She punched me in the arm and I laughed at her, but didn't continue teasing. "How's your new kick-boxing class? Getting on with the meathead coach?"

With a habitual flick she chased the blonde hair out of her face. "Class is good. The woman I thought was cute isn't my vibe."

Aspen's vibe was yet to be definitively identified, but that was fine. "Well, if the class is good, that's what you're paying for, I suppose."

"Yeah. How was your sword thingo?"

I flexed my hands. "I've got forearm muscles I haven't needed since I could buy my own vibrators."

She snorted and we curtailed conversation as we went into Maadai's office. She was on the phone, pinching the bridge of her nose. When she saw us, she mouthed *thank you* and then held up a hand, asking for five minutes.

We let ourselves out and back into our office where I did my best to smash out the critical parts of today's admin. Whatever Maadai was up to must've been more complex than anticipated, because she stuck her head in our door after fifteen minutes, phone beside her ear, and said, "You did fantastic, thank you. Are you okay?" I gave her a thumbs up and Aspen nodded. She waved and tapped her phone on the way out. "Yes, I'm here, and I'm listening, but what you're saying still isn't making sense."

Aspen let out a low whistle. "They're fucked."

Shepherd stuck his head in the door. "Who's fucked?"

"Whoever Maadai is reaming."

"That'd be the Bureau," he said, wandering in. "They want an anti-fae task force…and to cover up what's happened with Brown."

I groaned. Nothing good ever came of that kind of shenanigans. "Surely, anti-hypnosis charms would be cheaper?" I asked him.

"Ah, but what price do you put on their *egos?*" Shep asked me, grinning. "Where's Lilith at?"

"Remote," Aspen said, easily. "Where's Fritz?"

Shep waved a hand over his shoulder. "Video call. Got an incoming banshee who sounds like she's going to be a real one. Arthur says hi, Roars, and to tell you Janet's got her pottery class up and running if you've got any clients who'd benefit from it."

"Amazing." I made a quick note of it in our shared resources document, under *therapeutic arts*. "She'll be so good."

"He's pretty excited about the program," Shep agreed, his gaze going back down the hallway. "Hey O'Malley, what's up?"

I saw Taig appear on the other side of the hall, positioned over from the doorway. "The usual. I hear you folks have been busy."

I was closing down my work as they chatted. "We're good," Aspen told me, when I went to explain that to her. "I've got two phone calls to make that'll keep until tomorrow. We'll have a lot of time to catch up while we go to and from George. Which you don't have to do."

It was on the tip of my tongue to dismiss her worries again when I saw Taig, standing in the doorway across from Shep. I was on the way out and then I wasn't. *Ryan, smiling at me.* My heart sped up, my breath catching in my throat.

He was dead.

I crossed the room in two strides, grabbed Taig's hand and plastered a smile on my face, waving. Shepherd's lips moved, but Ryan's voice came out. *"I know things are difficult, Aurora."*

It wasn't real and I *knew* it wasn't real, but the flickers of memory were *right there.* I could still remember the way Taig had held those files and lured me back to him. The pizza that we'd shared. The flat soft drink he'd given me.

"Just breathe," he murmured, as the elevator chimed. "My car's just over the road. We'll be there soon."

The world tilted, but it was just the dipping elevator. *Plastic against my cheek. The press of crisply rolled up sleeves against my forearms.* "Remember that day? Cassius Gryffin's file. You brought it."

"I remember." He lifted my hand to his mouth. "Can you make it to the car, love?"

"Yeah." I could make it anywhere. I blew air out hard and drummed my hands against my thighs. It wasn't that day anymore. It never would be again. This was the day I'd got Jessica's uniform, and written her name inside of her sun hat because her dad couldn't, yet. I'd woken up hungover from ice-cream, with aching thumbs gaming all night, because that's how bad arse witches without a death wish partied. I'd tried to eat breakfast, except I hadn't had pancakes in days and everything else was dust.

The afternoon sunlight was warm on my skin and the air was still muggy, but a cool breeze made it less vile. It wasn't unbearably hot, yet. The city hummed around us. Taig opened the passenger door and I climbed in. As I peeled my fingers from their death grip on his hand, my joints ground together, locked in place from the force I hadn't realized I'd been using.

He stood beside me, blocking out the world, and squeezed a pattern on my upper arms. Left, right, fast, slow. I sucked in air and while my heart hurled itself against my ribs.

"I bought extra potatoes," he said, and I nodded, grateful not for the mention of food but normalcy. "I was hoping to steal some of that herb butter you made the other day, with the parsley. That was amazing."

It was butter and herbs. The man was easily amazed. I rested my head on his chest and felt the tattoo of his heart as it beat too quickly, carried along in my anxiety with me. "I'm okay," I assured him.

His hands moved up my arms to my back, but kept up the alternating rhythmic touches. *Tapping. It's tapping.* That's what he'd called it. "I know that. You know that. But your lizard brain doesn't." I felt him draw in a breath, hold it, then release it slowly. I tried to match his pacing, feeling my breath calming and his heartbeat leveling out. "Remember last time we had steak?" I shook my head, so he said, "Eclipse just about died of excitement."

I loved that cat to pieces, but I couldn't afford to feed her steak. I *could*, however, give her tiny pieces of mine. She'd sat in my lap purring while I ate, which probably was incredibly unhygienic but made my heart sing. Taig had slid some of his onto my plate for me to give her when I was done, too. That was true love, really. We'd agreed to do some research on what cats actually *should* eat. I hadn't, and I suspected he hadn't, either, though I had bought her fancy food the other day.

"I'm thinking Hasselback potatoes," Taig mused. "I feel like something a little fancier than mashed spuds."

I sat back, insulted. "Excuse me?"

"Don't 'excuse me' me. I'm Irish. I get the final say when it comes to potatoes." He gave my shoulders a squeeze. "I'm going to get in the car and get us home, yeah?"

I nodded, closing my eyes and sitting back, exhausted. He closed the car door after me and I struggled to get my buckle on. I didn't know why I was so fucking tired. I'd overdosed on sugar last night, but that was last night. I was fine now.

Rather than fight with my body I tipped my head back and closed my eyes. "Let me know if you want me to keep talking," Taig told me. "Otherwise I'm going to shut up."

The muffled road noise and the sound of his breathing was

enough. I felt like gravity had been cranked up. I didn't fight it, staying there until he pulled in and came around to help me out.

I knew he'd had a shit day, but right then, I didn't have a lot to give. "I'm going to shower," I told him, scrubbing my face. "I'll help with dinner soon."

"I can make steak and spuds, Rory," he said, waving me away from the bags. "And I can even put some in a container if you want to prove definitively that witches *are* heathens, and microwave it later."

I curled my lip in disgust. "Even suggesting that makes you liable to persecution."

"Anything for you, love," he told me, and I had a go at a smile, leading him up to my apartment where ice-cream containers and an empty bottle of gin waited beside my sink. Eclipse must've messed with the controllers, because one was in the middle of the kitchen.

Before abandoning the floor to him I did a quick tidy up, ignoring his protests as I emptied the dishwasher and ran the rubbish outside, then opened up the windows to get some fresh air happening.

I let myself relax under the shower, washing off the tacky layer of sweat that had clung to me all day and taking the time to center myself.

He'd had a rough day. I didn't need to go breaking down again. That'd only make it rougher on him. Anyway, I needed to look after me. I had to trust he was looking after himself.

My house smelled amazing when I opened the door from the bathroom. Eclipse walked over, rubbing herself against a random chunk of wall as she looked at me with her cutest expression. If she could've batted her eyelashes, she would've.

"How hungry are you?" Taig asked, appearing from around the corner. He'd ditched the jacket, but still wore the shirt and what was now a very loose tie. One of my tea towels was draped over his shoulder.

"I'm not," I admitted. "But you eat."

He shook his head, bending to try to pat Eclipse. She mewled and melted away, disapproving of his lack of steak, I assumed. "Tough crowd." He straightened, smiling at me. "I'm okay for now. Potatoes will take another half hour, veggies just need warming, and the steak is marinating."

In that time, I'd taken out the rubbish and had a shower. I put aside the guilt and focused on the good. "You work fast."

"It's not exactly a complicated meal. And the veggies are literally just dumped in a steamer thing." He followed me into my room, falling down on my bed. "Want to go for a walk or something?"

"Or something," I agreed, rummaging for a pair of comfy under-wear. The heat wave would pass tomorrow, and I'd be back to freez-ing, but right now… "How are you still in a *tie?*" I asked, fishing out underwear.

He ran his fingers down the tie, smiling a bit. "Kept you near me."

I stopped, one leg in, one leg out. I'd borrowed his tie at the Winter solstice and just about begged him to do me in my client's lounge-room in the process. We hadn't been a thing, then. More like a poten-tial thing. "That's actually the same tie?" I looked at it, sitting innocently against his shirt as if he hadn't smoothed it between my breasts like an erotic promise months ago. "I was just talking shit, earlier, because you never wear them."

"Same one." He was smiling, and I suspected he was back in that memory with me. While he was distracted, I sorted out the under-wear. "You danced with Lilith that night. You looked like you had a ball. I damn near broke Arthur's face for staring at you."

I'd been pretty torn up from a break up, but that had been a good night. I hadn't just jumped into bed with Taig, even though we'd both been physically okay with it. Neither of us had been anywhere near prepared for the emotional side of it. "See, I *am* good at self-care," I told him, proudly. "Still here, alive, and more or less whole."

Whether he followed my thoughts or not I couldn't tell. "Chalk and cheese from even just six weeks ago, love. Kicking goals."

Only Taig would tell me that after I'd lost my shit in the elevator at work.

My heart overfull, I climbed onto his lap, took his face in my hands, and pressed a kiss that was full of joy on his lips. "I'm fucking tired," I announced. "I'm hot, I think I need to detox sugar or some shit, and I feel like I have a million balls in the air. At some point I need to figure out this faerie shit with *nothing* to go off, and I still need to remember to pay my fucking bills and wash my clothes?" He made a noise of sympathy, and I loved him for it. "I thought as a kid that, like, there was always something going wrong. Adults went from one big drama to another."

Taig smiled at me. "We don't?"

"No, we don't. It's constant drama, all the time. The stakes change but the intensity doesn't. They made it look so *easy*, Taig. What the fuck?"

He made another noise of sympathy. "Would you like to report that?"

"Yes," I said, definitively. "Yes, I would. And while I'm at it, I want to report whichever arsehole decided that self-emptying dishwashers are too hard to invent."

"I can take care of it for you," he promised against my lips. Just like that the mood went from playful to sexually charged. "Since you're mine."

My breath got all tangled up in my chest. My peace was hard won and my buffer non-existent. But his arms folded around me, and they felt like home. I rested my forehead against his, letting myself relax against him. "I guess I am," I agreed, closing my eyes and breathing him in. When he let out a shaky breath I was reminded that it went both ways.

His hand cupped one of my arse cheeks and eased me in closer, so his hard-on was nestled at the apex of my thighs. "I like it when you get pliant, sometimes," he murmured, the words low and rough. "You don't give that to just anyone. I figure you know you're safe to be vulnerable, with me."

My former witch-hunter lover. I shivered, not entirely from arousal, and pressed another, slower kiss to his lips. He'd done nothing except share his own vulnerability with me. I didn't hit back with any sort of remark. The vitriol was there, at the back of my brain, but I didn't need it right then.

"Considering what we both know of the real world," he breathed, against my lips, "The fact that you're willing to let your guard down and let me in? That's pretty fucking amazing."

Maybe it was. Maybe he'd beat the odds by being worth that trust. His hand squeezed on my arse as the other slid up my back and I pressed closer, suddenly hungry. "What's my reward?" I asked him.

His chest lifted with his deep, indrawn breath. "I'll always have something for you," he promised.

See, now, if it'd been *me* behind the wheel I would've taken that as a challenge. The thought made mirth spark, deep in my chest. Because for him, it was a promise. "I believe you."

His quick breath and the way he ground his hips against me told me I'd said exactly what he'd needed to hear.

I let him encourage my spine to arch, knowing what he was going for and more than happy to play along. I'd learned my lesson well, last time. Taig made good on his promises.

His mouth on my breast made the wanting pool, low in my belly. It felt exactly right after so long. His beard prickled. The rasp of it was another layer of sensation existing only to contrast the velvet of his tongue and the warm wetness of his mouth. When Taig lifted his head, the air was cold against my nipple as he fell on the other like a starving man, teasing me with teeth and tongue until I was breathing fast. My world shrank to him and the blood beating hot through my veins.

As wonderful as the sensation was, I wanted more, and I wouldn't get it while we were stuck here. So I wasn't surprised when he tumbled me onto my back and pulled off my carefully chosen, maximally comfortable underwear.

The tie came off and was tossed onto my belly. I reached for it. He shook his head, laughter in his eyes. "Stay there."

There was something kind of nice about being able to relax back and know he was happy with me doing my ice cream puddle impersonation as he impatiently pulled his shirt over his head. He didn't undo his shoelaces, and I tried not to worry about how his poor shoes fared. But, given the day's temperature, he probably felt better without them on.

"I've got a lot of things I want to do with this tie," he told me. Still wearing his pants as he knelt on the bed beside me, unraveled the knot with quick, confident movements. "Not the least of which is watching you dance wearing it." He was beside me, the tie tight between his hands the way I'd hold a coiled rope.

I didn't feel even a shred of alarm. As someone who wasn't jumpy but had an excellent early warning system, I settled back, happy to enjoy all the energy he needed to burn. "Put your hands behind your back, under your hips."

I followed his instructions. It was a comfy place to lie, anyway. His gaze swept over me. Maybe others wouldn't have seen the pleasure in his eyes, but I did. It made me want more.

"I could look at you forever," he told me. "Maybe that's next time's mission, to watch."

His words conjured up a million possibilities. Before I could identify my favorite, he nudged my legs further apart and held the flat fabric of the tie against my clit. I drew in a breath out of reflex, but his hands were moving up and down, running the cloth against my core in a rhythm that turned my gasp into a moan. The cloth's drag was cut short before I lost myself. I heard him laugh, at some point, but I was beyond responding, feeling the tug and pull of it against me. Terrified it'd stop while knowing I needed just a little more. I teetered on the edge, frozen, until he straightened away from me.

"You're doing well," he told me, pressing a quick kiss to the inside of my knee. I fought not to grab him back as his attention turned to my drawer of toys. "We're in no rush, right? I've got dinner all ready to go once we want it, pretty much."

A sliver of anxiety crawled back into my belly. Some of the fog cleared from my head and I saw what he was pulling out, the various flared-base anal trainers, the large lube pump pack.

I was way too fragile to weather anything going wrong. The sensible part of me knew it. He wasn't a lot better. In fact, he might've been a whole lot worse.

I was trying to find words to tell him that tonight probably wasn't the best timing when he shoved my legs apart and closed his mouth over my clit, sucking hard before pushing himself away from my body. He vanished while I felt the orgasm fore-runners crash over me then retreat, leaving me shaking.

Taig returned with a towel and tipped me back, putting it under me. "Zero issues from me if things get messy," he said. "And now there's not even much to tidy."

I swallowed my misgivings, wishing I hadn't sworn off Share spells, and watched him watching me as he spread lube over the smallest toy. He'd expressed interest in receiving. He knew that was coming. Maybe he was just as excited to give.

He nestled it against me, then leant forward, pressing a kiss against my lips as I felt the first pressure of entry. "In case you're worrying," he said, as he waited for my body to adjust to the intrusion, "I'm happy to just play, here. I do quite like the idea of using some cum as lube." I held my breath as I felt the widest part of the toy press into me, but he held it there, hot and full. "Your eyes are so wide," he breathed. "I could do anything. There are almost too many options."

Not having that problem seemed like a blessing, right then. I felt him turning the plug inside of me and relaxed a little, closing my eyes. We weren't going straight to anything full on, and I was keen for more. Maybe not more in this specific direction, but as a side-dish, rather than the main meal, it had potential. Anyway, he had an impeccable track record.

"You're very quiet," he said. I felt him shifting about. "I don't know I trust that."

I didn't open my eyes, but I could feel every one of his movements. His fingers tightened around the base of the toy inside of me and then he slowly removed it. Almost instantly a new, colder intrusion was there, taking its place, stretching me.

My eyes flew open and his gaze darted up to mine. "Too fast?" he asked, softly, stilling.

There was no discomfort, really. Or at least, nothing close to pain. A sense of *different* wasn't bad, was it? I shook my head, and with one arm he scooped my legs up again, holding them against his chest as he rested his head against my calf, watching my expression with one of intensity. "We're going to get this one in, then take a break, okay?"

I nodded, unsettled and not sure if I was turned on or not. But I didn't tense up, and slowly I relaxed enough to let it all the way in.

With the weight of the foreign object in me, he pulled up my legs, turning toward me. I couldn't see his expression, but when he took up the tie again and held it taut between his hands, there was a little more space between his fists than there had been last time.

I was responded before the cloth even hit my flesh, arching up into his rhythm. My body flexed around the intrusion and ripples of pleasure ran through me. I arched my hips into the friction, wanting more, wanting it to go for longer, or go harder. He held me back until I was panting and straining, and then sat back for a new toy.

The slow pressure, the gentle rocking back and forth, made my breath catch. I didn't move into it, but I wanted to. The hand holding the toy stroked my flesh around the silicone and my whole world felt like it existed there, for seconds hours, or minutes, swollen clit and hungry orifices begging for more.

When it slid home into me I almost wept, and it had nothing to do with pain.

The black fabric wrapped around his fists. I lay there like a sacrifice, letting my head fall back and my body arch up, waiting.

The tie sang against my flesh and I struggled to breathe, every muscle in my body tightening as I careened toward the pinnacle only to have it whipped away again, leaving me panting.

His fingers dipped back to my ass to nestle the toy deeper. "Relax."

I tried to suck in air, but as soon as that fabric came down on me again spasms rippled down my thighs and up my torso. Muscles inside of me twitched and shuddered, wanting more or less or everything, I couldn't tell and couldn't figure out how to fix the problem. My hands fisted in the towel beneath me and he stopped. I finally relaxed and dropped back down. "That's better," he said. "That's good. Just let it happen, love. We're in no rush."

Except I couldn't breathe. I couldn't think. The fabric whisked up and down, the worst vibrator of all time because it wouldn't do what it needed to. I lingered on the edge, my breath coming in gasps, sobs in my throat.

But he took it away. He took it away and I was *so close* and all I could do was suck in air desperately and moan as he eased the toy out of me, waiting for the return thrust or the next size.

The next size wasn't cold silicone, though, but hot flesh that had less give and more girth. My eyes flew open again to see his gaze glued to my face, his expression one of fierce concentration. He still held my legs against his chest with one arm. The other was guided cock into me, and while it didn't hurt, it wasn't half as hot. He rocked back and forth, slow and gentle. All I could think was I wouldn't get the tie from this angle.

When he slid home his eyes flickered closed and his mouth fell open, as if in prayer. Maybe it was a Pavlovian response, but his quick breathing made my body light up again. I wriggled tentatively, hoping he'd start to move.

"Stay still, love," he said, shakily. "I need a moment. I think you might, too."

I'd had plenty of moments, but I gave him this one, relaxing back and feeling him relax into me as my legs took more of his weight. When his eyes opened, he nuzzled at my ankle, balls deep and sweet as pie.

His lube-free hand slid down from my knee. My body was alight before he reached my clit, resting his palm against my sensitive bud as he started to rock inside of me.

I felt like a doll, all my limbs dangling and flopping, but it was a far-off feeling. I didn't have space to worry about it, because my climax built rapidly. This time, there was no last-minute withdrawal. When I was gasping, he was, too. I lay there, totally pliant and riding over waves of pleasure as they built, crested, then built again, until it was all I could do to breathe.

He joined me, at some point, and eventually we were still and the buzzing noise in my head faded.

"Are you okay?" he asked, barely two seconds after withdrawing from my body. "Rory?"

I managed to flop a hand at him.

He vanished. Some point later, he returned. I could focus on him, but the glass of water he offered was beyond my meager skills.

"You need to drink, love."

"Tired." I curled up on my side and managed to wrap an arm around his leg and tug him toward me. He resisted. "Nap with me."

He did say something, and a kiss was pressed to my head. I couldn't decipher the words, but I knew, in my heart, what it meant.

We were home, and everything was okay.

CHAPTER 27

His hands were warm and gentle as they smoothed hair back from my face. I scowled at him all the same.

"You should have a drink, love," he said, gently. "And I've made potatoes."

Awake now, I climbed off the bed with less grace than energy, realizing I *was* hungry. My belly rumbled at the reminder, but I made my way into the shower. I hadn't washed my hair, earlier, and I didn't really want to now either. But Taig was good at keeping it dry when we showered together.

The toys we'd used were lined up and drying on my bathroom sink. He'd been up and about for a little while, apparently. My belly rumbled again. I couldn't smell the food anymore. "What type of potatoes?" I asked him, trying to remember where we'd been before we'd taken a very intense detour.

"Hassleback." He leant against the shower frame, muscles in his shoulders flexing and underwear riding low on his hips. My brilliant powers of deduction told me Taig had showered already. His hair was dark from the water, and finger-combed back. "Your legs are a bit wobbly there. Okay if I just hang out?"

I wanted to run my hands up and over his chest, but I also wanted to stuff my face, roll over and sleep. I could do neither, because I was in the shower. *How inconvenient.* It wasn't really fun if it didn't have some sort of clean up afterwards, right?

"If it's awkward I can head out," he offered. "But I've seen someone who went through a shower screen, and I'd rather admire you whole."

That thought chased away some of the lingering fog. "Don't these things have safety glass?" I asked him, lathering up.

"The newer, the safer, far as I can tell." He rattled the aluminum frame gently. "This one might be older than you."

The clean up wasn't too bad. Importantly, it wasn't painful. As for the shower, I highly doubted my apartment predated my birth but I didn't care to argue.

He folded me into a towel when I got out and let me flop against his chest. "I'm exhausted." My fingers threaded with his and I tugged him out of the bathroom. "We're done, right?" I asked, trying to rouse my brain. "I think I didn't say the end spell equivalent of our shenanigans."

A quirk of his brows pleased me. He hadn't thought of that yet. "I'm done. You done?"

"Super." I found my comfiest undies and took the shirt he passed me. It stuck to my skin where I hadn't dried off properly. He helped tug it gently into place. "Good work. Gold star."

There was a smile at his lips. "Told you we're a good team, didn't I?"

Had he? Probably. Would it be weird if I told him that was my first orgasm involving anal, much less the first multi? I shrugged it off. "I've heard of folks using the Share spells as a protective factor against improperly done butt play," I said, pausing to yawn.

He frowned at me. "It's pretty sad that's required." He passed a glass of water to me and I looked at the strange beast. I couldn't remember the last time I'd had a glass of water. A bottle, sure. But a glass?

"Potatoes are about done," he said, giving me a bit of a nudge. "I need to get the steak on."

Steak. Elders, my toes almost curled. If only it was ready right now,

I'd've died of happiness. Maybe that's why he'd waited on it. Death by happiness didn't seem like the most efficient option for today's festivities. "I'll clean up," I promised. "After you cook."

"Dishes'll be there tomorrow." I followed him out, drinking the water. He was right, it did feel good. "Feeling okay?"

"Sleepy." I wanted to groan as I remembered what I'd done earlier. "We seized an entire coven's *electronics*. I'm pretty sure there are policies protecting them."

He shrugged. "Someone else gets paid to figure that stuff out. I assume they knew Brown was dirty and just needed to prove it."

"You assume correctly." I refilled my glass of water and felt like an adult. "I'm not telling you this, but one of the witches came to us with some doctored documents. We're hoping the edits, paired with some very questionable emails and his call log, will be enough that they can throw the book at him."

"Fae?" Taig asked, tea towel over one naked shoulder.

From this angle I could clearly see the vamp mark on his back and I traced it with my eyes. "Yeah. Fae." There were dark flecks in the scar tissue. It didn't look like a burn, but it also didn't look like a healed cut. I tightened my hands around the glass rather than go over and run my hand up the gutter of his back. I could imagine fanning my hands over that mark and kissing it better. But kissing old scars didn't do shit.

"It'll be hard to nail him. They don't usually call people."

"Not my problem," I said, setting those worries aside. "I'm not the judge, jury, or the executioner."

He turned to half face me, tongs in hand and steak sizzling aggressively. "How's that sitting?"

I considered the question for a moment, turning it over in my head. "It's actually really nice. I was told to do the thing. I did the thing. I've mostly finished reporting on the thing. Then I'm done. And I get to hang out with some cool as shit lycans."

"Good." He turned back to the steak. "How about with George, tomorrow?"

My dinner sat heavily at the reminder. *Pix.* Her name had been

Felicity Martin, and the cops were still investigating her murder. Exactly how George felt about the investigation was hard to gauge. I doubted he himself knew. Hells, I couldn't blame him for that. I hadn't been the best witch on George's case, but Aspen had steered it, and I couldn't see where she'd mis-stepped. I couldn't see where my meddling would've been *helpful*. Not in this instance. Maybe, with a few years and some professional development down the road, I'd be able to reflect on what had happened and figure out how to avoid it.

And maybe not.

"I told him I'd be there," I said. "He's had a lot of people who haven't followed through. But also, I don't want to get into the habit of making promises I don't keep, you know?"

"I know."

Glad, I propped my hand on my chin, watching as he dumped uninspiring looking veggies on the side of the meal. That was probably something I should take over. He was a serial vegetable overcooker, and that wasn't ideal. "How about you? Okay with how today went?"

He shrugged. "I did what I could and what I needed to. There's one detail I didn't speak to, and it's looping in my head now, you know?" He opened the oven and slid the tray of potatoes out. My mouth watered. I kept that to myself, because it seemed like an inappropriate moment in the conversation to praise his culinary skills. "I can't stop running through the what-ifs."

"I hate that. I don't know what's worse, the lead up or aftermath what-ifs."

He made a noise of agreement, finishing plating up. "Good news is you shut down my brain pretty well, so I owe you thanks for that."

"Will accept all gratitude in the form of potatoes," I told him sagely, then accepted the plate he handed me.

His grin was quick and easy. "You're not sore?"

"Nope. You really want to talk about my butthole while we eat?"

He slid cutlery over to me. "I'm kind of partial to your butthole. Fantastic way to spend an evening."

I glanced at the time, then did a double-take. We were having a late dinner, apparently. "Wow. Okay. Nice trick with your tie, by the way."

His grin widened. "Thanks. Wasn't sure it'd work."

I spun my plate potato-first, looking at the golden, crispy deliciousness sitting in a puddle of butter. "I need to concentrate for a minute, okay?"

"You should," he agreed. "There's more butter, if you'd like some on top."

I flipped the spud and ran the tines of the fork over the crispy base of it. It was perfect top *and* bottom. I wanted to weep. I wanted to sing his praises. Instead I split off one slice and bit into it, moaning as the taste swamped me.

Eclipse leapt up onto the seat beside me and gave me her biggest, roundest eyes. "You are *not* getting any potatoes," I told her, turning my plate away. "I love you, but I don't love *anyone* enough to share this."

CHAPTER 28

"I should come too," Lilith objected, but didn't move from her comfy spot on my couch beneath Eclipse. "Anyway, I'd kill for some sushi."

I went to tell her that she didn't need to come, that I was fine, then caught myself. "Policy states that if we judge it fair and it could cause social backlash, we don't have to maintain the three-to-one ratio with all clients."

Her eyes narrowed at me. "Did you just quote policy at me?"

Pretty sure I'd paraphrased policy. It didn't say *social backlash,* but that was what it meant. "I don't make the rules," I said, holding up my hands. "Rocking up with one hot witch on your first day is one thing. Two hot witches, though?"

Her expression cleared. "You sure?"

"Yeah. And if you want the hours, we didn't finish submitting the last of George's transfer information. You could always get on that. We can go grab sushi when I get home and eat it in peace."

She twisted her fingers around her necklace. "Maybe. Wouldn't mind the cash from the extra hours, honestly. And if I don't buy sushi, well, that's basically making money."

Cash meant choices. She was trying to get out if she was saving that hard. "Fair. Want to stay for dinner? Taig was talking a big game about Moroccan chicken, or something." I needed to make a plan.

She rolled her eyes. "I don't want to third wheel."

"You're not third wheeling, he is, and he's happy fetching snacks and reading his book."

She hesitated a minute. "Sure?"

"Positive."

"Okay. Well, I'm definitely on a roll and I want to finish the third barn for our ostriches. So if it's okay, then I'd love to hang out."

"Great." I pulled on my jacket. "See you soon."

She waved and I let myself out, pulling up the hood to protect my hair from the rain. I figured out my route after I was on the tram headed in vaguely the right direction, then stopped to send Taig a quick text. He could opt in or out, but by letting him know what I'd told Lilith we were all on the same page. I also offered to cook, because he had a full shift. I was just doing a quick drop in.

Benson opened the door as I approached. I almost didn't recognize him with the standard hi viz top and work clothes in the place of his lumberjack aesthetic.

"I don't know why this is necessary," he said, annoyed.

"It gives them added incentive to keep paying you after your rates increase slightly, rather than replacing you with a kid."

He looked at me darkly, as if no one would dare to replace him. I wished it was that simple, but profit margins were narrow, and taking someone on for an apprenticeship was a big deal. Taking on an ursathrope was another layer of complexity atop all of that. So I rode in with him and met his boss, a friendly guy with dirt embedded in the cracks in his hands and freckles across his nose.

"Hey, Big Ben," the guy said, waving at Benson. "How's it going? And you'd be Lilith?"

"Rory." I shook the guy's hand and Benson followed suit. "But I'll take it as a compliment. You needed me to sign something?"

He waved it off. "Oh, I'll email it through. It's about your program, so it's not critical from our end. While the rain's eased we've got to get this gazebo up."

I glanced at the pile of wood, steel, and tools. Whether that was standard first day landscaping, I had no idea, but I knew Benson had done the induction work because I'd done it with him. He knew not to walk into a puddle with a toaster in it, if the toaster was plugged in. While I'd had to resist rolling my eyes at a lot of their information, as someone who hadn't grown up in our culture, Benson had really needed that course. None of us were *born* knowing this shit.

That was why I was a smidgeon anxious when Benson strode off, keen to get rid of me. I didn't cluck or anything, just gave his boss a polite nod, shoved my hands in my pockets, and made myself scarce.

The kids were with Trinity, the ursa delivered, the wheels were in motion. I'd taken Jessica to her new school yesterday to wander around and play on the playground. I'd take her tomorrow, or Lilith would. Maybe both of us, so we could debrief Benson at the same time. He preferred to be with the kiddos, so that'd work better. Then we could shuffle our Monday appointment to mid-week and that'd free me up to—

My phone rang and I dug it out, scowling at Nic's name. It was going to be a damned real estate request. Just because he didn't respect *his* Saturdays didn't mean I had to enable this. "What?"

"Please?" he asked, and I rolled my eyes. "All I'm saying is that it's important to me. And I already put in a sushi order at the place around the corner. I won't make it in time for the viewing *or* the food."

The fucking arsehole. "Nic, are you seriously Reading things that hard?"

"What?" he asked, innocently.

As if he didn't know Lilith wanted sushi. There were no coincidences with Nic, except what a jerk he was. "I'll see. Send me the address."

"Blessed be, Sunshine." He blew a kiss and I hung up, disgusted.

When I called Lilith, she answered on the fourth ring. "It's super awkward answering a call to you while I'm alone at your place."

"Well, Nic's asked me to check out an apartment for him and Aspen. They've been caught up and can't make it." I bet he was caught up drinking a coffee in a café being a meddling arsehole. "And they had a sushi order they can't pick up, too. He wants us to give it a good home." He'd fucking better, because that was my sushi now.

"Free sushi?" she asked. "I was feeling a bit of cabin fever."

Of course she had been. "Cool. Let's go judge this place's plants. I'll send you the address."

"How'd Benson go?"

"Yeah, good." There hadn't been much time for anything else. "I'm texting this through. See you soon."

I didn't question whether we'd make it to the location in time. But we were getting the sushi first.

"Who calls ahead to order sushi?" Lilith asked me as we let ourselves into the dinky little place fifteen minutes later.

Oracle asshats. "I have no idea," I muttered. "Hi, I'm here to pick up an order for a Nic Rubikeyv."

The person behind the counter smiled brightly at me. "Just a moment."

"Surely he can get here in time to eat it?" Lilith asked, looking at the time the place was open until.

"You'd think so," I agreed. "He said he couldn't, though, and I didn't ask questions." *Because he's a dirty rat.*

The bag was filled with a generous serving that, predictably, made Lilith's eyes light up. "No way. Is that *inari?*"

"Probably," I said, irritated.

Her eyes snapped up to mine. "What?"

"I'm grumpy," I said, waving a hand. My own very basic taste was also covered, of course. I took the tray and trudged down the road to the apartment they allegedly couldn't make. "I'm sick of looking at houses for other people."

"I get that," Lilith agreed. "There's no way we'll ever be able to buy in the city. Well, I can't." She glanced at me as if I might have a money tree in my back pocket. "At least with our wages now there's a chance of one day getting myself a little place at a retirement home."

Nic's words popped into my head. A dog and kids, property. "You and me, we'd be the life of a retirement village."

"Playing farming games until the late hour of ten thirty at night."

"Fucking oath." I stopped in front of the *Open* sign that was on a townhouse, not an apartment. *He said apartment, didn't he?* After a quick double check, I led Lilith in. "We're looking for anything I can whine about to Nic, and whether the roof could support Aspen's pole."

"She has a pole?" Lilith asked. "That's badarse."

They all thought *she* was the nice one. I scowled at the real estate agent whose smile made my face hurt just to look at it, gave over my name and number, and walked into the narrow little place.

The ceilings weren't as low as I expected, and while it was pokey it was also not the worst I'd seen. I wandered around, making note of nothing in particular, chomping on my ill-gotten sushi and trying to ignore the smell of mothballs and vacant house. The second story's floor creaked and the little courtyard out the back was cold and wet. It wasn't until I almost stepped on Lilith that I saw how wide her eyes were.

Fuck. "You like it, huh?" I asked, and shoved the sushi roll in my face to drown out the taste of betrayal. Maybe I ought to tell her she was being manipulated?

"I don't know." She looked over my shoulder into the little courtyard. "It's a lot."

"Nothing in this area is cheap." I nudged the window in the laundry. It didn't open. This *definitely* predated me. It made my bathroom look high tech.

"No. I mean..." she hugged the sushi to her chest. "I don't know what I mean."

That wasn't what I expected. Rather than waste my time looking at a house I couldn't afford, I watched Lilith. She ran her hand over the old banisters and gazed out at the sea of roofs from the grungy little window, her expression unreadable.

"Not a great day for it," the real estate agent announced companionably as they breezed in, inviting me to complain along with them.

"I love the rain," I told her. "I'm actually two percent frog." Lilith looked at me strangely and the agent's laugh sounded like a sitcom track. "I'll let you know if we have questions."

"That was unusually tactless of you," Lilith said, wandering again.

We'd been through the whole house more than once. I shrugged, trying to get a read on her. But she didn't say anything until we were done and on the way home and I said, "Well? What do you think?"

"The witch who taught me magick," she said, to her sushi. "She lived in a place that looks *exactly* like that, except the bathroom is different."

"Oh." I tried to figure out what that might mean. "That's good, right? If Aspen lived there, it'd feel kind of instant home?"

She shrugged. "I don't know. It should be. But it wasn't an easy time for me."

"Could go either way, I guess," I offered, and she nodded.

Well, fuck. Nic wasn't manipulating her, exactly. He was trying to figure out the best way forward so she'd be comfy.

By the time I'd finished making our coffees my face hurt from scowling. Lilith, efficient as ever, already had our farm loaded.

"You going to tell Aspen you like it?" Lilith asked, passing me a controller as I sat down. "The roof wasn't collapsing, and it had an inside toilet."

"The bar is in hell."

She shot me a quick look. "No, the bar was around the corner. They have decent wedges. I've got a friend who plays there. You'd like it."

I wasn't reporting back to Nic. No way. He was on his own. I had to be Switzerland, here. "Cool. Well, if they buy it, we can hit it up some time. We were hatching ostriches, right?"

"Right." The game came to life ahead of us and my cute little farmer set off. "I need to talk to Vince."

I kept my expression neutral. "Yeah?"

"Yeah." She shifted, tugging a blanket over her lap. "Things just got weird. His family is so good. He doesn't get that they aren't all like that."

I bought myself time by taking a swig of coffee. *Don't interfere. Don't interfere.* "Have you told him? Like, really stepped him through it?"

She shrugged, zooming amid the ostriches on her side of the screen. "Kind of."

"Either you have or you haven't. Mentioning it is different from saying, 'Hey Vince, you need to stop trying to test my boundaries with this because they're in place to protect me' or something."

She looked at me like I'd just grown a second head. "Did you seriously just *wise friend* to me?"

"Fuck, no," I scoffed, trying not to figure out if I should be insulted or pleased at the comment. "Are we out of chips?"

She looked suitably mollified by my reassurances, and we settled back in to share snacks and game, speaking only rarely.

When my phone pinged and Nic's name popped up, I ignored it on principle, focused on my adorable farmer cutting wood like her life depended on it.

Lilith glanced over, but I pointed to her side of the screen. "Cutscene."

"Hm?" she followed where I'd indicated. "Oh, I like this one. I haven't married this townie in ages. Maybe I'll wife her?"

"You do look super cute with her," I agreed, flipping my phone over and continuing on my woodcutting spree. "Things okay with your dad?"

She didn't look at me. "Yeah, fine."

My phone buzzed again and I resisted the urge to check it. "It doesn't have to be fine." Pretty sure that was Aspen's line, but I was borrowing it. "Let me know if I can do anything, won't you?"

"Yeah, like, there's nothing to do." She clicked through the dialogue options without reading them. She probably knew them already. "I've blocked him everywhere. Vince can do what he wants, but it isn't worth it to me."

I didn't ask her to confirm what that meant, but the implication made me feel sick. If Vince was going behind her back and trying to patch things up on her behalf with a sperm donor she didn't want to deal with, well, maybe I *was* team Nic.

"He's too sweet," Lilith said, quietly. "You know?"

"Yeah." Naive might've suited him better than sweet. "He shouldn't be discussing your stuff without you, though."

"He isn't, exactly, I don't think." She shrugged. "It's fine. You're right, I need to really sit him down and make it crystal clear."

My phone buzzed once more. I reached over to turn it to *do not disturb*. "I guess if you express important boundaries, even if he crosses them, it's clearer for the both of you."

She nodded. "Yeah, thanks, Rory. I'll let you know, okay?"

A call popped up. I debated hanging up on Aspen, but didn't.

Of course, it was Nic. "Hey, we don't have time to pop by. I just wanted to know what you both thought of the house, and if we should do our own inspection?"

"I thought it was a house," I said, unimpressed. "It had walls. They seemed stable. Same with the roof, but I'm no builder, so."

"Damned by faint praise," Nic said, heartily, but there was a question in the words and I couldn't help it. I looked at Lilith.

"I'd vote for it," she said, without looking at me. "It'll look after them."

I didn't know what the fuck that meant, and I doubted Nic would, either. He'd apparently heard, because he said, "Huh. Interesting. Well, maybe I'll call the agent, see if I can convince her to let Aspen do a walk-through later this week."

There wasn't small talk. We'd never been into that, thank the Elders. So when he hung up on me I wasn't surprised, but Lilith glanced over, brows drawn. "That was weird."

Yes, it is. "Nic is pretty weird." Feeling smug, I tossed the chips her way. "Did you actually like that house?"

She shrugged. "For me? I don't know. But there's something solid about it. Or at least, that's what I felt. It could be full of white ants, I have no real idea. But he wanted vibes, right?"

"Yeah, he did." I finished my woodcutting spree and tucked my little sprite into bed. While I waited for Lilith, I picked up my phone and, against my better judgment, sent Nic a text. *She described it as 'solid'. FYI you weirdo.*

A moment later, he sent back a sparkly heart and a hand flipping the bird. My world rightened, I got cozy again. The quiet wouldn't last forever, but while I had it, I was going to appreciate it.

CHAPTER 29

Jessica's school dress was neat as a pin. It might even fit her in three years. Apparently buying things to grow into wasn't just a human trait.

"Your dad will be there after school to pick you up," Aspen told her. "When the final bell goes at three-fifteen."

"I know," Jessica said, shooting Aspen a puzzled look, then sending a quick glance at her father who was impatiently wiping down the bench.

Benson and Jessica left without a backward glance. I opened up my emails, wishing information on the arseholes coming after the Hurtfields would magickally appear. Delyan and Taig had the case, and I knew they wouldn't be sitting on their hands. I also knew I'd hear immediately through informal channels if Taig learned anything even vaguely important.

Instead I had my first-aid refresher I needed to do, a bunch of care team meetings to attend, and some work calls.

Liam was on his back, his favorite doll held between his feet as he spun its hat one way, then another, then back again. Beside him, Lilith played with the kiddy tea set, making some of the other dolls pretend-tea and pretend-cake.

I could've called Delyan and asked some questions. Knowing I was still thinking about it might encourage them to revisit the case themselves and chase up any loose ends. To be fair, I *hadn't* asked Taig about it at all over the weekend.

But I could do that on the tram.

I sank down beside Lilith. "Could I have a tea?"

Liam paused, his eyes going to my hands, or maybe the rings on my fingers, as Lilith said, "Yes! Here you go."

I accepted it. "Thank you."

"You're welcome." She picked up the cake platter. "Would you like some cake?"

"I don't like chocolate cake," I lied. Then I shook my head. "I mean, no thank you."

"Okay." She turned to the doll beside me. "Would you like some cake, Mr. Frog?"

"Yes please," I said, out of the corner of my mouth, miming the frog doll take the cake.

We'd probably been playing for a few minutes when Liam's attention went back to his doll, but he rolled over closer to Lilith, holding his doll between his body and her actions. I saw Aspen watching from the bench, her eyes big and full of gratitude.

I shifted, uncomfortable. Instead I refocused on my frog who was currently eating his cake and having some sort of generic conversation with the astronaut beside him. I resisted the urge to excuse myself and my frog from the party to go chase up admin.

We went with Benson and Liam to Trinity's, where Liam was dropped off, then left Benson from there to see himself to work. He'd smoothed the late start over himself for the first week of Jessica's school.

"Maadai's confirmed we'll cover cost of Jessica's before school care for the first two months, right?" I asked Lilith.

"Already paid for," she told me, not looking up from her phone. "Speech pathologist shifted Jessica's appointment, Aspen."

Aspen groaned. "To what? Don't tell me, just email it through. I have to run. Catch you both after lunch!"

She jumped up and made her way to the tram door, waving as we called out farewells. I looked at my phone, wondering whether ringing Taig, who I knew was on duty, or Delyan was more appropriate to ask about the investigation. Really, it wasn't like I planned on having phone sex with him. It just seemed kind of strange to ask the guy who'd made me coffee in bed for a work thing.

Maybe I needed to think about that.

"Hello, Custodian," Taig said, his voice low, gravelly, and full of welcome. "To what do I owe the pleasure?"

I could just grab him and squeeze the guts out of him, he was so fucking amazing. If only I could reach through the phone. "Following up on Hurtfield's stalkers."

"Ah. 'Stalker' isn't quite the right word," he said, thoughtfully. "Not if we're going by legal definitions." I rolled my eyes and hoped he knew it. "Hurtfield is hardly at risk of victimization, and we both know it." That throwaway statement swept over me like a wave. "I do understand the question, though, and your answer is, not really."

I found myself oozing back in my chair, my energy drained.

Benson *didn't* look like a victim.

Did I?

The thought made the blood pound in my temples. A hard, hot band tightened around my scalp. I probably *did* look like a victim when I was tear-streaked at three in the morning in his oversized shirt.

But that wasn't when I'd been victimized.

My heart jack-hammered against my ribs and the air was too thick to breathe. *Hands on my shoulders.* I sat on the tram, swaying, remembering the night I'd woken from what had probably been a drug-induced exhaustion to a literal rift in the middle of the street. Had I looked like a victim as I'd kept everyone safe from the troll that had almost popped through, eating a late-night souva on the side of the road?

We could *all* be victims.

The thought made me feel sick as reason kicked in. The underlying concept Taig probably was trying to communicate was based on logic. Benson was a tough opponent. He wouldn't go down easily. Compared to plenty of the folks on our list…

But that didn't matter.

"The best we've got is a distillery in Port Melbourne that's leased to an employer of one of the identified people," Taig was saying.

The hopelessness rushed back and anger took its place. "Can I please get the name of that distillery sent through?" I asked, but there was still the edge of breathlessness in my voice.

Across from me, Lilith bumped her knee into mine. I met her eyes, saw the concern on her face, and shook my head.

I was a victim. That didn't mean I was weak.

"No, Rory," he said, amusement in his voice.

His humor left me feeling cold. Options coalesced in my mind like spells. He couldn't tell me. I wasn't a cop and I wasn't Retrievals.

"You've got sword training tonight, don't you?" he asked.

"Yes." He knew I did. I'd had to plan my evening around it, because I couldn't carry my sword around all day. He'd had the gall to give me crap about not having my *ceremonial* weapons secured.

Just because I could ceremonially cut someone's throat with those knives didn't mean they weren't foci, did it?

"Well, I might've found a safe that'll fit your sword and not require a key," he told me. "I'll show you later."

I didn't want a lock between me and my kit when crunch time came, and I certainly didn't want to give up wardrobe space for it. Suddenly I missed the years of bunking in the team quarters, which had been built with safety concerns in mind. I missed the team.

"We'll see. I've got some work to do before now and then," I told him, and there was an impatient edge to the words I hadn't intended to put there.

I hadn't told Taig about Benson's disclosure, not in confidence off the clock or officially as a Custodian.

How ironic that my dream guy turned out to be a fucking cop.

"I'll see you tonight." *Why couldn't I have fallen for a baker?* Catching myself before I gave the old school *blessed be,* I scowled at Lilith, who raised her brows in question. "Be good, Taig."

"Until tonight," he agreed, and while the words were neutral, his raspy voice could turn a deposition into a proposition. I was not wooed. Without engaging in the banter, I hung up on him.

"Ever wish you loved someone else?" I asked Lilith, before catching myself.

"Yeah." She locked her phone and leant in closer. The tram rocked and our heads bumped together gently. "Are you okay?"

The fury ebbed. I was close enough to smell the combination of her products and her perfume, and it made my eyes sting. "You gotta be more specific," I said, trying for humor.

"With what happened, at Samhain?"

Flattened grass beneath my feet on the boring side of midnight, the smell of cordite in my nose. The back of Ryan's skull was lifting away from his collapsing face.

"Yeah." I hadn't lost a moment of sleep from that and I sure didn't feel like Taig was a murderer. He was, but it wouldn't ever be my description for him. "Every now and then he'll make a comment about someone who's been in remand, though, or whatever." Every time a small comment was made, it stuck. It reminded me he actually *wasn't* safe. Not for everyone.

Her eyes were on my loosely clasped hands as we rocked along together. "I know Ryan was a bad guy," she murmured, into our private little bubble. "But vigilantes are only as good as their moral compass, you know?"

I resisted the urge to rest our heads together on purpose and breathed in deeply, putting aside my feelings for a moment. Traditionally, it was marginalized folks who suffered the brunt of discrimination, and I felt pretty gross that I hadn't even considered how that might feel for Lilith.

I couldn't reassure her, because her concerns were valid and I didn't know what the future held. I knew it was there, under Taig's surface. He'd never once had nightmares about what he'd done. He'd never expressed doubt, or even grief.

How many others had vanished? I didn't know.

"Tell you what," I said, quietly. "I'll nail him if he ever goes to the other side."

Her eyes raised to mine. "I'm not joking, Roars. He was too comfortable with it, you know?"

Maybe I was, too.

"Not the Ryan stuff," she said, waving it away. "But covering it up, acting like he'd done us multiple favors?"

I shook my head a little. "He has." It wasn't what she wanted to hear, but it was true. "Look, I'm hearing you. I agree." I agreed that her concerns were based on logic. "It's endless green flags with this man. Endless. And then..."

She waited, listening, her expression concerned.

I couldn't repeat what he'd said about Benson. I looked at her, the words swimming in my head, but they got stuck in my throat and the air was too thick.

He knew how to make people disappear.

There was no way Ryan was the first.

Sitting there, my belly full of dread and an ache in my chest, I said, "If you tell me you think things are going off the rails, I'll listen and I'll act, okay?"

She studied my face. "Are you offering cold blooded murder, too?" she murmured.

We both needed a hug so badly. I wished that hadn't been broken for her, so I could just wrap her up and squeeze her stress out. "Fuck, no." The thought was kind of funny, in a very sad way. "I don't do *anything* in cold blood."

CHAPTER 30

*L*ilith came with me to sword training. I'd seen her use a
spear, but the way she watched from the sidelines and the
questions she asked afterward reminded me that I didn't
know everything about this witch.

Taig was there when I got home, installing a big, fuck-off safe that
had a fingerprint scanner and code, as well as back up power. It took
up half of my wardrobe. He hadn't put it in the spot I'd given him, I
noticed. And something about the whole setup made me feel cold to
my bones.

"You didn't have a safe?" Lilith asked me, when I thanked Taig
through my teeth.

I opened my mouth to tell her I *was* the safe, then stopped when
Taig climbed up off the floor, dusting a smattering of cat fur off his
knees.

"Elders," she said, letting out a sigh. "You're going to fuck up one
day and they'll be able to nail you on technicalities, even if not the
actual crime. You know that, right?"

Ryan's face swam in front of me, creased in mock concern. He'd
intended to do just that. "It's a possibility." I was pretty sure they'd
have a hard time burning me at the stake, but I was also pretty sure

everyone thought that. "Look, I'm working on compliance, okay? It doesn't come naturally to me."

Behind Lilith, Taig sent me a quick look that made my belly knot. I cleared my throat, leading them out into the kitchen. "You want a cuppa, witch? I think tonight is salad and boring shit."

"No. All good." She tucked her hands into her pockets. "I'm headed home."

She didn't say anything else, but that statement had a ring of confidence to it that I hadn't heard from her in a while. So I nodded and followed her to the door, watching her boots hitting the ground with measured steps as she walked away.

I might've promised to violently deal with the man I love because of that witch. I didn't have a qualm about it.

"How was your day?" Taig asked, as I closed the door behind her.

How was my day? That question swam in the cotton wool that suddenly filled my head. "Yeah, good. I've hit a wall, though."

He nodded, opening the fridge. "You want to have a shower? Sleep it off?"

I was a bit more ripe than I liked from the sword training, and my muscles had that lingering heaviness from a good workout. "Shower. I'll be out soon. Happy to cook."

He waved me off. "So am I. Remind me we need cat food tomorrow."

We needed to have the budgeting talk, because he'd been doing more of the grocery shopping than I was happy with. Instead I poured myself under the hot water and let it pound away the stress.

I wasn't hungry, but by the time I got out there was food, and I managed to down some of it. I didn't want to analyze why my mood crashed, but it seemed like a no-brainer.

"Hey," I said, over a plate of chicken Caesar I was pretty sure I'd thanked him for, "It's low-key upsetting for me when I hear you making comments stereotyping folks."

He froze, his fork partway to his mouth. I could almost see the wheels turning in his head.

"I know the statistics," I said, before he could go on the defensive. "But it isn't that simple. And even if it was, it's literally my job to help marginalized folks." I wasn't the best at it, but I hoped I was getting better.

His fork dipped back to his plate. "Thank you for telling me. Can you point it out when I do it? Because I wasn't aware that I did, and while I'll be more careful going forwards, if I slip and don't catch myself, I'd appreciate you mentioning it."

Elders, the man was too damn perfect. He *did* have a spot of dressing on his lip, but still. "Yeah. Sure." I didn't feel better, and I didn't know why. Maybe part of me wanted a blow up. Maybe I had some maladaptive coping mechanisms. *Just a few.* "I'm feeling really shit," I said, honestly. "I don't know why. I'm going to try to sleep it off."

"Got a backup plan, for if you can't sleep?" he asked. There was no innuendo in it for me to weaponize against him. "We could go for a jog?"

I nodded, standing. I'd eaten, I'd washed, and I'd been physically active. If there was some sort of mystical Old Hag or Sky Daddy watching over me, surely I'd be able to sleep. "Thanks." I closed my lips over the *'and sorry'* I almost tacked on the end. I was allowed to feel shit. My requests were totally reasonable. "I'll clean this up in the morning."

He just nodded. "Let me know if you want me to come, tuck you in."

"No." I really didn't, right then. "But you're fine to sleep with me, later." Probably. If not, I'd deal with it then. "Thanks," I said again, and left before that damned *'sorry'* could escape.

I did sleep, eventually, and woke to my alarm and Taig's arm curled protectively over my waist.

He burrowed into my back, pressing a kiss to my shoulder. If I hadn't had to silence my alarm, I would've happily burrowed right back, but real life called.

While I tried to remember why the fuck I'd set an alarm half an hour earlier this morning I fed my poor, allegedly starving kitten.

Yawning into my empty coffee cup, I waited for caffeine to kick-start my brain.

It didn't want to be kick-started, but what the fuck did it know?

Taig hit the light and I squinted at him in the harshness of my kitchen fluoro. "What'd you do that for?"

"Coffee." He scrubbed a hand over his mouth, shooing me out of the way.

I let him, stepping back and pulling up my calendar. Benson was at the forefront of my mind, but it was actually a check-in at the bakery my banshee had landed a job at a few weeks ago. The banshee had reported it was going well, but the hours weren't great so I hadn't been able to lay eyes on him myself.

"Fuck bread."

Taig sent me a confused look. "Is this a yeast infection joke? Breakfast joke?"

"Work complaint." I pulled a face, though. "Yeast infections are not a joke. Not ever."

He held up a hand in peace. "No arguments, love. You just let me know if I'm doing something that'll upset the balance."

I couldn't even properly process that, making grabby hands at the coffee. "Weather?"

"Yes, there will be some."

I forgave him that comment because he provided me with caffeine, sussing today's temperature out on my phone. "Who doesn't know the weather?"

"You?" Taig asked, then dodged out of my reach, grinning. "Oh, come on, it was right there."

I flipped him the bird. It was supposed to be warm, so I took my coffee and bad attitude to my wardrobe, scowling at the safe taking up valuable real estate. On the bright side, since I had a banshee to visit, I could get myself something for breakfast. A flaky croissant sounded pretty fucking good right now. They probably sold coffee, too. It was basically a work expense.

Apparently Lilith had the same thought, because she was taking her coffee from the gangly kid behind the counter when I walked in.

"Aspen's running late," she told me, with a cursory flip of her hand in greeting. "Manager said they'd be here already."

"Oh, you want the manager?" the kid asked us, their eyes brightening. "That's me."

I hated myself for being so damn judgey that the first thing I did was try to figure out if they'd have to leave for school in two hours.

"I'm Lilith," Lilith said, offering a hand. "We spoke last Thursday?"

Fuck, we'd planned that far in advance? I breathed in the smell of Lilith's coffee and the fragrance of fresh bread and slapped my best professional face on. The manager reached up slightly to shake Lilith's hand. "Sienna. Hi! You're here to visit Chris, right? He's right back here."

She walked away from the coffee machine and I, ever the professional, did not stare dolefully after it. Instead, I followed her around the back and found Chris bagging loaves of bread. He fumbled when he saw us, blinking big blue eyes from behind long blonde bangs. "Oh. Hi."

"Hey," I said. It came out far too chipper. Lilith twitched beside me, but somehow her expression remained polite. I cleared my throat. "Sorry." And I again, with my impeccable willpower, resisted the urge to ask for coffee. "How are things tracking?" I asked the two of them in general, hoping I could steer the manager toward the front.

They made the predictable, polite responses as Lilith got into position beside Chris, watching his work. Coffee became the *perfect* excuse to get the manager alone. "Could I grab a long black?" I asked her. "While we catch up?"

"Sure," she squeaked. "I've got no complaints, though. Chris has been wonderful. He was only late once, and there was a traffic accident, so."

Shit, I'd been late more than that in the last two weeks. "That's awesome." I went back around the counter, watching her hands on the machine. "I believe it was Olivia who mentioned there was space to continue to the next phase of his apprenticeship if he has a good work ethic. Is that still available?"

"Uh, I think so." The kid's hands wobbled and I tried not to watch the paper cup bounce around. "We haven't taken on anyone else, so it should be, right?"

That was the theory, but the owner had been a bit slippery about exactly what the apprenticeship would entail, and how long Chris would need to work very short, very inconvenient shifts before he'd be given decent hours at decent pay. All of this was rushing back to me as I watched the kid make me a coffee that was going to burn my mouth. "Could I grab a splash of cold water, please?" I asked.

"Oh, of course." Her eyes flickered up to me. "Is there anything else you need to know?"

"I don't think so." I was going to remember it all the minute I stepped out the door. We needed to track down Olivia in the next few days. Chris was living below the poverty line with the limited shifts he was got, these people were taking his tax-free threshold for this job, and he was too hopeful of more to look for other options. They needed to shit or get off the pot. "So you're happy with his work ethic and productivity?"

"Absolutely," she said. "It's only been two weeks, but we're glad to have him in the Fluffy Top family."

No wonder I'd forgotten the name of the bakery. It didn't scream *bread,* but it sure screamed something. "Excellent." I had ammunition, then, to use against Olivia. No issues. One late start, which was able to be excused by… "You mentioned Chris was in an accident?"

"No. He attended one. Car accident, last week, over on Bourke street?" I shook my head, taking the coffee she passed me. "He was fine, just really shaken, you know?"

My heart sank. "Shaken, how?"

"Oh." She blinked at me. "Pale, jittery, you know."

Alarm bells rang. *I'm not jumpy.* "Oh yeah?" I asked, keeping it casual. "It must've been pretty intense. Did he recover okay?"

"I guess so." She frowned, going quiet for a moment as if running through it in her head. "He worked really well that day."

Fuck. "Did his color come back?" I asked, and I doubted it sounded casual, still.

"No. No, he was *really* shaken up."

Pale, jittery, and full of beans? *We have us an active banshee.* I hadn't done well enough in Supernatural Biology to explain how the banshee's Whisper both drained them and also rejuvenated them. I'd done well enough to remember the physical tells, though.

"I guess that's fair," I said, smiling, suddenly aware of the silence from the back room. "I'd be shaky too. I'm just going to pop back, see how they're doing. Lilith and I have another appointment," I lied, "so we won't keep you." *Unless I need you to talk to the cops.* I let myself into the back room, murder in my heart.

Lilith stood beside Chris, watching as he scooped a sliced loaf into a bag. She sipped her coffee, somehow and looking encouraging.

I watched from the doorway, tossing up whether I should just confront him directly. He wasn't pale, now, or jittery. His Whisper wouldn't take us out, but it'd do some damage. I felt like I'd lived dog years already, I didn't need him magickally bleeding off any extra time.

While I debated the best course of action, Lilith did the goodbye to-and-fro. I didn't *know* there had been fatalities. Maybe he just got juiced off of the adrenaline, or maybe there were lingering magickal by-products from people dying regardless of whether he'd killed them. I'd heard that was a thing, but never had it confirmed.

I'd reamed Taig yesterday for being a prejudiced jerk. So I kept my own prejudices to myself until we were out on the tram on the way back to work.

As soon as I saw the number of fatalities at that crash, I had to fight the urge to turn around and go save that average-coffee-making kid manager.

Seven dead.

Most banshees were happy to have nothing to do with death. It wasn't like the shift for a thrope, it was more like heroin for someone who couldn't face their reality.

Bro *was* living under the poverty line in a shitty job that was dicking him around.

"We've got an issue," I said, flashing my phone screen in front of Lilith's eyes. "Our banshee was in attendance."

Her lips thinned. "Seriously?"

"According to the manager. Pale all day, jittery, *and* high energy."

Lilith blew out a breath. "Better ring it in. It was last week. He seemed okay today, so he might've had a moment of weakness."

Which was the only reason I hadn't gone to rescue the manager who made too-hot coffee. Before business hours, I'd already spoken to way more cops than I anticipated. And that wasn't counting the one sharing my bed.

Aspen bounced in halfway through my second debrief with the detective from this district, eyes alight. She apologized, hastily backing out. I seized on the excellent opportunity to remove detective Dorrington from eating into more of my time.

"What happened?" I asked Aspen, finding her hovering beside her partially loaded teapot.

"We're putting an offer on a house," Aspen said, doing a happy dance with a squeak of excitement. "They're going to say no, I know they are. Nic wants to lowball them and oh my *God* I feel sick. I'm going to be paying him for like, seventy years, but it'll be so much better in terms of transport."

"If you can live with him," I agreed. I'd been there and done that. As housemates went, he hadn't been the worst. The barracks setup probably knocked most of our rough edges off. You had to learn to pull your weight in those situations, or you got gone. "That's super exciting!" I amended, when Lilith kicked me in the ankle. "Wait, you're paying him?"

"Yeah. Rent to buy, basically. He had the deposit, I have the current income. With our finances combined, we look like a decent invest-ment, apparently."

"Huh." I wondered what Taig's finances were like. It was a conver-sation I'd been dodging for awhile. I didn't know if I wanted to move in together. At the same time, we *basically* lived together and I sure as shit didn't want to bleed most of my wage into my landlord's bank account.

"Nic's coming across before lunch. You don't mind if I duck out to get this done?"

Lilith shook her head. "I've arranged to go to a Korean place with Vince for lunch. We could all go, if you want?"

"Oh, if you've booked a table for the two of you…" Aspen looked at me expectantly, waiting for me to do the polite thing and bow out.

I shrugged. Really, she should've known better. "I've got leftover chicken salad. Put me in the 'whatever' column."

Then I realized Nic and Vince would be in the same place, if this all went ahead, and my head pounded.

But Lilith was already settling in front of her screen. "Do you know how long it takes to rule out Banshee's whisper as COD?" she asked me.

"No." Their magick usually wasn't aggressive enough for them to have been a Retrievals target. "He's young, though. He won't be used to hiding it." If he'd called in sick, that day, and gone and nursed his high, we might never have known.

"Says the child prodigy who could cast Impenetrable Wards before she was menstruating," Aspen said, with a snort.

I winced at Lilith's curious look. "Not true," I said, at her look. "I just blew up charms and they wouldn't even think of letting me cast a curse. I didn't have a lot of options I didn't fuck up."

"Story of our lives," Aspen said, happily. "Find our way forward by first identifying every single dead end." She offered me her palm for a high five. "Thorough bitches stick together."

Lilith smiled at us fondly. "You're both adorable. And yes, of course come along."

Aspen ducked into the bathroom so I pulled up a chair beside Lilith. "You and Vince?" I asked, bluntly.

"Going to say 'I told you so'? Because it's totally your style."

My heart sat lighter in my chest. "No." How about that? I'd helped someone adult. Wonders would never cease. I pulled up my laptop. "What the fuck are we doing today?"

"You've got a ten-thirty with the asshole cop from West," she said, glancing at the time. "You lost the rock-off. Remember?"

I was trying not to. "Sure, whatever. Aside from that."

"We've got the kinder meeting tonight for Liam. Aside from that, normal visits." Lilith squinted at her email. "Oh, hold on. Looks like I'm chatting to some officers, too."

I peered at her screen, where a report sat, dated this morning. "Shit, they're fast on their paperwork, aren't they?"

"Constable Allen," she said, a smile tugging at her lips. "Interesting."

"Who?" She'd said his name like she'd say *gummy bear.* "Is he hot?"

Her smile widened. "I'll get back to you."

I leant further, watching Lilith type his name into the search function in our case notes archive. "I feel like I should know his name. Should I know his name?"

"All signs point to yes," Lilith said, clicking open the file on Jaye the lycanthrope. "I might need to chat to Shep."

"What's going on?" Aspen asked, coming back in.

"Remember that cop Wesley was pinning things on a few weeks ago?" Lilith asked her.

It clicked. "Wait, you couldn't find anything on him."

"Nup. I'd put it aside for a hot minute." Lilith's smirk hadn't moved, though. "I'd been looking too far afield. I only needed to talk to our own coven about it. Be right back."

I skimmed the report on Jaye this constable had signed off on. It was cop-speak for *no problems here, stop hassling the guy.* "Well, shit."

"Wonder if anything came out of Wes snitching on the guy," Aspen said, frowning. "You've got a ten-thirty, Roars."

I groaned. "I know, I know." I was going to miss out on all the fucking gossip and I hated it. "Catch me up at lunch, you future home-owning, bougie witch."

She let out an excited noise and did another happy dance, then stopped and propped her hands on her hips, deep breathing while I packed up my laptop. "I'm going to be poor forever," she said, horrified. "What if they say no? And we have to wait for our offer to be officially turned down before we can make an offer on something else? Our pre-approval only lasts for a little while."

I pressed a kiss to the top of her head, resisting the urge to squeeze her in a hug. "Cross that bridge when you come to it."

She nodded and waved me off, her eyes huge.

I opened up my phone and brought up Taig's number as I strode into the elevator. My fingers hesitated over the keyboard. *Hey, want to compare financial situations and see if we're compatible for the long haul* seemed like a bad text to send a guy. Knowing Taig, he'd take it with grace. Instead, I typed, *hey, you free for lunch? We're celebrating that Aspen's putting an offer on a place.*

The elevator door slid open and his response popped onto the screen. *Always down to hang out with happy, hopeful people. Just tell me where and when, and whether I can bring Delyan if we get caught up.*

Why was that the sweetest fucking response?

CHAPTER 31

*L*ilith was tucked firmly into Vince's side when I got there. They both looked happy as clams. I took the empty seat across from them, suddenly feeling awkward. Vince surely knew Lilith had been with me the whole time they'd been on the rocks, right? And that I'd help her bury his body in a heartbeat?

"Hey, Rory," he said. "How's it going?"

"Hey. I'm okay, how's your day?"

"Oh, good." He glanced over at Lilith. "Lil tells me you guys made big inroads in something?"

Allen. Right. I glanced over at Lilith, and she shook her head, sipping her drink. "When Aspen's here. I don't want to repeat it a million times."

There went my one conversation topic. *'So, what've you been up to while your girlfriend was living on my couch?'* seemed like a somewhat loaded question, but it was the only thing I could think of.

"Got a menu?" Lilith asked me, sliding one over. "I'm thinking of having the stew."

I seized on the conversational gambit. "Have either of you been here?" I asked them. "I'm all ears for recommendations. I don't know what I feel like."

It worked like a charm. They used to come here all the time, apparently, and chatted about past experiences until Aspen and Nic arrived. I realized, as Aspen excitedly told Vince all about the house they'd put an offer on, that I hadn't even asked which one. Of course it was the one Lilith and I had sussed out for them.

Nic sat beside me, since Aspen took the head of the table, but the grin he shot over to Lilith was simply friendly. He offered a hand to Vince. "Hey, good to meet you," he said, and seemed to mean it.

I wondered if I'd be that graceful, in his shoes, with my happily ever after lingering in the balance. He caught my look as the menu conversation kicked off again and quirked his brows. "You okay, Sunshine?"

I scowled, looking back at the list of food. "Yeah, except I want to hear about this cop."

"There's some issues with confidentiality," Lilith said. All eyes turned to Nic.

He tossed me a lazy look. "Come on. Vouch for me."

I ignored Aspen's laughter. She was giddy on hope. "Anything Nic doesn't know he hasn't chosen to figure out," I told Lilith, wryly.

"You're an Oracle, right?" Vince asked.

"You're going to ask me to read what you say next," Nic drawled. "It's going to be that you love that witch beside you, and you're going to get her another drink."

Vince's eyes widened. "I thought that was illegal."

Wrong boyfriend to be pointing that out. The whole thing was so common I had secondhand embarrassment for Vince. "Special licenses required makes it quasi legal," Nic assured him. "Taig'll be here soon. He's got Delyan coming. If you folks want to talk about this dirty cop with friends, do it now."

I held up a hand to stop him. "Hold on. Is Delyan a friend?"

He poured himself water. "She's a cop, isn't she? Taig doesn't count. You've got him wrapped around your little finger. I don't need to be an Oracle to distrust random cops. So." He settled in, pinning Lilith in his gaze. Even *my* head hurt at all that intensity, and I was used to Nic. "Tell us."

Lilith sat back. I had to close my mouth to stop from commenting over the long, unimpressed look she gave him. "I think I like you better when you're puking."

He grinned. "You wouldn't be the first."

She let out an irritated noise. Under the table, I gave him a bit of a nudge. He knew he freaked out the uninitiated.

"He's dirty," Lilith said, sourly. "I'm figuring out how dirty, and who I can pass the information on to. I think the call will need to come from Shep, because he's actually signed off on a report that he shouldn't have for Shep's problematic lycan. It's an obvious misuse of authority."

"I like the obvious ones," I said, surprised it was going to be so simple. "Not much of a threat, if he's working in plain sight like that."

"Well, Vince did a database search for me," Lilith said, shooting Nic a quick, distrustful glance, as if Nic wanted to get Vince fired.

I wondered if maybe he might.

"He's been involved in more than thirteen reports like that one in the last seven years," Vince said, his voice low. *"Thirteen."*

I resisted the urge to ask about fatalities, because a body count wasn't the best way to tally cost. Either way, it sounded like Shepherd was on it too, locked and loaded to make a report as soon as they figured out the best person to send it to.

"You don't have a coffee," Nic murmured to me under the lively conversation. "Or a torch and pitchfork. You okay?"

"Yeah." I wasn't even lying. "I mean, I won't say no to a coffee, but."

His expression softened as he gently tugged a single curl. "I like seeing you happy. We need to catch up. I'm sorry I haven't been around lately."

I didn't need to be an Oracle to know that statement was about the information I'd vomited at him when he'd been vulnerable. "It's fine, Nic."

He didn't respond, instead glancing up. I followed the direction of his polite smile and found Taig and Delyan coming to a halt at our table. "Ah, perfect timing. I was just going to order drinks. Taig, you can help carry. Oh." Nic paused, addressing the table as he stood. "What does everyone want?"

I could just about see what Vince was thinking, but he didn't issue his challenge out loud. I suspected the look Lilith shot him might've helped keep it inside his head. Meanwhile, I was far more concerned about Taig's neutral expression as he set his keys down, claiming the empty chair beside me. He'd never been territorial before, but I didn't love the way he looked at Nic.

I sat there as Nic took orders without bothering to ask me. That wasn't a flex, though. I was pretty sure everyone in Melbourne knew my standing order.

Taig didn't mention it, though he would've noticed. Delyan awkwardly perched between Aspen and Lilith, introducing herself around. I watched Taig's professional mask deflect Nic's shit-eating grin as they went to get drinks. What were they saying to each other?

"Does Taig know you and Nic were an item?" Lilith asked me, making ice chime as she stirred the last of her drink.

I saw Delyan's eyes flicker to me and wanted to kick Lilith. "Yes, he does, and he knows we're both happy to be friends."

Lilith's brows arched, but she turned to Delyan. "Busy morning?"

"Gorillas aren't cute," Aspen murmured, to me.

Except neither Taig nor Nic were beating at their chests and defending their territory, so that wasn't a relevant comment.

She didn't need to tell me twice. I opened up my phone, irritated. "I can't remember the address. Or anything. Search this place and let me have a second look."

Nic was the one who set my coffee in front of me when they returned. I refused to read into that, or be weird at all. Maybe there were no undercurrents and I was just jumping at shadows. "Have you seen the cute place they put an offer on?" I asked Taig, angling my phone.

He made an approving noise, his hand resting on my thigh. If it'd been a possessive move I'd have shifted away, but it felt reassuring. Maybe it was. I settled in and leant against him. "Good space. Even a courtyard. Do you grow your own herbs?" he asked Nic. "For your work?"

"I haven't been," Nic said. "But I'm looking forward to being home enough to learn how."

"Oh, that's a witchy thing I *can* do," Aspen said, enthusiastically. "I got you."

I wasn't jumpy, and I doubted I'd misread the signals. My refusal to acknowledge the bullshit apparently paid off, because conversations about real estate beat unnecessary shows of ownership.

Most of us had finished our lunch when Aspen's phone rang. I looked away from Delyan and Lilith's conversation about shoddy building practices to see the name of Jessica's school scrolling over Aspen's screen.

She was standing as she answered, heading outside where it'd be quieter. I watched her go, a sinking feeling in my belly. We had a meeting with them next Monday. Surely, anything non-urgent could wait a few days?

I considered organizing the bill now, but hesitated, watching out the window as Aspen spoke into the phone, a faint frown on her brow.

"Everything okay?" Taig asked me, following my gaze.

"No good reason for that call," I explained. He nodded his understanding.

Aspen looked up and met my eyes over the crowded restaurant. Ice went through my veins before her hand made quick, aggressive summoning motions. "Hey, Lilith," I said, over top of the ongoing conversation. "We've got us a situation."

Taig stood so I could get out. Behind me, they talked about the bill. I didn't know if I'd actually heard Nic insisting he'd get it, or whether that was just memories clashing together.

"...points of access?" Aspen was saying. She jerked her head toward the bus stop down the road and looked pointedly over my shoulder. "I understand, and I agree, but duty of care for her wellbeing this afternoon remains with you until she is discharged into the care of another adult."

Fuck. I stuck my head back inside to hurry Lilith, but she was already striding over. "Something's happened to Jessica," I told her.

Her lips thinned and we fell in alongside Aspen, who did her level best to make sure everyone kept doing their job while we headed over. I regretted not hitting Taig up for a lift as the bus rocked along, but he had his company ride so it probably wouldn't have gone down well anyway.

I could imagine the conversation between him, Nic and Vince would be fun right now.

"What's the last we heard on those stalkers?" Aspen asked me, as she hung up.

"Distillery in Port Melbourne." Even though I was pleased my brain worked, I didn't comment on it. "Taig wouldn't tell me more."

"Well, Taig is going to need to spill," she said, flatly. "Because someone just tried to sign Jess out."

My stomach turned over. I didn't need to tell Lilith and Aspen why that was so colossally fucked up. There were *only* bad options, and while Benson's disclosure had narrowed down what type of option it was, it didn't matter a shit. "They failed," I confirmed, and Aspen nodded. "Description?"

"A man. Forties, white, jeans and a band t-shirt."

That narrowed it down not a hell of a lot. "What band?" Lilith asked, and Aspen shook her head. "Seriously? They couldn't even catch that?"

"He had a Custodian license," Aspen said, the words clipped.

My head spun. "Well, if we can find him, that alone will send him to SuperSec," I managed.

"Wait. Wait." Lilith pinched the bridge of her nose. "He had a license, but they didn't let him sign Jessica out?"

"They called me. He wasn't listed, of course. He took off pretty much as soon as they started to sound suspicious."

Of course he had. "I'm letting Maadai know we've got a counterfeit license out there," Lilith said. "We got a name?"

"Josh Kelly." He'd even *chosen* an obnoxious name. "The school is contacting law enforcement, but there isn't much they'll do except put out an alert, I suspect. Maybe a patrol car, if we're lucky, to cruise around."

I listened to Lilith debriefing Maadai and ran over what I knew, which wasn't anywhere near enough, and kept my eyes up. The bus driver had music on, everyone had headphones, and the only other passengers weren't close. The chance of being overheard was never zero in public, but Lilith kept names out of it, using initials where they were needed. It was the best we could do.

"Benson's going to need a lot of support," Aspen said, quietly, leaning away from Lilith so as not to disturb her. "We might be on school pickup and drop-off for a while."

Relief rushed through me. Shit, I hoped they came at Jessica when I was there. "I'll clear our schedule so we can make that for the next two weeks."

"Thanks." Aspen blew out a breath. "I was having such a good day, too."

That was because I'd forgotten to mention we were probably about to have a banshee removed from our list and into SuperSec.

She unlocked her phone as I did. "I'll start re-booking tomorrow," she said. "You do Thursday. We'll see who finishes first."

"Deal."

Lilith was on deck helping manage schedules before either of us managed to finish our shuffling. We made it to the school with the whole week sorted.

In the office, Jessica was sitting outside of the room with the principal's plaque on the door. I waved to her as we came in. She had the fixed expression of someone who knew they were up shit creek and didn't trust anyone to give them a paddle. It made my heart break.

Aspen peeled away to go to her and I smiled at the clerk, flashing my *legitimate* Custodian license. "Aurora Gold."

"Of course." The receptionist looked over at where Aspen crouched in front of Jessica, who perched on the edge of her seat, pale with barely veiled terror. "This way."

"I'll wait here," Aspen said brightly.

Damn it, if anyone was punching stalkers in the dick, I wanted it to be *me.* But she'd called shotgun, so I followed the receptionist into the room she indicated, not allowing her to hesitate. I was pissed to see Lilith hung out with Jessica, too.

Everyone got to have fun *except* me.

There was no one waiting in the room, but I was told it wouldn't be long. So I sat and kept rescheduling what I could, copy pasting a default apology email and tweaking the details. By the time the principal walked in, I was on a roll. I put it aside without hesitation. "Why has she been pulled out of class?"

He looked over my shoulder, as if expecting Aspen to pop up and ask the same thing, except nicely. He was shit out of luck. "Jessica had already been summoned. We thought it was best she not wander the school grounds, under the circumstances."

"The call was twenty minutes ago. Surely there was *someone* who could've taken her back in that time."

His expression was falsely placating. "Benson thought it was best she remain present for easy pickup."

Oh, fuck. They'd already called him.

"Ms Gold—"

"Custodian," I cut in.

"Custodian Gold," he amended. "Where there are court orders in place, we're happy to support families, but we aren't able to differentiate licenses. That's not in our skill set, you understand."

"You're telling me you don't want to provide an education to a child enrolled in your school?" I asked him, coldly.

"Of course not, and I hope you appreciate—"

"I appreciate you called us," I said, cutting him off. "I don't appreciate you terrifying her father."

"As her legal guardian—"

I stood. "If I need to get the Department involved I have no hesitation. The safest place for that kid is in her class, leaving the issues to the adults around her. Given the depth and breadth of services involved, you have a *lot* of people watching." His expression said he knew I wasn't lying, and he fucking hated it. "Make sure that happens, and there are no issues." And, furious as I was, I couldn't tell them *not* to contact Benson. They'd called us first, this time. "Given the situation, the first call is to her father, the second call *immediately after* is to us." Elders help them if Benson arrived before we did.

The crash of the front door punctuated my thoughts. Glass crunched, and the principal's expression became fixed.

"Good thing you've got insurance," I told him, knowing damned well who'd just walked in. "I'll be in contact with the police about this. Thank you."

"We have a zero-tolerance policy," he told me.

I snorted. "Same, mate. Same."

CHAPTER 32

I stood in Trinity's backyard as Jessica watched Liam crashing trucks into each other, listening to Benson giving Trinity what I assumed was the run-down in their native tongue.

Someone had been sniffing around.

Someone who was a lycan.

Someone who Trinity identified as being linked to Duke, and Benson suspected might be linked to his stalkers.

Benson's breathing had slowed, now, and he wasn't white knuckled, but the fury was there, right under the surface.

I was helpless to do anything.

Maybe this was the by-product of doing my actual job, not Cop Lite, the way I had been. I didn't *know* all the criminal activity going on around us. How in the everloving fuck could Duke possibly be involved? It didn't make sense. Zane had mentioned his people had been sniffing around. I knew Duke's crew were linked to the illegal drug trade. I'd fucked his brother and his Melbourne branch, both, *and* made sure he couldn't get his hands on his kid. He absolutely had a vendetta against me. I suspected he was a businessman, though.

I wasn't making waves, and I no longer stood between he and family. I'd also taken out no small number of his people.

It would make sense if he was focused on his drug trade. It wasn't that far a stretch to trafficking, but it wasn't something they were known for. And how were the guys who'd been parked over the road from Benson linked in?

Lilith ended the call she'd been on and wandered over. "They found the license a block away," she said, quietly. "Half burned."

Duke's people hadn't been done for forgery, to the best of my knowledge. Another piece that didn't fit in the puzzle.

"Magickally burned?" I asked.

She shrugged. "Don't know yet."

I could've fucking told them. "Did it smell like petrol?" I asked, irritated.

"You want to call them?" she demanded, offering me the phone.

I kind of did, but I let it go, feeling sick as I watched those kids.

Duke didn't fit. Not because I didn't have my finger on the pulse, but because it was too different from how he'd worked in the past, what he'd been interested in.

Unless he was linked to the vamps who wanted Benson back. I didn't know what the odds were that Duke's people were competing with the human fertilizer who'd driven Benson from his home. I just knew they were never zero.

My thumbs itched to text Oma. I needed some charms.

I was too close to this. But damned if I was stepping back. *Not being close seemed like a crime.*

"I mishandled the principal," I told Lilith, the words bitter on my tongue. "I'm sorry. I might need Aspen to manage him going forward."

She grunted. "He looked a bit rattled."

"Sorry."

She shrugged. "Maybe he'll be less of a twatwaffle next time. He *earned* the bad witch routine." She made a noise of disgust. "Imagine not sending her back to class."

The kid in question glanced up at us and I remembered her hyper hearing. "You deserved better, Jessica. Sorry," I said. That apology was a lot easier than my admission to Lilith.

Lilith murmured her agreement, running her hands through her hair. She glanced over at where Benson and Trinity were deep in conversation, their expressions intent. She didn't voice her speculation, but she didn't need to. I could hear it all the same.

Did they know Jessica was listening to their every word?

We'd had a meeting booked for Liam's kinder this afternoon, but Benson didn't want to leave the kids and Aspen didn't want them privy to the entire meeting, and no one would accept a silence ward, so Aspen was taking that one solo to try to make *some* progress.

"Aspen probably wouldn't have been very polite if she'd gone in, either," Lilith told me. "To be fair."

"She would've been rude in a civil way."

Lilith snorted, folding her arms under her breasts and stepping back into the scant shade. I followed, about to comment on the heat when my phone went off.

I glanced at it, expecting to see Aspen or VicPol, but Shep's name was backlit. I answered, wondering if he was checking in.

The sound of crunching metal came from the other end. "Jaye's garage, Roars," he said, the words clipped. *"Low and slow prevent this show."*

Adrenaline roared through my veins. "On my way." I didn't know if he heard, though. The line was dead.

Trinity, Benson and Jessica were all staring at me and I paused for a moment, torn.

"Go," Lilith said. "I'll keep these three safe."

I saw Benson's eyes narrow slightly at that, but I didn't have time to argue about whether he needed our protection or not. "I'm calling Nic," I told Lilith, setting off. "And Aspen."

"Send me Aspen," she shouted after me.

No shit. I didn't say it, already out the front door and sprinting down the block to the nearest tram stop.

I'd had such a peaceful week. Maybe I *was* jumpy, but this seemed far too convenient a coincidence. Still, I wasn't leaving Shep and Fritz to deal with a lycan pack on the off chance someone was trying to divide and conquer.

We were harder to conquer than that, and would never be divided.

CHAPTER 33

The garage was ablaze when I got there. Fritz was bleeding from his forehead and sheltering behind a nearby car, talking into his phone. There were cops beside him, and sirens closing in. "Where's Shep?" I asked him, but it was a rhetorical question. A lycan was launched out of the building, fully shifted and pierced with shards of metal. Its claws ripped at the bitumen as it writhed in agony.

Nic wasn't going to make it in time. I kind of wished I'd called Arthur. He'd been semi-useful last time we'd been caught in a blaze.

So had Beo. Both the last blaze, and the last time I'd stepped foot in this garage.

I hoped he was doing okay.

"Widen your perimeter," I told the wet-behind-the-ears cop, but didn't bother waiting for an answer. I didn't have my fucking headgear, and while I had closed toe shoes my ballet flats weren't my boots. The best I could do was stuff my hair under my collar as I strode in, wand in my other hand. "Hey, betas," I shouted into the flames. "What did you do to my buddy?"

Crashing noises came from in front of me and a snarl was the only warning I got to raise my Impenetrable.

The lycan hit it like a cartoon creature, face to the side and expression shocked. I resisted the urge to punch it in the nose to make myself feel better. It had stunned itself, so I collapsed my spell and went in the direction of the noise.

Shep was pinned down, otherwise he wouldn't be in here anymore. I just had to get him, and get out. Easy peasy. I lifted the collar of my Lupetec shirt over my face and tried to breathe shallowly, my eyes watering in the smoke.

Clicking claws on metal made me throw up another ward, but the lycan remained hidden in the smoke.

My heart in my throat I thought I heard some spellcasting and adjusted my direction. The ground was hot beneath my feet and my head spun.

Shep came into view a moment later. I watched as his attention went from the lycan in front of him, to me, then over my shoulder.

As if in slow motion, his wand swung and my heart froze.

On pure instinct, I dropped to the ground. Before I felt the concrete, though, I was hit and pinballed against a car. Pain exploded in my head and fury was hot on its heels. Snarls and shouts, spells and scraping metal. I staggered to my feet, the world whirling. Nausea swept through me.

That was bad. *Your bitch is concussed.* I could taste the blood and it burned. I could barely breathe. Or maybe that was the concussion too. Shep kept coughing during his casts. His leg was caught under a car body and the lycans didn't seem to give a shit about little annoyances like the flaming inferno engulfing the whole garage.

I got it. Vengeance was a helluva goal. But if this was some kind of ruse to get me away from Benson, they were all so fucked they'd *wish* Shep nailed them.

Fury burned through my veins. I forced myself to move, trusting to adrenaline and sheer pigheadedness to get me through one more time as I ducked under Shep's line of sight so he didn't accidentally toss *me* through a wall.

The world swam. All I could taste was the copper of my own blood. I put my hands against the car pinning Shep to the ground and tried to hold myself up. *Pressure from crisply folded cuffs against my fore-*

arms. Disoriented, I felt another spell sweep past me. My stomach rebelled and my knees threatened to give way.

My phone buzzed in my pocket. In my mind's eye, Jessica's name danced across the screen. It wouldn't be her. I knew it, from far away. I watched from above myself, my head in the smoky rafters, as I set my feet and aligned my spine. The burn of my rage was palpable even from my vantage point in the ceiling. I imagined I could see smoke billowing out of my own mouth as I forced the car body off Shep with the scream of metal. *A zipper being lowered.* The world spun.

Shep popped out from under the car like a broken cork, leaving behind his jacket to float in the smoke. I needed to get him out, so I did, tossing him over my shoulders as I'd been trained to do. Smoke slowly swirled around us, a cinematic dream. From above, I looked like I was sprinting through that slow swirling smoke, but I was barely moving. I was burning up. I could feel it, even from my position above, in the the now-broken roof as it crumbled around us. I was burning up, and if I burned up, and I was holding Shep, he'd burn up too, and we'd never get back to Jessica.

A lycan came from the side, moving as slowly as I was, its progress incremental. I watched it closing on me, knowing I couldn't duck to avoid it without extending my time inside the death trap.

There was explosive stuff in garages, right? I was pretty sure there was. I didn't know if that was the cause of the fire, or if it was about to get a whole lot worse, and I didn't want to find out.

From my position in the rafters, I timed it perfectly. The lycan's jaws were wide and paws were off the ground, full-flight, totally committed, when I activated my blowback charm and sent it spinning into a car. I watched its arc until I popped free from the garage and into the sun.

I probably needed a hug. I'd have to see about that.

Whatever momentum I had, or whatever the fuck had happened, I lost it. *Speed wobbles,* Dad said in my head as my steps faltered. I staggered side to side, narrowly avoiding colliding with a panel van out front. Instead I hit the ute beside it with a crunch that sounded, even from the sky, to be not great.

"Down!" Nic shouted. My body listened to the instruction long before it filtered up to me in the clouds. The world started settling around me, like a snowglobe finally allowed to rest. There were gunshots. "Up!"

I climbed to my feet, Shep still over my shoulders. Everything developed that grainy quality of old film. The ground kept moving, but Nic was there in the center of the road, feet planted and wand out. A gray haired old cop stood beside him, her gun out and sweat running down her determined face.

I passed Nic and went straight to the paramedics. Vengeance was great and all, but I had people to see and shit to do.

CHAPTER 34

"You need to go home and rest," the ambo told me. "You've got a concussion and you've breathed in a lot of smoke."

I didn't smoke. My head swam. "I appreciate that, but I do need to do one more thing." She looked over my shoulder at whoever was checking my blood pressure and the whole world tilted. "If you get the waiver, I'll sign." I could make my hands work. I'd been concussed before. This one wasn't even bad. If I'd blacked out, it was only for a second. Yeah, sure, smoking was bad, but apparently I'd been in there for less than two minutes. That wasn't a big deal, right? It wasn't like I was a garage-a-day smoker.

I wasn't jumpy, but I was sure as shit not good.

A firetruck eased past, and I glanced up to see Nic closing in. "Go to hospital, Sunshine," he told me. "I'll go check on Lilith and Aspen."

"He can drive me," I told them, latching on to him as I tried to stand. My legs shook, but held. I ignored the world trying to kick me off. It wasn't the first time, and probably wouldn't be the last. Instead, I mimicked Nic's posture, trusting him to know where the ground *actually* was. "Waiver, please?"

Nic's expression grew intense as he looked at me, and I knew damned well he was Reading me. So when he nodded confirmation, I figured that was a good sign. Or a really, really bad one.

I was offered a clipboard and tried to focus my eyes long enough to see where to sign.

"Here," Nic said, holding me up with one hand while he pointed to a spot on the page with another. I scrawled something that didn't resemble my signature in the slightest.

Their liability discharged, they let us go without too much hassle. I stuck to Nic's side so I didn't faceplant on the way to the car. "They've got your wizard friends in the hospital already," he told me. I was pretty sure that shouldn't have felt like new information. "Lucky you've got such a thick skull."

Wow. So original. Much wit. I didn't try to get the words out, falling down into his car. He closed the door after me. When he climbed behind the wheel, I managed, "Jessica."

"She's fine tonight, far as I can see," he told me. "As if we wouldn't already be halfway there if she wasn't, Roars. Come off it." He threw the car into gear. The jolt made nausea sweep through me. "You aren't wearing your time charms."

"No." No, I hadn't been. Taig had ordered those STI tests ages ago. I needed to follow up on those. Or had he already told me? Maybe I could figure out how to juggle them so I could wear my sex protection and also time warp charms?

"You're moving fast, there, for a human," he drawled. "Got that under wraps yet?"

I was going to puke. "What?"

He glanced over at me and, in answer, flipped down his sunglasses to hide his eyes.

I didn't know what to make of that, so I fell back against the chair and tried not to puke. If Nic said Jess was safe, then Jess was safe.

Brandon wasn't. But Jess was.

I shook my head and regretted it with every fiber of my being. "Maybe I should get some healing done," I tried to say.

"You'll be more or less okay by tomorrow," Nic assured me. "It's the different magicks that're fucking you up. I thought you would've been training it."

Different magicks. I was helpless as a half-melted cappuccino ice-cream with the bottom bitten out of the cone. Or maybe I was ninety-eight percent cappuccino, two percent boysenberry. He accelerated through an orange light and I thought I was going to vomit. But if I had been, he'd've pulled over, for sure. So I didn't. No wonder I felt sick, really. Cappuccino and boysenberry? What a fucked up combo.

"Give me your phone, please."

I scrabbled at my pockets, my fingers like overcooked hotdogs. Maybe I was hungry. Maybe my blood sugars were no good. I didn't have blood sugar problems, but who knew, right?

My phone rang. Nic reached over, diving into my pocket with some muttered words about incompetent law enforcement and some-thing about Retrievals. "Hey Taig," he said. "Yeah, I got her. Yeah, I'm driving."

Amusement crashed over me. I could almost hear Taig telling Nic what sort of laws he was breaking by using a phone as he drove.

The next thing I knew the door eased open and I was scooped up. There was something so lovely about being scooped. I snuggled in and felt Taig press a kiss to my forehead before rubbing the soft part of his cheek against my temple.

"I promised her I'd go check on her coven," I heard Nic say, from a long way away. "Watch her cat, she'll be worried and get underfoot."

"Thanks, Nic," I heard Taig say, in his up-all-night voice. "I owe you."

"Pretty sure the Custodians owe both of us," Nic said. From where I floated happily in the clouds, I felt resentment curling through me.

"I can walk," I managed to say, but I wasn't given the opportunity to test if that was true.

Taig's steps hurt my head, and my lungs burned like hell. My heart felt better when he put me on the couch. Eclipse was immediately in my lap, inspecting me frantically. I drifted, feeling her weight settling over my aching chest and pinning me to the world. It hurt, but I knew it was the right thing to do. She purred on me, her reassuring vibrations making tears prick my burning eyes.

It was dark when I woke still feeling nauseous but more or less whole. Taig sat on the ground beside me, his phone showing pages of whatever book he was reading now.

As soon as I moved he glanced up, expression concerned. "Hey."

I was able to focus on him, which was definitely a good sign. I probably could've read the words, too, on his screen, if I'd wanted to. "I'm feeling better," I told him. "Thank you."

"I'm going to need to look into what fire extinguishing charms you can use," he said, frowning. "If you keep running into fires. Either that, or train as a smoke eater."

The first idea wasn't a bad one. I eased off the couch, hating the reek of smoke. "You don't have anything, right?"

"Like dinner?"

"Like an infection," I said, waving a hand in the direction of his crotch.

He shook his head. "I did mention it. You mustn't have registered."

"Sorry."

He shook his head again, walking slowly beside me toward the bathroom. "Not a sorry thing. I just didn't want you thinking I was withholding info."

I figured my brain did plenty of that. *You're not jumpy, though.* My skin crawled and I remembered the sound of metal screeching like a zipper. "I think I need to get in to see my therapist ASAP."

"Want me to send her an email?"

"No." Talking him through that, even digging up her email? That was too much work. "I've got it. Thank you."

He hung out while I washed. I was stable on my feet, now, just tired and mildly pukey with a pissing headache.

"Shep might need surgery on his leg," Taig said, from his spot before my partially open shower. "The bones aren't looking great."

I killed the water, remembering how I'd moved an entire car with one well aligned shove. Adrenaline was good stuff.

The towel in my hand was soft as I held it to my face. "I think I used fae magick."

He nodded, still leaning against the wall. "You've got enough charms no one will know."

He'd known. He and Nic *both* knew. Was that what they'd been comparing notes on? I shook my head, because I couldn't remember if they'd already known. Had Nic inferred it ages ago? Found out off Dad?

Fucking *Wesley* knew before me. Arsehole.

"Elders. Whatever I breathed in would kill a brown dog," I said, letting the water run off me into the bathmat. Apparently I channeled Dad when I got messed up. "Sick. I feel sick. That's what I meant."

"I'm stoked you're alive," was Taig's easy going response. "Is there anything I can do to help?"

I shook my head. The world stayed where it was supposed to. "Did Shep not get magickal heals?"

"He did. They're air-lifting an expert from Sydney, last I heard. Failing that, it's pins and plates to catch what the magick can't."

My mind skittered over the choices I'd made that afternoon, how I could've possibly gotten there earlier. "He's alive."

"He's alive."

That was about the best I could do, and it left me feeling hollow. "Richardson was there."

"Whisper network says she killed Jaye," Taig confirmed. "Nic held fire, I expect, so there wouldn't be unnecessary paperwork for him. He's already got to answer some questions, being there at all."

"Fuck." That pretty much summarized my relationship with Nic, though. Cleaning up my messes, making my excuses. "Poor guy."

"He's fine." I let Taig take a second towel and start patting me down. "Is there a reason you didn't call me?"

"You were on duty."

He paused, towel on my shoulder, and met my eyes. "Rory. Come on."

I wasn't wrong, though. "You'd lose your job."

He shrugged. "Maybe it'd be good for me."
"Maybe," I agreed, quietly.

CHAPTER 35

The clock read almost midnight and my phone display read *Bethany*. Adrenaline shot through me as Eclipse leapt off of me and onto Taig. He sat up beside me, switching on the light.

"Hey," I answered.

"Evening, Aurora," Bethany said. "I've got a felinethrope in Fitzroy tearing up a bar. Contract is pending, but you're going in hot."

My head ached, but only a little, and it wasn't distractingly bad. I was in better shape to deal with a felinethrope than whatever poor LO's were probably fighting for their lives.

But I was fucking *wrecked.*

Eclipse picked her way back over into my lap, purring.

"Not tonight, Beth," I managed, hearing the tears in my throat. "I'm a bit rough to be taking a contract."

She was silent for a moment. "Are you okay?"

"Yeah." Grief had claws like a huge cat. "I will be. Just not tonight."

"Of course. Thank you." And she was gone. My phone was a dead weight in my hand.

Taig pressed a kiss to my shoulder, silent. I swallowed tears and tossed my device aside.

I hadn't refused a contract since I'd been cleared to do casual Retrievals. I didn't know if it was the right call. I didn't know how many lives would be lost without me putting on my Lupetec and big girl panties.

Beneath my hands, Eclipses's fur was soft and warm. She pressed into my scritches, happily kneading the covers, and didn't mind if a few tears fell on her.

When I glanced up at Taig, his expression was full of compassion. One thumb swiped away a tear. "I'm proud of you," he told me, in that up-all-night voice. It was the sweetest statement I didn't need, but I received it with what grace I could muster.

I let out a long breath, feeling sick. I was going to need to avoid the news tomorrow. I didn't need to know the fallout. I'd never know if it came before or after that call, or what I could've done. So there was no point in borrowing that trouble.

"How long until our holiday?"

"Eleven days." He wiped away another tear. "Want me to tell you where we're going?"

I shook my head. "Just what to pack."

"Can do." He settled back. I went with him, finding the warmth I wanted in his arms and pressing myself close as the grief writhed in my chest. I wasn't grieving the people who might be dying. I was grieving the loss of my own sense of control.

I didn't like letting go.

His hair was soft between my fingers and I found his lips with my own, wishing I could just celebrate. *Yay, healthy boundaries.* He looked up at me, those pale blue eyes seeing right through my skull and tracking the course of my thoughts through my brain matter.

What I needed tonight wasn't to throw myself into more chaos, to kick off my fight-or-flight and spend the next days or weeks in survival mode. What I needed tonight was to find my way back into my own skin.

"Want to go for a jog?" he offered, softly.

I pulled a face. "Fuck, no." I found his mouth again and he hummed in pleasure, his tongue tracing the curve of my lips in a way that made my blood warm. I ran my hand across his chest, settling my arm around him and locking him close.

I dropped down onto the pillow so he raised up. I opened my mouth, encouraging the sweep of his tongue and feeling the affection turn to hunger with every beat of my heart.

"You're mine," he breathed against my lips.

I shook my head. "'Fraid not, buddy."

His laugh was short and pleased. "Can I kiss you better all the same?"

I sat up enough that I could wriggle out of the shirt I'd stolen to sleep in. Eclipse, underwhelmed by the jostling, leapt off the bed, but I knew she'd be back. This way I didn't have to worry about scarring her for life.

His touch was gentle and his hands sure. I let myself drift while he explored, kisses and caresses that moved down my body. I felt every single one of them from my home inside of my skin. The brush of his chest hair against my thigh, the wetness of his lips low on my belly, the weight of him settling between my legs, the curve of his skull in my palms.

I was treated like a delicacy. It felt exactly right. And when he brought me right to the edge, I pulled him up, locked my legs around his hips, and felt every stroke like lightning.

CHAPTER 36

My Lupetec smelt like smoke when I went to put it on. Not like wood smoke, which was a nice enough smell, but like *industrial fire*. There was no way I was doing that to myself. The soles of my flats were half-melted, which made sense, because my feet had a few small heat blisters. Enough that I wasn't keen on snug shoes.

It wasn't two-pairs-of-socks weather, but we'd make do.

"I've got a late shift this afternoon," Taig insisted, as I let him shoo me out the door. "I'll clean up your armor and get it drying. It needs to be good to go sooner rather than later."

"I've got my Retrievals kit."

"With you?"

"No. It's in the safe."

He ignored the disapproving look I sent him, watching me move with a critical eye. "You should be sleeping it off."

"There's going to be fallout. I can work a phone."

He let out a long, annoyed breath. "Why did I find your determination so enticing?"

"Genuinely? No clue." He opened the car door for me and I climbed in, dragging my skirt in after me. It wouldn't stop a knife, but it looked cuter than Lupetec. My Retrievals gear wasn't the same weave. It was much harder to accessorize.

Taig leant in and planted a kiss on my lips, his expression one of resignation. I mostly managed to hide my amusement and he closed the door firmly behind me, coming around to the driver's side.

My emails had blown up overnight, of course. I was going to need to do a thorough incident report for yesterday. That was going to be challenging, given how spotty my memory was.

I hadn't actively done harm to anyone, I was pretty sure, so it should be fine if I just skipped over some of it. I didn't have to prove self defense, after all. I'd barely even cast spells.

"What's news?" Taig asked, putting the car in reverse and glancing over at me as he did his head check. I looked up from the emails I was skimming, jolted back into the real world.

"Hm? Um. Looks like the arson team's been called in. I'm assuming Shep can't talk and Fritz didn't see the fire start." It was probably going to be magickal, though. Who didn't love a good fireball? Without silver, fire was pretty much the go-to for anything chompy and shifty. "One missing lycanthrope. Nic's team are actively pursuing." That would be why I was called last night to deal with the bar fight. "No news on the Hurtfield situation."

"No news is good news."

No news meant there was a creepy dude with a hard-on for shifters out there who knew where that girl's school was. "I suppose." I pointed up ahead. "Near that white van? If that works."

"It works." He pulled over. I climbed out, mindful of my aching feet. I accepted the kiss he blew me before he eased back into traffic and went to go scrub my Lupetec.

"Rory!" Aspen's shout made me turn. She was half-running, travel cup held awkwardly in one hand and horror on her face. "What the hell are you doing?"

"Taking Jessica to school." We'd agreed on this, hadn't we? That's why *she* was here.

"Lilith's coming." She picked some cat hair off my shirt. "Are you sure you're okay? I heard you got all fucked up."

"Bitch, I'm always getting all fucked up." I peered into her coffee cup. Whatever it was, it had a bag dangling out of the side and smelt like horse shit, so I didn't borrow any.

"Wow, I didn't know we were bragging about it," she said, giving me a hair flip. "Nice skirt. Where's your Lupetec?"

"It stinks. Trust me. Skirt is an improvement." I shouldered open the door to the apartment. "Lilith's probably already up there."

"Probably," Aspen agreed. "I cannot wait to live less than an hour away." She watched me like I was made of glass. I was sore, but not *that* sore. Maybe I'd end up heading off early, if my head got worse rather than better, but that was okay. "If you're concussed, you shouldn't be doing any reading or anything?"

"We'll talk about it later." Benson didn't need his faith in me shaken when our fragile trust was about to be tested.

Lilith was, indeed, already waiting. So were the Hurtfields, their faces grim. Only Liam was on the floor. He was playing with the frog toy and tea pot by tipping both of them toward the tea cup simultaneously.

I didn't know what Aspen had said to them, but Benson scooped up Liam and left with a long look at Jessica, and not a word to us.

There was no way a kid should be preparing to defend herself as she stepped out her front door. Or at all. Unfortunately, it was what it was. We escorted her to school and waited until the bell rang, trying to linger at an inconspicuous distance. Nothing was out of place.

"I want to talk to the cops who got this case," Lilith said, once the tiny people had all vanished into the big learning boxes. "This morning."

"We're going to have to do something drastic with caseloads," Aspen reminded her. "Shep's going to be out for a while, and Fritz can't work their stuff solo. Maadai is doing a full time job already. She can't just drop that and do fieldwork."

It meant we'd need to go down to two groups of two, probably. That was the whole reason Shep had ended up where he was now. Two people was a bad number. It was better than one, sure, but you really needed three people if things went south. *Afternoon sunlight.* Things were actually pretty volatile with a few of our people.

Fritz and Maadai were already in the break room. Fritz was cutting out names on pieces of paper and Maadai was making brief hand written notes beneath them.

She looked at us over her glasses as we walked in. "I've got advertisements going up for another Custodian position."

My heart sank. "Is Shep okay?"

"The magick couldn't fix everything. He's in having surgery now."

I wanted to ask about the specialist, but it seemed like a moot point. I sat down on the nearest chair to look at the client names we were apparently re-organizing. It probably made sense. Even if Shep was able to return in a few weeks he wouldn't be doing fieldwork for months.

"For now, we're cutting our lists," Maadai said, bluntly. "We can't do what we can't do. We need to focus on those who *really* need us, and transition those who don't back to their district magi."

My mood sank even further. I saw Aspen open her mouth to object, and Maadai shot her a hard look. "Policy had already been changed to allow two of you to attend a situation, but I don't want that happening if we don't feel in our guts it's safe. We're one team, now, not two."

Fritz didn't look surprised. He wordlessly passed Lilith a sheet and an extra pair of scissors.

"Four people in the field…" I let it trail off.

Maadai shook her head. "Four is too many. Three is already conspicuous, but those who we're more worried about social impact than safety, they're going to caretakers. Three in the field, one person doing meetings, answering emails, chasing up information, making bookings. We're going to need to flex and sway with this for a little while. We're reducing required check-ins under the emergency policy, but if they don't need weekly check-ins they probably don't need us."

Aspen looked at me, her expression unreadable. I didn't know how I felt about any of that, but we had to survive.

"I'm not hiring the wrong person," she said, flatly. "I'm sorry, I know our lives have been challenging because of staffing, but there has not been a candidate who was appropriate."

"Is it internal recruitment?" Lilith asked her.

Maadai shook her head. "It was. But now we've shifted the power dynamic, it's external, too. So tell everyone." She directed that, specifically, at Aspen. "They don't need magick to be effective."

Aspen nodded firmly. "Send me the listing. I'll circulate it with my old crew and ask them to pass it on."

"I want you in interviews with me, too," she said, to Aspen. "I can kick out a few wizards. I'd never wish ill on any of you, but if someone was going to get themselves crushed, it could've come at a worse time."

I hadn't realized how little control Maadai had been given, and it made upsetting the wizards even sweeter.

"So we're identifying critical clients for now?" Aspen asked. "And going from there?"

Maadai nodded firmly. "Whoever isn't in the field can support transition for our families who are ready."

I hated that we were here. "There are some families, like Zane's pack?" I glanced at Aspen and Lilith. "They're great. Super chill. But the kids are highly volatile and when things go wrong, they go very badly wrong." The memory of the lycan teen lying in a rapidly spreading pool of blood made me feel cold. Zane wouldn't call just anyone to help with hard situations.

Yeah, it was breaking the rules. I'd do it differently next time. But damned if I was letting one of those kids bleed out for policy's sake.

"Can we keep them on the list for now and just scale back support? For a month or two?" They barely drained our resources. I could see if I could call jiu-jitsu sessions a check-in.

"I know the pack is an old one of yours," Maadai told me, briskly. "There's no room for feelings in this. We need to work together." I opened my mouth to object. She silenced me with a look that made me feel like I was six. "But you're right. They're the reason I modified policy to allow greater time between check-ins. We're going to need to be very careful about making those check-ins quality, and hopefully do some phone calls between."

Relief rushed through me and I saw Aspen relax.

"All right, well." Lilith tossed Chris's name into the center. "He's being investigated for murder. We need to keep him, but he might end up being removed from our lists pretty soon."

"What?" Aspen demanded. "*What?*"

"I'll tell you later," Lilith said. "Let's get this done, because we're going to have to re-do a *lot* of schedules."

"I'll be interviewing as soon as the right application arrives," Maadai told us, firmly. "But from what I've seen, it might take awhile."

I scrubbed my hands over my face. My head hurt just thinking about our finely tuned schedule being tossed in the bin. "Is this human only?" Aspen asked.

"Of course not," Maadai told her.

She glanced at me, brow arched. "Hey, poster girl."

I cringed. "Fuck you." Maadai slapped a stack of names in front of me with a glower. "Yes, Aspen?" I said through my teeth, taking them obediently.

"Maybe it's worth you hyping the job at a few covens, encouraging caretakers *and* recommending they mention it to clients?"

I didn't love the plan, but it was not the worst idea. "If time allows, I'm happy to." I glanced at Maadai, and she nodded. "We're cutting down the district staff meetings, I assume?"

She nodded again. "We are. They're primarily to identify new clients that should come on, and while I'm not saying we *cannot* take on clients, we cannot take on any mid-tier clients."

It took us the better part of the morning to triage the two client lists. We didn't get to talk to the cops about the attempted abduction until after lunch. That turned out to be for the best, because the cops had become Taig, who had the original case with the Hurtfields.

"We're trying to print the license, but I doubt we'll get him that way," Taig told me. "The license isn't a very good fake, and isn't specialized enough that I think we'll be able to track it. We're trying.

Visiting the receptionist with some photos today, hoping we can get an I.D."

The fact that *he* was on the case told me they had enough to believe the stalker link. And I doubted I would've gotten all that if it weren't Taig. "Okay."

On the other end of the line, he was quiet for a minute. "Okay?" he asked, eventually.

"Yeah." I looked at the list of names in front of me, hoping like shit they'd all transition okay. "You've done everything I've thought of, and I trust you to do your job and think of a whole lot of stuff I haven't yet. So, thanks for the update, I guess? We'll continue to support pickup and drop-off until the situation changes." Which could be months. If they'd spooked and run, it might be forever.

They hadn't spooked, though. Guys who thought it was fun to hunt an ursathrope veteran weren't going to be worried about a school receptionist giving them the beady eye.

"That's unusually compliant of you, Custodian."

That low rumble wasn't quite as sexy when my head hurt and I felt like a nap. "I can play nice."

He hummed in pleasure. Despite myself I smiled. "Go on. Let me know if you get any I.D. hits."

"Will do. I'll see you about ten unless you'd rather not catch up," he said.

"Sure." Ten was whatever. "See you tonight." We really had to talk about moving in.

As somebody with wounded feet, they thought it'd be a good idea to keep me at HQ. By the time knockoff time rolled around we had shit more or less under control, my headache had eased somewhat, and I didn't hate them for it.

"The next few weeks are going to be a shitshow," Aspen said. "And you're going on holiday," she added, sighing. "Don't offer to cancel, I'll have to hit you. You should be able to take a holiday."

I should, but I still resolved to float the idea of rescheduling with Taig. One week of planned leave was different from a team member having a limb crushed. "We heard from Shep?"

Lilith opened up her phone. "Arthur said he was still in when I checked forty minutes ago."

"Still?" I hit the button on the elevator. "Wasn't he in at ten? How long are surgeries, usually? Is an eight hour surgery standard?"

"He went in at ten forty five, according to Arthur," Lilith said, tucking her hands into her vest. "I don't know what western medicine says is normal for surgery times post legalization. But it seems like a lot."

Aspen shrugged when I glanced over, her brow furrowed as she studied the screen of her phone. "No idea. Catching up on a day's worth of..."

I looked closer when she trailed off, then glanced down at the phone. The real estate agent's banner caught my attention. I stomped on my impatience, watching the color drain from Aspen's face as we stepped out into the ground level foyer.

"We got it," she said, her eyes huge.

"Got what?" Lilith asked, looking up. I was already grabbing Aspen in a hug, joy flooding me. She laughed, the happiness bubbling up and out of her chest as I rocked her. Her victory dance drove her knees into my thighs. I didn't even mind. "Elders, you got the *house?*" Lilith joined in and my eyes burned. *"You got a house!"*

"I own a motherfucking house!" Aspen crowed, and I saw a guy in a suit try to smother his grin as he walked past. If it hadn't been for Lilith locking us all together I'd've grabbed him too. "Oh my God. I have to call Nic."

Nic was busy and I hated that it'd happened this way. "We need to celebrate!" I declared.

"We do!" Aspen agreed, laughing. "Except I am so broke! And I really do need to call Nic. We need to sign things, and..."

We peeled apart, driven by real life to keep moving. "Nic's out with Retrievals," I admitted. "I'm pretty sure they aren't back yet."

Her face fell. "Oh."

Lilith met my eyes over her head. "Hey. We're here. Mexican?"

"Oh." Aspen laughed and waved it away. "Let's make a time for the weekend. Sunshine's still probably feeling shit, and—"

"Mexican at my place," I said, firmly. "Taig's working, so it's empty, and I have a cat."

She twisted her silver necklace around her fingers. "It's fine, really. Like, it isn't official yet. We can party when it's official."

"Fuck off." I resisted the urge to check over my shoulder for Maadai after that was out of my mouth. "We can have an unofficial party *and* go out when Nic can shout."

She looked at me thoughtfully. "That does have merit."

"Give me your orders," Lilith said. "I'm buying the food. And I'm going to go to mine and pick up a card game. It goes best with booze."

"Noted." I nudged Aspen. "Let's go, you bougie, landowning bitch!"

"Oh my God," she muttered, laughing nervously. "Okay. Why not? Let's go."

. , ' ' 0 0 0 \ ' ' . . 0 \ \ \ ' 0 \

FOUR HOURS, most of a bottle of tequila and some lukewarm Mexican later, I looked up from my hand of cards as Taig opened the door.

"Oh *no,* if Sexy Detective is back, we have to be *responsible,*" Aspen moaned, flopping back in her chair. Some of the cards in her hand fluttered to the ground. "I have to work tomorrow and I am going to hate myself."

"You can't hate yourself," Lilith objected. "You're too amazing. Hate capitalism. And hangovers. You want a shot, Taig?"

I grabbed my coffee and took a pull, hoping he wouldn't be upset by the alcohol as I crossed to him. So many things we needed to figure out. "Welcome home." I wobbled a little. He steadied my cup with one hand and a smile. "I should've given you a heads up."

"Not at all." He pressed a kiss to my forehead. "This looks like too much fun for me to come stomping in. Congratulations, Aspen." Another forehead kiss, and he was on the retreat.

I followed him out the door. I wasn't super coordinated, but it was because of my sore feet and tiredness. I'd done a tiny margarita hours ago. I didn't know how long the smell would linger, or whether he might have feelings about that. "Shep's out of surgery. He's got a lot of steel in him."

Taig shut the door gently behind me, leaving us in the hallway. Laughter came from inside my apartment, and I stood inside the circle of his arm, feeling the warm glow of all that affection angled my way. "I'm glad he's okay."

"That's it, isn't it?" I said, feeling disoriented. "He's alive."

"Yeah," he said, quietly. "That's it. You can improve from there. You should go in, love. Don't stay up late. You're mixing alcohol and a concussion already, you don't want to be pulling an all nighter too."

It stung a little but I tried not to let it. "Sorry. I should've warned you. And if it makes you feel better, I've had less than a standard drink all night."

He shrugged. "It's fine. Honestly. Other people's places, social things, it's fine." He stepped back a little further. "Your place feels a bit much like home, apparently. Or maybe it's just tonight it's not comfy. But it's fine, Roars." He kissed my forehead. This time, I suspected he was avoiding my lips. "I'm going to call you at eleven and if you aren't in bed I'm going to come back and toss you in."

That sparked some ideas. "Really?"

He grinned and opened the door behind me. "Go."

"Was that a promise, detective?" I asked, stepping back obediently.

"I'd never threaten you, love," he told me, quietly, and Aspen's drunken giggles made he and I both grin. "She's got a concussion," he said, over my shoulder. "Look after her."

"Oh, *what?*" Lilith demanded, standing and getting tangled in her skirt. "I got her, O'Malley, you go," she waved a hand, pressing the other to her mouth to mostly catch a hiccup. "You go."

"Going." The door shut firmly behind me, and I heard him jiggling the lock.

"I probably should organize a lift," Aspen said, sadly. "Sexy Detective is *boring.*"

"Capitalism is boring," Lilith corrected, cleaning up plates. "Vince is on stand-by, I can give you a lift?"

"God, no. It's like, a two hour round trip," Aspen said, with a snort.

"Bless your heart, though. I'll just—Nic!" she answered the phone I hadn't heard ring. "Nic! Oh my god, *Nic*, we got it!"

A blast of noise through the phone indicated that, yes, he'd known. I fell down on the couch, listening to their excited chatter dip around me.

When I woke it was to booming laughter and the crash of something breakable against lino.

"I got it, I got it," I heard Nic saying. I made it to my feet in time to see him dig out my dustpan and brush. "She'll have a million coffee cups. I'll get her a million more. Oh, hey, sleepyhead."

Aspen was perched on her chair, swaying, with a fond smile on her face as she looked at us. Lilith had her arm thrown back and was stretched out. The empty tequila bottle was now keeping a vodka bottle company. I squinted at the label, not recognizing it. "Is there a point to expensive vodka?" I asked them, picking my way around the shards of what had been one of my mugs. Nic was right about how many I had.

"Try some," Lilith said, sliding over another bottle. "Wait, no, you're concussed. You've had your one for the night."

"You're concussed?" Nic demanded, furiously. "What the fuck? I leave for a day, and—oh, wait."

I laughed at him. Drunk Nic could go one of two ways, and it looked like we got happy Nic tonight. "Congratulations, you jerk."

"Thank you." He pointed a finger at Eclipse. "Keep her back. Protect the toe beans."

"Protect the toe beans!" Aspen crowed.

Elders. I scooped my baby up, looking at the clock. Two in the morning. For perhaps the first time ever, I turned to the party and said, "It's pretty late, folks."

"You are *so* right," Aspen agreed. "When did you start doing that?"

"Wise friend," Lilith agreed, pouring another round. "It's messed up, isn't it?"

"Nah, nah," Nic told them. "She's always been wise, just like." He sniffed. "No one listens to you. Not even you. Right, Sunshine?"

I set Eclipse aside. "Okay, buddy. You go sit down. I got this. Last round, then you all need some water."

"It's basically water. With potato juice. It's a meal," Aspen told me, firmly.

"It's a meal you'll be cleaning if you puke it everywhere," I warned her.

She waved it away. "Wouldn't be the first time. I own land! I'm basically nobility!"

I didn't disagree, cleaning up and sorting out the immediate threat before confiscating the rest of their vodka and replacing it with watered down juice. "What is this shit?" Nic asked, after taking a sip.

"Don't you know?" Lilith asked.

"What? Of course I know," Nic scoffed. "It's orange juice. We have orange juice in the army. But she didn't put a shot in it!"

"Seriously," Lilith said, intently. "Don't party trick me. Doesn't it get old knowing everything?"

"That's why I don't look, sweetheart," he said, with a wink. "Leaves some spice, you know?"

Aspen met my eyes over the table. Her worry was stamped with comical exaggeration all over her face.

"It'd be so hard not to," Lilith said, quietly. "I don't know if I could resist."

I saw the writing on the wall. Nic had struggled with doing exactly that. Instead of alleviating his anxiety, though, it had only fed it. I was about to say something, anything, but he was already speaking.

"I could be the funniest guy. Or the smartest. Did it for a while. Knowing the right thing to say all the time? Fucks with your head." His words weren't crisp, but they were sharp with bitterness. "Do people like you for you, really? If you stop predicting everything, does it crumble? Is everything built on a single, shaky pillar? Is the world just fiction you've manipulated?"

Compassion swept through me. Aspen jumped in, knowing the dark places we were about to go, saying, "Come on, roomie. We need to sleep and you're on the floor."

"It's just another illusion," Lilith said, softly, and there were tears on her cheeks that made me ache for her, and she was looking at her hands, folded in her lap.

No fucking way was I being the wise friend in this situation. "All right, that'll do. Get up, Nic, you heavy arsehole, my feet hurt. Come on. You know what'll happen if I try to levitate you."

"She's crying," he objected, standing. "I can't just—"

"It's fine," Lilith said, laughing through the tears. "Whew. Too much for me. Sorry. Long week, hey."

The way they looked at each other made me feel like they were a mortar and pestle and I was today's spice.

"Such a long week, oh my *God*," Aspen agreed, putting her hand on Lilith's shoulder and giving me an exaggerated nod.

"Look, we got her." I pried Nic up. "We love Lilith. We won't let her cry by herself."

"I could cry with her," he said, softly, and I didn't know how the fuck to feel, except exhausted. I wanted off this roller-coaster.

"We can all cry together," I agreed, giving him another shove and hoping the words or the physical assistance would stop this situation devolving. "Move it, mate. Come on."

He went, saying, "I'm not that drunk, Rory. You've seen me way more fucked up. It was just a bit of booze."

"Good. Great." He flopped into my bed like a cold pancake onto a plate. I narrowly avoided getting kicked in the face as he tried to drag his big, stompy feet up onto my bed complete with big, stompy, *dirty* boots. "You could've wiped your feet," I said, just to make myself feel better. He'd picked up some bad habits since we parted ways, apparently.

"I did," he said, surprised. "Didn't I? I'm sure I did. I haven't been in your bed for a *long* time, Roars. It's kinda weird."

"What's weird is you making it weird." I yanked off one of his boots. "You're vacuuming my floor."

"'Kay." He settled back. "It does smell cute. Flowers and shit. These are fresh, right? I'd smell it if you'd been boned on them recently and that would be peak bizarre. I *am* weird, huh?"

In my head a narrator with a voice like Dad's said, *he was, indeed, weird.* "You're drunk."

"True." He helped me toe off his second boot. "Look at you, all responsible. First time we went drinking together you were on top of the table and I almost swallowed my own tongue."

I hummed in agreement. It wasn't the first time he mentioned this. I was pretty sure I'd been on top of the table with a bunch of other people, and only for a minute, because floors are better to dance on and that table had wobbled.

I wrapped him like the burrito I'd eaten for dinner, angling him so if he puked he probably wouldn't drown. "I'm not a teenager," he mumbled.

I rolled my eyes. "Go the fuck to sleep, Nic."

"'Kay. Since you asked nice."

In my kitchen, Lilith let out big, wracking sobs, doing her best to muffle it. Aspen was hugging her and rocking, tears on her cheeks, too.

Anyone else, I'd've thrown my hands up and gone back to bed. For Lilith I grabbed a box of tissues, some more juice, a puke bucket, and sat down beside her.

"She doesn't want to talk," Aspen said, tears in her throat. "Just big feelings need to come out, you know?"

"I know." I sniffed back my own, passing over a tissue. "We got you, witch."

She nodded, her face curtained by her hair, her shoulders shaking. I was pretty sure the next stage was either puking or sleeping. I doubted Lilith would overdo it enough to puke, but what did I know? I wouldn't have predicted she'd get so toasted she'd end up with snot strings, either.

"Come on. Cry on the couch. Eclipse needs hugs." With Aspen trying to help and mostly getting in the way, I relocated them to the couch, making sure the bucket was in easy grabbing range. I resisted the urge to give Lilith a hug that might make it worse, checking my phone surreptitiously.

Someone must've answered Taig's call, because my call log said one had been received at precisely eleven and gone on for seven minutes and change. I saw a text from an unknown number that had come through a bit after that and, seeing a voice note, hesitated a moment trying to recall if my identity could be stolen via listening to a voice note.

Rory, said a familiar young voice strangely calm for the hour. *Dad gave me your number in case he wasn't home before morning to warn you. But I thought maybe this would be better. Because he's been gone a long time.*

Aspen staggered to her feet. "What the fuck?" she demanded. "Was that Jessica?"

I waved her off. She was less than useless right now. "Look after Lilith, okay? I'll deal with this." My heart skittered against my ribs as I went into my room and fumbled at the damned safe.

Jessica picked up on the first ring. "Hi Rory," she said, primly. "How are you?"

CHAPTER 37

$\mathcal{M}$y heart. My motherfucking heart. "What's happened, Jessica?"

"He got their scent this afternoon," she said, matter-of-factly. "I didn't think I should put that in the voice note. I think the police wouldn't like it."

I was done. I was just a husk of a human. I'd never feel again and I didn't care. My Retrievals Lupetec was cool in my hands and Nic was snoring behind me. Not at all like old times. "Do you know where he went, Jess?"

"He shared his location," she said. "So I can see him. Mine's shared with him, too. I can send you a picture if you want. I think I can do that?"

"That sounds perfect. You do that." I put the phone down for a moment, gearing up as she did. My mind spun over the details.

Drunk coven. Even a drunk Oracle. Taig would be there in a heartbeat. Since he was home, I assumed he'd have his own weapons at hand.

Guess he could choose if his job was worth it all by himself. Or I'd get to see if he was always good at hiding bodies.

"You there, Jess?" I asked, jamming the phone between my ear and my shoulder.

"Yeah. I think I did it. Did it work?"

I opened the messages and found a distillery in mother loving Port Melbourne. "It did. You did great. And you've done the right thing. I'm going to call the police." Fuck, I could've used Aspen. But she'd kept pace with Lilith and Nic, despite being smaller. She'd still be blowing over point-oh-five come morning. "And the other people at my work, Fritz and Maadai. You haven't met them, but they're good people, okay?"

"I'm not opening the door," she said, firmly, but there were tears in her voice now. "Dad said."

She was safe. Scared as fuck, but safe. "I'm going to do my best to get your dad home tonight, okay, Jessica?" It was as close as I could come to making her a promise.

"He's been there since nine fifty-three," she said, and now the words were shaking. "He hasn't moved."

I tightened my belt over my hips, leaving behind my ill-gotten sword. "Jess?"

"Yes?"

There were tears in my throat, too, but damned if I was letting them out. "You keep you safe, okay?" Nic's keys were beneath the blanket burrito and in his pocket. He mumbled something as I dug them out. "You and I both know your dad is a hunter. He could be lying in wait. He's taught you to do that, hasn't he?"

She sniffed. "Yes," she whispered.

"Try to rest. Liam is going to need you tomorrow." There was probably a whole shitton wrong with me pulling that card but Aspen was curled up against Lilith's shoulder, both of them still and peaceful, tears on their faces. No one was awake enough to tell me off. "Even if your dad is home in the next ten minutes, he's going to be tired, right?"

"Right," she agreed, softly.

"So get yourself a drink, and maybe a snack." I pulled my door closed behind me and set off at a jog, hitting unlock on Nic's car keys. I watched for the telltale flashing lights, my heart in my throat but my voice even. I knew how to ride the adrenaline. Apparently, so did Jessica. "Snuggle up, and try to rest. Even if you can't sleep, rest. Keep your phone charged, and I'll call when I know anything for sure, okay?"

"Even if it's bad?" she asked me, the words small and fragile.

"Especially if it's bad," I promised, and for just a moment I thought that might do it. Had I thought I could *ride* this? Emotion rushed through me, jamming my throat, strangling me. *Birds screamed and so did Ryan. My nose was blocked. Supermarket body spray and pressure on my shoulders.* I paused, bracing a hand against the piss-scented brick and dragged myself brutally to the here and now.

I wasn't fucking *jumpy*.

The emotion was set aside. Tonight was none of those events, and this kid needed me.

Seconds crawled by. I swallowed, and hoped she couldn't hear it. But when I spoke next, there were no tears in my voice. "I won't hide anything from you, Jessica. No matter how hard it is. I promise."

"Okay." She sniffed, and there were tears in her voice, too, but I was hollow.

"Go rest," I told her. "I'll contact you as soon as I know anything." I set out again, mindful of my heart racing in my chest and cracks in my dam.

It would hold. I stepped up the pace to a controlled, loping jog.

"Okay. I can do that. Thank you, Rory."

"You're welcome." Lights flashed a block over. "I'm going to go now, Jess," I said, hoping she couldn't hear me running. "I'm going to be going as fast as I can, and calling people who can help, okay? You won't hear from me for what will feel like a long time, but I'm here, and I'm working on it." That was as much as I could give her.

"Okay. Okay. Bye."

I hung up, threw open Nic's car door, and almost screamed as the fury swept through me, but it was so intense it locked my jaw closed. I dragged that rage through my body, breathed it from my boots to my crown, and guided the car into the streets.

The rage ebbed as I started to plan. But into its wake rushed the dark, sticky shame. I should've seen this coming. I should've *known*.

I shook my head, trying to dislodge that bullshit. Rage was safer. "Not my fucking client, you don't." The words crackled with power and I aggressively moved my toes in my boots.

They'd fucked with the wrong witch.

CHAPTER 38

I adjusted the seat while the car was in motion and regretted it. Thank fuck the streets were quiet. Without fumbling, I found Taig's number and hit call.

He answered on the third ring. "What's wrong?"

"I love you so much," I said, but I didn't feel it. I didn't feel anything. It was a blessing, because I was involving him in shit that could end his entire life on every level.

He'd want to be involved. I'd benefit from him being involved. That didn't negate the cost.

How many of my fights would this man want to participate in?

"Where are you, love?" he asked, and I heard that exact same note of neutrality in his voice that had crept into my own as I'd been speaking to Jessica.

"I'm fine." I blew out a hard breath. "I have a situation and there might be bodies hitting the floor in the next twenty minutes."

"Location?"

See, this was *why* I loved him. "A distillery in Port Melbourne."

"Noted. Are you on route?"

I put my foot down to overtake a tiny car moseying along. "I am."

"Can I call it in?"

I followed the little blue navigation arrow on the map program, feeling sick. "Benson hunted them down, Taig."

He was quiet for a moment. Then said, "Shit."

"Your call. I haven't sent up the alarm." Maybe I wouldn't at all. But there was no way Benson's location was one of a scout. He was in the center of whatever that building was.

If we'd rolled a distillery a few hours ago, I could've saved Nic a few hundred bucks.

"Human assailants?" he asked me, and I could hear him moving in the background.

I hesitated. "Could be 'thropes. Zane inferred Duke's people were involved somehow."

"On it. Don't engage until I get there." I rolled my eyes at the phone and he said, "Rory. Promise."

"I'll see what I can see."

He muttered something vile. I accelerated through a light that was more red than it was amber. "A lesser man would threaten to take you over his knee."

"A lesser man than you wouldn't get to take me anywhere. Hurry up, honey, or you're going to miss the show."

"Your location?"

I read out the suburb, since the street name was lost to the app's audio narration that was being overridden by the call. "See you soon."

"I'm a solid ten minutes behind you. Scout it."

"Sure."

He blew out a noisy breath that was probably one of irritation. I didn't really blame him. I had no real intention of being a hero but I also wasn't going to sit on my hands in my stolen car.

The street was wide and dark. I cut the lights and regretted it instantly, easing up to a curb. I hoped I wouldn't have to explain to Nic how I'd lost his car. The thing was worth a few years of my salary. Well, it'd *cost* a few years of my salary.

As I climbed out, I wondered how Lilith felt about sport scars.

The distillery was on the other end of the block. I set off at a jog, pulling down my headgear. Taig would be ten minutes away, he'd said.

So I could figure out what area they were likely holding him, see if he was alive. If not, well, I may as well call the fucking cops.

Yeah, having had your heart pulverized had upsides.

The big, high up windows were mostly dark, but I could see a glow on the far side of the building. I ducked under the *staff only* boom gate into the empty car park, resisting the urge to take a photo of the van down the road that doubtless belonged to these guys.

If they'd taken Benson, they were a lot more dangerous than I'd given them credit for. Even if he wasn't pinned down, I was going to have to be careful.

A shipping container provided me cover as I peered around the building, identifying where the glow came from. I wondered how the fuck I was going to communicate that to Taig. Quickly, I dimmed my phone's screen to check the time.

Eight minutes.

Keeping my steps light, I began looking for a way in. I didn't need anything unlocked. I just needed a likely looking door.

I found one not too far along, a double door that was partly ajar. A cigarette butt burned on the ground nearby, discarded in the last few minutes.

Alarm skimmed up my spine. I sank back into the shadows, watching for movement around me.

Something crashed inside the building, followed with the clamor of metal against cement. A half-muffled roar made my adrenaline spike.

Come on, Taig. I had a way in. I had a location for Benson. He was alive, if likely restrained and injured. I forced myself to breathe and move further along, in case there was another door they'd left open.

They thought they'd caught the biggest threat. Arseholes obviously weren't clients of Wesley's.

Around the far end I found a small door and a ramp, but it was locked. Further along was a roller door. I checked my phone. Two minutes.

He'd park on the road. It'd take him a bit of time.

Laughter floated to me through the quiet night air. The place smelled like rust and dust. I moved into position so I had a view of the ajar door, crouching so my back was to the wall. My wand was in my glove, ready to use. My silver knife was loose in its sheath.

I was a patient bitch when I had to be.

I counted the seconds between breaths, listening to the quiet inside. Were they far in, so the noises were muffled? Was the party all-but over? I didn't know and I didn't like either option. After four minutes of crouching I stood slowly, moving my legs so they didn't go to sleep.

Tonight would be about the worst night to get pulled over for speeding. At least I didn't have to be worried Taig would be breatho'd and tossed in a cell for the night.

I checked the time again. He'd had three bonus minutes. I hadn't seen any sign of him. I didn't expect to, but I'd made it down that road in about a minute.

I took another breath, felt the hard-packed clay under my feet, and listened to my body. Because I had good instincts.

Separating out instinct from impatience was kind of a whole deal, though.

Uneasily, I shifted my weight again. Somewhere in the dark off to the side a frog croaked. The hum of a car passing along the freeway carried across to me.

Come on, Taig. I thought of Jessica, imagined her curled up around Liam, sleeping. I tried not to think of her waiting for hours for me to respond to her.

Gunshots went off, way down the road, and a fresh wave of adrenaline swept through me. The muted thump of something heavy hitting the ground traveled to me in wake of them. The shots hadn't been close. The thump had been loud.

Whatever had gone down was *big*.

My mind skimmed through options of beings large enough to hit the ground like a falling tree, but there was one explanation that leapt out at me. *Lycanthrope.* I wasn't just jumpy. It fit.

A small part of me wanted to flee toward those shots, because I knew who was holding that weapon. In my heart, I knew.

Luckily, said heart was a desiccated mess now, best roasted and sprinkled over your choice of meats. The smart thing to do was hit them while they were disoriented. I wasn't often accused of being smart, but every now and then I could pull it off.

A flurry of voices came from inside, but no shouts. Lights were turned off. The door was pulled shut.

Well, that was fine. I hadn't been planning on knocking anyway.

Gravity sucks, but I sure don't. I leapt, grabbing brickwork and hauling myself onto the tile roof, moving along until I figured I was above where the lights had been. Then I stepped back.

Fire seemed a bit much, and I'd already used the *smoke inhalation* square on my bingo card this week. I lifted my glove, focusing on an area a few meters away. *Gravity sucks, unless you're me, and then it blows.* Wood and tiles cracked. I turned back where I'd come, identifying one of the many chimneys. *Gravity sucks, but I sure don't.* It started to crumble. I closed the spell, casting my anti-gravity spell and hoping my distraction would work as I leapt down into the darkness.

More gunshots came from up the road. The darkness was complete.

Another, half-muffled roar came from somewhere to my right and I wished I could speak Benson's tongue as I tried to orient myself inside a building I'd never set foot in.

There was movement around me, scraping shoes and cloth on brick, the jostle of a body against crates. I closed my eyes and tried to listen, but my hearing was too mundane to get more than a vague idea of *they aren't in arm reach.*

"I think Watchdog is down," someone muttered, swiftly shushed in the dark.

"Make some noise, Benson," I said, as softly as I could.

Chains clinked and rattled. I started moving in that direction, the shadows layered so thickly I couldn't see my hand before my face. How he was silvered and shifted, I had no idea. But apparently, he was. It was the only way they could weaken him enough to hold him.

"Someone's in here," one of the voices said, forcefully. "That hole in the roof is too neat."

Too neat? If that was too neat, these guys had honed their weaponized incompetence into an artform. That roof was ragged as *fuck.*

Lights went on. I squeezed my eyes shut for a split second, crouching behind whatever was beside me while I adjusted.

"Are we going after Watchdog?" one of them asked.

"Secure the area."

Better me than Taig. Probably. Although a bit of chaos might've been nice. These guys weren't too shabby. I listened to their steps, confident now. Someone was going up stairs. I glanced and found a metal walkway up high. Machinery I couldn't have hoped to identify was sitting around in various states of disrepair. So far, I couldn't see any of them. That wouldn't last.

I started moving toward Benson again, my mouth dry and steps firm. *Be okay, Taig.* He had to have known what I'd do, surely. He would've done the same thing. He couldn't be bleeding out in the middle of the road. I'd heard two rounds of shots. He was alive.

I peeked around a corner, spotting the back of someone's head. A strap over his shoulder and the bulk in his hands told me he had a rifle.

That was good news. I liked it when people tried to shoot me with bullets. That was like being hit with a pillow in my Lupetec. It beat the shit out of, say, a Rot curse.

I glanced again and spotted, over the guy's shoulder, a thick chain leading down from a winch attached to a roof beam. As I watched, it rattled.

Gotcha.

I settled back, breathing deep. I felt the cement under my boots and the pressure of the headgear on my hair. Sweat made it stick to my neck.

Lifting one arm I locked eyes on a pile of wooden crates as far away as I could make out. *Burn, witch, burn.*

It burst into flames. I instantly ended the spell, allowing the fire to spread naturally. Shouts of discovery. Running steps. Maybe they weren't so crash hot after all. I stood, ready to bolt toward Benson.

And came face to face with that rifle.

"Cute."

I met his eyes, knowing he couldn't identify me through the head-gear, knowing time was ticking. I needed to get Benson and get the fuck out. And still, I wanted him to know which witch was about to kick his arse.

The muzzle dipped. The force of his shot made me stagger back. *Pillow. Just a pillow.* I struggled to draw breath and activated my blow-back charm. It didn't work.

I was inside Jaye's garage, inside the flaming inferno. *The car lifted away from Shep's body with the noise of the teeth of a zipper.* My stomach twisted and I shook my head.

I was grabbed from behind by the gunman. Energy roared through my veins and I drove my elbow back into something that crunched and swore. Freed, I turned to the hunter with a novelty t-shirt and bloody jeans.

Lost your license, Custodian? I didn't say it because I didn't have any air. I didn't need air to cast, though, and lifted my hand.

Before the spell could crystalize in my mind, pain exploded in my hand. The sound of a second gunshot made my ears pound. I could see, above Benson, the chain rattling.

I needed to get Benson out. That was all.

Come on, witch. But I couldn't breathe and the pain was every-where. *He's right there. Just melt his chains.* But he'd be in more than a single silver chain. Silver should've forced his shift. For him to be in bear form, they'd done something else. Or instead. Or as well.

I shook my head, trying to dislodge the bullshit. Fuckknuckle gunman grabbed for my headgear and I drove my forehead into those fingers. He swung the butt of the rifle at me. I dodged, driving my knee up out of sheer reflex. He smelled like beer. Of course he smelled like beer. Why wouldn't he smell like beer in a distillery?

Wait. Distillery means spirits. Fuckknuckle shoved into the crates beside me and bottles rattled as I fruitlessly kicked out.

I couldn't hear shit but I saw his hands cocking the gun again.

Much as I did prefer bullets to spells, I didn't need broken ribs. I was actually okay not joining in more pillow fights.

Through this dome none shall leave or come unless it is with me.

Dust puffed up satisfyingly around us in a circle. I stepped back as he leveled the gun directly at my face.

He was aiming for my eyes. They weren't protected by Lupetec.

I turned when he pulled the trigger, not watching the damage the ricocheting bullet would do to him. If it didn't kill him, well, he could hang out in my ward until I needed my magick back.

Another arsehole with a gun was between me and where I wanted to be. I lifted my fucked up hand. He fell back a step, his eyes going over my shoulder at whatever carnage I'd left behind.

This was why I didn't hate fighting folks who weren't fae. They hesitated. I liked hesitation.

Maybe my impulsiveness was my fae lineage. Or maybe I had undiagnosed ADHD. Or maybe I was wired weird. Who fucking knew.

Benson was flattened on some sort of mechanized platform. A large muzzle was over his nose and tied behind his head. His eyes glowed with whatever potion they'd hit him with. I could imagine him telling Jessica to call me come morning. I could imagine him putting their dinner in front of them, watching them eat it, and sending them to bed as he went off to assassinate the threat.

And here he was, white strings of viscous fluid dangling off his muzzle. *Plastic against my cheek. Supermarket body spray, wine on my tongue and hot afternoon sunlight. The slither of his belt and his hands on my shoulders.*

Something hit me from behind. I went down, my head spinning, my stomach rebelling. My arms were yanked, hard, and my shot-up hand screamed. "Don't let her point at you," I heard someone say.

Wrong. That's not how it works. I fought my stomach, not my captors, trying to get my bearings. The concrete under my face was blurry and that sure as shit wasn't good. *Taig, don't you dare even try to rescue me.*

I reached for a spell but realized my ward was still active. *As I will, so shall it be.* My headgear was being peeled off. I wasn't even sad about it. The air was a physical relief and if I puked in there I was in serious trouble. *Supermarket body spray and crisply folded sleeves on my forearms.*

"She's hot. Worth holding onto, maybe?"

"Bit dangerous," someone said. "Is Mick okay?"

"I don't know, man. I don't want to look."

Fair. Neither do I. I tried to put the pain aside. Reaching for spells, I sifted through them as I was dragged to my feet. It didn't take long for me to decide on my new plan. Pulling all my focus into sharp relief, I cast. *Gravity sucks, but I sure don't.*

The two guys holding onto me were dragged up into the air as I leapt, then, about roof height, I released them. They fell away with satisfying thuds. I landed beside Benson, making the platform shake. *Burn, witch, burn.* Whatever had been used on my hands as a restraint was now liquid. As it sluiced off me, the reek made my poor lungs hurt.

I heard a gunshot and ducked, suddenly furious they'd taken off my headgear. Beside me, Benson writhed. I didn't have spare air to reassure him as I put my good hand on the chain. *Burn, witch, burn.*

It turned white-hot and fell off him, slithering to the floor beneath with a long, drawn-out rattle-and-slide. I staggered without having that chain to bear some of my weight. Beneath where it'd lain against Benson's skin, deep welts were visible through his fur.

He shot up, ripping off the muzzle. I only just managed to keep my footing as he launched off the platform.

Fuck, I was glad I wasn't on the other end of that charge.

I stood, trying to breathe, and watched his claws rake across one guy's belly. Guts spilled over the cement. My eyes followed those glistening ropes to the left, where the muzzle Benson had thrown away lay. Strings of fluid I couldn't name still dangling off them. Further off, a camera sat on a tripod. On the wall behind it waited a smaller muzzle, and more chains.

I heard a man screaming and hoped there was no one to come to his aid.

The sprinkler system kicked in. I looked up, surprised to see the rafters full of smoke. *Well, fuck.* A fire that burned hot enough would erase all trace of us from this place. And if we couldn't be placed at the scene, then we were obviously home all night. I'd been drinking. I had an alibi.

The high-pressure spurt of an arterial bleed made me glance over at where a guy desperately clutching his torn open groin.

Too little, too late. My boots creaked as I walked. Every step threw up little droplets of water and I heard them fall like a meditation track. On the other side of the warehouse a gun went off, the sound layered with crunching bones. I wondered how bad Aspen and Lilith's heads would be tomorrow as I took the recording device off the tripod, flicking through the settings.

No internet connectivity. *Excellent.* They'd made content, but hadn't posted it. No face, no trace. I dropped it on the ground, nursing my aching hand to my chest. Benson, in all of his terrifying bear form, came to a halt in front of me so abruptly his claws left gouge marks in the cement behind him.

"Police!"

I rolled my eyes. "Stand down, Taig. I'm about to light this up."

"Got two dead lycans outside," he called through.

Lycans. Duke's lycans, that had been nosing around Trinity's? How the fuck was Duke linked with this? Had I been wrong, and this *was* his new business?

I was going to have to deal with that lycanthrope soon.

At least it wasn't fucking faeries.

I hesitated, looking up at Benson. He stared at me, frozen in time. His chest rose and fell in rapid breaths, but he stayed locked in place.

"Want me to burn them, too?" I asked Benson.

The water from the sprinklers ran down the ruddy fur of his brows and dripped red off his muzzle. He stared at me for what felt like a long time, in the artificial rain, panting, his eyes glowing eerily, his teeth bared. A string of that liquid hung off his cheek.

Maybe my heart wasn't completely desiccated, after all. I reached up and, slowly, broadcasting every move, wiped it away.

"Jessica's waiting," I reminded him, quietly. "I can choose for you, if you can't."

His throat worked. He made a noise that was somewhere between fury and grief. It resonated deep in my soul. I tried to swallow away my tears but they didn't want to go. I kept my feet glued to the ground when I felt like flying away to watch from the rafters. Benson stood with me, in the rain, watching me struggle to breathe and cry. That grief I could see in him, it was braided into my being, too. That fury was a bottomless poison well.

"I should be holding the space," I admitted, knowing I was failing pretty horrifically at this whole thing. "And also snitching on you."

He nodded and a hysterical laugh bubbled in my chest. Professional boundaries were important. I believed it.

I believed that if I took him to the cops what they'd see would be a dangerous, substance-effected sex worker who'd injured a bunch of the clients he'd illegally taken on.

I believed he was struggling to parent his kids because he was struggling to be okay. I believed this was only going to make things harder for him, and for his kids, regardless of the questionable justice that had been meted out tonight.

I believed I'd done everything in my power, thus far.

I believed I could help him, and I believed he might let me.

I believed in this big, furious, hurting person in front of me having a second chance.

"I'm going to burn this," I said, somehow. "Get out. Go. Wait. The potion. *Fuck.*" I scrubbed my hand over my face. "I know a witch who's good with potions. Or you can lay low until it wears off." He rumbled, low in his chest. I had no idea what the fuck that meant, but I doubted he'd want help, right now, and even as a bear I'd put money on him being able to hide until he was able to shift back. I knew what he cared about. I knew what he'd be thinking of. It wasn't his form. "I promise I will go immediately to your kids. I'm calling Jess as soon as it's safe, and I'll let her know you're okay."

He nodded, apparently content with that, stood, and walked out. I made sure he wouldn't ever have to look back if he didn't want to.

EPILOGUE

"*I* know," Aspen was saying. Benson's fist flexed between his knees. "But these sorts of negative social interactions are part of life, and we can't kill everyone who is ever mean to her."

"I could," Benson disagreed.

"She's got to learn to defend herself," I said, because Aspen had been doing this dance with Benson for a solid half hour and I didn't want to be late to my sword training. "You won't be here forever."

His eyes narrowed at me. "She can fight better than you."

"She kills the kid who's tormenting her, Retrievals come, and she's dead or in SuperSec for life." Or at least until the next fae invasion. "Come on, Ben. Trust her, if you don't trust us. She told you not to do anything."

He looked down at the floor between his knees and compassion for him simmered uncomfortably in my chest.

"What do I do, then? Talk? How does that help?"

"A loved kid has armor against cruel words," Aspen said, simply. "It's hard, if you haven't had that, to know what it's like. It's hard to know how to give that to her. Rory, can you be Jessica?"

Fuck. Roleplay. I blew out a breath and resisted looking at my phone. "It's nothing, Dad," I said, to Aspen. "Don't worry about it."

"If it's important to you, it's important to me," Aspen said. "But if you don't want to tell me, that's okay. I'm here if you ever want to talk. About anything."

He snorted. "And how is that useful?"

I nodded at Aspen. "Sure. Thanks, Dad." And I walked away.

"At least one of you knows what's likely to happen," he said. "This is a waste of time. I can find her a new school. I won't rip his throat out, okay?"

I turned around and went back to Aspen. "Hey, Jessica," she said. "You okay?"

"Sure. I'm fine."

"You haven't been playing much," Aspen said. "And you didn't eat all of your dinner."

"They have to eat their dinner," Benson said, flatly. "I can't afford the waste."

"I'm fine, Dad," I said. "It's fine."

"Okay. Well, I'm here if you need me," Aspen told me.

Benson scrubbed his hand over his face.

I came back and stood beside Aspen. "Hey, Dad."

"Yeah?" she said, without looking at me.

"I feel kinda bad."

"Thanks for telling me," Aspen said, the words low and quiet. "You can tell me why, if you like, or we can sit together awhile."

I sat down beside Aspen and didn't say anything.

Benson was silent, too.

"I'm glad you're here," Aspen said, nudging me a bit with her shoulder.

"Me, too." I hunkered down in the chair. "I don't want anyone to get in trouble."

"I don't, either," Aspen agreed. "But if you're worried about something, it's good to share. You can choose what happens, okay? As long as everyone is safe, I'll let you take the lead."

I nodded. "Everyone is safe."

"I'm glad." She nudged me again. "I love you."

"I know," I told her, and sat there in silence for a minute before getting up.

Benson watched as I paced away. "Are you done?" he asked, coldly.

Not even close. I did a loop of the room, trying to organize my thoughts. The first steps were easier for me to act out. I'd seen it often enough. But the next…

"Hey," I said, plonking down beside Aspen. "How was today?"

"Pretty good," she said. "My favorite part was hanging out with you at dinner. How about you?"

I blew out a breath. "Yeah, it's fine. I was just hoping to ask you about something."

"Sure," Aspen said, into the otherwise silent house.

"It's probably nothing," I warned.

"That's okay. You can ask about nothing."

I nodded and hunkered down. "I've got a friend at school. One of the teachers has asked her to do a lot of extra study and jobs at lunch and after school."

Aspen nodded.

Emotion rushed through me, cracks in my personal dam. I said, "I saw something happening. I think." Grief had thickened my voice. I didn't know *why*, but it was there, choking me. I sat with it. They'd know that wasn't part of the role-play. That was okay, though. He'd still learn. Maybe he'd learn from the role-play. Maybe he'd learn from me actually living it. "But the teacher said if I tell, my friend won't be able to do her extra jobs, and she really loves them. I don't want her to get in trouble. And he's really nice to us."

"That'd be really scary," Aspen said, quietly. "You look like you're really worried about it."

I nodded. Benson watched us with narrowed eyes.

"Thank you for telling me," Aspen said, the words holding a touch of concern. "I wonder if you can tell me more information, so we can figure out what to do, together."

I let out another deep breath. "I don't want to get in trouble," I said, hunching over.

"Without knowing more, I can't make promises," Aspen said. "But you know I love you, and I'll let you take the lead as long as everyone is safe, right?"

Before I could continue, Benson growled. "The kid made her *cry.*"

"Did he?" I asked, straightening and dropping the charade. "Because last time I heard her crying, she was scared about *you.*"

Aspen shot daggers at me with her eyes, but Benson's expression had cleared. "I'm fine."

I snorted. "Yeah. So's she. I've got places to be. You call us if you want to give your kid protection for the human world, mate."

Aspen tried to make nice but I waited impatiently by the door for her to stomp out after me. "That was a gamble," she told me, irritated.

"I'm feeling lucky." I hadn't told her what had happened, and maybe I should've. She was too drunk to remember. It was Benson's information to share or not. It didn't hurt us to walk Jessica to school while the investigative wheels spun fruitlessly, searching for assailants who no longer existed.

Aspen didn't argue. "I would be, too, if I was about to go on vacation with a Sexy Detective." She flopped onto the tram stop beside me, fanning herself. "What a mess. I hope you have a good break."

I heard the words between those statements. *It's going to be an even worse shitstorm when you get back.* I glanced up at Benson's apartment and saw him watching from the window. "I have a feeling I might be fielding a couple phone calls while I'm away," I told her, mindful of Benson's hyper hearing.

She followed my gaze. "Not if you're off the clock. You need a work-life balance."

"I do," I agreed, the bitumen under my feet so hot it was sticky. "I think I'm finding it." She looked at me in disbelief. But she didn't know what was in my heart. "I've got this," I told her, rubbing a reassuring hand on her shoulder. "I promise."

ACKNOWLEDGMENTS

When writing, I hoped the themes of *Met by Moonlight* would resonate with readers. I didn't expect the outpouring of emotion I received.

We aren't jumpy. We know it. And we've got this.

I learned about the concept of holding the space after I'd seen it modelled. I'd lived through the experience of having someone deliberately co-regulating with me when I most needed it without asking anything in return. That experience shifted how I approached things long before I started my trauma training and learned the proper why's and how's. Thank you, Wayne, for giving me the blueprint for the foundation on which I've re-built myself. It's all coming together.

My fellow ex-Owls (and those who are or were still Owls) have been a gigantic support. When life happened to many of my beta readers, Mindi Briar accepted my poor, battered old manuscript full of skipped words and typos and helped me find joy in the journey. I'm so grateful to Lisa Edmonds, Lilla Glass, S.C. Greyson and the whole parliament who sat on calls body doubling while we worked. I wasn't efficient during those chats, but they fed my soul. Knowing I've got a safe space to pop into has meant the whole world. I would've dedicated this book to y'all, except I couldn't figure out a collective noun that was appropriate.

I cannot ever adequately express my gratitude to Kristin, who took a very rough draft, held my hand, and walked through the polishing process with me. Thank you for your patience, thank you for the laughs, and thank you for sitting with me on this ride that I'm not sure either of us signed up for, but we're both determined to make the most of. Yes, I know that sentence was too long. Deal with it, I'm gushing.

A lot changed in my life between the original publication of *Met by Moonlight* and *Thunder, Lightning, Rain*. I cannot properly acknowledge every single person who helped with this transition, because the community support has been more extensive than I could've ever hoped. But if you've ever interacted with me, with my posts, with another Owl, or just in support of indies in general, I appreciate the shit out of you. It takes no energy to scroll past. When you don't, when you choose to opt in, we notice.

Thank you.